where lightning strikes

a BLEEDING STARS *novel*

A.L. Jackson

NEW YORK TIMES BESTSELLING AUTHOR

A.L. Jackson
www.aljacksonauthor.com
Cover Design by RBA Designs
Photo by Sara Eirew Photographer
Editing by Making Manuscripts

Print ISBN: 978-1-938404-96-2
eBook ISBN: 978-1-938404-94-8

where
lightning
strikes

MORE FROM A.L. JACKSON

$\mathcal{B}$right lights blinded from above and gleamed against the stark white floor. I hurtled down the narrow hall, desperate for escape.

With every pounding step, I felt the separation grow. A chasm rending and ripping until I felt myself splitting in two.

Gasping for breath, I stumbled out the building and into the vacancy of the deep, deep night. Wind gusted, tumbling along the surface of the ground, a stir of agitation at my feet.

Above, the storm raged. Clouds dark and heavy and ominous.

Lightning struck. A crackle of energy shocked through the air and wrapped me in coils of white-hot agony.

For a moment, I gave into it and let myself feel. I lifted my face to the tormented sky, hands gripping my hair as I screamed.

Screamed in anguish. Screamed in regret.

Screamed loud enough I would never forget. A crack of thunder opened the sky.

Rain poured.

My hands fisted at my sides. I buried the memory of his face and the memory of the way he'd felt in my arms in the deepest part of me.

Sealed it off and cemented my heart.

My spirit grasped and wove with the promise I made him. I will never fall in love again.

Not ever again. Not after tonight.

TAMAR

I pushed through the crowd roving the sidewalk.

What the hell was wrong with me?

Running?

Hiding?

This wasn't me. This wasn't who I'd worked so hard to become.

But Lyrik West made me this way.

Desperate to escape the overwhelming intrigue simmering in the sky.

Do you know what it feels like right before lightning strikes?

How you can feel the current running through your veins? The trembles of warning that ripple through the dense air? The crackling energy that bristles across your skin and shakes you to your bones?

It's as if nitrogen and oxygen have come alive.

As if every element in the air is combustible.

Explosive.

Your heart beats fast because you know you're in danger. It's instinctive. The awareness that in the mere flash of a second and without warning you could be consumed by the force. By nature and blinding light.

Incinerated.

But there is also an overwhelming exhilaration surrounding it. A power in standing below those foreboding clouds with your face lifted to their bloated, sagging bellies, as if you're issuing up the bravest plea.

Let me be a part of what you are.

You feel so small. Scared. Yet strong at the same time. As if you're witnessing beauty unseen. Touching upon an experience meant only to be observed from afar.

That feeling? I'd chased it for a long, long time.

The excitement.

The thrill.

Growing up, I'd been the girl who'd try anything once. I'd thought that attitude made me brave. Turned out, it'd just made me stupid. Naïve and unsuspecting and vulnerable.

In the end, it had only burned me.

Now, I did anything and everything in my power to stay as far away from that feeling as possible.

I sought safety from that storm in the walls I'd built up around myself. Behind the façade of this hardened exterior—tattoos and makeup and dyed hair—that had become my home.

No longer were they just a mask.

They had become *me*.

Yet somehow…somehow *he* kept reappearing at the fringes of my life, pushing and prodding and drawing me back into all those excited, convoluted feelings I didn't want to feel.

Lyrik West.

Cowardly, I ran, tracking him like a lunatic over my shoulder as I did.

A short yelp flew from me when I bumped into a guy in front of me. My face whipped back around to meet the irritation in his scowl.

"Think you could watch where you're going?"

"I'm so sorry," I mumbled. Too shaken to wait for his pardon, I ducked my head and quickly wove deeper into the crowd browsing the farmers' market set up along the sidewalk.

My nerves raced like a panicked dog as I constantly looked over my shoulder in fear he'd spotted me.

I had to be crazy. Insane. Every reasonable, rational part of me was screaming at me to stop and handle this like a normal human being.

There was absolutely nothing to fear.

Lyrik West wasn't Cameron Lucan.

Yet he made me feel things I couldn't allow myself to feel.

The Savannah afternoon was hot and the humidity thick. Trees that had been here for over a century overhung the sidewalk— their old branches stretched out, full of leaves and dripping with Spanish Moss—as if loaded down by the weight of wisdom. The June sun shone high, rays slanting and burning bright.

I felt flustered by the heat. Flustered by *his* presence.

I glanced again.

A crown of ebony hair bobbed through the mass as he ambled along the busy sidewalk, as if he were just another person meandering the quaint Savannah street.

It didn't matter he was surrounded by a crush of bodies. He might as well have been alone. Or more apt, under a spotlight up on a stage.

He stood out like a fiery bolt of electricity. A streak of light and a blanket of dark. So destructive and compelling it was impossible to look away, the boy poised to strike and set you aflame.

My eyes scanned for a place where I could cower and hide.

Shit.

You are strong. You are strong, I chanted beneath my breath.

I hated being this girl. Fearful and scared of emotions I didn't want to feel. But that's how this boy made me. Shaky and confused and losing the grip of the carefully constructed walls I clung to.

Like each step he took tipped my world further on its side.

He shouldn't have been here.

Not in my adopted town.

Not yet.

Last fall, I'd nearly dropped to my knees and shouted my relief toward the heavens when he'd returned to Los Angeles for seven months. He'd gone with the rest of his band, *Sunder*, where the four had been working on their latest album.

I'd known he'd be returning. But I'd thought I had another week. Another week to prepare and fortify and strengthen all my shields.

I needed that week.

And there he was, twenty feet away.

He paused beneath one of the many canopies set up along the sidewalk, grinning at a middle-aged woman offering her wares at her stand. He smiled, spoke words I was too far away to hear, but in the short distance, I was pretty sure the poor girl was melting at his feet.

I understood her pain.

His hair was thick and black, pieces chunky and unruly. Just as unruly as the near pitch-black of his eyes. I was convinced they'd be completely black except for the fact those darkened pools of obsidian were broken up by flecks of grays and browns that sucked you into their depth. Like sharp, cutting edges of crystallized molten flamed from within.

He was tall.

So damned ridiculously tall.

Lean but strong in a menacing way. *Bad* was written across him, just like the tattoos covering every inch of exposed skin. Each cocky grin was hand-delivered with a lethal dose of masculinity, and I was sure I heard every single movement of that sinewy body scream with the same warning:

Touch at your own risk.

That same feeling of endangered excitement shivered down my spine and flipped in my belly.

The buzz before the strike.

No. No. No.

Those dark, dark eyes suddenly snapped my direction. I yanked my attention back front and center. I pretended I was all too interested in the Red Delicious apples spilling out of a short wooden barrel turned on its side to make a display on the table in front of where I stood.

Damn it.

"Those are as fresh as they come," the man running the booth was telling me. "Picked them myself this morning." My head bobbed along in agreement as if I possessed the faculty to process what he was saying, while I fought against that warm sensation welling firm and far too quickly.

A bristle of energy and a flash of light.

Coming closer.

Growing stronger.

A tattooed hand darted out in front of me and plucked up an apple. He began to toss it in the air.

With nowhere left to hide, I conjured the *fight*. The promise I'd made myself that I was the one in control.

No man would ever hold the power to hurt me. Not ever again.

Eyes narrowed, I turned to glare up at him.

The air rippled and shook.

Or maybe it was my knees.

Lyrik smirked, amusement tweaking his red, full lips that I'd bet had to be just as delicious as the apple.

"Well, well, well, if it isn't *Red*."

Damn Sebastian Stone, lead singer of Lyrik's band, for giving me *that* nickname. I mean, come on, my hair was red. He could have come up with something more ingenious than that.

It'd stuck.

But the way it slid off Lyrik's tongue? It sounded as if it were one of the seven deadly sins. One he'd sell his soul to commit.

"What are you doing here?" I forced a sneer, praying he'd get the message and go on his way.

He kept tossing that apple.

Thump.

Thump.

Thump.

Right into his big, capable hand.

"Here for the big wedding. What do you think I'm doing here? And don't tell me you didn't miss me."

"Can't miss what doesn't even cross your mind."

"Ouch." He inflected the word as if it were nothing more than a joke, as if the idea were completely absurd. His laughter was cool and confident. "You really gonna stand there and tell me in the last seven months, you haven't thought about me at all?"

"Yeah, I really am."

Big, fat lie.

One I was taking to my grave.

And like there was a chance I'd crossed his mind. Even once. This boy didn't just look bad.

He was bad.

There wasn't a photo I saw him in where he didn't have at least two girls hanging on him, those arms wrapped around their shoulders with a lusty gleam in his eye. Not to mention, I'd seen him in action on more occasions than I cared to count at the bar where I worked.

It was apparent Lyrik West had a type.

Maybe I looked like it from the outside. Short skirts and high, high heels, dark-rimmed eyes, tattoos and lace.

But I was nothing like those girls.

It didn't matter how hard he tried to coax me into being her.

He chuckled, playing his game. This guy was so absurdly hot, so damned gorgeous, he rode around on a chariot of presumption.

He just reached out and took whatever he wanted, probably because he was so accustomed to *it* being thrown at him at every turn.

"That's a shame, Red," he said, giving another toss of that apple. "I was hoping when I got back, you and I could be *friends*."

My mouth dropped open with a snippy retort, but I made the

mistake of looking back at him again. The words froze on my tongue. My stupid, unfaithful gaze wandered up, then down, slower as it dragged back up again. He wore the tightest pair of black skinny jeans you'd ever seen, and an even tighter white V-neck tee.

Every exposed inch of skin was inked, a vast canvas of beautiful art etched on a darkly beautiful man.

I knew if he tore off that thin piece of material, his back was covered, too.

Beneath that extravagant, intricate ink was packed, solid muscle.

That attraction I'd been running from for months slicked warm and slow through my veins, this fluttery feeling I hated thrumming through my senses.

God, this guy was doing his all to make me break the promises I'd made myself.

I didn't want this. Didn't want to stand up against the allure and seduction. Didn't want to admit he made me feel things I didn't want to feel.

Things I hadn't felt in a long, long time.

Dangerous things.

Those dark eyes tracked the way my throat tremored and rolled as I glared up at him and tried to pretend I wasn't affected.

Brazen, he reached out. Callused fingertips glided down the hollow of my neck to my collarbone, as if he couldn't resist but call me out.

I should have been repulsed. But I knew those calluses were bred from years of playing across the strings of his guitar, forged in the music he made.

Tingles spread like wildfire.

That energy buzzed.

I shook.

"What do you think, Red? You wanna be friends?" he murmured, his voice a lure as he dipped his head closer.

I tore myself away and forced an incredulous snort. "Don't flatter yourself, *rock star*." I said it like a dirty word. "Not every girl is going to fall at your feet."

He tossed the apple once more, caught it in his hand, before he lifted it and took a big, crunching bite. He chewed, that damned smirk making a reappearance, red, red lips twisting like a decadent bow. "You sure you don't want a taste?"

It was pure innuendo.

"I'd rather starve."

He barked out a laugh. "Want to know what I think?"

"Nope."

I most definitely did not. That was my cue to make an escape.

I took a rigid step back.

He just inched forward, crowding my space, his head inclining toward mine the nearer he came. He ducked down until his nose nearly brushed mine and his voice went rough. "I think you are absolutely dying for a taste. I think that sassy little mouth of yours is watering and your belly is growling for a fill. And I think in order for you to finally get that stick out of your ass, all you really need is to get a sample of what it's like to really be *satisfied*."

My chin lifted defiantly in the same second my shoulders rolled back, my hard, rigid armor snapping into place. "And just what makes you think you could satisfy me?"

His grin was smug as he straightened and took another bite. "You brave enough to find out?"

My mouth dropped open, and I clamored around in my foggy brain for a response, for a way to shut him up and shut him down.

He called it brave.

I called it stupid.

He was smiling a self-satisfied smile when he dug in his pocket and pulled out a five. "Don't look so freaked out, Red. All you have to say is no."

Tongue tied, I could say nothing.

His attention turned to the man selling the apples, and he tossed the bill on the display table.

"Delicious."

He shot me a wink.

He actually *freaking* winked.

He turned and strode in the same direction he'd come, his

horrible, horrible promise floating on the breeze as he gave me a casual wave over his shoulder.

"See ya around, Red."

I was sure I felt the ground shake.

LYRIK

*L*oyalty.

It was an idea that meant different things to different people. Funny, because it should be a no-brainer. Require zero thought. But that concept covered so many bases it often became convoluted and confused.

Take the contrast of a man being loyal to his wife versus another man's best friend helping him cover up an affair. I was convinced that was nothing less than a contradiction, although some would argue it's the exact damned thing. Sticking up and standing by the person who means the most to you.

To me?

Loyalty was absolute.

There weren't questions or exemptions or exclusions.

Loyalty was the one unfailing moral I had. The one fucking thing I could count as good.

I pressed my cell a little harder to my ear, gritting my damned teeth, and wished I was back two minutes in time so I could mess a little more with *Red*. Dig that knife in a little deeper. Watch her splutter and fumble. Swim in those barely contained waves of lust before those blue eyes became irate.

Damn, I loved a girl who wasn't afraid to speak her mind while her body told an entirely different story.

That was the type of contradiction I craved. The push and pull. Hate bristling with want.

Sex with *Red* would blow my mind. I was sure of it. Which I was pretty sure was why I couldn't purge the idea of it from my thoughts. That girl was a bundle of fireworks, and I was certain we'd go boom.

But no.

Instead, I was talking to this asshole.

"Already told you, this isn't gonna happen. Not sure why you keep calling, because I assure you, *Mr. Banik*, it's a waste of your time." I spit his name as if tasting it was as nasty as this conversation made me feel, the *Mr.* lacking all the respect it normally imbued.

"Just hear me out."

I released a dark chuckle. "I hear you just fine. Basically what I'm getting is your balls are actually big enough to make the suggestion I leave my band. That sound about right to you? You ever heard the word loyalty before, Mr. Banik? How about betrayal?"

There it was. That word again.

Loyalty.

That's what this was all about.

My loyalty.

Baz's loyalty.

My stomach tightened in a gnarled knot, dread and worry and

staunch disbelief. I swallowed hard and he sighed, and I could just see the greasy piece of shit running his grimy hand over his bald head.

"The only thing I'm suggesting is you look at your options."

Eric Banik, manager of *Tokens of Time,* had been hounding my ass for close to a month. He wanted me to step into the shoes of their lead who had gone and bailed. I was all too sure the three remaining members were desperate to add a name to their roster who'd propel them forward.

"Those assholes should know exactly what it feels like for someone they trust to leave them high and dry. Put out an ad in the paper. Have fucking auditions. I don't give a shit what you do. Find someone else."

Tokens of Time had opened for *Sunder* a couple times back in L.A., and their lead had up and deserted just when they were finally catching on. He'd signed on as some pussy solo artist, wearing his own damned name like he'd earned the right to parade it like a badge.

"Your lead is getting married." He said it like he was trying to knock some sense into me. Like the consequences of that was clear as day.

"Sebastian is already married," I shot back.

"Married again or whatever the fuck they think they're doing. Maybe the first time it was just a test run and this time it's for real. But you know *Sunder* is as unstable as it's ever been."

Sunder had survived a thousand controversies. Outlived a million rumors. Made it through jail sentences and overdoses and the death of our drummer, Mark, which had been one of the most painful, tragic losses any of us had ever experienced.

We'd endured the bullshit Baz had gotten wrapped up in with Martin Jennings, an association that had gone deeper and darker than any of us had ever imagined.

The rest of the band—me and Ash and Zee—we'd taken up Baz's back during that time. Believed in him when everything around us was crumbling, our world tour cancelled, and the threat of our label dropping us hanging over our heads.

We'd made it, and I had to believe Baz wouldn't let us down

now.

My silence seemed to encourage Eric, and he continued, voice dipping in persuasion. "You're exactly what we're looking for, Lyrik. You're talented and you don't take shit from anyone. You have the vibe we need. You write the best damn lyrics we've ever heard and play the guitar like you were born with it. And look at you. You know as well as the rest of us you should be out in front. You need to lead. You're too good to stand in the shadows."

Long ago I'd adopted the policy not to give a fuck.

Shunning stress and worry and all the bullshit most people wore on their shoulders like some kind of burdened brand.

Me? I shucked off the weight.

Let's be real. Approaching life with this view? It was a whole fucking ton less painful. Learned that shit the hard way.

I had two exceptions to that rule.

My family—my parents, my baby sister, and my niece.

And Baz and the rest of boys who made up the band.

The few people in this world who I could count on to be *loyal* and I gave it in return. Guess you could say the guys had been grandfathered in. Granted a privileged spot in my shriveled, blackened heart before it'd been burned.

"Don't call me again."

I ended the call without another word and continued down the cobbled stones running in front of the aged buildings along the river walk.

I rounded the corner and darted down the narrow lane, strolling along the shaded street before I bounded the exterior staircase cutting up the middle of the old craggy building. Taking them two at a time, I deposited myself on the small landing leading to the two apartments occupying the top floor, their doors situated directly across from the other with the landing in between.

This secluded place sat right in the heart of the Historic District in Savannah, Georgia.

Was lucky as shit to nab it, too. Knew it was rented out most of the time, short-term to tourists and drifters like me who were just passing through.

My door was on the right, and I wiggled the key into the lock and let myself into my temporary home. It was a converted warehouse, now a trendy studio with exposed brick walls and high ceilings, a partition wall to section off the bedroom. Double French doors led out to a balcony I was guessing once upon a time had been a fire escape.

I tossed the keys onto the little table sitting just inside and raked a hand through my hair, shaking off the conversation and allowing my thoughts to go traipsing back to the girl.

God, that girl.

My blood was still pulsin' a little too hard for comfort, my dick all too eager to take a ride.

When I flew in to Savannah yesterday, I knew I would see her. Knew she was going to torture me a little more. Problem was, every time she told me I couldn't have her, the need she stirred in me just grew.

The girl slung drinks at *Charlie's*, the bar Shea, Baz's wife, had worked at when they'd first met. The same bar Shea's uncle Charlie owned. Every time I walked through the doors of that bar, a crazy feeling skimmed my veins, filling me full of some kind of foolish excitement I hadn't felt in a long damned time.

Didn't know what came over me when she invaded my space. She was like a red-headed siren, circling and circling and circling me on unsettled waters until I was trapped in some kind of vortex. It instantly flipped a switch in me and my dick started doing the talking.

And believe me, he was a *dick*.

Guess he didn't like being ignored. Shot down and rejected.

Neither of us were used to that shit. I didn't chase women. They chased me. Flocked in droves, really. And that wasn't my dick talking again. It's just the way it was. After a show, they were always there, doing their own circling, some acting coy and others' advances blatantly clear. But they all wanted the same thing.

Me.

But not *Red*. Every advance I made? She pushed right back. Hard.

It was no secret I loved women. Loved the way they smelled. Loved the way they tasted. Most of all, I loved the way they felt.

But I didn't *love* women.

Loving someone was like volunteering for heartache and sorrow and a lifetime of bullshit.

But I wanted one. I wanted her.

Tamar King.

We had a love/hate relationship.

I loved messing with her and she loved to hate me for it.

Just once, I wanted her to let go. I wanted the girl to come at me with the brunt of all the hostility radiating from that white, snowy flesh that peeked out from behind the pretty tats twisting down her arms. Tats I had the intense need to lick.

Yeah.

The girl looked like the perfect sin.

But there was something more. Something darker. Anger leached from her. The kind of anger that was real and not the angsty show all these other girls prancing around backstage liked to put on.

For one night, I wanted her to give it to me. Fight it out with me. Hands and teeth and bodies. Right in my bed.

My phone dinged and I glanced at the screen.

Ash.

You get Shea & Sebastian's wedding gift, asshole?

I tapped back a reply, grinning at one of my oldest friends who couldn't stay serious for five seconds. *Yep.*

Immediately it dinged. *You impress me.*

I could feel his sarcasm woven in the words.

Whatever, man. You'd forget your head without me.

Keep telling yourself that. We all know I'm the brains of the bunch. See you at 10.

I smiled and that same pulse of excitement vibrated through me. Nah, this little break wasn't going to be so bad after all.

TAMAR

Charlie's buzzed around me. Lights were cast low and the music turned high. Bodies pressed up to the smooth, antique bar, vying to get my attention as I scrambled behind it, filling pitchers full of microbrews while simultaneously shaking up a couple Purple Lamborghinis.

I slid the two martinis to the blondes commiserating their love-life woes over drinks at the end of the bar.

"Here we go. Two Purple Lamborghinis. Watch yourselves. Those go down fast and ride you hard."

The woman on the right smiled wide. "Mmm...after the day

I've had, fast and furious is exactly what I need. Keep them coming."

"Glad I could be of service."

"Hey, princess, how about another round of beers down here?" The same asshole who'd been eyeing me up and down all night shot me a smarmy smile. No doubt, it was supposed to melt my panties.

Gross.

My brow arched all on its own, tone going coy. I was getting good at this game. "Now...now... Do I look like a princess to you?"

"Nah, baby cakes, you look like a wet dream."

Let me reiterate.

Gross.

So gross.

And seriously, baby cakes?

What a douchebag.

You'd think after everything, I'd have picked a different work atmosphere. Away from men and sex and innuendo.

Or maybe it wasn't so strange after all.

Maybe I'd ended up here because it drew them into the light, the blatant advances and trashy pick-up lines dealt every night. I was always prepared. Never caught unaware.

"I'll show you a wet dream. When I'm finished with you, you'll be pissing in your sleep for the next month." It was all a grumble under my breath as I filled three mugs for him and his two friends, who were, surprise, surprise, just as douchy as the first.

"Easy now, sweetheart." Charlie's soothing voice came at me from behind. "I see someone's feeling extra feisty tonight. Don't need you chasing the customers out the door."

Charlie was the owner of *Charlie's*, a bar boasting a prime spot on the river walk here in Savannah. It was super popular, packed night after night, people flocking in to unwind at the end of the day and watch the local bands. I'd been working here for the last four years, first working in the kitchen before I was old enough to be out front.

He was also the owner of the apartment I'd been renting above one of his buildings for the same amount of time. The guy wore a ratty T-shirt and an even rattier gray beard, but not even all that facial hair could conceal the genuine smile peeking out from underneath. The guy was as good as they got.

Charlie was all about the saving. Without a doubt, he'd saved me.

He grinned when I looked back at him. "What has you on edge, sugar?"

I hiked a nonchalant shoulder as I strutted past him toward the value-pack of douches leering at my approach. "Don't know what you're talking about."

There was no holding back my sneer when I slid the assholes their beers.

Charlie snickered when I spun around and passed back by. "You sure about that?"

"Don't go playin' counselor, old man. I'm just fine."

One of his teasing chuckles rippled from him, and he shook his index finger at me. "I bet I know what has those knickers in a twist…you were out with Shea Bear this afternoon trying on your bridesmaid's dress. Bet you can't stand to put on a frilly dress for a day."

Shea and Sebastian had shocked us all when they'd gotten married in Las Vegas six months ago. They claimed that wedding was for them. This one? This one was to bring their friends and families together. A celebration of the life they were beginning together.

I was completely honored she had asked me to stand up as one of her bridesmaids. Escaping to this town, I'd never expected to find friends. To find kind, selfless people whose friendships would grow to the point where I'd consider them family.

So maybe Charlie was just glancing at the root of the problem. I actually didn't mind the dress. In fact, I kind of loved it. Shea was having a country chic wedding, everything casual and flowy and pretty, just like her personality, and our rustic dresses were no exception.

My problem was the asshole they'd paired me with. The guy I'd be walking the aisle with. The one I'd have to do that dreaded dance with.

He was the one who had my panties in a twist—tangled and tied and snarled, among other things that had me wanting to scream in frustration.

The one who evoked feelings I refused to feel. Things that made that brittle, fractured spot hidden away somewhere in my chest want to crack.

And...*shit*.

He was walking through the door.

An electric current charged through the air, blistering as it traveled my skin. Tingles lifted in stark awareness and the breath punched from my lungs.

Want.

Need.

Like the boy held the power to expose every weak spot in my armor.

I hated he had this effect.

But my body didn't seem to take my hatred into consideration when my heart hammered and sped. My stomach knotted in anticipation.

Catching my bottom lip between my teeth, I forced myself to focus on the task at hand. I rimmed four shot glasses with salt, poured tequila across them, garnished them with wedges of lime, all the while being painfully distracted by the knowledge he stood in all his rock 'n' roll glory thirty feet away.

The guys from *Sunder*, plus Shea, spilled in behind him.

Charlie bumped his hip into mine. "Look it there, sugar. Shea and the rest of the wedding party just walked in."

As if I hadn't noticed.

"Why don't you call it a night, hang out, blow off some steam? You should be with the rest of them rather than working your fingers to the bone the way you do for me night after night. I can handle the place."

Always the caretaker.

I fought the grin pulling at one side of my mouth, shook my head as I went to work wiping down the counter that was already gleaming. "Now there you go worrying about me again, old man.

I'm just fine behind this bar. Right where I belong."

Last thing I needed was to get in the mix of Lyrik and the rest of the guys.

"Pssh." He waved his hands at me, shooing me back. "Go on, girl. As much as you like to pretend you're happy with being a loner, you're just as much a part of that group as the rest of 'em. Besides, you know Shea's gonna come dragging you out anyway, so you might as well give it up now."

"Tamar." And there she was, calling my name.

"What'd I tell you?" Charlie said, lips twitching beneath his scraggly beard.

I tossed down the rag. "Fine." I pointed a warning finger at him as I backed away. "But I'm not calling it a night. One drink, and I'm back to work."

"Whatever you say, sugar. We all know who's the boss around here."

Charlie's was housed in one of the old cotton warehouses, the rafters in the high ceilings still exposed, the wooden walls aged to a near black from the years of smoke and bodies and a century of hidden mystery.

I strutted to the far end of the bar that took up the middle of the massive room, the ornate, carved mahogany the focus of *Charlie's*. My back was to the front door, and I used the time to prepare myself to come face to face with Lyrik West.

I knew it was crazy. Complete inane craziness. How I was terrified to face the man simply for the way he made me feel. For the way he made me want and desire and question all the promises I'd made myself.

Worst was being aware he enjoyed getting to me so much.

I knew it as well as he did.

He was playing me. Winding me up like a toy.

He'd get off on watching me spin, spin, spin, until I teetered and tottered and toppled. Used up and spent.

Cruel.

I was pretty sure that was the definition of Lyrik West.

I ducked under the small opening at the end, passing by the country band setting up on stage, and headed back toward the entrance.

There I was, pacing in the direction of the man my every cell repelled and attracted.

A chill slid through my senses. A premonition. A warning that magnetism was greater than any resistance.

Like an aurora of dancing, captivating lights that turned out to be nothing but a black hole.

Consuming life and light.

Those near-black eyes caught mine, almost stopping me in my tracks as they glimmered with that same dark mischief, as if at any moment he would strike.

Reach out and take me in his grips.

Devour and destroy and desolate.

Refusing to cave, I lifted my chin in challenge. I just prayed he didn't see the way it trembled.

I somehow managed to tear my gaze from the hook of his and turned it on my friend.

"Shea, I thought you'd given up your days at *Charlie's*," I tossed out like a tease as my lips stretched into a welcoming smile. With Shea, the truth of it was not so feigned.

The smile she returned was pure and relieved, and I knew without a doubt she was wearing it because Sebastian was back in town.

Shea came in for a hug, her baby bump prominent against my stomach.

Yeah. Shea Stone had to be about the cutest pregnant girl you'd ever meet, her six-month belly looking like she'd done nothing other than stuff a basketball under her dress.

No wonder Sebastian couldn't stay away.

I stepped back, squeezing her hands as I glanced up at her husband who edged in behind her, hands flattening possessively over her bump.

I arched a brow his direction. "Ah…the infamous Sebastian Stone. What are you doing here? I thought Savannah was safe from the likes of you and your boys for at least another week. We should be ringing the town alarm."

A playful smirk filled up his face. "Like my boys are any more dangerous than you."

Ha. Not even close.

Apparently appearances *were* deceiving.

"Besides," he continued, his voice going a little deeper as he kissed the side of Shea's head, "couldn't stay away a second longer."

Shea's smile lit up the entire darkened room. "He was waiting at the house when I got back after we did your final dress fitting. You should have seen Kallie's face when she saw her daddy standing on the porch waiting for us. I don't think I've ever seen that little butterfly get out of the car so fast."

As rough as it'd been for both of them, Shea had returned to Savannah with her daughter two months ago, leaving Sebastian behind while *Sunder* finished up in the studio recording their latest album.

Sebastian chuckled, nuzzled at her neck. "Don't think I've ever seen you get out of the car so fast, either."

"Can you blame me?" she whispered back.

A fresh wave of awareness rippled out. Targeted. My body marked by crosshairs.

That intensity wrapped and circled and ensnared.

I shuddered out a breath and tried to remain strong. But there was nothing I could do. I couldn't resist the power behind the stare I felt searing into my flesh.

That unsteady feeling trembled beneath my feet and hummed in my ears

My eyes flitted his direction.

Powerless.

Lyrik stood there looking at me, tattooed hands stuffed in his pockets. Everything about him was casual and unaffected. Yet striking and bold.

Severe and cruel and altogether aloof.

A damn enigma the very foolish side of me wanted to explore.

Layer by layer.

Touch by touch.

I swallowed around the rock sitting at the base of my throat.

I knew better than acting like a naïve school girl.

He would come like a plunderer, swooping in and tearing everything in his path to shreds, setting the world on fire.

With zero regret.

Zero concern for the mayhem he caused.

Zero remorse for his sins.

He reveled in them.

Like I said.

Cruel.

Ash's brash voice broke the tension. "Did any of you really think Baz was gonna hang tight in L.A. for two months after Shea and Kallie came back here? Dude was about to lose his shit. Slave driver had our asses in the studio nonstop for the last week to wrap things up so we could get back here sooner."

He stretched out his tattooed arms. "Of course, since we're talking about this group of badasses, wrapping up the album sooner was no problem. We make magic, baby."

Ash Evans had to be one of the cockiest guys I'd ever crossed paths with. Scary thing was, it just made him all the more endearing, added to the charm that oozed from him without a thought, the guy all charisma and dimples and ego for miles.

And he was gorgeous.

Poor girls didn't stand a chance.

But all that overconfidence? It was so different than Lyrik's. Where Ash's was friendly, Lyrik's felt like a direct threat.

"So I take it you're all here to celebrate. Let me grab some drinks." My eyes bounced over each of them, a little quicker over Lyrik.

How obvious.

Just awesome.

"Everyone want their regular?" I asked.

"Sounds good to me, darlin'," Ash was all too quick to supply. "But considering the magnitude of what we're celebrating, make them doubles."

"You do realize you always ask for doubles."

He laughed. "Then make them triples."

Good God.

These guys were nothing but a pack of trouble. All except for

Zee, who stepped up with an affectionate shake of his head, as if he were apologizing for the company he kept but wouldn't have it any other way. He gave me a quick hug.

"Nice to see you again, Tamar."

"Good to see you, too."

He headed for the secluded booth Sebastian had first claimed then *Sunder* had made their own.

Shea called, "Thank you," as Sebastian began pulling her toward the booth. Ash was all too keen to follow.

Lyrik seemed slow to conform as he cast me one more unsettling glance over his shoulder, as if he was making sure to drag my attention with him.

To torture me a little more.

Forcing myself back behind the bar, I filled three rocks glasses half-full with Jager.

The pour of the thick, dark liquid reminded me of the promise in Lyrik's eyes. A tempting, seductive vow of a night filled with delicious, carnal fun.

But that promise came with the consequence of a nasty hangover in the morning.

I did the same with Sebastian Stone's ridiculously expensive tequila he liked to drink and grabbed a bottle of water for Shea, then arranged everything on a tray. I wove back through the growing crowd.

Ash grinned up at me as I passed out the shots. "Ah...never thought I'd say it, but it is good to be back in Savannah. Tell me, Tam Tam, have these walls been missing me? How about those ladies? Tell me they've been asking for me. You know once I make an appearance, the place isn't ever gonna be the same."

I rolled my eyes. "Hardly. Half the female population is scarred from your last *appearance*."

"Oh come now. Don't act like you don't know my presence just makes everything better." The dimples in his cheeks deepened. "Kind of like bacon. Put it on a burger. Better. Put it on a salad. Better. Spread Ash around. Better."

I couldn't help it. Laughter escaped, all incredulous and full of disbelief, but there, nonetheless.

"See…" he prodded like he'd just proven a new theorem, "*better*. Admit you missed me."

"Okay, okay, if it'll shut you up then I'll gladly cop to missing you."

Ash was the first to lift his glass. "To Baz and Beautiful Shea, two people who love each other so much they think they need to get married twice."

Zee laughed, Lyrik grinned.

"But for real…the two of you?" Ash continued, "You've got something good. Don't ever give it up."

Don't ever give it up.

The words rang through my mind, and a flash of sadness threatened to swallow me whole and take me under. I squeezed my eyes closed, lifted my glass, and threw back the shot. A fiery burn rolled hot down my throat, wrapping me like a warm blanket as it settled in my belly.

Soothing the rough edges that kept trying to fray.

I refused to give in to the memories that raved in the depths of my conscious where I'd left them, struggling to find their way out. For four years, I'd done just fine. I'd stepped into the shoes of the girl I wanted to be and shunned it all.

The past was the past. I needed to leave it there.

But all that fear was fighting for a rebound.

I was no fool. I knew why. The proof of it was in the Facebook message I'd received two months ago on my inactive account. It was one I'd seen during a weak moment. Swamped in loneliness and regret, I'd signed on with my IP address turned off.

I'd just needed a glimpse of my family. To be reminded of their faces. To catch a hint of their voices.

To feel as if I were a part of their lives when I'd torn myself from it four years before.

As if those crumbs could ever be enough.

But it was the waiting message that had literally dropped me to my knees.

We need your help. We understand your hesitation, but we need any information you can give us on Cameron Lucan. Please contact me as soon as possible.

As much as I kept trying to pretend it didn't matter, that my getting involved wouldn't change a thing, those thoughts kept creeping back in.

Prodding.

Goading.

Spurring.

Forcing me to look behind at a past I'd done everything to forget.

Add Lyrik into the mix?

I could feel fissures splintering my walls, that firm foundation crumbling beneath my feet.

Giving them my best smile, I glanced over my shoulder. "Looks like Charlie is getting slammed. Better rescue the old man before things start to get ugly over there. I'll send one of the servers over to make sure you're all taken care of."

"Thanks, Tamar." Shea looked at me as if she were apologizing I couldn't stay, when in truth, I couldn't wait to get away.

I got back to work, letting myself get lost in the vibe, the urgency I fed on as darkness covered the room and the country band played on, quick to sling drinks and even quicker to shoot down advances from overly friendly men.

Maybe it was wrong it made me feel strong. As if for a little while, I was in complete control. Like no one could touch me or pollute me. Even though I knew it was nothing more than an illusion.

"Running low on Goose, Charlie. I'm gonna run back to storage and grab some."

"Not a problem, sugar. We're hanging in just fine up here."

I headed through the kitchen to the back storage room.

With my foot, I pushed the step stool over to the section with the different vodkas stacked on the shelves, and climbed up so I could reach a box of Grey Goose on the top.

Carefully, considering I was going down backward wearing five-inch heels, I maneuvered down, box balanced in one arm while I held on to the metal bar of the shelf with the other.

I turned around.

A yelp flew from me when I found the lone figure leaning up against the shelved wall.

My heart galloped like a sprint of horses, a riot of hooves beating against my chest.

Hands shaking so badly, I barely righted the box before it crashed to the floor.

Why are you doing this to me?

"What do you think you're doing back here?" I finally managed, the first words just as shaky as my hands, the last filling with indignant anger.

Why?

Lyrik let that lazy smirk take over his too-pretty face. Shadows played across one side, making him appear more dangerous than normal.

"Lookin' for you."

I pushed off the intrigue gathering fast, ignored the beat of my heart and the want in my belly as I forced out the words, sharp and severe. "Well, you can stop *looking* for me, because I don't want to be found."

"You sure about that?"

"What is it you think you want from me, Lyrik?"

I'd spent all of last summer dodging his advances, doing my best to repel him with every bitchy rejection I could throw his way. It was time to put an end to this.

My words were hard and harsh, fueled by the desperation buried underneath. I just hoped it wasn't the most apparent. "Do you want a quick fuck? Do you want me to drop to my knees and suck your dick and send you on your merry way? There are plenty of other girls out there begging for the job. Do me a favor and stop chasing me."

Riding on the rush of adrenaline, I stalked for the door.

Voice rough, his words hit me from behind, that overwhelming presence just as close. "Like those eyes chase me?"

Chills traveled my spine as the rest of my body froze.

Overtaken by this attraction.

Why did I want him so badly?

But I guess the saying was true. We always want what we shouldn't have.

Slowly I turned. That strong, beautiful body towered over me. Mine reacted to the nearness.

Heat.

Fire.

Need.

He hooked his finger under my chin, forcing me to look up at him through the dusky confines of the enclosed room. "You think I don't see you, Red. Watching. Wanting. Just because you refuse to let the words fall from your mouth, doesn't mean they're not true."

My teeth ground, every inch of me at war, my hatred of how he made me feel—hatred of that old, naïve weakness—up against the seeds of trust that wanted to make their way out.

It felt like a tornado gaining speed.

Lights flickered behind my eyes and a thrill rushed through my nerves.

No. No. No.

"What would be so bad about spending a night with me?"

And that was just it.

The only thing I'd ever be.

Easy, forgettable sex.

Another in a million faceless women.

A quick fuck that didn't even last long enough to be considered a fling. Hurt balled behind my ribs. Funny how his proposition felt like a rejection.

"Oh, I could think of plenty of things." Like my heart and the sanctity of my mind.

I struggled to resurrect the façade. To erect that rigid, impenetrable armor.

I wiggled the fingers of my free hand in front of his face and fired the words like bullets. "Believe me, I'd rather spend the night with these than with you."

He snatched me by the wrist.

My mouth dropped open in shock. At the heat of his hold. At the weight of his stare.

The man took full advantage of my momentary stupor, those dark eyes gleaming as he slowly sucked my middle two fingers into the fever of his mouth.

A panicked, strangled gasp wheezed from my throat, expanding my too-tight lungs.

Flames ignited, a fire set to my veins, spreading fast and coalescing as a hot melting point right between my thighs.

That smirk was in full force when he let my fingers free with a pop.

Then he went and shocked me again when he pressed my hand to his chest. It felt way too strong, and damn it, his heart had to have been beating just as hard as mine.

Something flashed in those eyes. Something soft. That was all it took, and something soft inside me wanted to give.

To give up and give it all.

Then that wicked mouth ticked up at the side, and he guided my trembling hand down.

Down.

Down.

Down.

While I stood like a sucker allowing it.

He stopped just above the obvious bulge straining from his too tight jeans.

"Oh, I'm sure your hands work wonders, but honestly, I had other things in mind."

My senses came rushing back.

Stupid. Stupid. Stupid.

That's what *soft* got me.

It left me no more than a pawn in an elaborate game.

I jerked myself free, begging my feet to cooperate as I scrambled for the door with all the confidence I had left, digging deep for the strength that was dwindling fast.

By the time I got to the door, my chin was lifted high.

Because I *remembered.*

Remembered who I'd fought so hard to become.

At the door I stopped and glared at him from over my shoulder. "Not on your life."

He just smiled that smug, cocky smile, as if he could see right through me. "All you have to say is no, *Red.*"

I raised a middle finger.

Take that as my no, asshole.

"You can go fuck yourself."

He laughed and those black eyes shimmered. "Nah, baby. Unlike you, I'm not so keen to go at it alone."

"You're such an asshole."

"And you, Red, are an uptight bitch."

He wasn't the first guy to call me a bitch.

Usually, it didn't bother me.

Hell, most of the time I took it as a compliment. An affirmation that no one would dare mess with me.

But Lyrik calling me a bitch? It was the first time it stitched these thick, suffocating threads of sadness and anger through my heart.

God, he was such an egotistical, shameless bastard.

And I was an idiot for allowing it to hurt.

I should have turned and walked.

Closed my mouth.

But I couldn't stop it from tumbling free.

"So a girl's a bitch just because she won't jump in your bed?" I was sure the shake of my head revealed too much.

Disgust. Disappointment. Defeat.

"You know what, Lyrik? Maybe I want more in my life. And I won't allow you to reach out and take what I don't want to give."

I was pissed.

Shaken.

Determined to put Lyrik back in his place.

They'd ordered another round of drinks.

I was quick to mix them, whipping up something extra special for one Lyrik West. Just because I *liked* him so much.

An hour had passed since he'd cornered me in the storage room, and just as much time had gone by since he'd returned to the booth, the table now sporting the addition of three girls.

Shea and Sebastian had called upon their good sense and

vacated.

Now Zee was sitting there basically alone, playing on his phone while one girl sat sideways across Ash's lap, arms laced around his neck, garnering all his attention.

It was the two hanging like sparkly ornaments from Lyrik's sides that had me on the rampage.

His arms were draped around their shoulders as he sat kicked back in the seat.

Not a care in the world.

A low growl gathered at the base of my throat.

Didn't take him long.

What a pig.

And why the hell did it piss me off so bad?

But it did.

Truth was, I was irate. Something about it left me feeling used and dirty and disposable.

Glasses clanked as I threw their drinks on the tray, and even though I wasn't a server, I was damned well going to deliver them myself.

I slithered across the floor, winding through the high-top tables, making sure my hips and ass were doing the talking as I stalked toward the booth. The most saccharine of smiles twisted my face as I slid the cosmos to the girls who were only out for a little fun, but somehow had managed to stumble into my path of fury.

They didn't even seem to notice the force in which I slammed them down.

Oh, but Lyrik did, eyes taking in his special drink. The bright red liquid sloshed over the rim and ran onto the table when I set it in front of him.

With that cocky smirk, he glanced up at me. "What's this?"

I pressed my palms flat on the table, leaning in close to his face, voice as bitter as I felt. "It's a red-headed slut. That's what you want, isn't it?"

This time the girls took note, glaring at me as if I was suddenly a competitor, my flaming red hair making it all too clear I was referring to myself. One had the decency to look offended when

Lyrik shot me a wry smile and opened that offensive mouth. "Actually, I was thinking I wanted a taste of a blue-eyed angel, but I'll take you however I can get you."

My blue eyes narrowed as I struggled to contain the hurt and rage and all these convoluted emotions I didn't want to feel, while his smile widened in satisfaction.

He lifted the glass toward me then threw back his shot.

Just as fast, he spit it out. Red liquid spewed across the table and dribbled down his perfect chin. Furious, he swiped his mouth with the back of his hand. "What the fuck was that?"

"That was a warning not to touch me again."

So maybe my secret red-headed slut recipe included a little cayenne and Tabasco. Nothing a real man couldn't handle.

In disbelief, he shook his head. "You really are a bitch, aren't you?" He pushed the girls off him, squeezed out to stand, gestured for them to follow. "Come on, we're out of here."

He dug in his pocket and pulled out two hundreds and flung them out in front of him, the bills fluttering down to land on the table. "*Thanks* for the drink," he seethed.

He stalked away like a howling, blackened storm, the two little bitches stumbling on their heels as they clamored after him.

Thickness crawled up my throat, supplied by the regret pressing hard against my chest.

You really are a bitch.

Why did I care? This was what I wanted, wasn't it? To chase him away. To throw out daggers and toss up shields, where I could seclude and conceal and isolate myself behind this barricade.

Where it was safe.

Ash shot me a knowing grin. "Oh, Tam Tam, remind me not to fuck with you, darlin'. Because you scare the shit outta me."

I swallowed hard.

Yeah. Sometimes I scared myself, too.

****

At 3:40 a.m., I pulled into my parking spot at the back of the building Charlie owned.

On a sigh, I cut the engine and stepped from my car.

My attention barely drifted over the bike parked in the spot reserved for Apartment Two, and I hardly registered the car parked awkwardly behind it.

The mental exhaustion clinging to my bones didn't allow me much thought other than the need to strip myself of these clothes and this mask of makeup so I could climb into the refuge of my bed.

I suppressed a groan when I heard the music pumping from Apartment Two as I drew closer, the lift of giggles and annoying female voices.

Awesome.

I had new obnoxious neighbors. Tonight just got better and better.

At least they never stayed since that apartment was used for short-term, weekly rentals.

No doubt, Charlie made a small fortune on those rentals, but he refused to rent my place out the same way. The day I'd come crawling into his bar desperate for a job without an address to put on my application, he'd sat me down and asked me the last time I'd eaten. When I couldn't answer, he'd fed me then put me in his truck and brought me here.

This stranger had set me up and given me a home.

It was the day the man had rescued a small piece of my shattered heart. Restored a little bit of my faith in humanity.

I climbed the stairs, pulling at the railing to aid my ascent, my feet sore and my body weary.

I was letting all this shit get to me, and I couldn't afford it.

I let myself into my dark apartment, kicked off my shoes at the door, and went directly to the bathroom to wash my face, then proceeded into my cozy room where I changed into a pair of sleep shorts and a tee before I flopped onto my plush, queen-sized bed with the pretty ornate metal headboard.

It was intended to exude comfort.

Instead I felt lost.

Hollow.

Alone.

With a glance to my earbuds on my nightstand, I hesitated. Why in the world after the night I'd had would I even consider torturing myself this way?

Apparently I was a masochist.

Sitting up against my headboard, I grabbed them, plugged them into my phone, and flipped into my music player. I went directly to my favorite *Sunder* album, the one that had the song I couldn't help but listen to again and again. Typically, Lyrik was the one in the background, there only to accompany Sebastian.

But no.

This song was all Lyrik.

His voice was so different than the screaming, growling lyrics Sebastian was known for. Lyrik's voice was deep and gravelly.

Yet somehow smooth.

Haunting and hypnotic.

It always made me feel as if I was being sucked into the song, mellower than their standard thrashing style, like a dark lullaby rocking me to sleep night after night.

I pressed the buds into my ears and let that voice wash over me, let it seep beneath my skin until it seemed as if the chords were played from somewhere within.

The first time I'd heard this song two years ago? I'd wondered what the man behind it was really like. If he actually was in the kind of pain the song bled. If the sorrow behind his voice was real. I wondered if he might feel the same way I did inside.

So full of regrets you didn't know who you were anymore.

Somehow, I'd felt as if I knew that man. Intimately. Wholly. A bond shared between complete strangers.

That had been nothing more than a wicked dream.

Because Lyrik wasn't anything like I'd imagined him to be.

Of course, at that time, I never believed we'd actually come face to face. Never thought he'd look at me and see something he wanted. Never thought he'd spark those old naïve fantasies.

Tempt me and tease me and trip me.

I bet he'd laugh when he watched me fall.

Cruel.

Breathing in, I closed my eyes, praying for the exhaustion to drag me into sleep. But instead I found myself feeling antsy. More uncomfortable in my skin than I'd felt in a long, long time.

When I couldn't force myself to sit still any longer, I slipped from beneath the covers and dropped to my knees in front of the chest at the base of my bed. Almost reluctantly, I lifted the lid, cautious of what waited inside.

I pulled out the black, leather-bound case. It felt heavy in my hands as I carried it to my bed and laid it on my crisscrossed legs.

It seemed like an hour passed while I just stared at it.

Finally, I conjured up enough courage to unzip the case and pull out the photos inside.

They were nothing controversial. Nothing obscene or secretive.

Just bright bursts of lightning slicing across each sheet.

There were hundreds of the black and white photos. Many had been photo-shopped with the splashes of colors I'd liked to add to them, changing the white strikes to purple and teal and any other color I could imagine, like colorful darts streaking through the sky and striking down against the parched ground.

These images? They represented me.

Before.

When I was so eager to look upon beauty. To chase it. To seek the thrill of being in danger. Putting myself in harm's way to capture these absolutely awe-inspiring images.

That was when I believed the world was out there just waiting for me to capture everything it had to offer.

I'd taken my first picture of lightning when I was five years old. I'd stood at my grandpa's side on our back porch while he pointed to the storm building over the mountains behind our house, explaining the stunning phenomenon.

That first crude image snapped with a cheap old camera soon developed into my passion. A representation of who I wanted to be.

Creative and bold. Positive and accepting. Sincere and honest and brave. Without skepticism or the deep-rooted chip now firmly embedded in my shoulder.

I'd captured my last at age twenty.

I'd thought they'd been an expression of what I found burning from within.

They were nothing but a lie.

After I'd come here? I'd convinced myself I wasn't the crying type. Tears were evidence of weakness. So I'd dried them and put on this bravado I found wasn't entirely false, tapped into this part of myself that I'd never known was there.

It was hard and brash and impenetrable.

Unbreakable.

Not like the unassuming girl who'd snapped these pictures.

Those tears I'd long denied pricked at my eyes, and a lump grew in my throat. It was a welling of emotion that my first response was to swallow down. But just for tonight, after the commotion of rioting emotions that had been stirred in me, I needed to set them free.

Just for a little while, I let myself remember who I once wanted to be.

****

I awoke resolved.

Last night had been a steppingstone instead of a stumbling block. A reminder I had to be careful or everything I'd worked so hard for would all have been in vain.

It was bad enough they'd tracked me down, asking questions about Cameron. Threatening the asylum I'd found in my new home. I refused to allow them to rip me from it.

I brushed my teeth and changed into my running clothes.

I picked the loudest, angriest playlist I could find and began to shimmy the same headphones that had transported me to the dark haven of *his* voice into my ears as I swung open my front door.

And I almost fell flat on my face.

It might have been better if I had. Maybe then it would have concealed the horrified expression that took me over in the two heart-wrenching seconds it took before the shock wore off.

I composed myself and plastered the sneer I'd mastered back onto my mouth.

Stumbling out the other apartment door were the two girls who'd been hanging all over Lyrik last night. Clothes wrinkled. Makeup smeared. Hair sexed up as they embarked on a walk of shame they obviously felt nothing of.

They actually looked rather proud.

And satisfied.

Jealousy flared.

That was the part I didn't want him to catch as his gaze ensnared mine.

But it was there, as obvious as the pang I felt in my chest as he stretched his arms above his head and held on to the top of the doorframe, all of his attention suddenly locked on me.

Don't look down. Don't look down. Don't look down.

It chanted like a plea as my eyes did exactly what I didn't want them to do. They swept down his bare chest. Like they were drawn and starving and without an ounce of the willpower I'd bolstered myself with just before I'd stepped out the door.

For a fleeting second, I gave in. Surrendered. Allowed myself the bittersweet treat of ogling the flesh covered in ink, the designs so intricate and intertwined I couldn't tell where one image ended and another began, although the really foolish part of me was dying to take the time to decipher them.

The jeans he wore hung so low I was certain there was no chance he had anything on underneath.

But it was more. More than that beautiful body. More than that face. It was as if he compelled me to look closer. Deeper. My self-preservation warned I wasn't going to like what I would see.

I ended my stare with a disoriented jerk of my eyes. Of course they had zero control and jumped right back to his too-perfect face, this guy so unbearably gorgeous I felt the magnitude of it shake me like an earthquake.

But this time there was none of that mischief glinting in his eyes.

They swam with pure, oppressive heat, a danger and lust that came with an undercurrent of desperation.

My skin prickled, and I shifted on my bright pink Nike's. I felt naked. Exposed. It didn't help I was standing there in nothing but a sports bra, my breasts squeezed and amplified where they swelled over the top, my belly bare and shorts short.

But it was my face that brought on the wave of insecurity. I didn't have on a lick of the makeup I usually wore and my red hair was wound in a haphazard pile on the top of my head.

Slowly, the smirk reemerged on his mouth, but where it normally bordered on aloof, this morning it trembled with an edge of hostility never before present. "Well, look it there, if it isn't my favorite *bartender*. Aren't you a clever, clever girl?"

"What are you doing here?" I demanded.

Dark eyes narrowed. "I could ask the same question."

"I live here."

"So do I," he shot back.

"God, are you kidding me?" Shaking my head, I rubbed my temples between my thumb and middle finger as I took a single step out onto the landing.

A dry chuckle rolled from him. "It seems we run in the same circles. Charlie owns this building, remember? Considering my best friend and his niece went and got hitched, that practically makes us family."

I wanted to fume. Charlie was *my* family.

"And you just had to pick this apartment?" I accused.

Shrugging, he leaned against the doorframe, for the briefest flash of a second distracting me from my anger when he crossed those strong arms over that strong chest.

Damn him.

"I wasn't about to intrude on Anthony's place considering his wife and kids are coming out to stay for a week or so during the wedding. I'm going to be here for a couple of months and I needed a place to crash. Charlie had a place he needed rented. It was a win-win."

Not for me, it wasn't.

"Besides," he continued, "I figured I was due some privacy. It feels like I've been living with the guys for half my life. Figured I'd come here and lay low."

Lay low?

I scoffed, my chin indignant as I jutted it toward the sound of the car engine just starting up from the parking lot below. "Looks like you're lying low to me."

An incredulous smile ticked at the corner of his mouth, and he cocked his head.

"What, are you jealous, *Red?* If I recall, I made it pretty clear I wouldn't mind it being you slipping out my door this morning. You were the one who said I had *millions* of girls just begging for the position, aren't you?" he demanded, rubbing it in like the arrogant bastard he was. "I was only acting on your advice. Two for the price of nothing. Just the way I like it. But I was willing to make the exception and make it a single rather than a double if it meant I got to play with you."

"You're disgusting."

"At least I don't prance around pretending like I'm not dirty."

He might as well have slapped me across the face. My entire being recoiled and a sharp gasp rushed from my lungs as the voice I'd give anything to forget whispered viciously in my ear.

Dirty.

The memory hit me in an audible wheeze of shock and humiliation and hatred.

"Fuck you," I whispered. The disabling pain stabbing through my body sucked all the animosity from the delivery. I was sure I sounded like a sniveling baby.

I slammed my door shut behind me and tore my gaze from his, thanking God I was in running gear and this was exactly what I was supposed do.

Run.

Because even if I'd been wearing heels, I was pretty sure I would do the same, and I couldn't bear to make the vulnerability oozing from me even more glaring. I bounded down the steps, my hand gliding swiftly down the railing as I made my escape.

Run.

"Goddamn it!" The roar hit me from behind in the same second I heard the crushing blow, his reaction sending a tremor through me even though I refused to look back. I knew without a doubt it was his fist landing a punch against his door. Wood clattered as the door crashed into the inside wall before he roared again and kicked it shut.

The air trembled and shook.

I could feel it. The ripples of danger. The threat enclosing in from above.

Run.

A storm was coming.

Frantic, I pushed the buds into my ears and hit the sidewalk, seeking refuge in the steady thud of my feet.

LYRIK

In my heavy black boots, I paced back and forth across the worn hardwood floors then did it again.

Rays of harsh light found their way in at the edges of the curtains drawn across the windows, like the sun crawled along the exterior walls of the house, seeking a way inside our little pit of darkness.

The song just wasn't coming.

Or maybe I wasn't in the mood.

Maybe my hand was still throbbing like a bitch and my mind was still reeling with what had gone down this morning.

"*Dude*," Ash drew out all frustrated like. "Are you intent on wearing a hole in the floor of my brand new house?"

Brand new? Hardly. It was a century-old mansion not that far from the apartment I was renting, and really close to Shea's place. The house was absolutely ridiculous, boasting something like eight bedrooms, and considering it would only be Zee and Ash and whatever chick Ash suckered in for the night, no one would argue it wasn't outrageous.

But Ash had to be about the damned most impulsive person I'd ever met. Yesterday, we'd been rolling down the street in the Suburban with Baz, heading to Shea's after we'd taken care of some wedding shit, when Ash had yelled out for him to stop.

He'd bolted from the truck like he was chasing down a long-lost friend, arms open wide, going right for the steps leading to the wrap-around porch in this over-the-top house. He'd wandered around like some kind of freak before he called the number listed on the *For Sale* sign staked out front.

He found out the house had once been condemned then completely restored.

Something about that fact appealed to Ash, said the place had called to him, which was the reason he'd found it or some kind of *psychopath* babble like that. Next thing we knew, which literally was like four hours later, Ash was forking over the cash to take it in the clear.

Claimed we'd have to be spending a ton of time in Savannah anyway, coming out because Baz wasn't going to want to be away from Shea, Kallie, and the baby, so it was a *necessity*.

Of course he still had all kinds of paperwork that needed to go through, but considering the house was unoccupied and already furnished, he'd somehow managed to swindle the seller out of the keys.

Dude had skills, that was for sure.

"Making me dizzy, man," he continued from where he sat on the couch with his bass balanced across his lap, face upturned toward the ceiling as he searched for the feeling neither of us could seem to find.

"Sorry," I mumbled, forcing myself back to my guitar. The

plush chair I was sitting on was pushed up close to the coffee table with my notebook open wide.

Blank pages.

No surprise.

I cradled my black electric guitar. She was my baby, after all. My favorite. My constant companion. She was a little beat up, worn down by the road, like she'd witnessed a whole lifetime condensed into a six-year blur of cities and shows and passing, forgettable faces.

A whole lot like me.

Ash's attention flew my way. Blue eyes overflowed with excitement, as if he'd been suddenly struck with a well of inspiration.

"Hell yeah. I got it. Know exactly what we're missing. It's the *vibe*, man. This old house? She's been barren for years. Needs some life breathed into her. A heartbeat. Let's christen her…best fuckin' party this city's ever seen. I mean, a real rager. The kind that will go down in rock 'n' roll history. Make it legendary. Introduce these old walls to what music really feels like. Songs will start flowing from us."

Scratch the inspiration thing.

Ash was just being Ash.

I huffed out a sigh, resisting the urge to roll my eyes like a thirteen-year-old girl. Considering Ash was acting like a kid, he deserved it. Problem was, I was usually game, the first to step to his antics. But since the second I got back, I just hadn't been feeling it.

"Or maybe it's just you storming in here with all your negativity," he accused, looking like he wanted to throw out a pout because I was raining on the goddamned parade the guy never stopped marching in.

"Who the hell pissed in your Cheerios, anyway?" He eyed me over the bottle as he took a long pull, eyes narrowed in speculation. "You not make it back with those two chicks last night? Because that looked exactly like your kind of poison."

I shot him a scowl. "Did you not see us leaving together?"

A grin that came completely at my expense took over his face.

"Hey, man, a girl can always come to her senses."

"Believe me, neither of them had any sense to find."

"Hmmm," he mused, obviously not going to disagree with that logic. He took another drink before he tilted the bottle my direction, like we were playing get to the bottom of Lyrik's piss-poor mood. "Couldn't get it up?"

"Fuck you, man." That was just damned offensive. And it wasn't even close to being the issue. Sick part? I'd gotten it up fantasizing about *Red*, blood roaring south when I thought about tracing the sexy tattoo that covered up the whole outside of her left thigh with my fingers, my mouth watering when I moved on to imagining doing it with my tongue.

There was something about the tattoo, the bright red apple with the serpent twisted around it, that had me wanting to dive in, dig deep into this girl and find out all her secrets.

Get *dirty* with her.

Shit.

Ash cracked the most victorious smile. "Ah, man, sounds like we are talking about my Tam Tam."

That time it wasn't a question. It was shoot, sink, score.

And his Tam Tam?

I couldn't stop the scowl.

Catching my expression, the asshole fucking howled like a banshee, laughter ricocheting against the walls as he slapped his knee. Punk ass couldn't catch his breath as he tried to speak.

"That…holy shit…now that was *legendary*. Couldn't top that if I tried. God, I think I might have fallen just a little bit in love with her last night. Anyone brave enough to pull a stunt like that on the likes of you? That one's a dream. Hotter than shit, too."

Mention of her had me gritting my teeth.

And kinda wanting to take him by the throat.

Still couldn't believe she'd slipped me that drink. At first, I'd thought she was finally stepping up to play when really she was just inciting a war. Truth was, I'd had no intention of taking those girls home.

Not that I owed *Red* anything.

Wouldn't owe a girl. Not ever again.

But my thoughts had been too worked up on her, my skin still itching with the lust she'd caused to pulse through my veins, the need to get lost in all that flesh and seduction, eyes the color of heaven, body like she'd been summoned directly from hell.

Temptation.

Hadn't felt it so strong since the night I'd given in and lost it all.

Ash tsked. "Should have known you were up to no good last night when you claimed needing to take a piss and didn't come back for twenty minutes. You were just asking for it. Hasn't that girl shot you down enough? I mean, seriously, that ego of yours has got to be hurtin'. When's the last time *the* Lyrik West heard the word *no?*"

"I have zero problems with my ego."

At least when I compared it to the size of his.

"And I was just talking to her."

The expression contorting his face said it all. *Are you kidding me? Remember who you're talking to.*

I'd willingly admit to myself I'd crossed a line, sucking those delicious fingers into my mouth, pressing the heat of her hand against my straining body and wondering just how far she'd let me take it. It'd been a desperate measure, really, me begging her to put us out of this misery, because honestly, I was ready to get this girl off my mind before she made me lose it.

That was part of the problem. No matter how many times I asked her to, the girl just wouldn't tell me no. It was like she got off on the chase.

But after that drink?

Bringing those two chicks back to my place was the obvious revenge. And this morning had presented the perfect opportunity to drive it home just that much harder. To make a point she was the one suffering by her shunning the attraction that blazed between us.

I'd just carry on.

Business as usual.

Except taking those two girls did nothing to quell that fire.

Only Tamar had the power to put it out.

Ash chuckled with a shake of his head. "What'd you do, man, take her in the restroom then let those girls go crawling all over you? I'd be tampering with your drink, too. That shit ain't cool. This is Tam Tam we're talking about. Not some random chick you aren't ever gonna see again. Where's your head, man? She's like family."

Family? I had all the family I needed.

"So maybe I said some shit she didn't want to hear."

"And you thought it wise to promptly go and pick up Candi and Bambi?"

I quirked a brow. "Oh, was that their names?"

"Dude, you're a straight-up asshole."

"Who was their friend?" I sent out the challenge with a smirk playing at one side of my mouth.

Caught, he laughed. "No clue, man. Birds of a feather flock together and all that shit. Don't you know anything?"

Apparently I knew nothing.

I'd thought I had it all figured out. Thought I had all my shit under lock and key. But when it came to Tamar, I felt like I was slowly but surely losing my head.

It was indescribable. The crazy sense of power, the thrill of ego and pride, that gripped at my chest when I heard *her* door rattling this morning at just the perfect moment. It was a feeling like I was conquering some unknown feat when that fiery ball of red got tripped up at her door just as I was shoving the two blondes out of mine.

Yeah. I knew she lived next door when I'd rented the place. So what?

Of course the joke was on me, when she'd come stumbling out, wearing next to nothing, hair a total mess where she had it tied on top of her head.

Holy fuck, the girl had the tightest body I'd ever seen. Heavy on the tits and ass, this curvy little bombshell I knew would fit perfectly in my needy hands.

But that wasn't what'd rendered me speechless.

I hadn't ever seen her bare before. Void of the makeup I had no idea could possibly alter her appearance so much.

It'd been like a punch to the gut, finding out just how gorgeous this girl really was—all natural and soft—exposed in a way I doubted she let many see, those blue eyes wide with shock and brutal honesty, and for a fleeting moment flashing with something that looked like innocence.

That was a description I'd never associated with *Red* before.

Innocent.

Angel.

The thought had gone sailing through my head and struck me dumb.

Then I'd gone and said it, just another jab that got to the heart of what I wanted.

I liked to get dirty and I wanted to get *dirty* with her.

But shit. I wasn't sure I was ever going to forget the horrified expression that had shut down all the fierce intensity that normally radiated from her and something else entirely took her over.

Like I was being slammed.

Wave after wave.

Hurt.

Shame.

What bothered me most was I thought I saw something that looked like fear.

Ash plucked at a few notes. "Did you really think hooking up with those girls wouldn't piss her off after you'd just gone propositioning her?"

"That was kind of the point."

And God, it made me feel...bad.

"You just love messing with her. You do realize you've been doing it since the night you called dibs on her when we first started hanging at *Charlie's*? One of these days, you're going to regret it."

Regret. Remorse. Those were emotions I didn't allow myself to feel. Not anymore. They just made you susceptible to all kinds of bullshit and pain.

Fuck.

I jerked my hands through my hair, yanking at the longer pieces on top as I went, before I threaded my fingers at the back of my neck.

I had no idea what I'd done so bad. But whatever it was, it was damned wrong.

And there it was.

Regret.

Remorse.

This heavy, sick feeling that gripped my chest like an iron fist.

Didn't like feeling it.

Not at all.

But with her?

I did.

"What, are you really seriously pissed at her for that drink? That shit was classic, man."

A roll of bitter, confused laughter bled free. "I don't even know. She just..." I trailed off, not sure what kind of label to put on it.

The amusement drained from Ash, this tenseness I wasn't used to feeling filling up the air.

Exactly the reason I tried to stay away from all this bullshit.

My shoulders lifted to my ears in my own confusion. "I said something really shitty to her this morning. Hurt her. Saw it the second I said it. She freaked the hell out and took off."

What scared me most was I'd had the overwhelming compulsion to chase her down and kiss the hell out of her, and kissing was a no go. That shit was too damned personal.

But maybe it would have been enough to warm whatever had gone cold.

It'd felt like the chill of snow. The freezing of rain.

The heat always boiling between us had evaporated and morphed into razor sharp shards of ice in less than a blink of an eye. So I'd put a hole through my door with my fist instead. My throbbing hand was nothing less than an effective end to that delusional, dangerous impulse.

"You...hurt her feelings?" Ash drew out like he was trying to decipher the details to the most difficult equation, because adding a chick and worrying about hurting her feelings was something that just didn't compute for either of us.

I pushed out a sigh.

Why the hell was I letting myself get sucked into this conversation? But that was Ash's way. Couldn't keep a straight face to save his life. Always smiling. Living life. But he got shit no one else did. Knew things no one else could.

He blew a puff of air from his nose, eyebrows drawn in outright bewilderment. "You like her?"

"No." I denied it faster than my mind could process. But my heart had plenty of time.

God, I wanted to fucking hate her, that sick, twisted side wanting to make her pay for having the ability to affect me this way.

Making me want and desire and question.

But like her?

Liking her would be slanting a little too far into the emotions than were allowed.

"Holy shit." Ash chuckled low. "You *like* her."

I lifted my gaze, halting the progression of the humor cutting lines all over his face, dimples denting in his cheeks and chin.

Don't.

It was a silent warning.

He fucking knew better.

This time he huffed in disappointment, roughing his hair back from his forehead and looking at the far wall for two awkward beats, before he turned back to me with his head cocked to the side. "When are you going to give it up, man? Are you going to hang on to it forever? Are you going to let it continue to fester and rot until there's absolutely nothing left of you?"

I swallowed hard.

He jabbed at my notebook with his finger. "You think I don't know what comes out in the songs you write for us, Lyrik? In your words? You think I can't hear that pain? It's going to ruin you."

Too late.

"You made a mistake," he pressed on when I didn't respond.

A swirl of anger twisted through my gut, my voice thick and hard and filled with hatred. "A mistake? A mistake is forgettin' to pay your cell phone bill. Fumbling on the frets during a performance. Putting a ding in someone's car and not telling them.

What I did? That wasn't a *mistake*."

It was wicked.

Inhumane.

Unforgiveable.

A somber smile spread across his face, while I shifted in discomfort.

I watched the thick bob of Ash's throat when he began to speak. "You know, every guy gets his heart broken at least once. We all get that defining moment when we find out the world really fucking sucks. That it's always gonna take more than it gives. Maybe it's a kid's dad to first break his heart when he comes at him with fists flying. Or maybe beating on his mom. Maybe it's the day the dog he's had his entire life dies. Maybe it's the girl he would have cut his heart out for trounces all over it instead."

His own regret traveled his expression, his jaw clenching. "Most of us? We just break our own damned hearts."

He and I both knew that all too well.

"You know as well as I do the past can't be undone. Maybe it's time you moved on from it. Because you aren't fooling anyone."

Move on?

Ash knew better.

There was no fucking moving on.

Stagnant and stale.

Stuck back in that day.

That's where I was gonna forever remain.

Diverting, I shook my head, because I wasn't about to go there. "It's not anything like that. I just feel...bad."

Weird. Different. Unsettled.

He shook his head. "Whatever you say, man."

I clasped my hands between my knees. "What do I do?"

He scoffed like it was obvious. "Maybe start by saying sorry."

Right.

Sorry.

Guess I fucking was.

Ash readjusted the bass on his lap. "Are we going to do this, or sit around acting like pussies all day?"

"Yeah, let's do this."

Because this? It was why I lived. I'd sold my soul for it, after all.

TAMAR

A slight sheen of sweat gathered at the nape of my neck. My hair was pinned up in a red bandana headband, the humid Savannah summer laying siege to the city. Birds flitted through the trees, the slight breeze rustling through the branches the only reprieve to the stifling heat. Rays of sunlight wove patterns on the ground as they glinted through the leaves like a kaleidoscope projected on the earth.

Rounding the corner, I headed back toward my apartment, an antsy, anxious feeling taking me over as I approached.

Knowing what I would find.

Of course it was there.

That menacing-looking motorcycle parked at the curb in front of our building. It didn't matter how many times I found it there. It managed to stutter my breaths each time. Managed to fill me with hesitancy and fear, a shaky sense of excited apprehension that thrummed through my veins.

The thrill I was terrified to feel.

The last week and a half had been an exercise in evading him like the plague.

Because no question.

The boy was a disease.

The kind the came on strong and crept in slow.

No. I wasn't proud of the fact I'd spent a whole lot of that time watching him through my blinds like some kind of deranged stalker. I just couldn't stop myself.

I had this sick compulsion to track him when he'd come sauntering out his door in all his notorious rock-star glory, stealing more of my breath when I'd catch a glimpse of his dark, wild hair, those big hands shoved in his pockets, body powerful and jaw rigid.

Harder still was stoically pretending he didn't exist during the few times he'd come into the bar. I really hated admitting the pang of displeasure I felt when I realized he'd decided to pretend I didn't exist. To respect my wishes to leave me alone.

It was what I'd wanted, after all.

Until it wasn't.

Because worst of all?

It was the time spent sitting on my living room floor with my back propped against my front door.

Lost in his deep, haunting voice.

It floated on the dense air, as if the sadness it bore was alive, its ethereal fingers slipping through the cracks of his apartment into mine during the deepest, loneliest hours of the night.

As if voice and guitar wept as those vapors wrapped around me like ribbons of his sorrow. Each time, he'd play the same song. It was a song I'd never heard before, other than coming from within the walls of his apartment, the lyrics muted and obscured, though the message was clear.

Sorrow.

In those few foolish moments? I hazarded this idea we had become partners to the other's void. Filling up that dreadful, hollow space. As if we somehow fit.

Because the anguish in his voice?

It promised he was as empty as me.

That emptiness was blatant in the times I caught him watching me, too. In the moments when the intensity in those dark, cryptic eyes spiked with something regretful and real. Overridden in shame. Gone before I could give it a name.

Like I said, foolish.

Shaking off the thoughts, I grabbed the railing and jogged up the steps.

A loud clatter coming from his apartment slowed my ascent.

"Shit, shit, shit," he cursed in a quick panic, his unmistakable voice coming from his open window.

Cautiously, I edged up one step and then another.

My heart was beating like crazy when I hit the landing, a gasp shooting from me when his door suddenly flew open. A billow of smoke came filtering out.

"Shit," he said again, his door standing wide open while he disappeared back inside, clearly not noticing my presence.

At a loss to stop myself, I inched forward.

The old, broken pieces inside me flailed, fighting to break free, that naïve, ignorant girl led by curiosity.

And that was the root of it all, why I knew I should stay away.

Lyrik West threatened to zap her back to life.

"God damn it," I heard him mutter.

Another shiver of unease wound with the pique of interest that traveled my spine.

The buzz before the strike.

In hesitation, I sucked in a breath, held it in as I tiptoed forward.

Drawn.

Like one of those ditsy actresses in a horror flick you knew was walking straight into a trap.

You know the kind. That senseless girl who runs up the stairs where there's obviously no possible chance of escape, stumbles and falls flat on her face the second before she has a knife impaled through her heart?

Yeah. Her.

So rash and predictable, yet here I was, inching closer.

The pull.

How was it possible this man held some kind of spell over me? But it was there. Invisible strings tied in all the wrong places, to my heart and my mind and my spirit, those wicked eyes tugging and tugging and tugging until I stood helpless before him.

Run.

But I found I couldn't.

I stood at his open door. And just like that ignorant girl in the movie, I stepped forward in a daze.

My eyes widened as I took in his apartment that looked as if the Tasmanian Devil had come spinning through.

Smoke billowed from the oven, and Lyrik was tossing down potholders next to a burnt cake he'd yanked out and dumped on the stovetop.

"What happened in here?" Concerned words I had no business speaking were out before I could stop them, and Lyrik's attention snapped toward me.

Shirtless.

Of course he was.

Could I have hoped he'd be any other way?

The sad part was I really didn't know the answer to that.

He came closer, waltzing back to a small round table where another cake rested on a platter.

My eyes flicked to where a streak of chocolate frosting was smeared across one sharply angled cheek then down to the dab on his shoulder where he'd obviously tried to wipe his cheek without using his hands.

I had the overwhelming urge to lick it.

I sent up a thousand silent curses.

Dark eyes narrowed, and a flash of that same mischief lit them up.

I felt their spark from across the room.

"Oh, I'm thinking the better question would be what the hell are you *doing* in here, wouldn't you, Red, considering you're standing uninvited in my apartment? Lookin' like a pin-up girl straight outta my favorite fantasy, no less."

The words came out sounding like he didn't know whether to be angry or amused.

I glanced down at my attire, at my sleeveless floral-printed button-down blouse with the bottom tied just below my breasts that revealed a thick strip of my belly, to the flare of my short shorts, down to my little white loafers.

"It's hot out," I mumbled almost incoherently, completely caught off guard.

"Obviously a little too hot," he muttered just loud enough for me to hear.

He turned right back to the high crystal cake platter, a white pastry bag with a swirly tip positioned in his tattooed hands. He bent over and his tongue poked out to the side in concentration as he applied another flower.

Okay, so maybe I hadn't stepped into a horror flick.

I'd stepped right into the Twilight Zone.

Ripping my eyes away, I made a quick pass over the normally immaculate rental. The trendy furniture was covered in tissue paper and ribbon. Boxes were upturned and on their sides, shopping bags of fabric and yarn and sewing supplies dumped out on the couch and chairs.

His suit for the wedding day hung in a plastic garment bag over the French doors.

My stunned gaze moved on to the kitchen where every cabinet door sat wide open, every tool and small appliance cluttering the counters, the sink overflowing with dirty dishes.

"Seriously…what in God's name are you doing?"

So maybe this time I was concerned for his sanity because I was sure this rock star had dove right off the deep end.

"What does it look like I'm doing?"

"It looks like you're baking a cake."

"Baked a cake," he corrected with a shrug of a muscular

shoulder. "Now I'm decorating it."

"And…why would that be?"

"What, I don't look like The Pillsbury Doughboy or Betty Crocker or Paula Fucking Dean?"

A chunk of that silky hair flopped over one of his eyes as he inclined his head, his too-pretty face entirely trained on the task at hand.

I laughed.

Shit.

I laughed.

He was right. He was asking the better question. What the hell was I doing here?

A million warnings shouted in my head, but still, I found myself taking another step deeper into his apartment, a forced lightness twisting through my words. "Uh…no. Not even a little. Should I be concerned? Call someone? I'm worried for your safety. You could have burned the place down."

A soft chuckle rolled from him and I watched the subtle rise of his brow that was still level with the cake.

"You're concerned for my safety, huh? I figured you wouldn't mind one bit if it all went up in flames…me included." His teeth tugged at his plump bottom lip. "Hell, I bet you'd be the first in line to strike the match."

"Well, I kind of like my apartment, so I wouldn't be happy if it *all* went up in flames."

I felt the smile pulling at my face.

Damn. Damn. Damn.

Now I was joking with him.

That same smirk he loved to wear curved one side of his mouth, before something set in those jet-black eyes. Like twilight taking hold. Dimming the world in an aura of severity.

He set the pastry bag aside and blew out a weighted breath as he pressed both hands flat to the table on either side of the cake.

"Listen… There's something I've been needing to say to you."

Uneasily, I swallowed. "Yeah?"

"Yeah." Dropping his eyes, he breathed again. "I…uh…fuck."

A harsh laugh escaped him. One filled with pure disbelief.

Obviously directed at himself.

He rocked back enough to study his bare feet between his outstretched arms, those vibrant designs dancing above the sleek, rippling muscle of his back and chest and arms.

"I don't do this…" he finally said.

I crossed my arms over my chest in the same second I lifted my chin.

Searching for the shield.

"Don't do what?"

He looked up, hands clutching the edge of the table, the air loaded as he pinned me with his unwavering stare.

"Care."

The word struck me like an electric prod. My pulse went haywire and that same shiver of adrenaline prickled across my skin.

Was he even capable of caring?

My thoughts traveled to the song.

To his voice.

To the intangible words inscribed with mourning.

How could he not?

Straightening, he raked a hand through his hair. He glanced off to the side, before he reluctantly looked back at me.

"I don't usually give a whole lot of thought to anything." He frowned. "The things I say? The things I do? I do them without a second thought. Without concern. And the girls surrounding me are usually game. No questions asked. And I was wrong…thinking that same standard applied to you."

"You assumed I was easy?" I forced it out like a tease, tamping down the quiver of unease.

He cast a coy grin. "Isn't everyone?"

"Wow…you really are a charmer."

A shot of bemused air puffed from him as he set his hands on his narrow waist and looked to the ceiling with a shake of his head. He dropped his questioning gaze back to my face.

"But I'm starting to think there isn't one easy thing about you, Red. And whatever the hell I said the other morning…"

In discomfort, he gestured behind me to the stoop between our doors, and I did my best at not revealing how vulnerable he'd had me in that moment.

Did my best to keep up the walls.

"I'm fucking sorry. I didn't mean to hurt you, and I *saw* it, how badly I did. God…you don't want to know how fucking bad I don't want to care that I hurt you. But I do."

His admission stabbed like a stake to the heart.

For him.

For me.

Could we really be so much the same?

"I don't know whether to take that as a compliment or an insult." My attempt at a joke fell flat, the words as wispy as they were dry. I struggled to remain aloof, to grasp onto the bratty bitch who cared about nothing. To align myself with the same kind of indifference usually given by this man.

But right then, he was giving me *more*.

Is that what I wanted? Is that why my skin tingled and my heart hammered every time he was near?

God, it was foolish.

But I wanted to give it, too.

He huffed. "Take the apology however you like. Just know they're rare and chances are there won't be another one where that came from. But we have to do this wedding thing, and I don't see much use in the two of us wanting to kill the other."

I forced a playful smile, pretending as if I didn't feel little pieces inside unraveling.

Coming undone.

"Are you asking for a truce?"

"I guess I am."

"Then I'm sorry for the drink."

He quirked a brow. "Are you really?"

"No." I felt the smirk taking hold, this one not so feigned. "Not at all. You totally deserved it."

"Guess I probably did, didn't I?"

That deadly smile reemerged.

My insides shook.

It had to be my favorite kind.

"You're a dangerous woman, Tamar King."

"Only to those who are a threat."

I plucked a wrinkled black tee hanging from the back of a chair and tossed it his direction. "Here. If we're going to be friends, you need to put on a damned shirt."

He snatched it out of the air. "You know, when I suggested we be *friends*, this wasn't exactly what I had in mind. How about you take off yours and we'll call it even?"

I tapped my foot. "Sounds like someone's gettin' thirsty. Do you need me to whip you up another drink?"

He tossed his head back and laughed.

Gone was the sorrow I heard at night. For once, his expression was totally carefree. He looked back at me with a smile that threatened to shatter my stringent little world.

Because just for a little while, I wanted to fall into his.

To know this other side of him. This irresistibly sexy badass rocker who baked cakes.

He pulled the tee over his head. The tight material stretched across all those perfectly cut ridges and planes, doing nothing but accentuating just how perfect he was.

He roughed his hands through his mussed-up hair in an attempt to tame it. "I think I'll stick to my regular, thank you very much. Don't think I'm up for any more surprises from the likes of you."

"Oh, come on, you're a big boy. You can handle it."

He grabbed the pastry bag, and I focused on the way his fingers curled around it. A large red rose covered the back of one hand and a skull covered the other.

But it was the words *sing my soul* tattooed across his knuckles that twisted me somewhere inside. Without reason or doubt, I knew this beautiful man sang from his soul. Knew there was something greater than the shallow surface he showed.

As if I got an inch deeper, I'd be in a different plane. In a place where emotion reigned and shut down the superficial.

"Nah, I doubt it," he said as he went back to work. "Might not look like it, but I'm a routine kind of guy. Same drink. Same friends. Same kind of easy lay. Write some music, hit the studio before I hit the road. Rinse and repeat."

"That sounds horribly *boring*." Sarcasm dripped free as I made myself at home and walked toward the table.

"Sounds stupid, right? But it all becomes mundane. Predictable."

I glanced at the cake sitting between us.

"And baking. You can't forget baking."

He laughed. "Right?"

Then his expression shifted into something soft as he stared across at me.

And again, that rigid place inside softened.

Apparently I'd launched myself into a perfect swan dive, right into a downward spiral. Dipping my toes into dangerous territory. Immersing myself in the realm of new. For a few ignorant seconds, giving into that feeling of being free and uninhibited and spontaneous.

Needing a breath, I turned away from him, my feet searching for safer ground. I began to snoop through the things strewn around the living room.

We were *friends*, after all.

"Seriously, what are you doing, Lyrik?" I asked with my back to him. "I have to admit when I broke into your house, this was not what I expected."

A lumbering sigh filtered through the air, and I could sense the severity of his hesitation. He barely glanced my way when I peeked over my shoulder at him. He shifted, waging what to say. "My mom…"

My heart clenched at the sudden shift in his tone. At the bald affection that infiltrated it and the expression of love that flickered fast across his face, the fleeting vulnerability woven in between.

On a self-conscious laugh, he dropped his eyes back to the cake. "Jesus…why am I telling you any of this?"

I realized I was holding my breath. "Because I asked."

"My mom…" The words tightened, coming thick and heavy from his mouth when he finally began to speak. "She always told me 'make it if you want it to matter'."

He shook his head, the words strained and choked when he admitted, "*And I want it to matter.*"

Caught off guard, I twisted my upper body toward him. "This is for Shea and Sebastian? For the rehearsal party tomorrow night?"

"Yeah."

That buzz hummed.

The air was so full, my strained breaths skidded in and out of my lungs. My chest trembled with a heave of confusion.

Unable to continue looking at this perplexing, infuriating, beautiful man, I turned away again. Pretended I didn't feel the roll of the ground as it shook beneath my feet.

But it was there.

Intensity skating the space just below the surface of my skin.

Something significant and scary.

Something powerful and bold compelling me toward twilight.

As if I was drawn to the darkness that set around him as if he held the power to cast away the light.

And I knew I should pack it up and leave. Run because running was what I did best.

Instead, I got sucked deeper into his living room, unable to tear myself away.

My fingers played along the pieces of cut fabric, trying to make sense of what I'd walked into. Trying to make sense of this menacing, dangerous boy who *wanted it to matter*.

My attention caught on the crude patchwork teddy bear on his couch. I reached for it.

"Don't touch that."

The dark desperation in his voice stalled my hand that was already wrapped around the thin body. The mismatched pieces were tied and sewn together with brightly colored yarn to create a long, lanky bear in a way that had to have been taught but never perfected.

I could feel the deep furrow pulling between my brows as I looked his direction. Dumbfounded, I held it out toward him. "Is this for the baby? You made this?" It came out almost an accusation.

Pain flashed across his face, before it hardened. "Put it down."

I shook my head. "Why?"

He threw the bag of frosting down and stalked toward me. "I'm warning you, Red. This truce only goes so far. I said to put it down."

Good God. Who was this guy?

I blinked, searching desperately for my shields, but my heart was hammering, blood pulsing in my ears as he neared, that towering boy pressing his hard, hard body into mine.

He pried my fingers from the bear and tossed it back onto the couch. In the same movement, he had me backed into the wall, hands planted above me to keep me caged.

"What do you think you're doing, *Red*?"

My head rocked back to see his face, his ridiculously tall body obliterating mine.

I felt so tiny beneath him. Small and insecure.

Fearful and brave and vulnerable.

For the first time in forever, I wanted to feel that way.

I needed to remember what *living* felt like.

Whatever hid within this boy compelled me to trust.

Dark eyes glinted like black diamonds, as if they could cut through my hardened exterior and find the girl hiding beneath.

As if he could reach out and *touch* her.

I grappled for an answer.

"I'm getting to know my new friend," I whispered, voice shallow and hoarse.

I watched him vacillate in indecision, watched the thick bob of his tattooed throat as he swallowed, before he brought his thumb up to trace my bottom lip. Back and forth. Back and forth.

Those intense eyes were transfixed on the motion, and his tongue darted out to wet his lips.

He seemed torn as he leaned in, body rigid, simmering in doubt and uncertainty and the same insane attraction that refused to let us go. Tension wrapped us, filling the air, covering and coaxing and begging.

That dark, dark pull beckoned me closer.

Lyrik West was going to kiss me.

And God, I was out of my mind, because I was going to let him.

I whimpered when instead he dipped his thumb inside my mouth.

Lust—this hunger that'd simmered since the moment he'd first walked through *Charlie's* doors—flamed through me like a flash fire, twisting my stomach and throbbing between my legs.

Fueling my fears.

Feeding my desire.

He pressed against my tongue, and I knew exactly how giving in to him would taste. The sweet, sweet seduction. The danger. The promise of the most mind-blowing bliss.

Scariest of all was I could already feel the throb of the wounds he would leave behind.

This boy was nothing more than a wicked dream.

"We're not really friends, now are we, *Red?*"

With his head cocked to the side, he murmured the warning up close to my face. "You and I both know better than that."

He dragged his thumb free and trailed it down my neck.

My chin lifted and my stomach quivered as he headed toward my chest.

The callused pad of his thumb ran a path over the distorted heart tattoo that peeked out between the top buttons left undone on my shirt. He traced the inscription on the tattered ribbon that wrapped around the heart as if he were reading Braille.

Ante omnia cor tuum custodi.

Deciphering the words.

As if he could possibly understand my meaning behind it.

Guard your heart.

He suddenly stepped away. "Go home, Red."

My body slumped forward at the loss of his, and I gasped.

Disoriented.

Rattled.

Mortified.

Anger and humiliation engulfed me, and I fumbled to gather my bearings as I staggered into blinding afternoon light. Inside, I begged for the walls to come up. For the mask to hide the hurt on my face.

What the hell just happened? What did I just allow *to happen? Again.*

I turned to glare back at him. "You're such an asshole."

He laughed this horrible, cutting sound.

"I think we've already established that."

My body was on fire and my mind was reeling with the memory of how the crude, simple bear had felt in my hand. I was engulfed in emotion—hate and want and a crazy drive to know a man I didn't come close to understanding.

Was I stupid for wanting to?

My chin lifted and I forced any connection I thought we shared aside.

Drawing blood, I bit at my bottom lip to keep it from trembling. "It's a good thing your apologies are rare…because they don't mean anything anyway."

TAMAR

"Well, damn." On an exaggerated sigh, Ash plopped down into his chair between April, Shea's long-time best friend, and me.

Twinkle lights were strung through the trees above. They draped across the space to create the illusion of an outdoor ceiling over a clearing in the wooded area behind the church where the ceremony had been held. Round tables were set up along the perimeter, making a horseshoe around the dance floor and stage that had been constructed in the center.

A cool breeze blew through the night. It rustled the leaves, mixing up the voices and laughter from the reception with the faint trickle that could be heard from the stream running in the distance.

The scene was breathtaking.

It was no wonder Shea had chosen this spot.

"Damn what?" Anthony lifted his drink, eyeing Ash with a grin from across the table where he sat beside his wife. Anthony was *Sunder's* long-time manager, but I knew he was more of a friend to all the guys than simply a business partner.

Next to him on the other side, almost lost in the shadows, was Lyrik. Sable eyes severe. Dark and confusing and twisting me up just a little tighter. Right into that knot that'd refused to leave my stomach since he'd been *so kind* to make a fool out of me in his apartment two days ago.

But what did I expect? I knew the games those kinds of boys liked to play. And I'd willingly stepped right into the ring.

I wouldn't be making that mistake again.

Ash huffed in astounded frustration. "I thought weddings were supposed to be all about the hooking up? Lovely ladies for miles. A buffet. A smorgasbord. Only single women here?"

He hooked his thumb over his shoulder toward a table on the other side of the dance floor. "Three chicks I already bagged back in L.A. So that leaves April and my Tam Tam."

He waggled his brows between us. "Which of you knockouts wants dibs? One night with a rock legend." He stretched his arms out to the sides, offering that overabundance of cockiness, dimples lighting up in his cheeks. "All-access pass."

April curled her nose in disgust. "Ew, no...just no."

He turned to me, blue eyes gleaming. "Guess it's just you and me, then, Tam Tam. Only thing I ask is that you not chop my dick off in the middle of the night." He grinned. "You kinda scare me, but I'm willing to take the risk."

I lifted a teasing brow, playing along. Funny how I could spar with Ash without qualms or sweaty palms or fear slicking down my spine. "Feeling awfully brave, now, aren't we?"

Leaning on his forearms, he spun the heel of his half-empty rocks glass on the table. "Brave?" He acted as if he were in deep contemplation. "No...No...I believe the correct description would be horny. Yes, yes, that's it."

"Ew," April said again with a shake of her head and shove on his shoulder. He jostled into me and I pushed him back.

"What, can a man get no love around here? Does only Baz get this privilege, the lucky bastard? This is just not damned fair. Someone help a man out here."

I laughed. "Looks like you're going to have to help yourself out tonight, buddy, because it's sure not going to be me."

"Sounds like someone else I know…taking matters into their own hands." That dark, smooth voice cut through the air.

My eyes flew Lyrik's way.

Was he really going to go there?

My stare narrowed in warning and hatred and a flash of hurt I just couldn't keep at bay. I knew what he was implying. Going back to that night when he'd backed me into a corner in the storage room. When I'd turned him down then days later he'd turned around and done the same to me.

I thought both of us would finally have had enough and thrown in the towel, giving up this stupid, futile game. Quit hurting each other for sport.

Because neither of us were going to win.

But, no.

He just kept right on like he wanted to go another round. Watching me as if he couldn't stop.

Big question?

Why?

Why wouldn't he give this up?

That fierce gaze shifted between hunger and remorse and an apology I didn't want him to speak.

Not that I'd be foolish enough to fall for it again.

Casually, he sat rocked back in his chair, as if he were just another person in the small group gathered at Shea and Sebastian's wedding reception.

As if he wasn't single-handedly setting fire to my safe little world.

Lights from above glowed against his face.

Like a halo bestowed on a dark angel.

Under his scrutiny, I felt as if he was slowly killing me. Piece by piece. Thought by thought.

I could feel him sinking in. Slipping deeper. That disease taking hold.

How could it feel as if this dangerous boy was becoming my last dying wish?

Shadows played across the defined cut of his cheeks, accentuating the sharp angle of his jaw, his tie loosened as he kicked back in that delicious suit the man should have been forbidden to wear.

Because on him it was nothing but an irresistible snare.

Potent and provocative.

My insides quivered and shook.

Did he have no shame?

I lifted my chin. "Maybe some people choose to go at it alone because they don't need the added disappointment. They've had enough of it already."

His brow rose. "Maybe they're looking in the wrong places."

"Oh, I have no doubt they're looking in the wrong places. And then in a weak moment they think maybe…just maybe they found something they wanted, that maybe they were looking in the right place after all, and the next second they're shown their instincts were right all along."

If I wasn't locked in this stare down, I might have missed the way he winced at the jab I threw.

We both knew my thoughts had gone right back to his apartment, where I'd sought him out and ended up against his wall. Where I'd so stupidly been giving in.

Succumbing.

Falling right into that trap.

Silence stole over the table, and everyone looked between us. They weren't fools to the discomfort.

Ash tsked, a smirk stealing onto one side of his mouth. "Oh come now, you two, this is a wedding. It's supposed to be all about the lovin', and here you are, fighting like cats and dogs."

Ash let his eyes trail over me, over the gorgeous dress that was pretty, sweet, and delicate up against my hard, rigid armor.

"Considering our Tam Tam here is nothing but a sex

kitten…"

He turned and widened his eyes at Lyrik. "And you, my friend, are nothin' but a dog, we know you two can't help yourselves. But before you go ripping each other to shreds…or more likely, each other's clothes to shreds…let's have some respect for the sanctity of the evening, shall we?"

He glanced between us, smirking wide.

A scowl gathered on Lyrik's face—attention still directed at me—before he grinned at Ash. "Just makin' sure these ladies know all their options."

He looked back at me. "Wouldn't want them missing out on the good things in life."

Ash chuckled quietly. "Sure you are, my friend, sure you are."

Some weird moment transpired between them, Ash's chin tilting up and to the side. Lyrik gave a short shake of his head.

Just awesome. Now I was a part of some silent manwhore conversation. It made me itch in discomfort. Shift on my seat.

Had Lyrik been talking about me?

Kallie, Shea's little girl, suddenly came flying in from across the dance floor, screaming, "Uncle Ash!" with her hands thrown in the air.

Thank God for small miracles.

Ash turned and swooped her up just as she flung herself into his arms. He propped her on the table facing him while he squeezed her, tossing an exaggerated wink out to everyone watching. "Now this here's my real date." He smiled back at her. "Little miss maid of honor."

"Today I'm a butterfly princess," she said with a resolute nod.

He poked at her belly and she giggled, trying to catch his finger. "Stop it, Uncle Ash. That tickles way, way, way bad!"

"Well, that's what tickle monsters do…they tickle." He tickled her more, lightly, before he touched her nose. "Are you saving your first dance for me?"

"Yep, yep, yep! Just like we practiced."

"Good girl."

He set her on her feet, and she kept moving. She pushed up on her toes to press a kiss to my check. Warmth spread through me.

The child was so sweet.

She rounded back to kiss April, doing the same to Anthony and his wife Angie, before she made it to Lyrik.

Only he didn't lean down to accept her kiss.

No.

Instead, he pulled her onto his lap.

Pulled her onto his lap.

Hugged her and whispered words I couldn't hear but made her giggle and pressed gentle kisses into the wild curls on top of her head.

Who was *this* man?

I took a big, steeling gulp of wine and tried not to watch them. Tried to pretend I wasn't witness to something so sweet and soft. Tried to convince myself I wasn't witnessing this convoluted, wicked man *caring*.

God, he made me insane.

He looked up at me from over the top of her head. He held me in the grips of his stare while he held the precious little girl in the safety of his arms.

The air trembled and shook.

No. No. No.

This jerk would wreck me. I could feel it in my bones. In my marrow. In that hollow space inside that no matter how hard I fought it, just kept aching to be filled.

Every part of me was at war. Hate and fear up against the need to be touched. To feel a part of something. Of someone.

I craved it.

Missed it so much it hurt.

Loneliness was a bitch.

But loneliness was safe.

And there was nothing *safe* about Lyrik West.

Hand in hand, Shea and Sebastian worked their way back over to the wedding party table after making their rounds personally thanking their guests for coming.

Ash raised his voice in a tease as they approached. "Ahh…it's Baz, the man of the hour, going and stealing my Beautiful Shea away."

"Damn right." Sebastian grinned.

"Just how many girls are you going to claim?" April asked with a laugh.

"As many as will have me, of course."

Shea stepped forward and dropped an affectionate kiss to Ash's head. "One of these days a girl's going to steal your wild heart and you aren't going to know what to do with yourself."

"Not a chance, darlin'."

"God, please let someone do it." Zee walked up, breaking away from the conversation he was having at another table.

"I'm not sure how much longer I can handle the likes of him with the endless string of girls parading in and out of the house. Woke up with a girl curled up next to me this morning...one I never touched, mind you...she just forgot which bedroom she'd come out of when she'd gone to the kitchen to get a drink of water."

Ash howled and pointed at him. "Hey, man, you're welcome for that."

Zee just shook his head and muttered, "Asshole," under his breath.

Lyrik chuckled in that low mysterious way, the sound wrapping me whole.

Don't look. Don't look. Don't look, I chanted in my head.

Right now what I needed was to shield and protect and fortify. Reinforce the steel barricade guarding my heart.

Yet I held no power to stop myself.

How could I?

Not when I heard Kallie giggle again.

Warily, my gaze flitted their direction, and that wicked, menacing, malicious man was bouncing that angel on his knee.

Dark and light. Corrupt and pure.

My heart clenched in the center of my chest and I could feel those rumbles under my feet, could feel it in the air when that murky gaze locked on me.

I desperately tried to pretend as if he had no effect.

No control.

No intrigue.

All the while that overwhelming awareness spun around me with the force of a windstorm.

Winding and twisting and whirling.

Catching me up in a cyclone of energy.

In his intensity.

In those eyes that saw too much.

He tore his gaze away and looked at Shea, full lips tweaking in affection. "I think there might be someone here who is ready for cake."

"Me, me, me!" Kallie yelled, as if everyone didn't know he was talking about her.

"Really? Are you sure you're ready for cake?" he said while peppering a bunch of loud kisses to the side of her face.

Oh God.

Why? Why? *Why?*

Sebastian swooped her up and tossed her into the air. She squealed. "Then I think it's time to get my Little Bug some cake."

He glanced around at everyone. "You all ready to get this party started?"

"Hell, yeah," Ash said.

I rolled my eyes at him. Was anyone surprised?

Ash pushed to his feet, lifting his chin to the band who had been playing quietly during dinner. The song they played trickled out and he bounded up the three steps and onto the stage, accepting the offered mic.

Shea stepped behind me, leaned down, put us cheek to cheek. Her voice was a whisper. "Thank you so much for being a part of it. Of this day. I know it's not your thing."

I blinked hard.

Because this totally *was* my thing.

Back before I was who I was today.

"I wouldn't have missed it," I promised, my words a little clogged.

As foolish as taking part in this wedding was, it was true.

I wouldn't have missed this.

Not for old insecurities.

81

Not for stolen dreams and not for undying fears.

Not for a boy who had me so spun up I was having a hard time recognizing who I was supposed to be.

Ash's voice rang from the speakers, and everyone turned to face him. "How did everyone enjoy their dinner? Delicious, right?"

A murmur of approval rippled over the exclusive crowd of Shea and Sebastian's friends and family. No question, the wedding was small. They had kept the event secret, away from all the prying eyes of Hollywood and the paparazzi that would all too happily wreak a little more turmoil on their lives.

I had to admit, if our roles were reversed, I'd absolutely hate it. Constantly looking over my shoulder. Worried someone was watching me.

I worried about that enough.

"Shea and Sebastian are just about ready to cut the cake, but before then, I want to say a few things."

"Of course you do," Anthony yelled.

Laughter rolled, and I felt the smile pulling at my face, all the while being completely aware of the man who sat across the table behind me.

As if the heated gaze roaming the bare skin of my back was palpable.

Like I could feel the caress of his callused fingertips.

I shivered.

Ash continued, "As you all know, we're here to celebrate one of my best friends, Sebastian Stone, and his gorgeous wife, Shea."

He gestured with his head in their direction. They had moved to the cake table. Sebastian's arms were wrapped around Shea from behind, his chin rested on her shoulder, hands on her belly while little Kallie jumped around at their sides.

Emotion thickened.

"How the guy got lucky enough to marry my Beautiful Shea, I'll never know," he cracked with his smirk ticking into place.

"Hey, watch it, man," Sebastian hollered with a wide smile, holding Shea just a little tighter.

"Just speaking the truth, my friend." Ash grinned. He held his hand out in a placating fashion. "Now, don't worry, y'all. Sebastian made me promise if I was going to stand up here and talk to you, I had to be on my best behavior. As if I could ever be *bad*."

He winked and I laughed with a shake of my head.

You had to love Ash.

He sobered and glanced around at the guests. "Me and my crew? We've all known Sebastian for most of our lives. We all grew up together. Suffered tragedies. Made too many mistakes to count and learned a ton of tough lessons."

Behind me I felt that severity swell, and I had the overpowering desire to look at him. To see what expression I would find on Lyrik's face. To know what he'd suffered.

Because I knew it was there, beneath all that bad.

"But we also got to experience some of the best times of our lives." Ash chuckled low. "Now I was pretty sure none of us were ever gonna get hitched. I thought we had an unspoken pact that the four of us were never falling into that trap. But our boy here definitely did, and he couldn't have fallen with someone better than Shea."

He lifted his glass and everyone did the same. "To Shea and Sebastian, may you forever keep falling together. May all your *bests* be yet to come."

"Cheers!" echoed through the night, winding with the wind.

We tipped back our glasses, and I swallowed hard and tried to find even ground.

To slow the pounding of my heart.

God, I wished I could leave while a huge part of me wanted to stay.

I felt torn in two.

Shea and Sebastian proceeded to cut the cake, joking around as they fed it to each other while my little world spun on.

Tighter and faster and denser.

So close to spinning from its axis.

And it was that magnet that pulled, pulled, pulled.

I drew in a staggered breath as I felt Lyrik rise to stand behind me.

He strode around the table. His steps were long and strong and purposed, that suit clinging perfectly to his lean, muscled body.

83

The man was so compelling, there was no looking away as he headed for the stage.

He climbed three steps to the top, grabbed an acoustic guitar from a stand, and pulled up a stool in front of the mic before he sat down.

Shit. Shit. Shit.

Lyrik and a guitar would be my demise.

Frantic, my gaze flitted around the space, desperate to find a focus.

Anywhere but on him.

He cleared his throat.

I looked back.

Enraptured.

A gust of wind arose, stirring through the trees, and the twinkle lights danced above.

With his index finger, he scratched his temple. As if in that moment this bold, arrogant man felt out of place. He scanned the crowd and let his eyes land on Shea and Sebastian.

His words were deep and wispy and I felt them in my gut. "Baz...like Ash said, I've known you most of my life. We've had some good times. Victories we never expected. We've celebrated and rejoiced and lived this crazy lifestyle to its fullest."

His tone deepened. "But you were also there at my lowest."

Sebastian stilled, like he was surprised by the admission.

Lyrik's throat bobbed as he swallowed hard. He seemed to have to force out the words. "I want you to know I'm forever grateful that you gave me what you did. Because sometimes one moment...one memory is more important than all the rest combined."

Baz ran his hand through his hair and looked to the ground. So clearly he was caught up in the rawness of Lyrik's declaration.

In the vulnerability he showed.

My pulse spiked and my mouth felt dry.

"I can never repay you, but I can say there's not a soul who deserves to have found what you did. That you got a girl like Shea to love you and she somehow came with an extra bonus of that sweet little girl."

Kallie danced around, grinning up at Lyrik as if he was the sun.

As if he wasn't dark and wicked.

As if he didn't come as a destructive force.

"So tonight, I wanted to play something for your first dance."

He hooked the heel of his shoe in a rung and adjusted the guitar on his lap. That shock of dark hair flopped to the side and across his forehead as he leaned forward.

Enthralled, I watched as he wrapped his big hand around the neck, tattooed fingers taking the frets. His hand with the rose strummed one echoing chord as his eyes dropped closed.

"To me, a song has always meant more than anything I could ever say, anyway. May these words always be true for the two of you."

I felt a tug right in the center of my chest.

That thrill shimmered in the air.

The buzz before the strike.

Lyrik plucked at the strings and, in that moment, the only thing I wanted to know was what he kept hidden inside. For him to show me everything.

I stood.

I couldn't help myself. My feet took me to the very edge of the shadows that hovered around the dance floor.

Drawn.

There wasn't a soul who would have noticed. The rest of the guests did the same, gathering to watch as Sebastian led Shea onto the center of the floor. Where he pulled her into his arms and danced with her for the first time as husband and wife.

Like the rest of the guests, I should have been watching them.

But I couldn't.

Because Lyrik leaned in and finally pressed his sensual mouth close to the mic and began to sing.

He was singing Ed Sheeran's *Thinking Out Loud.*

But his voice.

His voice was raspy and low and filled with emotion so thick I could taste it. Filled with what I could have sworn was prominent in those lonely hours of the night when his songs wept with pain.

I swallowed hard. Desperate for my armor. For all the shields to come up so I could block him from my mind. From the places he was seeping, sinking and submerging and overwhelming.

I was going under.

His entire body tensed as he sang.

Wind whipped through his hair.

Those dark, dark eyes opened and they landed directly on me.

Was it possible he felt this, too?

His voice traveled the air, wrapping me in soft, soft ribbons. Spinning and spinning and spinning. Until they got tighter and tighter.

Suffocating.

Like he was the only thing I could breathe.

Tremors of panic rolled through my body. My heart galloped as he peered at me in the darkness and continued to pour himself into the song he sang for his friend.

He held his voice as the song came to a close. Awe filled the night. Voices silenced.

And I wondered if they could feel it, too.

Lyrik stood, and I remained frozen beneath his gaze.

The hired band reclaimed their spots. Their singer spoke into the mic. "We'd now like to invite the wedding party to share a dance with the bride and groom."

This…this was what I'd dreaded.

But now that dread shivered through me in little shocks of excitement.

Dazed, I took two steps forward onto the dance floor.

At the same time, Lyrik strode down the three stairs, dark, dark beauty radiating from each step.

Tattoos peeked out from beneath his tailored suit. The perfect opposition of gritty and straight-laced.

God.

No man should look that good.

He stalked my direction as the band struck up.

I trembled. Fisted my hands. Hands that seemed desperate to touch.

Was I really going to just stand here and let this happen?

Whatever *this* was?

Hot hands landed on my sides.

I felt as if I'd been electrocuted.

A bright burst of light flashed behind my eyes.

Body alive.

He tugged me closer, up against his heat and hard and destructive beauty.

I pressed my hands to his chest, desperate for space. For a way to keep from feeling like this. Instead, my fingers curled into his suit jacket.

He pulled me tighter, wrapping me in strong arms.

They felt safe.

His breath tickled across my face, lips brushing the shell of my ear.

"I have never seen a girl look as good as you look tonight," he mumbled at my temple. "Stole my breath when you stepped through that church door and started down the aisle. So fucking sexy, dressed up like an angel when I know you've got a little bit of demon hiding underneath."

He splayed one hand across the small of my back. The other set a trail of flames as he ran it all the way up my spine until he was cupping the side of my neck. Forcing me to look at him. Long fingers twisted through the curls that had been ironed into my hair. "Can't stop thinking about you. Can't stop watching you. Can't stop wanting you. What is it you think you're trying to do to me?"

That palm at the small of my back drew me closer. Up against his cock that pressed hard into my belly.

Oh God.

My knees wobbled, and that fear trembled free. But it was overshadowed by the want roaring through my veins. Stomach tight. Legs quivering.

"This...this is what you do to me. One fucking look, one touch, and I'm dying for something I know I shouldn't have. Because you," he chuckled darkly, "you do things to me you shouldn't. It's driving me damned near out of my mind knowing you're just a few footsteps away, right outside my door, and I can't have you."

I fought for my senses, clutched his jacket a little tighter. "We're a terrible idea."

Hard, harsh laughter rocked from him, so low that only I could hear. It came at me like a warning. "Make no mistake, Red. I don't want an *us*. I'll be the first to admit it. I'm an asshole. I'm not wired that way. Not anymore."

Not anymore.

God, I was a fool. Self-preservation floored. Because right then? All I wanted to ask him was what that meant. To dig deep and sink in.

Discover who was hiding underneath.

I knew it. Felt it.

He was just like me.

His voice dropped lower, a wisp at my ear. "But what I want is *you*. I want to take you back to my place, unwrap you like a gift, and look at you laid out on my bed. I want to touch you and taste you and explore you. Make you lose your mind, kinda the way you've been making me lose mine. Tell me what you want, Red."

Shivers slid down my spine.

He pressed his mouth to the side of my neck and mumbled the words at my skin. "All you have to say is *no*. Say no and I'm gonna walk and never going to look your way again."

I got the feeling he was begging me, begging me to say no.

A loud guitar strum reverberated through the speakers. The song played out. Over.

"All right, all right," the singer shouted, his voice amped up as he spoke into the microphone. "It's time to get things shaking around here. Everyone on the dance floor."

It shook us both from the daze and back into this painful reality.

They launched into one of those seventies disco songs that no generation could resist.

I took two fumbled steps back and stared across the short space at the man who was panting. Looking as if he was ready to pounce. To destroy, plunder, and desolate.

"*Uncle Wyrik...Uncle Wyrik,* dance with me! Dance with me! Imma butterfly!"

Kallie was at his side, jumping up and down with her arms in the air.

Warily, he looked between us, his chest heaving. He lifted her. Her grin grew wide with joy as she wrapped her arms around his neck and her legs around his waist. He cast me one last pleading glance before he turned away and started dancing with her.

Bouncing her and swinging her and making her howl with laughter.

Tremors rolled and the air turned cold.

Fear gripped me tight.

I can't feel this.

And like a coward, I turned and ran.

After all, running was what I did best.

I drove directly to my apartment. I cut the engine and sat in the silence for a few moments, trying to reorient myself.

To regain control.

Pushing out a breath, I opened the door and stepped into the night. Gusts of wind stole the peace, cutting through the trees and tumbling along the ground.

Climbing the stairs, I held the railing, slowly pulling my weary body up. My heels dangled from the fingers of my free hand, my head lowered.

Staggering loneliness swamped me.

Rushed over me.

Wave after wave after wave.

I hated how bad it hurt.

I wanted to put up my shields and lift my chin and paint that hard, fierce scowl on my face.

But I was getting weak.

The faintest flash of lightning lit up somewhere in the far distance and my hair whipped around my head.

I mounted the last step onto the stoop and headed toward my door.

A deep, hard rumble echoed through the air. Drawing closer. Coming nearer.

It trembled through me like energy and light and life.

God.

Was he chasing after me?

Why was he doing this?

I knew I should *run*. Lock myself in my apartment and never come out.

But I was frozen with my hand on the doorknob.

A bright light blinded my eyes as Lyrik eased his bike into his spot. He planted his feet as he came to a stop. The engine grumbled and rolled, the sound beating through my heart and pulsing through my veins.

He killed the engine and the headlight dimmed.

The street lamp filtered in from above in a milky haze. Playing across his face as shadows.

And I wondered if I was wired wrong. If I gravitated toward assholes and manipulators and those who would only bring me pain.

Because my want for him was greater than the fear that clogged my throat. Greater than the knowledge that when he was finished, he was going to leave me behind.

Desolate me.

It was all supposed to be contained.

Concealed and buried and camouflaged.

The perfect masquerade.

All feeling corralled.

Suppressed.

With the man staring up at me and me staring down at him, I dug deep for conviction. For the confidence I'd found. In who I'd become.

I was *Tamar King.*

And Tamar King was nobody's slave.

I held complete and utter control.

But Lyrik West single-handedly made me feel as if I was losing that control. I could feel it unraveling. Pieces splintering. Ripping and snapping.

He lifted himself from the bike and straightened to standing.

So tall and menacing and beautiful.

Alarm flashed.

"You left," he said, voice hard.

"And you followed," I whispered back.

Every promise I'd ever made myself rolled through me on a vicious cycle. The ones I'd made to myself when I was just a little girl. When I was bold, excited, and brave, and had wanted to experience everything in life at least once.

They clashed with the ones I'd made when I was twenty. When I'd turned my back on the girl of my youth and became this hard girl who needed absolutely nothing in her life but herself.

Lyrik slowly mounted the steps.

Relentless.

He stopped at the top. His dark eyes swallowed me whole.

In the distance, thunder rolled. I looked that direction.

"A storm's coming," I murmured quietly. I could feel it, gathering in the air. I kept my attention trained on the furor gaining speed, not sure I could continue looking at Lyrik without completely succumbing.

He said nothing as he came closer.

I finally looked toward him as he moved to back me against the door. His hands went to either side of my head.

And again, this dangerous man caged me in.

And I felt vulnerable and small and brave.

Those little girl promises swirled.

I didn't want to be scared anymore.

Didn't want to be alone.

"Give me one night. Show me who you are. Show me that anger. Show me why. Fight it out with me with that hot little body." His words were harsh and desperate. "Or tell me no, *Red*, tell me no. *Say* it, and I'll walk away."

Fear blasted across my skin, mixing with the fire Lyrik had set.

Together, the two were combustible.

My breath heaved from my lungs.

"I can't."

seven

LYRIK

I inched forward and pressed her closer to the wall. She looked up at me with wild blue eyes. They roiled like a tormented sky. I brushed my nose along her temple and inhaled. She smelled so damned good. A touch of cinnamon and a whole lot of spice.

This girl made me lose my head. Fuck. She *made* me lose my head.

If I were in my right mind, I would walk. I would turn right around and walk away and never look back. Just like I'd promised her I would. I knew it deep. Knew it like the setting of the sun that led me into the darkness night after night.

This was gonna end bad. Just the fact I was chasing her was evidence enough.

But right then? I didn't care because I wasn't close to feeling sane.

It seemed no matter how hard the two of us kept trying to fight it, pushing each other off when the other got too close, the next time we just got closer.

Closer and closer and closer until there was no going back.

I couldn't.

Not anymore.

Sitting up on that stage and playing that song while watching the ripping expressions tear across her features had proven that.

For one night, I wanted it. I wanted her secrets. I wanted to sink my fingers in and take for myself. She was the exact kind of contradiction I craved.

The push and pull.

But this time the pull was too great to ignore.

I traced my thumbs along the delicate slope of her neck. Dragged them across the soft, soft skin. Her pulse was racing with a violent beat. I forced her to look at me while my entire body ran hot.

"Tell me what you want, Red." It slipped out in a rough murmur.

In the distance, thunder rolled. Those blue eyes flashed. Flashed with courage and fear.

Something about it made me shake.

Almost defiantly, she lifted her chin, and she reached up with her small hands and grasped me around the wrists.

"I want you to kiss me."

Motherfucker.

Leave it to Red to ask for the thing I didn't want to give. Memories cut a path of panic through my consciousness. Reminding me of what I'd done. Of why I could never get too close.

Of where my loyalty truly lay.

Clenching my jaw, I gripped her tighter. My heart was giving its all to reject *this*. Screaming at me to wise up and to do it fast. To turn my back and walk away. No doubt, my feet had officially crossed into the forbidden zone. Out of bounds.

Red was trying to take me places I didn't want to go.

On the inside, I struggled like a goddamned madman. Torn between lashing out like I'd done the last time she'd been tempting me with the need to sink inside her, to discover the countless secrets she had lying underneath, and gathering her up and letting her in on all of mine.

I was at an all-out war with my instincts. The fucked-up thing was I didn't even know what those were anymore.

Not when it came to her.

Wavering, I rocked forward in indecision then rocked back. Getting closer to those full red lips with each pass.

Her attention flitted over my face. They jumped from my eyes to my mouth and back again. She fisted my suit jacket.

"What do you want?" she demanded, turning the question on me. Her voice was a brazen, needy mix of the siren who had no issue with putting me in my place and the soft vulnerability that kept seeping through.

My tongue darted out and swept across my bottom lip.

Dying for a taste.

"Fuck it."

Figured she was going to kill me, anyway.

My mouth came down hard on hers. At the same time, I drove my hands into ruby-red curls.

Yes. No fucking question. This was what I wanted. Every hesitation left me.

I twisted her hair tight and yanked her head back to grant better access to the pouty mouth that had starred in more than just a few of my fantasies. I *needed* to take more of this girl.

Because hell, if I was giving in, then I was getting it all.

"Red," I groaned as I edged back for a second. Diving back in, my lips closed over her plump bottom lip that'd been seducing me for months.

Goddamn, she was delicious.

I tugged and sucked at it, before I turned to the top and did the same.

A hard breath left her, and tiny pricks of pain just wound me higher as she dug her nails into the back of my neck.

Tamar was short, and I found myself smiling against her mouth as she pressed up on her toes to get closer to me, just as I was pressing her into the wall. Trapping her against my dick that had been hard for her for days—for a damned year, really.

But God, it'd been unbearable since I'd tossed her out my door two days ago. I'd been desperate to keep her out when I knew full well she'd been trying to break through. Back when I'd been a big enough fool to think there was a chance we weren't going to end up right here.

Her tongue touched mine. Tentative at first. Like maybe it'd been just as long since this girl had kissed someone as it'd been for me. Like it was foreign and too much and too little, all at the same damned time.

Then she opened more. Needing more.

Her tongue flicked against the intrusion of mine. She moaned.

Sexy as fuck.

"That's it...show me, Red," I coaxed at her mouth. "Show me what you've got."

My dick throbbed, and I yanked her from her feet so I could get her legs around my waist. Right where they belonged. And this fucking dress...this fucking dress that'd nearly brought me to my knees when she'd come walking through the church doors and down the aisle, was bunched up over her thighs.

With her pinned to the door by my body, I spread out my hands and let them slip firmly down her sides. One single target in mind. My thumbs flicked over the hard pucker of her nipples that peaked through the thin fabric of her dress.

Shit.

"Lyrik." It was a gasp.

I groaned through a grin. My entire body vibrated with a fresh flood of lust. "Give me a few minutes, baby, and you're going to be screaming that name."

I was going to make sure of it.

Shivers rocked her, and I grasped her by that ample ass before I moved lower to take her by the thighs.

I was right.

This curvy bombshell fit perfectly in my hands.

My palm moved hot over that tat of temptation. The apple and the serpent painted on the outside of her thigh.

I wondered who of us was who.

I kept kissing her because she tasted so damned good, kept grinding up against the tiny slip of silk between her thighs. Winding us up tighter than we already were.

"So good," she murmured almost in confusion.

The inflection of her voice? I wanted to swallow it down and somehow make it a part of me. Maybe just as bad as I wanted to devour her. Just as bad as I wanted to taste and take every inch.

Shit.

I felt like a dog on the hunt that had no clue he was about to get bit.

By a tiny red viper, nonetheless.

I pressed harder against her, aching in a way I hadn't for years. Maybe ever.

She was hot.

So damned hot.

Her tight little body radiated heat. Skin on fire.

"Red." That nickname floated out on the delirious, lust-inducing need she managed to work up in me.

On that one single word, we lit.

We were suddenly a blur of desperate hands and straining bodies.

Mouths and tongue and teeth.

She ripped at my suit jacket, trying to get it over my shoulders in the same second I fumbled with the knob of her door.

I couldn't wait to get in this girl.

I wanted to be everywhere.

In her mouth.

Her pussy.

Her ass.

I was taking it all.

For one night, I was letting myself get mixed up in this confusing contradiction of a woman.

Fuck the consequences or the feeling or the lingering regret. Fuck all the bullshit she evoked with a mere glimpse of vulnerability.

Like this blue-eyed angel got me in a way no one could.

Because right now…right now gone were the traces of soft and the innuendos of sweet.

And this red-headed demon had been tempting me for too long.

The door gave and it banged open behind her. Her weight was suddenly completely in my arms. I hiked her up higher and she clung tighter.

We stumbled in, and I kicked the door shut behind us and pressed her up against the nearest wall. "Fuck…Red…I need you. I need you in a way that's just not right. You have me so messed up."

I yanked her back, carrying her toward the hall.

"I know…I know…I know," she chanted, still kissing me mad, two of us banging into walls as we went.

"Oh my God…this is crazy…what am I doing…what am I doing?" she mumbled into our frantic kisses.

"Taking what we both need. Taking what's been coming. What's been coming since the second I walked into *Charlie's* and saw you behind that bar." I kept moving, fumbling toward the bedroom that was just like mine. "Knew then I had to have you."

A soft light glowed from above the partition wall that didn't come up all the way to reach the ceiling, her room sectioned off in the back.

My heart was racing. Too hard. Too wrong.

Still, I continued on, carrying her into her room and tossing her onto the center of her bed.

She bounced on it and whimpered a tight, "Lyrik."

Shit. I liked the way that sounded. Too much.

My eyes raked over the girl who was exactly my kind of perfection. Curves and big tits and round ass. Slender little waist just right for cinching my hands around.

Her head shook slightly on her pillow, and her chest lifted and fell in tiny quakes. For a second, her expression tripped me up,

97

jumping through so many emotions I couldn't catch up with them. Not when I couldn't catch up with my own.

But tonight wasn't about deciphering. It was about giving in. About taking. About surrendering for one minute when it was clear neither of us had a day to give.

I crawled over her. My hands slid up the outside of her thighs as I went.

Her head pressed back and she whispered a moan.

Everything rushed, my blood pumping hard.

Her nimble fingers freed my already loosened tie then tore through the buttons on my shirt. Shrugging it off, I went for her neck. I kissed at the snowy flesh, her pulse alive beneath my tongue. All the while I worked the zipper down on her dress and lifted it over her head.

As soon as I did, I pushed back onto my knees and flicked the snap between her tits on her strapless bra.

It fell free.

"Shit," I hissed, taking a good look at the girl who I'd been desperate to have for the last year. She lay there shaking in nothing but her barely there panties. "You're the best fucking thing I've ever seen."

Ever.

Tamar always looked like a pin-up. Exactly the kind I had pinned up on my walls when I was just making that transition from boy to man. When I was just getting an idea of what I liked. Girls who were red-lipped, sassy, and full-of-steam.

But this…this…

Her.

She was hard and soft. Tattooed and clean. Vixen and angel.

Dirty and pure.

The war I'd been fighting regrouped for another battle. Screaming at me to run. Because my stomach twisted and my heart fisted tightly. A foreign feeling I barely remembered formed in my chest.

Gritting my teeth, I forced it down and instead pulled the rosy-bud of one of those tits into my mouth. I sucked at the pink, pebbled flesh, rolling it around my tongue. Flicking and tasting and teasing.

She arched and gasped.

A growl rumbled in my chest. "So damned hot…fuck, Red…fuck…you are every girl I've ever wanted."

I didn't even know what I was saying. The words were a mumbled mess. Logic not quite fully firing from my brain. All rational thought had been stripped from me as I made a move across the tattoo on her chest and on to her other tit. I lapped across the top of the curved swell before rising up to take that nipple in my mouth.

Nails scratched at my back and her hips bucked against mine.

Begging.

When I couldn't take it a second longer, I climbed off the bed and unbuttoned my pants, stripping myself to my underwear while I watched Red writhe on the bed. Eyebrows drawn and pulled up tight. Hands fisting in the sheet below her.

Knew I was about five seconds from setting off that bundle of fireworks that sizzled and burned.

I crawled back over her and knelt between her legs. They were trembling. Rolling with need and lust. I gripped her knees, her skin hot and flushed and making my mouth water. My hands slid down and my fingers traced over the serpent and around the apple on the outside of her left thigh as I watched her blue eyes flare.

At the contact, she released a tiny cry.

The sound had me straining harder. I leaned forward and bent over her leg so I could dip down and get a good taste of that tat. My tongue dragged over its lines, across her skin. I just kept moving, taking a path over the top of her thigh and to the inside. I sucked at the tender skin that met the edge of her panties as I gathered the tiny bit of material at her hips in my hands.

They needed to go.

I started to drag them down.

Red whimpered again, and there was something about it that sent a tremor of unease through me. Her legs clenched down around my sides.

Not to hold me close.

But to keep me at bay.

They were shaking. Almost as badly as her arms were shaking at her sides.

I jerked my head up to look at her face.

"Red," I whispered urgently. At the sight of her expression, I scrambled back like I'd dipped my fingers in flames.

Blank panic.

Her eyes were wide and trained on the ceiling. But somehow I got she wasn't really there. Not with me. Not anymore. Her body was rigid and tears streamed unchecked from the corners of her eyes and into her hair.

This time when she whimpered it sounded more like a sob.

"Red," I whispered again. A whisper that was close to begging, because I'd beg if it'd bring her back from wherever she'd gone.

My heart pounded. Fuck. I was so far out of my element, I didn't have a single clue what to do. I moved back enough to give her space.

To let her breathe.

But there was a piece inside that wouldn't let me get far. Even under the warning roaring in my head to fucking up and run. It was the piece that urged me to comfort her. To soothe her. To take it away.

Some fucked-up piece that got all twisted and mangled when I looked at her like this.

When she was completely vulnerable and exposed.

Angel.

Innocent.

She rolled onto her side and drew her knees protectively to her chest. Her head just kept going deeper, burrowing into the pillow.

Her body wracked and shuddered, heaving with sobs that got louder as she curled tighter. Like she'd give anything to disappear.

Again, my heart fisted in my chest. Painfully. So tight I couldn't breathe. Like this *thing*—like a monster inside me—was suffocating me. An inhuman swell of protectiveness I couldn't afford to feel. Rage set up a slow boil just under the surface of my skin.

Get out. Go. Go. Go. You can't do this.

Helpless, I climbed to my feet, searching her room. For what,

I didn't know.

An answer.

Or maybe a name.

Yeah.

A fucking name. Because I was pretty sure I needed someone to kill. To hunt down whoever had hurt her.

I looked back at the girl who was lying there half naked, shivering like she'd been left for dead out in the snow. I grabbed a blanket and covered her.

"Red," I whispered. Cautious, I ran my fingers through her hair. She flinched but didn't freak out like she had before.

"Red, baby, Red. It's me...it's Lyrik, I won't hurt you...I promise, I won't hurt you," I kept murmuring as I gathered her in my arms.

Crossing another line.

I carried her to the big plush chair she had in the corner of her room and settled her on my lap.

She kept crying and trembling in my arms.

"Red." I rubbed my hands up and down her back. Rocking her. Shushing her. Anything to take it away.

To make it better.

Fuck. Why couldn't she have just said no?

I'd begged her to.

Then neither of us would be here. Right where we shouldn't be.

"I'm so sorry." Her voice was a hoarse rasp. So desperate and small, I felt it rattle my bones. She buried her face in my chest and clutched me like I was her lifeline back from the dark. The brash, bitch of a girl who tossed drinks at a dive bar was long gone. "I'm so sorry."

I ran my hand down her back and pressed a bunch of small kisses to the crown of her head, my voice lost in her hair. "Shh...don't apologize. You've got nothing to apologize for. Nothing. You're safe. You're safe."

"Lyrik." It was pain. Torment. Regret.

"Shh...baby...I've got you...I'm not gonna let anything happen to you."

I cringed as soon as I let it pass from my mouth.

I looked to the ceiling and squeezed my eyes closed.

What the fuck had I gotten myself into?

"Promise?" she whispered like she was just a scared little girl.

"I promise."

It was a lie.

Truth was, I couldn't keep anyone safe.

Because guys like me?

They bred destruction.

I felt everything break apart while I held her. Held her until her whimpers trailed off and her tense body finally relaxed. Meanwhile, mine threatened to snap.

When I was sure she was asleep, I carefully carried her back to her bed. Cautious not to wake her, I laid her down in the center of it still curled in the blanket. A moan bled through those red lips, and she snuggled back onto her side. All that red hair tumbled out behind her.

I brushed my fingers through it and anger pulsed.

Unstoppable.

What the fuck was I going to do?

TAMAR

I couldn't keep my hands steady. Glass clattered as I fumbled for two beer mugs from where they were hanging on the iron racks suspended above the bar. I pulled in the deepest breath, a vain attempt at settling my heart and my mind and my hands. It did nothing but stir my nerves more.

I should have called in sick.

I should have stayed curled up in bed all day. Just the way I'd found myself early this morning when I'd awoken alone in my bed wearing nothing but my underwear.

Or maybe I should have packed up all my stuff and thrown it

in the trunk of my car and ran.

My heart throbbed in a resounding ache. *That's exactly what I should have done.* I knew it. I couldn't stay here much longer. In this place that had become my home. Where I had friends. People who cared. Those who had become my family.

That was the problem. It was getting too hard and I was getting too deep. But I didn't want to leave. I didn't want to start all over again. I couldn't imagine welcoming a loneliness greater than the void I already drifted in.

Why, after all this time, had I given in?

Above all, why had I given in to *him*?

Turmoil raged through me like a sizzling firestorm. My insides were aflame with the aftermath of Lyrik's touch. With the way he'd made me feel. That chaos was only fed by my pathetic reaction last night. I'd never anticipated *that*. But I'd let myself go. Let myself get lost in feeling and touch and hungry words.

Lost in everything I'd wanted and refused myself for the last four years.

I'd gotten lost in Lyrik before I'd gotten lost in the recesses of my mind. Lost in the dark corners I wanted to pretend didn't exist.

I focused on pushing the air in and out of my lungs as I filled the mugs with draft beer.

Lights strobed from the stage. The rest of the bar was dimmed and dark, the energy alive. Normally, this was exactly the type of vibe I thrived on.

Not tonight.

The band playing on stage was loud and gritty. Every word the singer sang grated on my ears. Every chord of the guitar felt like the screech of nails dragging down my spine.

My entire being was twitchy and antsy and out of sorts. My concentration shot.

Foam spilled over the sides of the mugs. "Shit," I hissed and set the beers aside, frustration bleeding through when I grabbed for a rag and aggressively wiped up my mess.

"You think I could get that beer over here, or are you not even capable of that one little task?" The snub hit me from the side.

I had no capacity for bullshit tonight.

Narrowing my eyes, I grabbed the beers and turned my attention to the jerk sitting at the far side of the bar. A guy who was probably in his early thirties. Attractive. Clearly, that was the only thing he had going for him.

He shot me a sweet, mocking smile. "Is it really that hard? If you need help, all you need to do is ask. I'm really *good* with my hands."

Insult me and try to pick me up all in the same breath. What a prick.

My top lip curled. "I think I'm plenty capable, thank you very much," I tossed back with all the restraint I could muster, doing my best to keep it in check when all I wanted was to unleash the hostility roiling inside me on this asshole. With a sneer, I slid the beers to him and his friend and cocked my head. "Satisfied?"

His brow lifted, his voice smooth. "Not even close. Why don't we find a dark corner and you can make it up to me."

Like he'd struck me, I paled and took a trembling step back.

"Oh come on…look at you…don't play coy. You know what you're good for. You need me to pay?" His eyes gleamed with lust, as if I was there for nothing more than his entertainment. "I'm good either way."

Those flames roared, that storm spinning and spinning and spinning. Or maybe it was the room.

I was shaking, searching for the breath I had lost. My chest grew too full and blackness threatened at my eyes. I felt stuck somewhere between that vulnerable, stupid girl who I never again wanted to be, and the bitch who wanted to lash out at the world. To jump across the top of the bar and rip out this guy's throat. To make *him pay.*

Like instinct, my hand wrapped around the neck of a big bottle of Jack.

I felt a solid arm around my waist, pulling me back, a placating voice at my ear. "Whoa there, sugar."

Charlie.

I slumped with my back against his chest, catching the breath I was searching for in a wheeze.

"There now, there now," he murmured as he hauled me away.

He dipped us under the end of the bar and led me through the swinging door to the kitchen. Off to the left was an old grungy office, a single dim lamp burning from the desk that sat in the middle. He snapped the door shut behind us when he had me within the quiet.

He turned me around with his hands on the outside of my upper arms. I cringed when I saw his expression. His mouth was slack, those kind brown eyes filled with concern and completely lacking their near-constant ease.

His brows knit tight. "Hey there," he soothed. "You in there, sugar? What's going on with you tonight? You damned near clawed that guy's eyes out."

I huffed, though it was shaky. "He would have deserved it."

"Have no doubt about that. Already have Nathan on it. He's out. Don't need scum like that mucking up my bar."

He squeezed my upper arms in his hands. "But you and I both know well enough you deal with trash like that on a nightly basis. Normally you handle it without even a ruffle of your pretty little feathers, and tonight you're about as agitated as my momma's old washer."

I ran an unsteady hand through my hair and glanced at the floor as I blew a puff of air between pursed lips. Reluctantly, I looked back at him. "Sorry, Charlie. I'm not exactly at the top of my game tonight."

A tender smile appeared, and his voice dropped in sincerity. "Don't expect you to always be on, darlin'. We all have a bad day every now and again."

Creases dented his forehead. "But I don't think I've seen you lookin' so lost since the day you first came stumbling through *Charlie's* doors. And you damned near broke my heart that day. Tell me what's put that haunted look back on your sweet face."

Sweet?

Is that what he saw when he looked at me?

Slowly, I shook my head, swallowed over the lump lodged at the base of my throat. I was searching for that smirk I loved to wear, but it just wouldn't come. Instead, my bottom lip quivered. "It's nothing."

"Don't go lyin' to me now. I know you better than that." His eyes narrowed. "This have something to do with Shea and Sebastian's wedding last night? Knew it was gonna be hard on you."

Knew?

How?

Did this man see right through me?

A frustrated sound jetted from between my lips, and I roughed a hand through my hair. "No, it wasn't that."

It was everything surrounding it. The stepping out. The putting myself on the line. The dangerous boy who'd seemed to haul in the monstrous load of my baggage with him.

"You looked beautiful, sugar," he attempted. "Real beautiful."

His head drifted just to the side. "Hope one day you'll be lettin' me walk you down the aisle, just like my Shea Bear gave me the honor of doing yesterday."

And I knew he was digging, trying to get to the heart of *me*. Just the way he'd always done. I struggled to find the mask just as an excruciating pain clamped down on my chest.

Everything in Charlie's tone was fatherly. Caring. Hopeful for my future.

Daddy.

Memories barreled through me. I was too weak and raw to stop them.

Charlie didn't even know my father existed. He thought my parents were gone. Dead. That I was alone. I'd lied to this selfless, generous man who'd only ever cared for me, thinking it was the only way to protect myself.

And I kept doing it because I didn't know any other way.

That hollow loneliness radiating from within was worse than I had felt in four years. Maybe in all of it combined. As if it was creeping in like a lost ghost, looking for a home, settling heavy within my soul.

Because I felt this life of pretense coming to an end.

I pasted on a teasing smile. The edges were a wobbly mess, clearly just as fraudulent as the flimsy, impetuous words. "Don't hold your breath, old man. You and I both know that isn't about to happen. This girl flies solo."

He lifted my chin. The tweak of his lips was genuine and knowing. "Just who do you think you're foolin', sugar, because it sure ain't me."

"Charlie—"

"Don't think for a second I don't see you, Tamar King. That I don't recognize loneliness when I see it. I've been livin' in it for too long myself."

God.

"Lonely recognizes lonely, don't you see?"

I tried to speak around the lump clogging my throat. Diverting and obstructing and pretending as if what he said didn't hit me like a landslide.

"I can't count the number of times I've seen women flocking here just to see the likes of you, Charlie. Pretty ones, too," I tried, going for casual and knowing I failed miserably.

He smiled a somber smile. "But none of them will ever be my Sadie."

His words clawed at my chest.

"Don't break my heart, old man." It came out on a breathy, teasing plea.

His brown eyes softened. "Looks to me like it's already broken."

I recoiled.

"Don't you dare," he warned with a big palm cupping my face.

"What?"

"Run. Don't keep running from whatever you've been running from."

Quickly, I shook my head. "I'm not sure I know how to stay."

Softly, he eased in and kissed my temple, before he turned and walked to the door. With it open, he paused and looked back at me over his shoulder. "You keep running and whatever you're running from is just going to keep running right after you. Only way to stop it is to turn around and cut it off head on."

Fear flashed through me. I couldn't. I wasn't ready. And after last night, I wasn't sure I was ever going to be.

I blinked as images flashed.

Lyrik kissing my thigh.
Too close.
Too much.
Shaking.
Terrified.
Engulfing darkness.
I gulped around the remnants of fear.

Would it always be that way?

Charlie clicked the door shut behind him. A hard breath pushed free, and I turned away as I slumped forward with my arms wrapped around my waist.

As if I could shield myself from the turmoil.

But I was coming to realize the shields did nothing to protect me. They gave me nothing more than a counterfeit sense of security. And I was breaking down beneath them.

The door swung open again.

"Charlie," I whispered, still facing away. "I can't—"

Shivers pricked across my skin just as awareness pressed in.

On a gasp, I flipped around. My mouth dropped open wide and I fumbled back.

Lyrik stood in the doorway with his hand on the knob. Shock waves pulsed, and his intense, severe energy surged. Slamming and striking and stealing my breath. Those licking flames he'd left behind blazed to life, singeing me in regret, fear, and a rush of unwelcome relief.

No.

That dark, menacing boy stood like a shadow beneath the hazy light, his face all harsh lines and blunt curves. Even from across the space, obsidian eyes flared. In them, I felt the resistance, like maybe he was fighting the same battle as I and neither of us knew which side we were supposed to be fighting for.

I wanted to scream at him to go *and* beg him to stay.

Humiliation shivered through me. God, I couldn't stomach the memories of the way I'd clung to him. Begging him to make it okay like a weak little girl.

I'd ruined everything.

I stepped back, my voice quiet but hard. "Please, just go."

Panic spread when of course he didn't listen. Instead, he edged the rest of the way into the office and shut the door behind him. He seemed to ride in on a whirlwind of anger, his jaw clenched, muscles strained and tight. The click of the lock snapping into place resonated in the tense air.

"You know that's not going to happen. Not now. Not after last night."

My feet fumbled a step back when he began to advance.

He'd left me sometime in the night. I'd thought maybe he'd had enough. That he'd let me be. And Lyrik West leaving me be was the only thing I needed and the last thing I wanted.

I pressed my hands flat against the wall behind me that prevented my escape. Tremors rocked beneath my feet with every step of his approach. A halo of darkness surrounded him, his potency trembling in the air.

The buzz before the strike.

That feeling just increased as he came nearer and nearer, until he once again had me backed into a corner. Caged. Breathing his breaths and feeling the rapid beat of his heart.

I tried to keep my attention downcast. To hide some more when he'd already witnessed every single thing I hadn't wanted him to see. But I couldn't resist when he just hovered over me, not saying a word. As if he were prying whatever answer he sought from my silence.

When I couldn't take it any longer, I looked up. My gaze tangled with his. Hatred. In his dark, expressive eyes, I could see unfathomable hatred.

But it wasn't directed at me.

Because they were protective, too.

Somehow he managed to delete another inch between us. Completely closing me in. His voice was rough when he spoke. "Someone hurt you?"

My entire body winced, and I jerked my head away. His hand found my chin, his touch gentle while everything else surrounding him was harsh.

"Please." I squeezed my eyes closed when he forced my chin up.

"Red." The way he said it twisted through me like a hot knife. The pain forcing my surrender.

"Don't shut me out," he murmured, and his thumb traced along my trembling bottom lip. "You think you can pretend last night didn't happen? Even if you can, I can't."

Hard laughter rocked from me and my eyes flew open as I released the bitterness from my tongue. "I've been pretending for years."

"How many?" he whispered with that same voice that haunted me night after night. "How many years you been pretending? How many years has it been since you let a man touch you?"

I whimpered.

"How many?" he demanded.

"Four."

I couldn't keep the word in. It was as if he pulled it from me.

I watched the thick roll of his throat as he swallowed hard, and his attention shot off to the side as if he needed to gather himself, before he looked back. Something desperate coated his severe words. "Did you want it? To be with me?"

The answer was a tight rasp when I finally forced it from between my lips. "Yes."

The scary thing was how much I'd wanted it.

"Do you still want it?"

Maybe he saw the answer in my eyes, in the way my lips parted and a needy breath left me. Because in a flash, his mouth came down on mine, and his big hands wrapped around both sides of my neck, his fingers extending all the way around to the back.

Possessive.

The shock died on my tongue when he licked at it in a dominating dance. Energy stirred, that thrill I'd lived for speeding free and fast, igniting every nerve ending and skating across my skin.

I moaned, fingers tugging at his hair. "Lyrik."

"Tell me," he mumbled against my lips, "tell me you still want it."

"Yes."

It was all the response he needed.

He kissed me like I wasn't the fragile, broken girl who'd crumbled in his arms last night.

A small piece of me fell for him. Right then. Right there.

His spoke between his kisses, his voice raw. "I'm here for the next two months. Let me spend it erasing every memory of that bastard from every inch of you. Until he no longer exists and I'm the only thing you know."

A breath escaped me, and my heart beat so hard I could hear it pounding in my ears, this constant boom, boom, boom that raced to keep up with my speeding thoughts.

Because there were some wounds that went too deep they could never be erased. But God, I wanted him to try. To erase some of this acute loneliness. To sate some of this inescapable attraction.

All I wanted was to feel and to touch and to be touched. To love and to be loved.

But I was no fool. Lyrik wasn't going to *love* me. Not like I needed to be.

Pulling back an inch, he cupped both sides of my jaw. His eyes searched my face. "Yeah? We take it as slow or as fast as you want." He squeezed. "All you've have to say is no."

My tongue darted out to wet my dry lips, and the raspy, imploring words tumbled out before I could stop them. "What if it hurts…when you leave?"

God. He must think I was pathetic.

Darkness flashed, those eyes setting like the sun, and one side of that delicious mouth tweaked with a half smirk that tore at my insides. Because it was every kind of sad.

"Baby, I promise you, I'm not worth the pain."

"We're a terrible idea," I murmured in some kind of last-ditch effort for him to come to the senses that neither of us seemed to be able to find, wishing I could push him away when I just kept getting closer.

Sinking deeper.

Our voices quieted with each word we spoke, the tension increasing. Thickening the air. Our breaths strained and our bodies stretched tight.

"Yeah. A terrible, terrible idea," he said. "All these months you pushed me away? You were right…everything you said. I'm rotten to the core. And fuck…know I should stay away…tried to all fucking day. Told myself again and again to leave you alone. To let you be. And here I am. I told you last night…I can't stop thinking about you. Can't stop wanting you. And I can't stop thinking that maybe you might need me just as bad as I need you."

He reached out and ran his knuckle down the side of my cheek, turning it to lift my chin toward him. I didn't flinch, just blinked up at this beautiful, dark, menacing boy who didn't seem so menacing after all.

We seemed to be set to pause. Hung up on which direction to go. Whether to push rewind or flash-forward or delete.

"I don't believe you," I finally whispered, so soft it was barely heard. I reached up to clutch the neck of his T-shirt, exposing more of the ink littering his body across his strong chest and climbing up his neck.

I trembled, wanting to touch and taste and explore. For a few moments, to feel like the old me. That was the problem with Lyrik West. He zapped that brave girl back to life. But I wasn't sure who she was anymore. "I think you might be a little perfect underneath it all."

I could almost feel his heart rate increase. "Believe me, it just gets uglier the deeper you get."

It felt a little like it was his last warning.

"Funny, because the more I see, the more I like."

A small smile kicked up at the corner of his mouth, and he shifted and wrapped one arm around my waist, pulled me close, up against all his hard and heat and danger, the other palm coming soft against my cheek.

"*Blue*," he whispered.

Blue.

My nose scrunched in confusion.

He smiled wider and ran his fingers through my hair. "Wild, wicked *Red* and sweet, beautiful *Blue*."

Oh.

Shit.

Yeah. A little too perfect. And every single kind of wrong.

Chewing at my bottom lip, I let loose a soggy laugh. As if maybe I could float away from the heaviness of this world, as long as I was safe in the security of his arms. "Are you accusing me of being bipolar?" I teased, my feet barely touching unsettled ground.

He laughed, a throaty sound I felt in my belly. "All I'm accusing you of is being every single thing I like. Rough and hard and brash. Sweet and soft. This sexy little contradiction I want to decipher, bit by bit."

My insides shook. "Now you're just asking for trouble, rock star."

He leaned in close to my ear. "And I can't wait until I'm drowning in it."

Lust pooled low and I clutched him tighter.

The truth was, I wanted that, too. To know this perplexing, infuriating man. Inside and out. Mind and body and soul.

Would he let me?

"This is crazy," I said.

"Probably."

A smile wobbled on my mouth as I looked up at him. "I'm not even sure I like you."

He laughed a rumbly sound. "Sure you do. At least a little bit."

He brushed his full lips across mine. I was right. They were just as delicious as that damned apple.

Softening, he ran his thumb over my cheek. "You're so damned pretty. You make me lose my head."

No, *losing their head* was all on me. Because there was no question. I had to be insane. Completely, totally insane.

Because I knew better than this. Was stronger than this. Had rebuilt my world to become who I wanted to be.

And with a touch, Lyrik brought it crashing down.

Straightening, I put an inch of space between us, needing a breath so I could try to make sense of this complicated situation. "How does this work?"

He shrugged. "However we want it to." My favorite smile worked its way on to his mouth. The deadly kind. The kind that could desolate whole cities unaware. Just a flash and you were *owned.* "Think we should start by you getting back over here so I can kiss the hell outta you. Now that I've started, I'm not sure I want to stop."

My eyes dropped into slits. "Just you and me? Because there's no chance I'm going to sit inside my apartment watching a flock of sexed-up girls stumble out your door every morning."

A low, satisfied chuckle rolled in his chest and he edged closer, hand cinching tight on my hip. "There she is…*Red.*" He dipped down closer. Sincerity wove through his expression. "That was wrong, Blue. Pulling that shit with you. Shoving something in your face you didn't deserve to see. Two months…just you and me. And I promise you…you're the only girl who'll be in my bed."

And Lyrik kissed me.

Kissed me like he didn't want to stop.

I guess I really had lost my mind.

The distorted heart engraved between my breasts throbbed.

Guard your heart.

Guard your heart.

Because I was worried this boy might just be the one to steal it.

LYRIK

I slid into the secluded horseshoe booth with my crew. Ash was sitting directly across from me and Zee was stuck in the middle. His eyes flicked between the two of us.

I got why his nerves were all kinds of rattled.

Zee was the blameless of the bunch. Not a malicious bone in his honest body. Sometimes I wished he wouldn't have stepped up to stand in his brother's shoes. Mark had gotten messed up, mixed so deep in the corruption that was our lives, he'd lost his in the middle of it.

When Mark died two years ago, Zee took his place as drummer.

He wanted his brother's legacy to live on through him. I totally got it. That didn't mean I was okay with him seeing the ugly shit that defined our world. With this kid getting tainted by it. Not when it felt a little like he was our responsibility.

"She good?" Ash asked with a rigid lift of his chin. The lights strobing from the stage just barely lit up the lines set in his face. Ash was normally as casual as they came. Nonchalant. Everything a fucking joke. Until the shit going down wasn't funny at all.

"Yeah. She's good." I swallowed down some of the violence still screaming through my veins. Seeking a release. Because if I was being honest, I wasn't sure she really was. "Is that piece of shit *good?*"

Ash shook out his right hand, flexed his fist. "Yeah, man. Taken care of. I don't think anyone's going to see the cocksucker hanging around *Charlie's* any time soon."

I nodded tight, because I really wanted it to be me who got to beat the asshole bloody. But Ash knew me well enough to know when I needed to be sidelined. Saw it the second I was about to come unhinged and things were going to get ugly.

Last night when I'd left Tamar and gone back to my apartment, I'd tossed and turned all fucking night. Worried about her when I didn't have the right to. Fought the goddamned overwhelming compulsion to track down the fucker who'd hurt her and inflict whatever pain he'd caused her a hundredfold.

What I'd fought against hardest was the need to go back to her place and wrap her in my arms. Hold her and soothe her pain away.

And that right there was what led me to the decision to walk. To turn away and never look back. Just like I should have done in the first place.

I couldn't afford to worry.

To *care.*

I had convinced myself getting involved in her mess would just make it messier.

Get her *dirtier.*

And I knew without a doubt this girl didn't need that. She needed no part of my black, filthy heart.

She needed the good shit *I* couldn't give.

Funny how it hadn't taken Ash all that much to persuade me to head down to the bar for a couple drinks. Not after I'd spent the entire damned day watching out my window for a glimpse of her. To make sure she was okay. Guilt ate at me like some kind of flesh-decaying disease, because no question it was me who'd pushed her over the edge.

I'd had the stupid compulsion to apologize again.

Instead I'd pressed my back against my wall to keep myself concealed when she'd come out her door, looking like the best thing I'd ever seen. Like everything I couldn't have. So I'd convinced myself again just to let her be.

Of course that'd been shot straight to hell when Ash, Zee, and I had come strolling into *Charlie's*. She hadn't seen me, but I'd caught the tail end of what the piece of shit had said to her.

Worst of all was I'd seen the look in his eye.

Like she was dirt and he was about to get *dirty*.

Charlie had intervened with Tamar, because I was pretty damned sure I'd seen the girl just about to lose her cool, while Nathan, the big-ass, burly bartender who doubled as security, started to haul the piece of shit out the door.

I'd seen *red*.

It was instant. The spike of rage that pierced me like a fiery arrow. It'd come on like a hurricane. The need to protect this girl. The need to hurt whoever hurt her.

I was right behind Nathan.

I knew it was the aftereffects of last night. Of feeling so fucking helpless when all I'd wanted was to track down the bastard who'd struck that all-consuming fear in her.

Nothing had prepared me for the look of absolute horror—fear—on the normally fierce, beautiful Red.

Ash had intervened, got in between us and shoved me back. He knew from experience. If I unleashed the fury there would be no stopping its force. He told me to go check on his *Tam Tam* while he and Zee took care of what needed to be done. Charlie'd been game and pointed me in the right direction.

Wasn't supposed to end up with her pressed against the wall with my hands and mouth all over her lush body, words falling from my tongue that didn't belong.

But the second I'd seen her slumped over, like she was giving it all to hold herself up? I couldn't stop it.

It felt like holding her might be something right.

Like maybe I'd be doing something *good*.

So yeah, I wanted to fuck her. Wasn't gonna lie. I knew a piece of me was just being greedy. Wanting something I shouldn't have.

But maybe two months would give her more than that. Maybe it'd give her back something she'd lost. Maybe for once I'd be counted a benefit rather than a stain.

I studied Zee whose knee was bouncing around with enough amped-up energy to light up the town.

"You okay?" I asked.

He shrugged a single shoulder. "He had it coming."

Ash gestured at him. "One of these days he's going to jump in."

Zee cracked a smile. "Looked to me like you had it handled just fine."

Ash laughed. "Dude was a pussy. All he needed was to be taught a little respect. Nathan and I were all too happy to give him a lesson. Pretty sure he's feeling it in all the right places."

"Thanks, man," I said to Ash.

"I've got you," he returned seriously before a knowing smile came sliding back to his face.

Great.

My gaze slithered over the darkened space. The crowd churned, doing their best to get up close to the stage, and a mob swarmed the bar.

Tamar had pulled herself together and gotten behind it. Fingers fluttered over her shirt to smooth it out, swept through that wild red hair to tame what I'd spent the last fifteen minutes mussing up.

She caught my stare and a tic of one of those sexy smirks curved her sweet mouth. But there was timidity, too. She waved a bottle of Jager my direction.

You want?

Hell yeah, I most definitely did *want*.

I lifted a chin in acknowledgment.

Sure.

Ash clucked. Heaviness gone. Pot-stirrer firmly back in place. "So, did you ride in there like a knight in shining armor and save the damsel in distress? Kind of ironic because my Tam Tam just doesn't seem the type. Looks to me like she is perfectly capable of doing a little ass-kickin' herself."

That's because he didn't know her.

Not at all.

And by some miracle...I did.

I hiked my shoulders, not about to betray what she'd somehow trusted me with last night. "We talked. She's good. And I'm sure she could have handled herself just fine."

His brow lifted like maybe he suspected more. Like he'd sniffed out my bluff and was getting ready to call me on it. "You sure about that...the two of you were just talking? Wanna tell me what the hell happened last night? Tamar up and disappeared right when the party was getting good."

He smiled wider. "And so did you. After you were both looking like you might reach across the table to kill the other. And here I was thinking you'd met your match. Thought you said you didn't *like* her?"

I scowled at him. "It's nothing like that."

"No?"

"No."

"Then what's it like?"

I gritted my teeth. "It's like it always is. I fuck. I leave. Simple as that."

But simple wasn't close to describing what *this* was.

Ash knew it just as well as I did. Knew I was acting a fool. Stepping into territory where I didn't belong. Everything about it felt miraculously right and profanely wrong.

He sat back in disappointment. "You're an idiot."

Leaning forward, I cocked my head to the side, my voice dropped low. "Even if I wanted something more, did you up and forget who I am? What I did?"

He huffed in frustration. "I know exactly who you are, my friend. And you're nothing but a fool."

Tamar took that moment to duck under the bar to come strutting our way, looking like my favorite fantasy. Flimsy-white blouse, tight black leather pants, five-inch killer heels. She stirred up a tornado in her path. She turned every damned head in the place as she went, every guy panting for a taste when the girl was only looking my way.

Red.

That side of her was in full force.

Damn. The girl was a gorgeous nightmare.

My chest tightened like a fist.

Maybe I had met my match.

She balanced a tray on her hand, all fire and sass when that gaze bounced around our table. She set a tiny shot of Jager in front of Zee. "There you go, handsome," she said.

A ripple of embarrassment bled out in Zee's laughter. "Are you trying to make me look like a sissy boy? I know I'm the youngest and all…but seriously, I think I can handle a whole shot."

He was grinning full by the end.

"Nah." She smiled at him with a wink. "I just know you're way smarter than these two who seem to think it's a good idea to drink their weight in alcohol night after night."

"Ouch." Ash slammed his hand over his heart. "Just what are you implying, darlin'?"

She placed a tumbler down in front of him, the short, fat glass swimming full of near-black liquid. "Don't worry, you know I love you."

Ash gave her his best dimpled smile. "Oh, Tam Tam, you are my dream girl. Bringing me drinks without even having to ask for them."

"And it's a triple," she said.

"I'm in love. That's it, someone find me a ring. I'm dropping to one knee and proposing right now."

She laughed and pushed at his shoulder. "Save your breath, buddy."

Ash grabbed her hand. "Come on, Tam Tam, we'd make magic together. Almost as good as the magic I make in the studio. Let's do this."

He slanted me a wide-eyed glance, baiting me, while Zee looked at me with a sly grin. "You gonna sit there and let him talk about your girl like that?"

My girl?

What the fuck?

Assholes. Both of them. Goading me like I had something to give.

Both of them were so good at pointing out what wasn't there.

As if I'd ever deserve her.

Tamar's expression softened when she turned toward me. Everything about her seemed to turn timid. She leaned down and looked at me from under her lashes and slowly slid a drink toward me. It was completely unlike the others.

Bright neon-blue liquid danced within the walls of the glass.

Hypnotic.

Just like her.

At the thought of the *special* red-headed slut she'd made me, I eyed it warily, though excitement went twisting through my gut at the same time. "What's this?"

"It's a Blue-eyed Angel." She whispered it close to my ear, where only I could hear. Her warm breath tickled at my neck. All my blood went stampeding south.

Blue.

And I got it. She was offering a side of herself to me that she didn't let anyone else see.

The innocent side.

The side that was broken and soft and pure.

And she was trusting me with it.

I grabbed the drink and tossed it back.

Yeah. Assholes were right. At least for a little while, the girl was mine.

TAMAR

I glanced at the clock.

Five minutes to go. I felt anxious. Excited and nervous as if I was welcoming an old friend home, mixed with an undercurrent of fear.

Standing in front of my full-length mirror, I took in my appearance, my skinny jeans ripped at the knee, tight-fitted black tee with a cool print, and the only boots I owned that didn't have a heel.

Yeah, my hair was pinned up the way I knew Lyrik liked it,

because when it came to him, I was a sucker like that.

Wear something comfortable because I want you on the back of my bike.

That's what he'd told me while we were saying goodbye at my door last night. He'd insisted on following me home after work, then informed me he was taking me out today since it was Sunday and I had the next two days off.

He'd shot me one of those deadly smiles and dropped a peck of a kiss against my lips, before he'd backed away while I'd melted against my door.

I'd been disappointed he didn't ask to come in.

I guess that was the answer to all my questions, what-ifs, and internal warnings.

I wanted him.

I wanted what he was willing to give, even though I had the sinking feeling it was never going to be enough.

This boy was going to scar me in an entirely different way.

Three knocks echoed from the door. Taking in a deep breath, I strode from my bedroom, then opened it without all the reservations I'd expected to feel.

That breath left me in a whoosh.

Lyrik stood in my doorway. Filled it, really. His presence so thick and potent it shook my knees. Black hair blowing in the breeze. Eyes playful.

"Hey," he said with a smirk ticking up at the corner of his mouth. A hint of that cockiness made a resurgence as he leaned his shoulder against the jam and let his gaze wander over me.

I quirked a brow. "Hey."

He grinned. "Hope you're ready."

"Yep." I stepped outside and locked the door behind us. "Care to tell me what I'm ready for?"

"Well, to get things started, I have a little surprise for you. Thought after that, we'd give the normal couple thing a whirl and grab a bite to eat." He shrugged. "Then I figured we'd head back to my apartment and make out like teenagers."

Leaning in close, he whispered in my ear. "Maybe if you're up for it, I'll make you come."

124

Tingles touched me everywhere.

Desire I'd never expected to feel.

Security I'd never thought I'd find.

And again I loved he didn't tiptoe. Loved he didn't treat me as if I were breakable. As if I would fall apart with one wrong look. I struggled to maintain casualness. The tease. "Wow, guess you find no need to beat around the bush. You seem awful sure about yourself, rock star."

Easy laughter rumbled through the air and thrummed through my chest. He wrapped both his arms around my waist, making me sigh, and he tugged me against him. With a glimmer in his eyes, he raked his teeth over his bottom lip. "What, you'd rather go back to your place? I'm okay with that."

"Oh, you think this is about location? I was thinking more about your ability to *please*."

"Baby, I know all about *location*. And there's no question about my ability to please. You just let me know when you're ready for it."

My own laughter rolled, and I wound an arm around his neck. It felt too easy. Too good. The two of us batting back and forth. Though now it was done without an ounce of the animosity it'd held before. I blinked up at him with wide eyes. "I'll be sure to let you know."

He gave me a grin I felt rock the earth, before his expression shifted. It filled with a softness I was just coming to recognize in this man. He ran his fingers through my hair, his head tipped back enough to fully take me in. "Thank you."

My throat tightened, and I felt the crease form on my brow. "For what?"

He glanced away, as if he were struggling, before looking back. "For trusting me. It's been a long time since someone has."

He seemed to shake himself off, and he took a step back, grabbed the helmet he'd left waiting on the ground, and extended his hand. "Come on, let's go or we're going to be late."

"Late, huh? Should I start making guesses at where you're taking me?"

"Nope." He glanced back at me as he led me down the exterior stairs. "Have you ever been on a bike before?"

A pang hit me hard and I stumbled a step. I forced it down and buried it where it belonged. "Yeah…a few times."

Back when I was brave and believed the world was at my feet. Back before *he'd* ruthlessly brought me to kneel at his.

"Good…then I won't have to go easy on you, *Red*," Lyrik said with mischief.

A light chuckle rolled from me. Not that I ever imagined this boy would.

In front of his bike, he turned to me and placed the open-faced helmet on my head. Those eyes flicked all over my face as he worked the straps under my chin. Taking my hand again, he straddled the bike, his long legs stretched wide for balance, the man so intensely beautiful for a moment it stuttered my heart.

I sucked in a steadying breath. He never let me go as he guided me to climb on behind him.

I trembled a little when I did, old memories coming fast, just as fast as my downfall had. Instinctively, I wrapped my arms around Lyrik's waist and pressed my nose into his T-shirt right below his neck. Breathed in his severity. His heat. His danger. And somehow I didn't feel scared.

He kicked the engine over, and his Harley rumbled to life. Gleaming chrome vibrated with power. A little like the man at its helm. "Hold on tight," he yelled as he tucked me closer, his hand protective on my thigh. Right over the serpent tattoo he seemed a little obsessed with.

Temptation.

This tattoo had come later.

I got it as a reminder of how easily we can be blinded by the things we might want. By the things that might not necessarily be good for us.

Like that extra piece of candy I had always wanted that my mother would have warned would be too much because it might cause a belly ache or rot my teeth.

Lyrik rolled us back with his feet, before he took to the street.

And I knew I was defenseless to this temptation. Whatever path he led me down, I would follow, whether he would hurt or heal.

Somehow I knew he would bring me both.

The bike ate up the road as Lyrik traversed the quaint Savannah streets. Heat blasted at my face and the engine roared. Shade blinked across my eyes, the trees tall and proud and offering their relief from the intense summer warmth. Still, I blistered with it, my insides on fire, my skin alive, as I held on to this menacing boy as he took me for a ride.

Wherever he wanted me to go.

Trust.

It was a precarious thing. But it was there.

Five minutes later, he eased into a parallel parking spot running the street in the Historic District not that far from our apartments. The sign hanging outside the shop on the ground floor of the old building directly in front of us boasted it's offering.

Tattoos.

A stir of unease twisted through my stomach.

Lyrik helped me off, and I just waited while he unfastened my helmet and hooked it over the handlebar.

He eyed me, the bright gold and gray flecks reflected in the black. "What's wrong?" he finally asked.

Wringing my hands, I looked warily toward the shop. "We're getting tattoos?"

Smiling, he tugged at my hand and walked backward in some kind of excitement as he edged toward the shop. "Figured it'd be fitting, right?"

I hesitated.

"Come on, *Red.*" A razzing tease coated his tone. "Don't tell me you're afraid of a little needle."

He let his gaze travel my body that was not nearly as inked as his, but still, it was blatantly clear I was no stranger to the gun.

"No...I'm just..." I blinked as I searched for the right description. God. This was stupid. What was I supposed to say?

"I'm happy," I settled on, hoping that would pacify him.

He quirked a brow, his words slowed as if he couldn't possibly keep up with my craziness. "And you...don't get tattooed...when...you're...happy?"

I'd always gotten tattooed for one reason and one reason only.

I did it to cover up what Cameron Lucan left behind.

That feeling stirred through me.

Fight or flight.

Funny how I'd thought I'd been fighting all along. Standing tall. An impenetrable fortress that could never be knocked down.

Really, all I'd been doing was running.

For far too long.

I sucked in a deep breath, hiked up on my toes, and pressed a kiss to his flirty mouth. "Let's do this."

Grinning, his excitement reappeared. He turned to pull the door open and gestured for me to go ahead of him. He stopped me just as I was passing the threshold, and he dipped down so he could whisper in my ear. "What are you going to get?"

What was I going to get?

Lyrik was smiling. This complex, complicated, infuriating man who I wanted to dig inside of until I discovered all there was to find. Until the only thing I knew was him.

Or maybe until he turned my reflection back on me.

Yeah. I was going to get something I should have gotten a long time ago.

"How about instead of telling you, I let you see it later?"

His smile curved into a smirk. "Ah, Red, I like the way you think."

Neither of us had showed the other our new tattoos, the art covered and taped up throughout the rest of our *first date*. If that's what you wanted to call it. But it felt like one. Like we were just beginning even though we'd put an expiration date on whatever *this* was.

Dinner had been easy. The two of us had joked around the entire time, never traversing into the serious topics that seemed to hover unanswered around us.

The truth was, I couldn't help but feel this niggle of pride at what I'd gotten permanently etched on myself. It was so different than what I typically used to conceal the damage. So different from what I wore as armor.

It was hope.

Because for the first time in a long time, I felt it. Because for the first time in a very long time, someone had taken the time to break that armor down. To really step back and look at me.

Now I held tight to his beautiful body as we rode the streets. Heat comforted like a familiar caress as the wind whipped against our faces.

Lyrik made a few quick turns back in the direction of our apartment building, his movements fluid and skilled. When we neared, he slowed, and his feet came out to balance us as he eased into his spot.

He killed the engine.

Silence swallowed us whole and a hushed anticipation trembled in the heavens.

Or maybe it was my hands and the butterflies that wouldn't sit still in my belly.

God, this wasn't me. A bundle of anxious nerves. Not until Lyrik West rode in and changed all the rules.

I hugged him tight one time, as if I needed to give myself a buoy of reassurance. Slowly, he swiveled a fraction on the seat. Those dark eyes were appraising. As if he could see right through me to every fear I had hiding inside.

Slowly, he unwound my hands that were clamped around his waist and guided me to stand. Never releasing me, he swung his leg over the bike and stood.

Rising to his full height.

Stealing my breath. My thoughts. Overtaking my mind.

I was on such dangerous ground. I could feel it shaking underneath.

He brushed the back of his hand across my cheek. His potency both sweet and severe. "You say the word, and this night ends right here."

I gazed up at him. My heart rate sped in fear and adrenaline and want. And again, I didn't want to be afraid. "I don't want it to end."

Not at all.

Thoughtful eyes gauged, before he leaned down and pressed his lips to my forehead where he murmured his promise. "Slow."

Slow.

Overwhelming gratitude welled in my chest. It was crazy how this intimidating boy could so easily set me at ease.

Giving me time when I'd had no idea until two nights ago just how desperately I was going to need it.

He glanced back as he led me up the stairs. "My place or yours?"

"Yours."

He turned the key in the lock and led us into the waiting darkness of his apartment. Muted lights from the Savannah street outside his French doors trickled in from below, the living room cast in dancing shadows.

He moved aside. "It's all yours."

I wandered into his living room. Over my shoulder, I looked back at him when I realized the disaster I'd stumbled upon last Wednesday had been cleaned.

With his index finger, he scratched at his temple. There was something absurdly endearing about him when he seemed unsure of himself, and another rigid part of my exterior creaked with the pressure.

"Uh…I picked up a bit since the last time you were here."

Funny how that day seemed a lifetime ago.

I smiled back at him and tried to force a tease as I looked around the space. "Ah…it looks like you need to add Mr. Clean to your list of alter egos…or did you really sneak someone in here to get this place in shape to impress me?"

My smile faded when I looked back again to where he lingered near the door. My head drifted to the side to take him in as his expression shifted through a thousand emotions.

Regret. Sorrow. Lust.

And a longing that nearly brought me to my knees.

Desire trembled through my body.

I wanted to crawl inside him.

To discover every secret.

Even though I got the crushing feeling *knowing* him would be the end of me.

Cautiously, he edged forward.

Tall.

Beautiful.

Strong.

The air filled up with him. So thick I wasn't sure I could breathe.

Gently he wound his fingers through my hair. Not so gently he tugged my head back and pinned me with that stare. Slowly he dipped down, my stomach in a thousand blissful knots as he left a dizzying trail of kisses down my neck.

Soft, silken lips.

Little flicks of tongue.

Tingles spread in a wildfire of sensation.

Then his voice was at my ear. Whispering belief. "*Blue.*"

Blue. Blue. Blue.

She was so scared and unsure and innocently brave. Because *she* wanted all the things I'd learned the hard way the world didn't have to give. But *she* wanted me to fight for them anyway.

Callused fingertips trailed down my sides, and I trembled when they edged under the hem of my shirt. Skin to skin.

"Is this okay?" he asked, his voice like gravel.

My answer scraped from my throat. "Yes."

Lyrik pulled my tee over my head, slow but sure.

A cool rush of air sent a rush of chills skating free across the flames. My chest heaved as Lyrik stared down at me in my jeans and bra. Eating me up with that irresistible intensity.

I knew my eyes were wild as I looked up at him. My pulse hammered and my spirit thrashed.

"Blue," he murmured again as he went down onto his knees. He peeked up at me every few seconds as he worked the bandage free from my side. My belly shook as he peeled the bandage away and exposed the statement that had been etched into my side over my ribs, from my hip bone to just under my arm pit on the left side. And I knew the area needed to be cleaned. But somehow right then, I didn't care.

I just wanted him to see.

The four simple letters were written in a big, scrolling font, and swirls and flowers extended from the first and last letters.

Rise.

Lightly, he drummed his fingertips over the design, not quite touching the raw skin.

His unyielding gaze latched onto mine. "I think you already have."

Uneasily, I shook my head. "No...for a year, you've been chasing a runner. All I've done is hide while pretending I was strong." A pained breath left me. "But that's not me, Lyrik. All of this..." I waved my hand over my body, "it's just a show."

He pushed to his feet. His body moved in a slight sway. Mine followed. That magnet I couldn't escape.

I was helpless to this fascinating man.

He placed his palm on my neck, and his thumb traced along my collarbone. "No."

Obsidian eyes flashed, and he leaned in closer. "This girl...this bold, brave girl. She's a part of you. I see her. She's real. *Red*," he murmured on a sigh, brushing his lips against mine.

He pulled back to look at my face. "But maybe...maybe you're just outgrowing that season of your life. Maybe you don't need her as bad as you used to and now *Blue* is bleeding through. Maybe she wants to be heard, too. To have a voice in your life."

Blinking through the tears, I shook my head. "How could you know?"

It wasn't a rebuttal or defense.

It was concession.

Surrender.

His mouth fell against mine.

Hard.

Unyielding.

His big hands wrapped around me, way up high, heated palms flat at the center of my upper back. Lifting me to him.

I sank all the way in. Into his kiss and his hold and his violently beating heart.

"I don't know who he is...what he did," he muttered, the words almost maniacally interwoven with our kiss. He never broke for air. Instead, he was stealing it. Stealing everything. Sanity and light and fear.

"But with me? Your safe word is no. You got that, Blue? None of that playing games bullshit. This...this is real. And if it gets too much...you say it. You say it. All you have to say is no."

He pulled back, lines carved into his face like a plea. "Do you hear me?"

Affection poured free.

"I hear you."

My fingers dug into his shoulders because I could no longer stand.

A needy sound slipped up my throat, and he pushed me up against the wall.

It was so familiar to where we'd been two nights ago.

But everything...everything was different.

An age gone in the understanding of his touch.

And he was soft and gentle and rough.

Careful yet challenging.

And he was suddenly back on his knees.

My back pressed against the wall for support as I panted for breath.

Unzipping my boots, he pulled them off, then his adept fingers were flicking free the buttons of my jeans.

Those palms were suddenly on my bare thighs, gliding down to rid me of my jeans. He placed kisses at my belly as he did.

I gasped and bucked.

His mouth turned gentle and soft as he breathed at the front of my lacy underwear.

Oh. God.

He hooked his fingers in the edges. "All you have to say is no."

133

But I had no breath or words, and if I did, I would have been begging him for more. Instead, I wove my fingers through the softness of his hair.

Drawing him closer in a silent plea.

He groaned. "Blue."

Cool air hit me as he dragged my panties free. His hands slid all the way down to twist them from my ankles, then slid all the way back up until he was gripping me at both thighs, staring up at me with all that darkness. Pulling me deeper. Taking me further.

Leaning in, he licked deep in my folds and dragged his tongue all the way to my clit. Never once did he break the fierce gaze.

A shudder and a moan and a whimpered, "Yes."

That was all the approval he needed. He hooked my leg over his shoulder and pulled my ass away from the wall, his hands gripping it as he hauled me closer and devoured every last sensibility.

Barreled through every wall and shattered every defense.

He licked and sucked and fucked me with his mouth until I was a quivering mess in his capable hands.

Until I could feel the current running through my chest. Until I could feel the trembles of warning that rippled through the dense air. Energy crackled. Bristled across my skin and shook me to my bones.

As if nitrogen and oxygen had come alive.

As if every element in the air was combustible.

Explosive.

The buzz before the strike.

I was aware that in the mere flash of a second and without warning I could be consumed by the force. By nature and blinding light.

Incinerated.

He pushed two fingers into my sex.

I exploded beneath the intensity. Carried into the storm. Into heat and fire and blinding light.

Flash after flash after flash.

Powerless.

Burned.

Branded.

I slumped back and slid down the wall. Right into his arms.

He held me, kissed me, and ran his fingers through my hair. "Blue...brave, beautiful Blue."

My world rocked, I kissed him back. I rose onto my knees as I steadied myself on his shoulders.

A frenzy hit me.

Need. Need. Need.

I yanked at his shirt. He lifted his arms so I could tear it over his head, our kiss broken for the flash of a second before I was back on him. Our chests mashed together. Desperate for the connection.

I rocked my body against his, every big, beautiful inch of him hard and begging.

"Slow," he murmured at my mouth, and I smiled against him. It was a wistful smile that sent emotion billowing through my insides.

In that moment, I fell for him a little more.

This cruel, dangerous boy with the softest heart.

I urged him to lie back on the thick, plush rug that took up most of his living room floor.

It was my turn to see what he had hidden on his side.

Kneeling over him, I slowly peeled back the bandage. Through the double French doors, light filtered down in a dusky haze, illuminating his body.

But what I couldn't seem to look away from was his face. It was screwed up as if he were in physical pain, his eyes pinched closed and his back arched from the floor.

As if he were bracing for war.

Ready to defend himself.

Agony.

It was written there, in the rigid set of his muscles, in the shield that I knew all too well.

I stifled my gasp when I saw what he had imprinted on his side. It was in an area that was already heavily tattooed. It seemed impossible another would fit or stand out.

But it did.

Come winter she'll be gone.

The intense flare of jealousy that slammed into me was something I most definitely could not afford.

Because I knew this confession was not intended for me.

And I was nothing but a fool for even contemplating the fact.

Shit. Shit. Shit.

This was bad.

What if it hurts when you're gone?

Baby, I'm not worth the pain.

Those words came crashing down.

Because it already hurt.

I made to crawl back. To get away. To find a wall or a shield or more importantly a door.

I could already feel myself ripping apart.

Lyrik's arm flew out and he gripped me by the back of the neck, stopping my escape.

"Don't." A plea was wrapped up in the hard demand. Lines pulled between his brow, and he struggled for words. "Two months, Blue...we've got two months...and two months can't take you as deep as that goes."

And I ached and I hurt and I wanted to make it better. To offer him what he was offering me.

Refuge. Asylum. A sanctuary until I was strong enough to find a new path. To find myself. Whoever *she* was supposed to be.

Even though I knew doing so was just setting myself up to be broken more.

With my spirit pulled in every direction, I gave in and placed frantic kisses all over his chest, across the swirls of ink, and down the sharp cut of his abdomen. A canvas of beauty with so much hidden pain.

I jerked through the buttons of his fly.

"Shit," Lyrik hissed, both shocked but still completely turned on. His cock jumped free when I pulled his jeans down to his thighs.

I shuddered a little at the sight of it. It was just as big, bold, and threatening as the rest of him.

My stomach knotted and my mouth went dry.

"Red," he whispered on a moan when I wrapped both hands around him at the base, stroking up his length and gliding back down.

Everything shook. My heart and my hands and the room. Because I wanted this even though I was afraid.

Desire twisted through the fear as I watched the glistening bead appear at the tiny slit.

Maybe I was a fool, but I loved I had the ability to affect him this way.

I moaned as I leaned forward so I could taste. So I could experience this man. Of my own free will.

My. Choice.

That moan became a rumble in the back of my throat as I drew him deeply into my mouth. As far as I could take him. Both my hands began to work him in sync with my mouth.

I felt powerful and beautiful.

Real.

He bucked and arched and groaned, his hands tangled in my hair.

Exhilaration simmered in the air.

The thrill.

"Blue."

A rush of energy captured me, and I kept on driving him higher and higher and higher. Until I knew he would break.

"Fuck," he mumbled.

He clutched me tightly when he came. "Blue...Blue...Blue."

I swallowed, riding with him through every last wave. Because I knew without a doubt, with him was where I wanted to be.

We both jerked and trembled with the aftershocks.

I collapsed forward onto his chest. Panting. Reeling.

Lyrik flung his forearm over his eyes, the other still rustling through my hair. Faint sounds of the traffic made it feel as if we were elevated above it all, our breaths and the pounding of our

137

hearts and all the questions still roaring through my head the only sounds in the room.

His voice broke through the sudden quiet. "That was…unexpected."

I chewed at my bottom lip while I let my fingertips play across the bristling muscle of his chest. "Yeah," I whispered softly.

My need for him had hit with the force of a desert storm.

Because there was a piece of me already tethered to him. This piece that screamed we were the same. That we belonged.

Like Charlie had said, lonely recognized lonely.

And my heart recognized him.

Almost shyly, I peeked up at him. He grinned a sloppy grin.

Sated and satisfied.

"You, beautiful Blue, just completely blew my mind."

"I think it's you who continue to blow mine."

He shifted me a fraction so he could readjust his pants, and I moved, turned my back on him.

Hit with a rush of awkwardness, I dug through my jeans and found my panties, then pulled them back on.

What are you doing, Tamar? He's going to wreck you.

Destroy and plunder and invade.

My hands were shaking when I fumbled with my jeans. I froze when I felt his hot mouth moving slowly across my shoulder blade and kissing down my spine. From behind, he unwound my fingers from my jeans and dropped them back to the floor.

"Don't get dressed," he whispered against my skin. "Don't hide from me. I want to feel you."

Oh God. This man.

He saw right through it all.

How did he get me?

Lying back down, Lyrik took my hand and pulled me with him until I was completely sprawled across him. Chest to chest. He tucked my head under his chin. He let his fingers draw lazy circles down my back, and I shivered as I curled more deeply into his hold. His gentle touches explored, until he was moving across the skin of my lower back just above my underwear.

I flinched as he ran them purposefully across the old scars. As if he already knew they were there.

"*He* did this?" His voice was hoarse as he brought me back to my admission from earlier, and I could feel the tremor of violence that came with the question. I could feel his hatred for the man who had stolen my innocence and belief.

"That was my first tattoo," I admitted into the stillness, clutching his side as he continued to caress across the scars.

Sometimes I wondered how the long-healed wounds that now were barely palpable could remain so profound.

"When I came here…to Savannah…I was so scared. I had no idea who I was or who I wanted to be. I only knew I didn't want to be that stupid, naive girl anymore. I dyed my hair, changed the way I dressed, did my makeup differently. Anything so when I looked in the mirror, I didn't see simple, unsuspecting Tamar."

I drew in a breath. "And as soon as those wounds were healed enough, I went and got them covered. There was something about it that made me feel brave. Stronger. As if I'd put some kind of separation between him and me. A barrier. As if I'd blocked some of it out."

A tremor rolled through Lyrik, and his hold tightened in time with the hard breath he released. "Who was he? Tell me, baby. I need to know."

Somehow his question sounded like both encouragement and a threat.

A part of me wanted to tell him two months couldn't take him as deep as those scars went. To throw his defense back in his face. Part of me wanted to hide behind the same kind of walls he hid behind.

There was no question now.

I heard it in his voice at night. In the words he sang and the sorrow it imbued. In the words etched on his skin. Most of all, I felt it in his touch.

But the stronger part of me? I just needed to tell someone *something*. But it wasn't just *someone*. It was him. This beautiful, terrifying man who filled me with such trepidation and fear and need. The one who felt like peril and air and belief. The one who broke me down and exposed what was underneath.

That girl?

She wanted to lie here in the security of Lyrik's arms and whisper her secrets into his darkness. Somehow I knew he would keep her safe.

No, I couldn't take him all the way. That name had been a secret on my tongue for far too long. But I couldn't stop myself from speaking. From giving him the pieces I wanted him to hold. "When I first met him, I thought he was everything I wanted."

Like he'd been struck, Lyrik flinched. "You knew him? You were with him?"

I shuddered with the onslaught of memories, and I realized Lyrik had absolutely no clue about my past other than the fact I'd freaked out when he'd touched me. I wondered how many different scenarios had played out in his head. "Yeah."

Old pain wove through me like a rusted needle.

Tamar King wanted to stand up and crush it. She wanted to lift her chin in defiance and sneer and shout to the world that no man had the power to hurt her.

Instead, I turned my head so I was speaking against Lyrik's thundering heart, my voice barely above a whisper. "On the outside, he was a lot like you. Dark. Dangerous. Beautiful."

Warily, I glanced up at him. "That's why I hated that you made me feel the way you did. I hated the fact that the first man I was attracted to in four years physically reminded me so much of *him*. That you made me feel excited and alive. So I fought back the only way I knew how."

Squeezing me, he pressed a fierce but tender kiss to the top of my head. "I would never hurt you."

My insides quaked. I was sure that wasn't true. This man was quickly gaining the power to destroy me in so many ways. But I knew that wasn't what he meant.

I nodded against his chest. "I know."

His silence urged me to continue. "He was older than me by more than ten years. At first, I wanted to be with him so badly…wanted to experience the intense way he made me feel…that I ignored the warning signs. I was such a fool. I look back now, and they all were there. I ignored my parents when they begged me to stop seeing him. I isolated myself from them so I wouldn't have to hear the worry in their pleas for me to see reason."

I stared unseeing into the shadows that played along the wall. "I think my mom knew it the first time she met him. We were always so close, and I couldn't wait for her to meet my new *boyfriend*. Because all the boys I'd dated before had been exactly that. Boys. But *he* was a man."

The words turned shaky and regretful as I thought back to that day. The memory so clear. Vivid. "I'd been so excited…proud to introduce him. My mother…she'd paled the second she'd touched his skin when she shook his hand. I can still almost feel it…the cold dread that had filled our tiny kitchen. I'll never forget the look in her eyes…the fear. After he left, she'd grabbed me by the arm, pleading, warning me he was dangerous. If only I would have listened."

He swallowed hard. "Blue."

I just kept on, my voice a whisper as I told Lyrik things I'd never told anyone. "He was a monster. Twisted in the worst way. At the beginning, he'd taunted me that I was too young…too inexperienced…that I couldn't handle his lifestyle and I'd just turned right around and promised I could."

A lump grew so thick at the base of my throat I could barely speak. "I had no idea what I was promising. And I *couldn't* handle it, Lyrik. No one should. It started out as rough play. Things I wasn't really comfortable with, but didn't really hurt me. But before I knew what was happening, before I could stop it, it was torture."

Rage. It was tangible. The way it expanded and surged, rolls and rolls coming from Lyrik's body.

"I hope he's burning in hell right now," he said as he tightened his hold. Like he would never let me go.

"I wish that were the truth."

141

I wished he were dead or rotting behind bars, right where the sadist belonged. But no. He was free.

Because of me.

Because I'd thought I was brave and it'd turned out I was nothing but a coward.

Lyrik lifted my wrist and pressed the underside to his mouth, over the scars that remained there from where I'd struggled and fought to break the ties, where ink disguised the evidence of my bonds.

"The scars are my enemy," I whispered hard. "I covered my wrists next, and again, it felt good. It became this sick pattern. Every time I got scared or felt small, I would get another tattoo. Even after the exterior wounds were covered. Until I'd built up this guise that warned everyone off. I never wanted anyone to see."

He tucked his chin and at the same time he lifted mine toward him. Intense, knowing eyes darted all over my face. Searching. Seeking. Defining. "But you let me."

A roll of soggy laughter rolled from somewhere within. "Maybe that's because you're the first person who refused to let me hide."

Maybe it was because he was all the things I had always wanted, but shouldn't have. *Couldn't have.* The darkest light. A disturbed safety. Stony and impenetrable and devastatingly soft.

I smiled a wistful smile. "And I think I'd been running from you for so long, when I finally stopped, you crashed right into me and ripped everything open wide."

And it just kept spilling out.

"You revealed things I didn't even know were still there." Tears gathered in my eyes. I swatted at the one that fell. "I hate being this person. Weak. Fragile. Powerless."

He held me tighter, the words a breath at the top of my head. "No...sweet, brave, beautiful Blue. Pretty sure you might be the strongest person I know. You're here. Alive. Living. Strong enough to open that gorgeous mouth and voice what the sick bastard did to you."

The words dropped low. "And now you're here, lying with me. You were strong enough to *leave.*"

I looked up at him and revealed the one thing I wasn't sure I wanted him to know. "I didn't leave…I escaped."

And I'd been running ever since.

Darkness clouded around his features, a storm gathering strength. "I want to know who he is. Just a fucking name. That's all I need."

The words trembled. "And I just want to forget. I want you to *erase* him. Like you promised you would."

Not drag him out into the light.

Because I wasn't ready. And I wasn't sure I was ever going to be.

Pure menace rumbled at the top of my head. "*Erase* is exactly what I want to do."

This man. Menacing and terrifying and intimidating.

And I'd never felt safer.

I drew in a breath and let my fingertips play over the bars of the song that wound up his arm. I wondered if I could decipher his song. Flowers and leaves climbed in between, and in the muted light, I squinted, focusing in on the name hidden within.

Brendon.

My gut twisted in a slow, sinking dread as I carefully traced the lettering.

As if I'd touched an apparition, fingers disappearing into the misty vapors.

I knew the moment it struck him. A pain so brutal I felt it splitting through him and crashing into me. And again Lyrik was flinching. Deflecting. Shielding and shuttering. Shutting me out.

Two seconds after I'd let him in.

Slowly, I withdrew my shaking hand and tried to reassemble some of my well-practiced, hardened exterior. Because my insides felt raw and achy and sore. As if I was bleeding out. Bleeding for this boy when he was only going to cut me deeper.

God, this got messy and fast. And I knew better. I knew it all along.

"I should go," I muttered as I rolled from him.

He snatched my wrist. "Stay."

143

I gasped, and he loosened his hold. Those dark, penetrating eyes swam with turmoil. "Please," he said.

"I have no idea what you want from me. What you're asking of me."

"Two months, Blue. I'm asking you for two months."

Could I cope with that? With getting this small piece of him and maybe finding some of the missing pieces of me?

Tenderly, he ran his fingers through my hair. "Please."

"Okay," I whispered, because with him *no* didn't seem to exist.

TAMAR

*I*n the near darkness, I sat at the tiny desk in my bedroom. I stared at the blackened laptop screen. Willing it to stop screaming at me to search for what it had concealed inside.

I couldn't sleep. Couldn't focus.

Since Lyrik had torn me open wide two days ago, it was as if my past was nipping at my heels. Razor-sharp teeth bared, waiting for the perfect moment to sink right into my Achilles heel. It was going to be a hard fall when I finally hit the ground.

But I could feel it. Advancing and encroaching and invading. Like a dark cloud that ate up the earth and was getting ready to swallow me.

I knew it was Lyrik who'd brought it to the surface. He'd made me stop and contemplate when all I'd been doing for the past four years was running just as fast as my feet could take me. Across the country. Away from my family. Burying myself in obscurity and unfamiliarity.

And just like that night two months ago, when I'd signed onto Facebook, the need to brush against something from my past was almost overwhelming. Unavoidable. As if my family was *right* there. Pleading with me to turn around.

Unease stirred through me when I thought back to that message.

We need your help. We understand your hesitation, but we need any information you can give us on Cameron Lucan. Please contact me as soon as possible.

It was from a DA.

A DA in Tucson.

From my home.

Where Cameron Lucan lived.

Yeah. Everyone thought I was from L.A.

Just another lie.

I was so good at letting them fall from my mouth.

I wondered now if anyone was good with believing them. I was beginning to doubt it.

Since then, I hadn't looked again. But like that night two months ago, I found myself drowning in an unbearable ache. The loneliness so acute it was alive.

Fear and hope and insecurity wove a pattern of despair through the fibers of my being, trying to tie me back to that girl.

To make me her.

Tamar Gibson.

I'd spent a lot of time hating her. Blaming her. But the crazy thing was, I missed *her* too.

Early morning light spilled in through the sheer drapes of my window. Subtle warmth before the heat of the day.

His voice…his deep, mournful, haunting voice still lingered in the air. Still brushed across my skin.

Although this time it wasn't the wispy tendrils of his presence that used to filter through my walls as if they were seeking a way inside, piercing me and pervading my senses.

No, this time I'd been on his living room floor with my back propped against his couch while he'd sat on it and played into the silence.

I guess I shouldn't have been surprised he didn't play the song. The one I instinctively knew curled up his arm, the cryptic notes and bars naked to the eye but obtuse to the ear.

The songs he did play had been quiet, yet somehow powerful and moving. And I'd felt as if he'd done nothing more than make love to me with his song before he'd touched my cheek, my chin, and sent me home with the softest kiss.

The man was slowly killing me. I was sure about it. Stripping me bare until I had zero defenses remaining.

And now I sat in one of those weakened moments—when I needed a glimpse into the past.

I guess I could blame the temporary insanity on him.

With a trembling hand, I slid my finger across the pad, and the brightly lit screen popped to life, slicing into the darkness. Seeping into my room as if cast with the mission to rob me of my air. Of the safety of my half-lived life.

Quickly, before I lost my nerve or my mind, I clicked onto the Internet with my location disabled, the way I always did, and I signed into my old account.

I told myself I just wanted to see my mother's face, a grave urgency to feel her touch from across the boundless void.

Despite all the messages being marked as unread, I still recognized a new one from her. I'd memorized her words from the last time.

But it was the new message from the DA that consumed my attention. An unsettled part of me shouted its criticism. Because this was so stupid and reckless. I had to be mad. Raving mad. Which I seemed to be proving more and more often lately. I just kept stepping out and putting myself on the line. But there was a part of me that had to see.

Ms. Gibson, numerous attempts have been made to contact you. We're pressing forward with the case. We're requesting you contact us ahead of a subpoena being issued. It's my greatest hope not to have to turn that direction. We have the video. We just need you to answer questions. You don't have to agree to go on the stand. You don't have to be afraid.

They were instant. The tears that flooded my face. Nonstop. Because that's all I'd ever been.

You don't have to be afraid.

Afraid.

I wasn't afraid.

I was terrified.

I blinked through the bleariness, and quickly marked the message as unread, before I clicked into my mother's message. Her messages were always the same.

Come home. We miss you. It wasn't your fault. You can't blame yourself. Not for what happened to you. And not for what happened to her. *Please.*

Her words felt like the sharpest knife, impaling the deepest part of me.

I'd written my mother only one letter as I'd hitchhiked across the country. One to tell her I was sorry. To assure her I was alive and would survive. I asked her not to worry. But I knew even then that request was nothing less than selfish. Of course she would worry.

Quickly, I marked her message as unread.

I gasped when another immediately popped up behind it.

I know you're there. Please, Tamar, call me. They're looking for you. You need to come home.

Like I'd been burned, my hand flew back and I slammed down the screen. Panting. Blinded by the tears that kept streaming from my eyes. Frantic, I scanned my room, as if I could find a place to hide.

I jumped up and began to pace.

The fear was suffocating. I couldn't breathe.

I gripped my hair.

How could they ask this of me?

I couldn't.

I couldn't face it. Couldn't stare him down and voice the horror of what he had done.

Because I'd been weak.

I *was* weak.

Pathetic.

Just a naïve little girl.

And it didn't matter how many false exteriors I wore. That was all I was ever going to be.

LYRIK

*T*here are times in your life you know without a doubt you're doing everything wrong. That tiny little spec you call your conscience? It's still loud enough to assure you you're making mistake after mistake. It's loud enough to call you out on bein' a sinner and selfish and a little bit twisted and sick. And there's not a question left in your mind all those mistakes are hurting the people you care about most.

Yet you're just that selfish to keep right on making those mistakes without a whole lot of contemplation of stopping.

That's why I'd chosen a long damned time ago not to care.

To keep everyone out except for the few who'd already secured a spot inside the brittle, hostile place that made up my heart.

I'd told her as much.

Warned her.

I didn't do it often.

Care.

But when I did? It seemed I did it in a way that instead of doing something good, it just turned around and threw me back into the sickening depths of that selfishness again. It was a goddamned vicious cycle. Take, take, take until there's nothing left but what you've destroyed.

And when you did have the guts to stop? It was *you* who was left destroyed.

It was a no-win.

Yet here I was, desperate to piece those broken bits of her back together. To patch it all up with her strength, beauty, and bold, blinding colors. To mix up every hue of red and every shade of blue. To somehow help her paint a picture that made her whole.

Even though the truth of the matter was I already saw her that way.

All the while, I was doing my best to shut her out. Every day, I was fumbling, trying to protect this flimsy understanding we were teetering on and wanting more of it, all at the same damned time.

Fuck.

I wanted more. She was a complex riddle I wanted to keep sheltered in the palm of my hand.

Tamar had shared secrets with me I knew she'd never told anyone before. I also felt confident we'd barely made a scratch. But I also got the unsettled feeling if I discovered all of what she had buried, I might not be able to handle it. It was a little disturbing, the rage that slammed me every time those bright blue eyes dimmed, when they went dark and haunted, and my insides felt like they were being squeezed and ripped apart.

I would thirst for vengeance and blood, while at the same time I quietly promised her she was brave and strong and everything was going to be okay.

The girl brought out the best and worst in me.

Ash was right.

I liked her.

I fucking liked her and it was every shade of wrong. A glaring mark against the most important promise I'd ever made. But for now? I couldn't seem to put on the brakes or take a turn.

And God knew it was too damned late to throw it in reverse.

Like I said.

Selfish.

But I had two months. That was all the time I'd been given. Two months to put that look on her face. Two months to touch and tease and *erase*. Two months to pretend I had the right to be doing it.

I knew it was going to run out. Faster than I wanted it to. This good thing gone. Two weeks had already been eaten up, and I was getting greedy. Antsy. *Selfish*. I wanted all her minutes and days and most of all her nights.

I was determined to make the most of them.

Because she was the first real thing I'd felt in years. The first person to chip away at all that hate. The first to make me want to do more.

Be more.

It wouldn't last.

But for now, I needed it just as damned bad as I knew she needed to break free from her past. For someone to believe in her. To see her the way I did.

Strong and sweet and with everything to offer this world.

So much more to give than slinging drinks behind a bar.

So much more to gain than sleeping alone night after night.

Sitting in the oversized plush chair in Ash's living room that I'd somehow claimed as my own, I tried to pretend I wasn't affected. Tried to pretend I didn't like it so damned much that she was sitting on the floor to the right of my legs with her back propped on the chair while she hung with my friends.

Like she'd always been there and she was always gonna be.

But maybe she could feel that same connection I swore was there every time she walked in the room, because she swiveled a fraction and looked back up to where I sat, red hair aflame, lips painted the same lust-inducing color. She shot me one of those sexy-ass grins.

That single look was enough to get my dick hard.

And I hadn't even gotten inside my little red pin-up yet.

Crazy, because she was hands down the best non-sex I'd ever had.

But I could feel it building. The two of us were getting ready to go boom. Without a doubt, this girl was going to blow my mind.

One of her legs was tugged up to her chest and she sipped at a beer, laughing easily at the stupid story Ash just couldn't keep to himself.

I tried not to stare at her, but that was a damned near impossible feat.

Yeah, she was beautiful.

But it was more than that. I felt this compulsion to look at her. To look at her closer than I'd looked at anyone before. Because there was more to her than just that surface beauty. Something bold and intriguing and begging to be made whole.

She made me want to explore the forbidden.

Dive into my own debauchery.

Swim in sin.

Because being with her? It wasn't anything less than that.

Sin.

Ash waved his hands in the air like the madman he was, his voice lifted as he fed everyone what I was sure were a few exaggerated lines.

"You guys had to be there. Literally, I was running for dear life. Like, I thought I'd seen my last day and was gettin' ready to see the light when I was trying to get away from this crazy-ass chick. She just wasn't going to give up or take no for an answer. She kept ripping at my shirt and informing me she was a VIP. Like that actually meant something. And somewhere in her jacked-up mind, she actually thought that meant I was hers. Free rein. I mean, she was hot and all, but that shit was scary."

A mild chuckle rolled from me. I learned a long time ago the guy couldn't be blamed. He couldn't help himself. He was a fucking clown I'd give my damned life for.

All of them.

Sebastian and Zee and Ash.

Laughing, Sebastian pointed the neck of his beer bottle toward Ash, taunting him. "What, you can't protect yourself from a girl?"

"Girl? This chick was some kind of bodybuilder or some shit. You should have seen the muscles on this thing. It just wasn't natural." He shuddered.

"That's because chicks kick ass, right, Tamar?" Shea piped in, grinning in Tamar's direction.

When I looked down at Tamar, my chest prodded somewhere deep, this sort of fucked-up pride that didn't belong. But I liked that she was enjoying herself, that she felt comfortable and safe while being in my space. The mood was light and easy, and Ash's old house only added to the relaxed atmosphere.

But maybe that was just the issue I had, always watching for *Blue* underneath all the *Red*. Worried something would trigger her and she'd go spiraling down to that desolate place where I couldn't stand for her to be.

Didn't know why I had this crazy visceral reaction to protect her from going to that place. Like somehow it'd become my responsibility. My duty.

Right now, though, she was all *Red*, and she glanced at me quickly and cracked one of those smirks that damned near drove me out of my mind, before she turned back to Ash.

"I'm sure you have this all twisted around, Ash," she teased with a cock of her head. "She was probably protecting herself from the likes of you. I have seen you in action, you know."

Ash slammed his hand over his heart. "Oh, Tam Tam. Do you really have that little faith in me?"

Tonight we were actually supposed to be practicing, and surprise, surprise, it'd turned into the Ash Evans Show.

Sebastian and Shea had gotten back from their two-week honeymoon a couple days ago. Considering we only had six weeks until we had to head back to L.A. to finish up the tracks, we decided we'd better keep ourselves up to par before we let the easy, slacker life take us over.

We weren't getting a whole lot done.

I knew Shea would be coming along since the song she and Sebastian had written would be showcased on the next album. That and the fact he pretty much wouldn't let her out of his sight.

Honestly, there had been no hesitation on my part when Sebastian had suggested we consider the song for the album. Shea had a voice unlike any I'd ever heard. It'd be the last track. One to round out our expected thrashing songs, this one soft and sweet and slow, just like Sebastian's girl.

Tamar had been in tow.

Should I have been pissed? Resistant to her unconsciously weaving her way into my tight-knit group?

Maybe.

But the truth of it was, I wanted her there.

And I just sat here and pretended it didn't mean anything.

From where he was sitting on the couch across from me with Shea curled up on his lap, Sebastian lifted his chin, and I turned to catch him watching me watching Tamar. His eyes narrowed in question. In curiosity.

I gave him a short, quick shake of my head.

Don't even.

Not a chance in hell was I about to let him go there. Not any more than I was going to let Ash or Zee, for that matter. Yeah, so what if this was the first time any of them had seen me with a girl. In fucking years. Not since when I didn't want to remember.

And I wasn't talking about the ones that came and went faster than I could catch their names.

I was talking about one being at my side while I stood at hers.

But six weeks from now? This would all be over. In the end, would she be just another nameless, faceless body?

A swelling of emotion locked up my throat.

No.

This girl.

This girl was unforgettable.

"So anyway, before I was so rudely interrupted," Ash tossed out at Tamar, his blue eyes glaring wide, "this crazy bitch was suddenly on the dirty, grimy floor. I don't know if she tripped or launched herself at me, or what, but there she was, wrapped around my leg while I'm trying to shake her off like a bad dream. I fucking panicked. Like panicked. Started hauling her ass across the floor while she's hanging on."

He shook his leg to demonstrate.

"Then she turns tactic and starts pleading with me that she'd seen a psychic and I'm her soul mate and I just don't know it yet, but we were gonna have three boys named Kurt, Kaleb, and Kyle, and we were going to live on a farm in Missouri. At that point, I literally had to pry this girl's fingers from my legs because I'd had enough psycho for the night."

Somehow he both shivered and grinned. "I mean, I know I'm irresistible and all, but come on, a farm in Missouri? And three boys? Pssh. This girl obviously didn't know me at all. She had to be lyin'."

I busted out laughing. "You think she was lying, huh? What clued you in? And since when are you so selective?"

"Since this one could probably break me in half."

Ash took a swig of his beer, forehead bent up like he was deep in thought. "In all honesty, I totally get it and I don't blame the girl." He stretched his arms out wide, smiling like the cocky bastard he was. "Girls can't resist grabbing on and going for a ride."

"Seriously, Ash!" Tamar shook her head, stirring me up with the throaty lilt of her laugh. "Did you ever hear of this little thing called humility?"

He frowned. "What's that? It sounds like a terrible disease. I pray I don't catch it."

"You're such an asshole," she teased with a smile as she took another sip. That mouth wrapped around the lip of the bottle, and I squirmed in my seat.

Damn.

With her arms draped around Baz's neck, Shea grinned at him. "Come on, Ash, don't act like we can't see your hand. Your poker face isn't all that great and Tamar and I are totally onto your game. Look at this big old house begging to be filled up with a bunch of babies. Before you know it, you're going to have a herd of baby Ashes running up and down the stairs."

Her eyes bounced around to everyone. "Y'all just wait. I'm

putting down bets. A hundred bucks."

Zee hopped up and clapped his hands together. "I'll take that bet and raise you a hundred, because there isn't a girl in her right mind who's going to stick around here long enough to put up with his ass."

Ash smirked at Zee. "All except for you."

"Dude...so not cool. Not cool at all," Zee said with a slow, offended shake of his head.

Ash swiveled and pointed at Shea's belly, and his voice slanted in artificial sincerity. "And in case you all hadn't noticed, Baz Boy up and went and stole my girl...my dearest, Beautiful Shea. I had to bear the crushing news that baby's not mine. All my chances have been shot to hell. Heart broken. Happiness gone."

He feigned a gasp and a heart stab with a slow, agonizing death as he dropped to his knees.

On all things holy, it had to be Ash who was the nut job and not the girl.

Giggling, Shea ran her hand over her belly that seemed to have doubled in size since the wedding. Baz set his hand protectively over hers.

Tamar had her attention on Shea, focused on the two-intertwined hands on her belly. She smiled their way. It was soft, sweet Blue that shined through in her expression while I was doing my best to look away.

It wasn't like I didn't like kids. I fucking loved Kallie, that sweet little girl who tagged around at our heels like we were the coolest things in the world.

She was always telling me wild stories about butterflies and fairies and all things unattainable, her tales always chasing after that absurd happily ever after. The kind she hadn't been around long enough to know not a whole lot of people ever found. Funny thing, I didn't mind listening. Maybe it was because she reminded me of my little niece.

But there was something about Shea's protruding belly that left me feeling cagey. Itchy and agitated whenever she was around. Still, I'd gone and gotten stupid and gave her that damned bear like doing it could possibly be a good idea.

But this was Baz's baby we were talking about.

And Baz deserved it.

He deserved it all.

I attempted to shake off the thoughts. That was one rabbit hole I didn't need to fall down, even though lately Blue had seemed intent to drag me into it.

Instead, I tried to relax and stretched my legs out on either side of her. She wound her arm around my leg and pressed her head to the inside of my thigh. She shifted her head back and looked at me upside down.

Those big, blue angel eyes were wide and playful, and she whispered so only I could hear. "For the record, your friends are crazy." She pointed at Ash. "That one...bat-shit."

With the way she was looking at me? Everything inside went haywire. All abuzz and alive and excited.

Fuck.

I liked her.

"But you love them," I countered, one corner of my mouth lifting.

Everything about her softened. "Yeah. I do."

I touched her face and she sighed a breathy sigh, and my dick twitched again. Fuck, maybe it was me who was twisted. Because I wanted this girl in a way that just wasn't right.

"I'll match that, Zee," Shea said, still messing with my crew. "Two hundred bucks says Ash is going to be painting all the upstairs bedrooms pink and blue."

"You're on," Zee shot back.

Tamar's smile was soft and hinting at things I didn't want to see. At things I couldn't give, and again I was wondering just what the fuck I'd gotten myself into and how the hell I was going to get out of it.

Still, I got stuck there, in that warmth of those wells of blue, trapped by the body of a red-headed enchantress.

Temptation.

I felt it in my gut and trembling around my blackened heart.

I looked away, to the ground.

Loyalty.

That was the one thing I had. The one thing I got to count as good. I had to cling to that.

My phone buzzed in my pocket. Three times in quick succession.

Blowing out a breath, I dug it out and swiped across the screen. I tried to hide the irritation I felt flash across my face.

Motherfucker.

I told this asshole not to bother me again. Appeared he didn't get the message.

I scrolled through his texts.

Have you thought any more about our offer?

Have it on good word your boy Stone is about to split.

Don't let this opportunity pass you by.

What the hell? This guy had to have been a used car salesman in a former life.

And it didn't matter what he had to say. What he threatened Baz might do. Still, I felt it in the knots that suddenly tied my insides, this thick band of defensiveness for my crew all mixed up with a dangling thread of dread.

With a dry chuckle, I tapped out an answer.

Fuck off.

That was about as clear as I could be.

"Care to let us in on the joke?" Ash asked.

Probably should have before. In private with just the guys. But I guess now was as good a time as any.

"Joke is, this bastard Banik…the manager of *Tokens of Time*?" I said it like a question, talking while I looked down at my phone and pressed send. "He somehow thinks I'm gonna up and leave *Sunder* and pick up for their piece-of-shit lead who left the rest of the band high and dry."

Funny they were basically asking me to do the same.

Silence fell over the entire living room. Tension whipped through and filled up the old walls, a dense cloud of it sagging from the ceiling, making it hard to breathe.

Guess I really should have said something earlier. Their shock was palpable.

Stagnant.

As if any of them could think for even a second I could walk away.

Confusion and anger pulled tight across Ash's face. "And why the fuck does he think you'd go and do something like that?"

Warily, I looked around the room, gauging how much to say. Sebastian was on the couch, still as stone, like he was preparing himself for what I was getting ready to say.

I gestured to him with my chin. "Banik seems to think Baz isn't going to stick around all that long, and I might as well cut my losses before *Sunder* goes south."

And maybe it was fucked up, because I was staring Baz down while I said it, searching for his reaction, just waiting for which way this was going to play out. Wondering how I was going to feel.

Because I was willing to let him go.

I wouldn't even put up a fight.

Maybe it was more of that selfishness. The need to pay off a little part of my debt. Or maybe it was because I cared enough that I actually wanted him happy. Part of me wanted him to make a break for it because I'd been feeling him needing to cut ties for a long damned time.

Why wouldn't he when he had something so damned good?

Baz shook his head. "Asshole has not a clue what he's talking about." His gaze bounced between Zee and Ash and me. "Any of you really think I'd up and leave without warning? Without talking this through? We've been through too much shit together for that to ever happen. Banik is full of shit. Anything he's trying to lure Lyrik away with is nothin' but assumption."

My eyes flicked between him and Shea and her belly, and the words were tumbling out before I could stop them. "Baz, man, you know we've got your back. Whatever you decide. None of us are going to blame you for leaving, because songs aren't ever going to be as important as family. We owe you that."

Five years ago, I'd promised him I'd be there while he was in jail. I'd promised I'd take care of the band in his place. Watch over his brother. Make sure everything didn't fall apart when he'd sacrificed and gave me the one moment I wasn't ever supposed to have.

I'd do it again. And I'd keep doing it.

Still, admitting it out loud felt like I was stabbing myself in my own damned back.

I shouldn't have been offering it right then, anyway. Not with an audience. Not with Shea. Least of all with Blue.

She'd shifted, facing me more. I felt pinned beneath her stare. Beneath all the questions and concern and outright confusion pouring from her. I felt trapped with the way it felt like she were digging her fingers into my skin, sinking in and going deeper.

Invading.

Intruding.

Penetrating.

Fuck.

The entire room jumped when a beer bottle slammed against the wall. It shattered the silence. Shards of glass rained down and pinged across the hardwood floor. My attention flew to Ash who glared down at me from the middle of the room.

Anger.

Disappointment.

Sympathy.

I sucked in a steeling breath.

It was the last I hated most.

I'd dug my own fucking grave.

"What the fuck, man?" he accused, head cocking to the side in contention. "You get to make that decision for the whole band? You made it before, remember? You just fucking walked away and look where that got you."

I was on my feet before I processed the action. Anger rippled through me on roaring waves, and I was fucking shaking, trying to hold myself back. Bitterness fell sharp from my tongue. "I came *back*, and look where *that* got me. It wasn't the leaving that was the issue."

Furiously, he blinked, and he dragged both hands down his face in frustration. "Seriously, man…you think that was because you came back? It was because we were fucked up. All of us. We fucked up and a whole ton went to shit. And I know you bore the brunt of it. Lost the most. But five years are gone, man, and you're still making us pay for it."

"Ash," Sebastian uttered a low warning as he untangled himself from Shea and climbed to his feet.

Ash pointed at him. "This needs to be said, Baz. Out loud. Too much time has been spent tiptoeing around this shit. Pretending it doesn't follow us everywhere we go. Pretending Lyrik isn't still stuck back in that day."

He swung his attention back to me. His voice dropped lower and strained with the plea. "It's time to let it go."

My entire face pinched. Pain sheered through my chest like that day was yesterday.

Because he was right.

I was still living in that day. I woke up every morning just to die over and over again.

"Let it go?" The words grew louder, my cool evaporating like sizzling mist. "Let it go?" I demanded as I took an incredulous step forward. "I lost everything. *Everything.* And I'm going to be paying for it for the rest of my life."

Because there were some things you weren't ever going to make amends for.

Ash knew better than pulling this shit. Throwing it in my face. Especially with outsiders looking in.

"But that's what you don't get," he said. "You don't have to keep paying for what you can't change. And I can't sit around watching you suffer for one more day. Not when being free of it is *right* there. Right in front of your face, and you refuse to see it."

He made no secret of the fact he was referring to Tamar. Like I could ever actually have her. Like I could ever be with her the way she deserved.

Anger and hurt rolled over me like a heavy, roiling storm. Closing in. I could feel myself coming unhinged. Fiber by fiber. Memory by memory. It was a loss so intense it almost knocked me to my knees.

Fuck.

I wanted to scream. To beat something or someone.

I shouldered passed Ash before I did something stupid like launch myself at him.

The fucked-up thing was he was the same guy part of me couldn't help but blame, even though I knew none of it was his fault.

All of it was on me.

"Lyrik, man, come on…don't fucking do that," Ash called behind me. "For once, stop being a fucking hothead and listen. All of us…we just care about you."

Care.

Nice.

Glad he was doing such a bang-up job of *caring* in front of those who had no business in any of it. Bringing it out into the open for them to see. Shedding light on what was written on me like the blackest stain.

"Lyrik," he shouted.

I ignored him because I was finished with his bullshit. I shoved through the old-fashioned double doors that led to the massive kitchen and stormed into the renovated space that was larger than the apartment I was renting.

Inside, it was dark. Except for the moonlight streaming in from the big windows overlooking the sprawling backyard, the milky rays striking against the silver flecks in the white and gray granite countertops.

Pressing my palms to the island that took up the center, I dropped my head between my shoulders and tried to catch my breath. To purge the memories from my mind. To stop the barrage of images from slaying me. Cutting me in two. To stop the assault of their faces that struck me again and again.

Thunderbolt after thunderbolt.

The loss.

The loss.

The loss.

The swinging door creaked and let in a flood of light as it opened, before it swung closed.

I was no longer alone.

The air grew thick. A charged intensity shimmered through the room. It only added to my agitation.

The girl was doing her best to completely destroy me.

"Go," I gritted out.

I squeezed my eyes closed.

Shuttin' the world out.

It was for the fucking best. And I sure as hell didn't need her to see me this way.

Pissed and vulnerable and hurting. But it seemed ever since she made her way into my life, all of it was there, just simmering below the surface.

High heels clicked on the wooden floor. Blood pulsed through my veins, harsh and hard. Beating faster and faster with every step of her slow, guarded approach.

My lungs squeezed.

She hesitated, her presence full and soothing and probably one of the damned most frightening things I'd ever felt.

I couldn't do this. I needed to fucking stop before I fucked this up more than I already had. Before my guilt grew greater and I had nothing left to stand on.

She wrapped her arms around me from behind.

I stuttered out a breath.

God, she felt so good.

She pressed her face to the middle of my back.

"It goes both ways, you know." Her voice swam through the room, honey and warmth. My body processed it like a song.

"I was so alone. Not just lonely, Lyrik. But *alone*. Hollow. Without anyone who understood. And then there was you...this beautiful, terrifying man who was pushing his way into my life. Demanding I let him see me for who I really was and not what everyone else saw. Now I'm standing here begging him to invite me into his. To let me *see*."

I gripped her hands that held tight to my stomach. "You can't go there, Blue."

Over my shirt, she scattered a bunch of light kisses across my back. Still, they singed and scorched and seared.

Scarring as she silently begged.

"Blue." I took her by one wrist and pulled her in front of me. "You walk into the room..."

I swallowed over the lump in my throat when I saw the

complete understanding on her face. Lifting her, I set her on the edge of the island and forced my way between her legs that were eager to accept me.

I cupped her face. "You walk in the room and I don't recognize myself. I forget who I am. Forget who I'm supposed to be."

Blue eyes searched my face and she flattened her palm across my racing heart. "Maybe you're finally beginning to see who you really are." Her voice softened. "The man I see when I look at you."

My mouth came down hard on hers to stop her from talking.

I drove my fingers into all that silky red.

I kissed her mad.

Just like she was driving me.

Tongue and teeth and desperation.

Fuck.

This was stupid.

Needing her this way.

But I felt like if I moved back even a fraction, I wouldn't be able to breathe. That if I let any space come between us, it would be the end. That without *this* I couldn't take one more step.

Which was why I should walk the fuck away.

Instead I slid my hands down her sides and wrapped her legs around my waist. She sighed a greedy sigh and crossed her ankles at my lower back.

Then the girl rubbed herself on my straining dick.

Torment roared like the howl of a wildfire in my ears.

Deafening, consuming flames.

But this fire?

It felt so fucking good, I couldn't let it go. Not when I had it for these moments that were fleeting fast.

I lifted her from the island and carried her toward the narrow second set of stairs leading from the kitchen.

She clutched my shoulders and held on tighter. "Where are we going?"

"Upstairs," I mumbled at her mouth, refusing to come up for air because I might lose *this*. I might lose the feeling that I had something real for the first time in what seemed forever.

Fingertips dug into the base of my neck. "Are you sure that's a good idea?"

"I think it's a very fucking good idea," I grunted at her mouth. My cock begging at the seam of her jeans seemed proof enough.

I pressed her harder against me, loving that was all it took to make her moan.

I needed her. Needed her touch and her smile and her panted breaths.

"I want to make you come."

She whimpered a sound that shouted yes, while her words poured out their reluctance. "That's not going to erase whatever just happened back there. Talk to me. Please."

I kept kissing her as I took the stairs. *Erase.* That's what I was going to do. And I was going to write myself over that bastard's blemish. Over the anguish and damage and ruin.

For once…for once I wanted to have something good to offer.

I wanted to offer it to her.

Every remnant of what I had left to give.

Her fingers dug deeper and her nails sank into my skin.

And I knew…I knew she wanted to give it, too. But the difference between us was I didn't ever want to forget.

I hit the landing of the stairs at the back of the hall and fumbled with the knob of the door at the end. It knocked open and I was quick to kick it shut. The drapes on the windows facing out back were drawn open wide.

I laid her in the center of the bed and stood at the side.

"Whose room is this?" she whispered into the quiet.

"Mine."

That was the thing about Ash. We fought. We fought like brothers. Because that's exactly what we were. Not by blood. But by every single thing that counted. He'd had me pick out one of the rooms and told me no matter where I went, I'd always have a home.

Blue eyes flickered with some kind of hope.

Stay. Stay. Stay.

Every rational part of me knew I needed to stamp it out. Tell her no. Warn her we had six weeks to go.

That was it.

The end.

But I couldn't make the words form on my tongue. Instead, I pulled off one of those sexy-ass heels and kissed the inside arch of her foot, then turned and did the same to the other.

Shivers rolled through her body and lust curled in my gut.

I wanted to fuck her more than I wanted air.

To experience all she had to give.

To taste her courage.

To swallow her insecurities.

"Lyrik." It was a breath. A question.

"You're so damned pretty." Part of me wished she wasn't. Truth was, it was getting harder to look at her. Because I just kept wanting more and more. Asking for trouble. For heartache and pain.

I knew better.

I'd learned a long time ago to shuck the worry and the bullshit chains. Life was so much easier to glide through with nothing weighing you down.

I already carried more than I could bear.

Still, my heart picked up a beat when I leaned over and flicked the button of her jeans. The ripping sound of her zipper echoed against the walls. She whimpered and lifted her ass from the bed, making it easy for me to drag her jeans and underwear down her legs.

I didn't even try to hide my moan. The girl was so insanely hot. A promise of heaven and a temptation sent directly from hell.

Right where I belonged.

Setting a knee on the bed, I leaned over to the side so I could trace that serpent tat on the outside of her thigh. My tongue ran along the lines while I slipped my hands beneath her shirt and dragged it up. My tongue followed the path as I lifted it over her head.

My entire body shook with quickly unraveling need. Control disintegrating.

Red was in nothing but a lacy black bra, which had to be illegal in all fifty states. Cruel and unjust punishment, because I just might die if I didn't get to touch.

Those tits spilled out over the top while the distorted heart tattoo wept in the middle.

Ante omnia cor tuum custodi.

Urges hit me. Ones to kiss it until it was perfect and whole.

Shit.

I was losing my head. My foundation.

Consuming need twisted through me when I licked over the aching red, and I stole one hand under her back to undo the clasp. I moved back far enough to pull it free.

Her pulse ran wild and her chest heaved.

Quick to dive back in, I took a pink, pert nipple in my mouth. I sucked it deep, flicked at it with my tongue.

She wound her hands in my hair. "Shit…Lyrik…that feels so good." She released a confused groan. "Why do you feel so good?"

I grinned against her skin. That's exactly what I wanted to hear. That she felt *good*, that I was the only one making her feel that way.

My mouth trailed down the side of her breast. I lingered at one spot, drawing the silky flesh deep into my mouth. Maybe a little harder than necessary, but I was making sure to leave a mark. Because that's what I promised her I would do.

Both my hands cupped the fullness of her tits, squeezing and lifting so I could tease and torture and make her squirm as I turned to the opposite nipple.

"I need you," she said as she clawed at my shirt. Cool air hit my back as she tore it off, and those fingers sank right back into my skin. Begging as they burned and scraped and pleaded for more.

This was the more I could give her.

She deserved more, but I'd give all I could. *For her.*

I wanted her to trust me in a way she hadn't trusted anyone since that bastard had broken her. For her to know she was beautiful, and what he'd done didn't have the power to define her.

Didn't have the power to destroy her.

I wanted her to know I saw something beautiful.

Something good.

A precious gift given to this world.

My head spun and my heart hammered a warning in my ribs. It

caught time with the beat of hers, wild and erratic and violent, her breaths just as harsh.

Frantic, she dragged my mouth back to hers.

Tingles rolled across my flesh, and this achy feeling compelled me I was doing something wrong. Violating a promise. But I did nothing but kiss her back.

Because I couldn't fucking stop.

Her tongue slipped past my lips in a delicious tease, tangling around mine. Eager and demanding.

Every inch of me lit.

A hazardous frenzy thundered through my veins, and I pressed up onto my palms. My head dipped down as I kissed her wild. My jean-covered cock pressed into her bare pussy. Underserved need squeezed every cell, filling my breaths and my lungs and my head.

No.

I squeezed my eyes closed and she kissed me more. Fevered hands searched my skin like she might find a weak spot. A way in. Access to what was buried inside.

"Lyrik," she breathed as her hands trailed down over my shoulders. Her touch sent shock waves burning across my skin. Fingernails scraped down my chest before they were working at my fly.

And I felt fear slipping over me. Something haunting and dark. While everything else came alive.

A tortured contradiction.

But that's what I craved.

The push and the pull.

I wanted. I wanted it all. Wanted to know every inch.

Her body. Her heart. Her mind.

Easing back an inch, I glanced up at her face, then I looked right back down, gaze intent on where I palmed her sex, watching as I pushed two fingers inside.

So fucking wet and warm and perfect.

Her walls clamped down and she arched off the bed. Her mouth parted on a silent moan.

Gorgeous.

Ripples of anxiety surged. I wasn't ever going to get enough.

I rushed back to take more of that mouth.

That sweet, sweet mouth.

I kissed her and kissed her while I struggled to pump her slowly. To keep control when all I wanted was to let go. I wanted everything. Everywhere. All at once.

To consume and devour and lay all her fears and reservations to waste.

To take and take and take.

To give and give and give.

Delirium.

I let my hand go trailing back.

Fingers slick.

I pushed two into her tight, perfect ass.

I wanted there, too.

She jerked and I did the same, jumping back just in time to catch the fear in her expression. Those blue eyes had gone dark, the girl getting sucked back into that depraved place.

Shit.

Shit. Shit. Shit.

What the fuck had I been thinking? Getting reckless with this girl? I should have known. And that tiny spec that was my conscious screamed I was making mistake after mistake. It screamed I was a sinner and selfish. That I was twisted and sick. And I knew right then I didn't have the guts to let her go. Not yet. Not when she was this close. This close to being *free.*

Tears slipped free from the corners of her eyes, wet streams streaking down and disappearing into her hair, while my heart went frantic with regret and hate and the need to slaughter whoever had hurt her this way.

I wrapped her in my arms.

"Don't leave me," I murmured harshly, clutching her tighter. "I'm right here. It's me, Blue. It's me. Baby, you just have to tell me no. I'm not ever going to hurt you."

But the way her eyes flicked all over my face? I already knew. I already fucking knew I was hurting her because I wanted to take everything and I couldn't offer her the same in return.

She bucked up. The head of my dick poking out from the waist of my unclasped jeans rubbed against her. Still crying, she burrowed her fingers into my shoulders, as if she were transferring some of her pain over to me.

"Please...just...fuck me," she begged.

That sick part of me? He wanted to. The part that wanted her so fucking bad I'd take everything and anything I could get. But instead I was kissing her again, murmuring "slow" at those red lips. Thanking God she was with me. That I hadn't messed up so bad she was a curled up ball in the middle of the bed.

But this was what I did.

I found the little bits of good hidden behind a mask, sought them out, and brought them into the light.

Then I destroyed them with one crushing blow.

"I trust you," she said, holding me tighter and rubbing her bare center against me.

Trust.

Motherfucker. I wanted to weep. I felt it. Emotion gripping my chest like I was being strangled. A noose around my neck.

Frantic, I pushed my jeans down to around my thighs, because I was just greedy enough to take a little more.

"Slow," I struggled to say.

Slow. Slow. Slow.

I kept chanting it in my head. Even though she was begging for it, I knew Blue wasn't ready for sex.

I was starting to wonder if I was. If I could handle her. Even though I was dying to sink into her.

I slid my bare cock against her, gathering all the slick desire coating her center, and clutched her shoulders while I rocked against her.

A small gasp escaped her. Confusion and desire.

I did it again, getting her closer because I couldn't seem to get her close enough.

No. I never moved enough to fuck her, even though with one slip, I'd be home.

I just moved against her like some twisted fuck who needed to get off.

I made sure to drag back far enough so the ridge of my

throbbing head flicked across her clit.

Our faces were a breath apart, our lips just touching, eyes wild and open and vulnerable.

And I rocked and rocked and rocked. Using up this girl who was supposed to be using me.

I was beginning to wonder who of us needed who.

"Lyrik." She gripped me harder, pressing her tits to my chest as she tried to get closer.

"Let it go," I whispered at her ear.

She shuddered below me when she did, nails breaking skin, the little pricks of pain the perfect conflict up against the pleasure that had my body wound up tight. Tighter and tighter.

So warm.

So wet.

Too much.

Fuck. Me.

Burning, agonizing bliss.

I came all over her belly with a groan.

My head dropped and I buried my face in her neck, sucking in any air I could find.

All of it was her.

Every breath *Blue.*

Reluctantly, I shifted and gazed down at her. I brushed the back of my fingers down her cheek. Those blue eyes swam as they stared up at me, tears still streaming over her temples and into her hair.

Blue.

Sweet, soft, trusting Blue.

"I'm so sorry," I said quietly.

She blinked and swallowed hard, voice sincere. "I'm not."

.

TAMAR

I drummed my fingertips across my top lip.

Paced.

Then paced again.

The blinds were drawn in my bedroom, the dwindling sunlight beyond breaking through at the edges. I glanced back at my desk where my old Canon sat like a beacon to my past. Like a bridge to everything that once had been and everything that felt just out of reach.

It was as if I simply dragged my fingertips across the divots and grooves, I'd be transported back there. With a twist of the rings,

I'd be focused on their faces, dialed into all the things that had once been important to me.

My goals and hopes and dreams.

I'd thought they'd been obliterated. Wiped out.

But there they were...waiting just below the surface. Where Lyrik kept scratching and scratching and scratching. Exposing more of who I once had been.

My spirit throbbed with possibility.

Scariest part? All those possibilities had begun to revolve around him. Coming to life under his touch and his words and those dark, mesmerizing eyes.

But I never claimed to be sane when it came to him.

Three sharp knocks at the door and my heart rate spiked. The few threads of reservation snapped, jarring me forward.

Before I lost my nerve, I scooped up my camera. For a moment, my eyes squeezed closed as I cradled it like a lost child. As if I was holding a missing part of myself.

A loss regained.

A casualty resurrected.

Another knock rang against the wood, and I spun on my heel and headed toward the door.

Eager.

Hopeful.

Different.

I twisted the lock, and before I could turn the knob, Lyrik was pushing his way across the threshold.

I gasped, then giggled like a giddy schoolgirl when he came for me and wound both of those strong arms around my waist. Pulled me up close against his overpowering body. His presence so thick and heavy and bold.

I'd once taken it as a warning.

A foreboding omen of the danger that was to come.

I never would have imagined it would be safety I found in his arms.

Big hands slid up my sides, traveling all the way to my neck, leaving a trail of chills in their wake. He urged my head back so he could kiss me. Quick and hard. Stealing my breath.

He pulled back. Ebony eyes flashed their light.

Mischief and mayhem and the promise of a blinding, blissful ride.

I was *so* ready to take it.

"Hi." A smirk took hold of that lush mouth, full lips hovering, strands of black hair flopping across his forehead as he bent me back. Clearly, the arrogant, cocky boy had come out to play.

No one would see me complain.

I loved when he was this way. Loved when he was playful and free.

But I loved it just as much when he was intense and vulnerable. Loved when he protected and loved when he pushed.

Shit.

I gulped over the disturbance that rumbled in my chest and climbed my throat.

The energy suddenly manifested in the form of a shiver across my skin.

The buzz before the strike.

"Hi," I whispered back, the word hoarse.

He'd moved his hands to my ribs to keep me steady, and edged back and let his gaze travel down my bowed body.

"There's my girl...always lookin' like my favorite fantasy. Little red pin-up sent to drive me right outta my mind."

My girl.

God, how I wished.

The errant thought twisted in my stomach. They'd been coming too often. Thoughts of what could be. Of how *good* this beautiful man was for me. And there were a few crazy, rash moments when I thought maybe I could be good for him, too. That as I let him discover me, he'd let me discover him.

How good we'd be together.

But this boy's heart was an unstable place. Hard and dark and impenetrable. No question, broken. Fragments patched together in bitterness and shame. But it was all the goodness that kept pouring out from the cracks that swept me away.

I forced myself to latch on to his tease and nudged him back. "I aim to please."

He helped me straighten, then reached out and tugged at my red bikini top where it peeked out from the black tank I wore over it.

The suit was a fifties throwback. Just his style.

A single finger trailed down the side of my neck and across my collarbone. He edged in closer, nose brushing mine. "And please you do."

His tingling touch traveled all the way down until he wove his tattooed fingers through mine, all that ink dancing over rippling muscle exposed on his arms.

He gave me a firm tug. I giggled as I stumbled forward, right back into that delicious, lust-inducing body.

God, he had me so spun up.

"Need to get you out of here, or we're never going to leave," he said.

I slanted him a flirty smile. "That sounds like a fine enough plan to me."

Four weeks of *this* had passed. Four weeks of us exploring and learning and tempting each other's bodies. Dipping our toes in heated, boiling waters. Standing at the brink of ecstasy. But Lyrik had started to seem reluctant to take it past that.

Maybe we both were beginning to worry when we finally dove in, we were going to get burned.

"Don't temp me, woman. The boys will have my balls if we don't show up."

A single brow arched. "Fine…we wouldn't want your balls to go missing, now would we?"

He growled and buried his face in my hair, nose running along the shell of my ear. He nipped at it. "*Red.* Do you know who you're messing with?" he whispered like a threat. Hands cinching tighter at my sides, he yanked me up against all his hard. Voice raw. Dripping with seduction. "What I'm going to do to you? How I'm going to make you beg and scream, and then you'll be begging me to do it all over again?"

Ah. There he was. That bad, bad boy. All that darkness and menace and severity. All while he held me in the security of his capable hands.

Because I knew without a doubt, the only thing in danger was my heart.

I tipped my chin up. At the look in his eyes, my breath caught in my throat. The thunder of need and lust crackled like a chemical reaction where they battled with flickers of something more.

"I already am," I told him.

Begging.

Needing.

Surrendering.

He wove his fingers through my hair and pressed his lips to mine. Closed-mouthed and hard. He dropped his forehead to mine, before he took a step back and offered me his hand. "Not kidding around…need to get you out of here. Now."

Accepting it, I slung the strap of my camera over my shoulder and followed him out the door to his bike waiting downstairs.

I put on my helmet while he straddled the gleaming metal.

That was a sight that could never get old. Lyrik's tattooed hands gripping the handlebars.

Those words.

Sing my soul.

I ached a little every time the statement written across his knuckles passed through my vision. His lithe body so powerful. Frightening and foreboding. Still, an unshakable haven.

The engine rumbled to life and the ground shook beneath my feet.

With a glance, my world rocked.

Tamar *King* was nowhere to be found.

Trying to regain my senses, I placed my camera in the saddlebag and climbed on behind him. He tucked me closer, the way he always did, ensuring my hold was tight where I wrapped myself around his back.

He turned us in the direction of Tybee Island and rode toward the seaside mansion where Lyrik and the rest of the guys had stayed when they'd first come to Savannah a year ago.

Anthony, *Sunder's* manager, owned the place, and he had come out from L.A. this weekend to check in with the band. He'd invited everyone over to his place for a BBQ and bonfire on the private beach before he went home to his family tomorrow.

I hugged Lyrik closer and breathed him in.

Four weeks left.

That hollow place inside me moaned like haunted gallows.

I didn't know how to sustain the loss.

The inevitability of losing the first real thing I'd felt in years.

It terrified me how desperately I didn't want it to end. But I refused to count this time as a mistake. Not when this man was slowly breathing true life back into me.

Awakening a soul I'd believed condemned.

No longer did I feel so...angry. Funny how I had to give this infuriating man credit for that.

Wind whipped his hair into chaos, and the ground was eaten up beneath us as we traveled the short twenty-minute trip to the beach house. He pulled his bike around the large, circular drive and stopped at the front. Lyrik helped me off, and I quickly removed the helmet and grabbed my camera as he killed the bike and flipped down the kickstand.

I pulled in a deep breath. The scent of sea and salt and summer heat filled my senses.

"Wow, that is some house." I eyed Lyrik from the side before I looked back at the extravagance before us.

This was a part of Lyrik's life I didn't see. The money, the fame, and the limelight he barely acknowledged. He was strangely modest when it came to those things. But I had an inkling Savannah had become his own haven. Reprieve from the fans, stardom, and the endless roads and tours and cities that ruled his life.

While here, for a few brief moments, he could settle into some kind of normalcy.

I'd started to count it an honor to share that time with him.

Lyrik pecked me on the mouth. "What...you gonna go and get greedy on me?" It was pure tease. "And here I was thinking you were one of the good ones and not easily impressed."

"Not easily impressed." I looked over at him. Seriously. "But I am impressed."

He frowned.

"By you," I added, brushing my fingers over his tight T-shirt, across that confusing, conflicting heart pounding underneath.

"You're so different than anything I expected." My words came out soft.

He turned toward me, and for a second, he just stared. Then he set a big hand on my cheek. "You are everything I never expected. Never anticipated. Everything I never knew I'd need."

Sadness flashed across his face. He was giving me a glimpse into something intensely private. Something real. I knew it. I also saw in his expression he didn't want to *need* me. And I knew deep in my spirit he would refuse it.

I gave him a shaky smile, before I forced it into something sexy and coy. "Come on before your crew sends out a search party. I do believe Ash is a little needy when it comes to you."

"Poor guy wouldn't know his hand from his ass if I wasn't there to look after him."

I knocked my shoulder into him, and he hooked his arm around my neck and started to walk.

"And here I thought it was Big Bad Baz that looked over all of you," I said as I threaded my fingers through his where they hung over my left shoulder. I brought the back of his hand to my lips.

So simple.

So easy.

"Pshh…" He smiled down at me. Affection played around his mouth. "I think we all know better than that. Baz is as soft as they come. Boy has his balls zipped up in the front pocket of Shea's purse."

"Is that where you were afraid they'd leave yours, too?"

He laughed, one of those ones that came from his belly, and I burrowed deeper into the warmth of his side.

He led me around the side of the house and toward the beach. Voices drifted along the breeze. Rounding the corner, the ocean spread out in front of us, with sandy dunes piled up in front of it before they gave way to the shore. Tall wisps of wild grasses grew from mounds of sand and the tufts waved in a gentle sway.

Twilight threatened on the horizon. A twist of pink and purple hung low in the sky, a reflection of the sun as it set behind us in the west. Ripples of the easy waves sparkled in the waning day.

My pulse quickened at the sight of the storm brewing in the distance. A toil of building clouds. Heat continued to cling to the humid Georgia air, but it was no longer unbearable as it mixed with the cooling breeze lifted from the ocean.

Raising my face to it, I inhaled. "It's so beautiful out here."

"Yeah," Lyrik agreed with a short nod. "More peace out here than I've felt in a long, long time. So different than L.A."

I slanted my gaze toward him. "Better or worse?"

Maybe I was digging. Looking for that connection. But it was already there, pulling taut between us. Tugging and stirring this yearning within me I'd never before known.

He hiked a shoulder. "Different. L.A. is what I know. The beat of the city. The rush. The road. Bein' here just feels like an extended vacation. You know when you get to some awesome getaway, a country you've always wanted to visit or an island you'd only ever dreamed of, and the second you get there, you're thinking just how nice it'd be to stay? To say fuck it and forget all the rest. But you know at the end of the week, you're going to be packing your bags, boarding a plane, and heading home. It's unsustainable. The dream sounds real nice. But that's just what it is. A dream."

"But you dreamed hard enough that you do what you love. Every day."

"But that dream comes at the greatest cost."

My brow pinched. "Sebastian has both. Is *living* both."

Lyrik shook his head. "Baz is in limbo. He'll be at a crossroads soon. You get one or the other. Life doesn't give you both, and he's going to have to pick."

"What if you're wrong?"

He started to speak, but trailed off when Shea shouted my name.

I looked to where she stood down on the beach, holding Kallie's hand.

Little Kallie's voice mixed with hers. Higher and more excited the closer we came. She jumped around at her mother's side. "Uncle Wyrik...Uncle Wyrik! Are you gonna go swimmin'? It's way, way, way warm. My daddy already took me and I'm gonna go again. But my mommy said we have to eat first because dinner is almost all done!"

A rush of something sweet rolled through him. Something tender. It didn't matter how hard this boy was. There was no question in my mind that another part of him was alive beneath the impervious layers he wore on the outside. A place soft, shielded below the calluses. A place reserved for something great waiting to break through.

"Heck, yeah, I'm going swimming, as long as it's with you. You have me all to yourself as soon as we eat. How's that sound, Kallie Love?"

The skin felt tight across my ribs. "What about me?" I said with a tease, though my throat was tight, too.

Lyrik shot me my favorite smile. The deadly kind. "Oh, you'll have plenty of me later."

Sure hoped so.

He guided me up the side steps and onto the large wooden deck attached to the back of the house. Red umbrellas were open wide to guard from the waning sun, the deck a pattern of shadows and comfort. Anthony piled a heap of fat steaks on a platter Sebastian held as he pulled them off the grill.

Ash came out the French doors carrying a stack of plates just as we made it to the top.

He grinned. "Oh hell, yeah, Tam Tam is here. Day. Made." He shot a feigned glare Lyrik's way. "Of course, you had to go and show with this asshole."

He looked directly at Lyrik. "Why do you always have *my* girl on your arm like she belongs there when we both know she belongs to me?"

Lyrik's nostrils flared. "Watch yourself, man."

Ash just laughed.

After the fight they'd had two weeks ago at Ash's house, I wasn't sure how things were going to look between them the following day. But they'd come into the bar the next night, thick as thieves, acting as if nothing had happened.

Soiled water swept under an unwavering bridge. Washed away.

But I was no fool. I knew whatever had passed between them

had been overwhelmingly significant. Something beyond my boundaries, where I sat on the outskirts and looked in like a stranger.

Whatever had incited Lyrik was why he'd go dark and shut me down when I dipped my toes too deep. When I got too close. When I asked too many questions. Why he'd stiffen when I trailed my fingers over his left arm covered by the bars and notes of that unspoken song and the hidden meaning woven within.

"Ready," Anthony called as he shut down the flames on the grill.

A huge spread of food was laid out on the outdoor kitchen. Everyone made their plates and took a seat at the round tables beneath the umbrellas, conversations light and laughter easy as we ate and watched as the day slowly faded away.

"All done!" Kallie called with a flap of her hands.

I nudged Lyrik. "I think that's your cue."

"I do believe it is."

He pushed back his chair and pulled Kallie right out of hers. "You ready for that swim, Kallie Love?" he asked as he ran the knuckle of his index finger under her chin.

"Yes yes yes!"

Ovary explosion.

I'd kind of forgotten I had them.

Then Lyrik West burst into my world.

A frown pulled at Shea's forehead. "You know what my grandma would have said…no swimming right after you eat or you're going to get a cramp."

Anthony laughed. "Oh come on, Shea. Just how long have you been living in the south? I'm pretty sure that's about the oldest wives' tale ever told."

She feigned offense. "I'll have you know, my grandma was brilliant."

Sebastian's smile was soft as he set his hand over hers on the table. Their exchange was silent, like a million words passed between them in the simple glance. "She'll be fine, baby."

Worry flitted through her eyes, before she looked up to her daughter where she was held protectively in Lyrik's arms.

"Go on, sweetheart. Have fun and hold on tight."

"Wouldn't dream of letting this one go."

He looked down at me. "You want to come?" he asked.

Did he realize he'd let an edge of hope slip into his tone? Did he have a single clue what he was doing to me?

The ground trembled beneath my feet.

God, what was I doing?

"I'll be right there," I promised.

I needed a moment.

Space.

Clarity.

Sebastian stood. "I'll come with ya, man."

Ash and Zee both hopped up. Ash peeled his shirt over his head. His body was a mess of thick muscles, tattoos covering the entirety of his arms and shoulders, his back and chest bare. He grinned. It had to be the dimples denting his cheeks that were his greatest weapon.

"Hey now, don't be taking off without us. We all need some Kallie time, don't we, Kallie?"

She giggled and clapped. "Yep…it's Kallie time!"

There was no stopping my smile as I looked over at them. The overwhelming comfort in being part of this exclusive crowd.

Home felt closer than it had in a long, long time. The loneliness seated so deeply within me diminished with each day, with each layer I shed, with every old feeling I allowed myself to feel.

My gaze stayed locked on them as the whole mass of gorgeous guys ambled down the boardwalk to the beach.

Anthony began to gather the plates, refusing help, so Shea and I settled into the quiet. A breeze blew through, gentle, churning with the soft gusts from the approaching storm.

"It's hardly fair, is it?" Shea mused. She had her attention trained on the guys plodding through the sand.

In question, I swung my attention toward her.

She shot me a scandalous grin.

"All of them…looking that way. The whole lot of them are kind of irresistible."

I turned back toward the group. Lyrik took that exact moment to glance at me over his shoulder. In the distance, those dark eyes glinted. My insides quivered. "No. Not fair. Not at all."

A soft snort left her. "He might be complicated and a giant pain in the ass, but I know he's a good man." She said it as if she knew I needed to hear it.

Slowly, I nodded, because I didn't question that. "But only part of him is there."

With meaning, her brown eyes drew thin. "You realize I see the same thing when I look at you?"

I flinched but she continued, "Maybe both of you are the missing piece...what the other has been looking for."

I forced the off-handed laughter. "Come on, Shea. Let's not pretend we all don't know what's happening here. That boy's just looking for a little fun while he's in town. Who better to pass it with than me?"

I shot for the blasé, badass girl Shea'd worked with for years behind the bar. The one who took shit from no one. The one who was game to play as long as she won.

But who the hell was I fooling? Because I had the overwhelming urge to touch my throat. To soothe the way it throbbed when I said it.

She just rubbed a tender hand down her swollen belly. "Sometimes fear shouts so loudly it drowns out everything else."

Well, I sure as hell wasn't fooling her.

We both turned our eyes to the beach. There was no mistaking her apprehension as she watched Lyrik with her daughter in the ocean. They'd gotten deep enough the waves lapped at his waist.

The little girl squealed and clapped and kicked in her excitement.

I wondered if it was torment for her to watch, for her to feel out of control, knowing how easily she'd lost hold of her little girl in the waves around this time last year. Thank God Sebastian had gotten to her in time.

"How do you let it go? The fear?" I asked.

A mix of unease and comfort traveled over her. She lifted a shoulder. "I think it comes to a point where you have to allow hope and belief to outshine the fear. Because I don't know if the fear ever truly goes away. We all feel it. It's up to us how we handle it. We can hide or we can live." She looked over at me, her tone emphatic. "And I want to live."

Emotion welled and wound with the discomfort already lodged in my throat. I swallowed over it as I watched the man who shouted all that hope and belief but somehow couldn't hear it himself.

Sebastian stood at the edge of the waves. He hollered at Shea, "Get that sweet ass down here and take a swim with me."

Life lit in her expression. She leaned forward and yelled back, "Believe me, no one needs to see that. I'm just fine right here."

He scoffed. "You lost your mind, baby? You've never looked better. Now get down here before I come up there and throw you over my shoulder."

Giggles rolled from her. "All right, all right, I'm coming."

Wow. The guy really had to twist her arm.

I laughed lightly as she pushed to her feet with a little more difficulty than she used to have. "Come on, I'm not going down there unless you do, too."

Shaking my head, I snagged my camera and joined her. No doubt, I wasn't going to get out of this.

I wasn't sure I wanted to.

Our footsteps thudded against the planks of the boardwalk.

Night had drawn near, clouds deepening to a fiery pink where they hugged the horizon. Waves rolled in, growing stronger than before as the storm encroached, rising from the south.

I set my camera on the blanket spread out by the fire Anthony was building. Kindles grew hot. Flames jumped and licked as they climbed toward the sky. Coming to life.

Lyrik had passed Kallie off to Sebastian since neither of them were willing to let her stand on her own feet.

My heart rate sped when he turned around as if feeling my approach.

Waiting for me.

Ink covered his chest and stomach, scrolled all the way down his arms and onto those hands I wanted nothing more than to feel on my body. Droplets of water dripped from his jet-black hair and those eyes were severe. Pinned on me as if they could see nothing else.

My breath stuttered.

He looked so dark and wicked.

Daunting, vicious beauty.

But I recognized more.

Energy swirled, stirred up by the sea. Drawn, I peeled off my tank and jeans and edged out into the lapping waves.

Lyrik didn't look away.

Cool water hit my feet and climbed higher and higher up my legs as I slowly made my way to the man who stood waiting for me.

So ridiculously tall.

Striking.

"Come here," he said when I was within two feet of him.

I squealed when he shocked me by grabbing me and pulling me deeper into the waves. He wrapped me up in his arms and buried his face in my neck. "There's my girl."

And I fought for reserves. For my shields. For the barriers. Because for so long I'd believed vulnerability was my enemy.

I felt it greater now than I ever had.

Not in the way Cameron Lucan had made me feel.

No.

I felt it in a way that was profound.

Life-changing.

As if an unsure hand was holding my heart precariously.

A heart that could be nurtured or crushed.

Lyrik had become so capable of both.

He broke the intensity by lifting me then tossing me into the air. Water swallowed me, and I sank to the bottom before I propelled myself up. I swiped back the drenched hair sticking to my face.

"Lyrik!" I sputtered and shouted. I gave a good punch to his stomach. "You're such a jerk."

But there was no anger.

No venom.

Because I no longer believed that assertion myself.

He jumped back, his abdomen flexing, his body rolling with laughter.

Carefree and light.

Shivers spread, and that need in the pit of my stomach kept growing stronger.

He smirked that cocky smirk.

God, I liked that, too.

"What's the matter, *Red*. You think a little water's going to hurt you?"

Anticipating this very thing, I'd only put on gloss before I'd left. My face was void of the makeup I normally wore, not even caring everyone would see me this way.

Romping in the water with a boy.

A month ago, who would have ever thought?

Who would have thought I'd splash him back? That I'd laugh and dodge when he retaliated with the same?

Who would have thought it would feel so good? That I'd crave the mouth hovering an inch from mine? That I'd hunger for *his* touch?

Who would have thought I'd need a man?

Want a man?

I clutched his sides.

I did.

I needed him.

Needed the safety I'd found in his arms.

Needed the belief that shone from his eyes.

Needed all that bad and that unfailing good.

It was there.

In him.

His nose brushed at my jaw, voice raw. "Blue…you make it feel different."

There was something so inherently sad in his statement, that voice twisting through me with the intent to tie.

But that was okay.

I was pretty sure I wanted to be bound.

We all played and splashed as the sun slowly slipped from the sky. Darkness wove a pattern within the clouds. In the distance, the faintest flashes of lightning flickered within the storm.

My heart twisted and mourned and begged.

Suddenly overwhelmed, I took a fumbling step back.

In concern, Lyrik's grin fell. "You okay?"

"Yeah, I'm fine. I'm just going to go dry off by the fire."

Telling him I was fine was nothing more than a lie.

Because I was staggered.

So close to feeling courageous.

More than brave.

Whole.

I spun around, fighting my way through the waves as I climbed back up the beach. The fire roared, logs aflame where Anthony stood guard.

Kind of the way he seemed to stand guard over all the guys. Their protector. Supporter.

I guess even the baddest boys needed one.

I flung my hair back and heaved out a breath as I approached.

"How was the water?" Anthony asked.

"Glorious," I replied.

Or maybe it was the air and the sky and the excited feeling that shimmered over the earth, my own secluded world set ablaze.

I sank down onto the blanket next to the fire.

The people who'd somehow become my family continued to play in the water. Zee and Lyrik and Ash wrestled in the waves like teenagers, while my sweet friend who I'd come to adore wore a white bikini with her baby belly on display. She clowned around with her husband and daughter, so free and unrestrained.

A tender smile pulled at my mouth and prodded at my fractured spirit.

Long gone was the snark and sneer.

Anxiously, I glanced at my camera. My pulse spiked and blood coursed through my veins. I ran my palms over the blanket to dry them. They were shaking by the time I finally got the courage to pick up my camera.

This hopeful feeling came over me when I focused the lens over the water and on the little family that brought a pang of hurt and hope beating through my spirit.

Four years ago, I made a promise to myself I'd never take another picture. Like a morbid punishment for the fool-hardy choices I'd made.

My little brother's face wove through the deepest recesses of my thoughts, my mother's words so clear.

Come home.

I wanted to because I missed them.

Because I wanted to do the right thing.

Because I wanted to be that girl.

Tamar Gibson.

I almost felt like her.

I just didn't know how to let hope and belief outshine the fear that was so intense. Didn't know how it could ever blot out the shame. How it'd ever make up for my guilt.

But staying only amplified it.

Sucking in a stealing breath, I clicked.

I wanted to sob as I broke that promise.

A promise that had been faulty.

Profane.

Misdirected.

Another way I'd allowed Cameron Lucan to steal what I had loved.

It was a single tear that slid down my face when I snapped the first picture I'd taken in four years. A darkened image of a family that represented joy.

Joy. Joy. Joy.

Lyrik was suddenly standing over me.

His expression both hardened and softened when he looked down at me. My face was wet from the waves. But I knew…I knew this man recognized my tears.

"Blue," he whispered.

I turned the lens up at his striking face and my lungs felt like they just might implode. I focused on that pouty mouth and the sharp angle of his jaw and those hypnotic eyes.

Click.

I was coming apart while a broken piece of me came together.

He stretched out his hand. "Blue…come here."

Shakily, I let him help me stand. How could I refuse? No longer did I want to.

No.

I wanted to experience and feel and love.

I wanted to *live*.

He leaned down and gathered the blanket from the ground.

He didn't say a word as he led me down the beach. Our footsteps marked our path where we walked several feet from the ebbing tide, our toes sinking into the damp sand. Wind whipped around us as the storm drew closer and we walked deeper into the night, away from the lights of the houses behind us and to a secluded section of the beach.

When we were completely isolated from the houses, he led me up a dune where wild grasses grew high at the bank. He flung the blanket down on a barren spot.

He helped me down. Immediately I pointed my camera at the horizon. At the billowing clouds that gathered higher and higher.

Lightning flashed, and a soft gasp left me as I captured the image.

God. It'd been so long. Never could I have imagined it would feel so good.

Like freedom.

Like exoneration.

"Blue," Lyrik whispered as he climbed down onto his knees in front of me. We both still wore our suits, the fabric wet and clinging to our bodies. He nudged me back onto the blanket. He straddled my waist with his knees still bearing his weight.

Holding me down in a way I was pinned but I knew I was free. I snapped and snapped that gorgeous face, while my insides shook with the impact of each click.

"Blue," he whispered again. Gently he pried the camera from my hands. Shadows danced around us. Grasses blew. Black hair whipped and his big body eclipsed mine.

"Tell me what's happening, baby."

The confession tumbled from my mouth. "Pictures were my passion. My grandfather taught me when I could barely hold a camera."

Emotion clogged my throat. "I took pictures of the most beautiful things. Storms and the desert and the people I loved. But I felt most alive when I was out in a storm. Capturing its beauty. Maybe it's dumb…but my pictures represented everything I wanted to be. Who I wanted to be and how I wanted to react to the people and things around me. They represented who I *was*. Tonight…tonight is the first time I've taken a picture in four years."

Understanding dawned in those inky eyes. Twilight and the sunrise.

He turned the camera on me.

Flinching, I jerked my head to the side.

He dropped the camera an inch and peered over the top. His stare burned into me. Digging deep while I tried with all of me to hide.

"Tell me…show me. You said this camera only held the most beautiful things. That's what you are. Don't you get it, Blue? You're so fucking gorgeous my breath gets locked up every time I glance your way. That's what you do to me. One look and I'm gone."

More tears seeped free and ran down the sides of my face as I looked back up at him. "I don't like my picture taken."

"Why?" he prodded.

Unearthing and exposing and uncovering.

My voice was gravel. Pained. Locked up.

"Because that's what he liked."

Confused, Lyrik blinked. "He liked taking your picture?"

My entire face pinched, my eyes squeezed closed while I admitted some of the horror etched in my spirit. "He took pictures of me tied up against my will. He…videotaped me while he let another man rape me."

Memories spun, too close, too fast. "Then he made me watch it. Made me look at the pictures again and again."

Shame.

Hatred.

Fear.

They threatened to take me hostage.

Lyrik stiffened, his anger so fierce it ignited in the wind.

Something wild and violent. I could feel the beat of it as it surged into me, silent but extreme.

"Tell me he's dead."

With the tight shake of my head, my eyes squeezed closed again, then slowly opened when I felt him aim the camera at me once more. The words falling from his mouth came in a rush. "What do you want, Blue? You're in control. This camera is yours. What's on it and who sees it. All you have to say is no. Do you hear me? Do you *hear* me?"

I hear you.

I hear you.

I hear you.

Splayed open wide. That was me. Lying there looking up at him.

"I don't know how to say no to you."

Right then? I knew I'd never want to.

Click.

Energy sizzled in the air.

The buzz before the strike.

Lyrik looked down at me as if he'd seen the sunlight for the very first time.

My heart flailed in my chest. Anticipation and need and the greatest sense of being free.

Wind barreled down and lightning flashed.

Yes.

A storm was coming.

LYRIK

*I*n some sort of frenzy, we stumbled up the stairs of our apartment building. Tamar was one step above me, and she was kissing me like the sex kitten she was. Ferocious and wild and a little bit scared. She struggled to get closer, all the while trying to drag me up the steps.

We made it to my door, and I fumbled with the knob, eager to make it inside. The door flew open. It banged against the interior wall.

I tossed my keys, because I damn sure had better use for my hands. I drove my fingers back into ruby locks just as my mouth

193

was diving back in.

Drowning in this girl.

She was sweet.

So fucking sweet.

"You taste so damned good." It was a groan at her mouth.

Red, delicious lips. Tart little tongue.

Red.

She moaned.

My movements were frantic, desperate as I edged her into my apartment and flung the door shut behind us.

Darkness swallowed the room. All except for the glittering lights of Savannah filtering through the balcony doors. That and the flashes of lightning blanketing the sky.

With each one, short gasps would escape Tamar's mouth. Those hot little sounds wound me up tighter than I'd ever been. Tension curled between us. It was this fierce energy blistering across my skin that I couldn't shake.

Sucked into her turbulence.

So hard and brash and sexy as fuck. Simple and sweet and good.

Couldn't even begin to make sense of the enigma.

Instead, she let me discover it. Bit by bit.

Rain pelted against the windows and beat against the roof. It echoed through the walls, a pounding rhythm. It filled up the air with need and lust and an insistent greed.

My dick strained. Pressing hard and hot at the seam of the jeans I'd thrown on right before I'd practically dragged her back to my bike after whatever the fuck had happened on the beach.

After she'd lain out there in the night and let me snap picture after picture. Let me urge her to show me what she wanted me to see. Her expression had knocked the breath from me. So full of faith and hope. And still brimming with the old pain that threatened to split me in two.

Eradicating it had become like some kind of twisted, fucked-up Holy Grail.

Never had I wanted to destroy someone the way I wanted to destroy that bastard without a name. Had never ached for vengeance. For blood. For revenge.

Scariest part was why I wanted it so fuckin' bad. Why I felt like I needed to wrap up this girl and keep her safe from all the atrocities of this world.

The rational side of me knew I should be pushing her away. I needed to shut down this insanity before it went any further.

But that logic became a dull, nagging sound against the roar to wrap her up and protect her. To coax her out of that shell. To let this girl shine because she was the most vivid thing I'd ever seen.

A rush of dizziness swirled through my head. I needed her so damned bad.

Fucked. I was completely, irrevocably fucked.

Touching her felt like a tease. Like torment.

I couldn't help but wonder if she'd been sent as additional punishment for what I'd done.

Because not a soul was perfect. But goddamn, if this girl wasn't perfect for me.

And soon she would become another piece ripped from this half-life.

Guilt clenched my heart, and I pushed her up against the wall, a little rough. Just as my hands gently cupped her face.

Conflict and contradiction.

"Red."

Flattening myself to her body, I rocked against her, my hard cock begging at her belly.

A tiny moan rolled from her tongue, and I got lost in her intense blue eyes as she stared up at me.

In emphasis, I squeezed her face. Giving her an out.

No question, both of us would fare a whole hell of a lot better if she took it.

"Going to fuck you tonight, Red. I'm not going to stop until I make you mine. Until I erase a little more of that asshole from your skin. Not unless you tell me no. Tell me no and you can walk right out that door."

Walk away.

Please.

She fisted both hands in my shirt. "I wouldn't let you stop if you tried."

On a growl, I spun her around and started backing her down the short hall, kissing her like the madman she made me while I pulled her shirt over her head. Under it, she still had on that tiny piece of red fabric she liked to call a bikini.

Truth?

The barely-there slip of material was my utter demise.

Her tits swelled over the top and the tat engraved just above them heaved with every breath she took.

"Don't stop," she pled at my mouth. She slipped her hands under my shirt, her palms flat on my stomach as she pushed it up and dragged it over my head.

Tremors rippled at her touch.

Mother. Fuck.

A torrent of emotion swam across her features. "Don't stop. Please, Lyrik, make me feel. Let me feel everything. I never thought I would again. Not until you."

Blue. *This* was Blue.

Innocent.

Vulnerable.

No trace of the mask.

And I needed to keep my cool. To take it slow when I was overwhelmed by the urge to tear into all her snowy flesh. To devour and consume. To conquer this girl—heart and mind and body and soul.

Because maybe it'd been me who hadn't felt anything in far too long. Instead I'd just been living out this never-ending hell of hollowed-out regret and overwhelming blame. All the bodies that'd been under me and over me? I couldn't remember a face.

Meaningless.

Not a name. Not one.

Not until her.

Red.

Unforgettable.

Blue.

"Tell me what you need."

She bit her plush bottom lip and her brow pinched with the magnitude of her confession.

"I need you."

Fuck.

I picked her up and she wound her legs around my waist. Nose to nose, I quickly carried her into the bedroom and laid her sideways across my bed, keeping her legs wrapped around me where I stood at the edge.

The lights were off. The window shades drawn.

The storm raging outside lit her up.

She'd told me that was where she felt safest.

Freest.

So yeah, there were no doubts in my mind it was stupid and selfish. But I wanted her freedom found with me.

In me.

Even when I'd remain in chains.

Edging back, I pulled her shoes and socks from her feet as something heavy pulled at my heart. I leaned in close, inhaling deep and filling my senses with all that cinnamon and spice, pressing my nose to her bare stomach as I undid the button and zipper on her jeans.

Intoxicating.

Maybe that's what this was.

A spell.

A curse.

A red-headed demon sent to crucify and slay.

Because her fingertips were mercy and her touch was misery.

What the fuck had I done?

Letting her get to me this way?

I knew better, but there was nothing I could do to stop this, and I was all too eager to yank her jeans down her legs.

I dropped them to the floor, leaving her in nothing but the red suit she'd been tempting me with all night.

"Do you have any idea how gorgeous you are?" I murmured. I smoothed my palms up the outside of her thighs, gripping a good handful of those lush hips. "Do you know, Red? How I have to tear myself away from you night after night? How I can't fucking sleep because I know you're just across the landing, lying in your bed. Alone. And then here I am, left thinking that's right where I should be?"

A shaky breath and a brush of her fingertips down my cheek. "Why do you leave when you know I want you to stay?"

Need and something I didn't want to feel knotted my guts.

Pulling back an inch, I let my gaze wander over her body.

Her skin was white and snowy, all except for the color inked across her flesh.

Long locks of red were strewn around her head like a fiery halo.

Just like my girl.

An angel.

A siren.

Rise swirled up her ribs in that pretty font, and my fingers trailed over the statement before I slid my hands under her back and freed her bathing suit top and tossed it to the floor.

"Goddamn," I hissed. I palmed her tits, bunching them up and pressing them together. I ducked down and brushed my lips across the hardened tip of one nipple. Breathing a breath of hot air across that perfect flesh.

Red arched and she fisted her hands in my hair.

Tugging hard. "Oh God...please."

My dick damn near exploded.

I did the same to the other, making sure she was a squirming mess of need.

Ready for me.

Because on all things holy, was I ever *ready* for her.

I moved back, knelt down and unlaced my boots, before I stood and shed my jeans. I stood before her in nothing but my tight underwear, my cock so fucking hard.

Begging.

Needy.

Desperate to take this girl.

Body and soul. Spirit and flesh.

Everything.

I had the depraved, fleeting thought that maybe I'd find a little bit of freedom in her, too.

Under her unyielding stare, I pulled my underwear down and kicked them from my feet.

Blue eyes roamed my body, up and down. The girl knew exactly how to undo me. Her tongue darted out and swiped across her lips when her heady gaze locked on my dick that was pointing to the sky. But then she let it trail back up, over my body that was covered by my story. The good and the bad. The deranged and the beautiful.

She looked to my eyes. Like she was both in the dark—willing to give up anything to read the fucked-up pages because she couldn't quite see, and in the light—where she still got all the important stuff anyway.

"It's you who's beautiful, Lyrik. Fascinating. Talented. Broken while you take the time to rebuild me. To make me remember what it feels like to be cared about. Taken care of. What it's like to feel unafraid."

Care.

I did.

I fucking did.

My jaw clenched. "But my time's running out."

Pain and hope lashed across her face. "It doesn't have to."

But it did and it would and there was no use wishing for things that weren't ever going to be.

I cinched my hands tight around her narrow waist and tugged her closer to the edge of the bed. "It's gonna end, Red. You and I both know it. Tell me right now you're okay with that. Otherwise, you need to get up and go, because I'm not the type of guy who's going to stand here and feed you lies. Think you know me better than that by now."

Shit. Why did saying it cause a ripping ache to slice through my insides?

But she knew what this was. Right from the start.

She squeezed her eyes shut. Her head nodded harshly as I ran my palms under her ass, kneading and squeezing,

"I want everything you have to give. Even if this ends right here, it's more than I ever thought I'd have."

Resting her ankles on my shoulders, I leaned down and worked the red bottoms free from her tight little body. She lifted her ankles just enough so I could pull them from her feet.

Lust lit up behind my eyes and saturated every cell. What was left of my senses took a sharp turn south.

Her pussy was pink and bare and damp. I parted her with my fingers and watched her expression as I plunged two fingers inside.

Her hips shot from the bed. "Shit…Lyrik."

"Love my name coming from that smart mouth." The words scraped up my throat.

I kept pumping my fingers, and her head rolled back, mouth dropping open the more pleasure I brought her.

That mouth.

That mouth.

She cried out in frustration when I suddenly pulled my fingers free. The sassy red vixen came out to play. Blue eyes flashed, and she made to sit up. "Damn it, Lyrik…don't you dare—"

I cut her off by pressing my fingers into the well of her hot, hot mouth.

A mumbled moan rolled from her as she sank back down onto the mattress. The needy sound vibrated up my arm and through my body as her tongue played across the pads of my fingertips.

I slid them out, back in.

"Fuck…you're so hot, Red. Don't know how to make sense of you."

I kept fucking her mouth with my fingers and she kept bucking up, pussy rubbing against the tip of my dick.

Energy thick. Heavy. Anticipation and apprehension and desire.

I pulled all the way back and stared down over her.

Red writhed on the bed. Her delicate hands were fisted in my sheets.

Soft and unbelievably fierce.

Strong and unbearably sweet.

This girl was my ruin.

"Get in the middle," I demanded.

She scooted back. Her breaths came sharper and harder as I opened the top drawer of my nightstand and grabbed a condom. I tossed it next to her on the bed.

"I'm going to fuck you until the only name you know is mine."

Made her that promise once, and I intended to keep it.

She arched as I crawled over her. Her heart was pounding. It was this wild beat that stirred something deep within.

Beyond the window, lightning flashed.

I sat back on my knees between her trembling legs, and rolled the condom over my cock. I reached down and held my hand over that tat of temptation, before I ran it up her leg and hooked her knee over my hip.

I set the opposite hand next to her head to hold myself up. Our faces were a foot apart.

Breaths mingling.

Hearts stuttering and hammering and racing.

Tension wound fast, my muscles going rigid with restraint. My eyes locked on the girl. "Do you hear me?"

Did she?

Could she?

She burrowed her fingers into my shoulders. "I hear you."

Her back bowed, her tits mashing into my chest as she clung to me. Like she was giving me everything and I was giving it in return.

Trust.

Hope.

A little bit of life she didn't have.

Something *good*.

This time she turned her mouth to my ear.

"*I hear you.*"

That confession hit me like an earthquake.

I wedged my hips between her thighs.

I grabbed my cock at the base and ran the tip through her center.

Cautious. Watching every insinuation and implication. For any sign of fear or panic. I remained still while I watched the emotion wash through the girl who was trusting me with something I didn't have the right to hold.

But fuck.

I wanted it to be me.

Couldn't stand the thought of this moment belonging to another man.

A moan shuddered from her when she lifted herself and rubbed against my dick. Needy and breathless.

I pushed inside. Barely an inch.

"Shit." The harsh word left me as my stomach coiled. A flash fire of pleasure roared across my skin. Singeing. Swallowing me whole.

Her nails sank deeper into my shoulders and her blue eyes locked on mine. Anxious, but lacking horror or fear.

"No girl should feel this good."

She stuttered out a disbelieving laugh, half-choked with desire. Then she shot me one of those flirty grins. All sex and seduction. She lifted her chin. "And you haven't even felt me yet."

My lips curled into a smirk.

"I'm about to change that."

I slid all the way home.

Taking her knocked the smirk right off my smug face. My body heaved with the impact. Like I'd just dived into an endless abyss of bliss, and even if it cost me my life, I didn't ever want to come up for air.

I stole the throaty moan escaping from between her parted lips with a kiss. My entire body pulsed like a live wire while she trembled and shook, adjusting to my size.

Edging my head back, I looked down at her. "You okay?"

A smile trembled around her luscious mouth, dancing between awe and hope and faith. The same way she'd been looking at me back on the beach when I'd snapped that first picture.

"Saying I'm okay would be nothing less than an insult."

My chest tightened, and I struggled for a breath. I pressed up onto both hands and let the rest of my weight fall to my knees.

Our eyes tracked each other's gaze, flicking down at the same time to where we were joined as I drew out.

Slowly.

A strangled, needy sound slid from her tongue.

"Yeah?" I asked, giving her a nudging taunt.

"Yes," she whispered frantically.

I rocked back in, hard. Her walls clenched around my dick as I took her as deep as I could go. I shifted and clutched the caps of her shoulders, tight and tender and trying with all of me not to completely let go.

But she felt so good.

So damned good I couldn't see.

Couldn't grasp on to reality or sanity or that dwindling sense of loyalty.

Couldn't feel a single thing but Tamar.

Tamar.

Blues and reds and blacks and blinding light.

For a year, I'd been dying to get inside this girl.

The first time I saw her, I knew sex with Red would blow my mind.

She was like a bundle of fireworks just waiting for a match.

Now I was standing in the flames.

I fucked her, relentlessly, while she panted and moaned.

"Lyrik. Lyrik. Lyrik."

A tingling feeling weaved through my chest and compressed my ribs.

Was it wrong how much I liked that?

Hearing her cry out my name. Struggling to get closer while I was filling her so full each utterance left her mouth on a panted breath.

Pleasure wound fast. It spread across my lower back and tugged at my balls.

"Blue. Need you to come, baby. You feel too good."

It'd been five weeks since I'd been in a girl. Worse yet, it'd been my whole life since I'd been in this one.

Sick part?

If I could, I'd keep this moment forever.

Keep this girl.

Like I could *ever* deserve her.

"Touch me," she whispered.

Inching back a fraction, I slid my hand between us and rolled my finger across her clit.

That was it.

All she needed.

My blue-eyed angel lit.

Tamar screamed my name.

I pumped harder and faster as she came, her body nearly floating up beneath mine. My hips snapped against hers. Frantic and uneven as intense feeling swept over me. Head to toe and everywhere between. Something bigger than I'd ever felt.

Something both blinding and bright.

Energy and life.

Boom.

TAMAR

Rain patted gently on the roof, and Lyrik pulled me deeper into his hold. My back was to his chest and his breath was all around me. The pound of our hearts had finally begun to settle like the waning storm.

He pressed a kiss to the back of my head. "How do you feel?"

On a heavy exhale, I let myself be drawn closer. My mind and body drifted on the comfort. Light and free.

I braided my fingers through his where he had his hand pressed over the tattoo centered on my chest.

"Amazing." It was a reverent whisper as I lifted our entwined hands and pressed my mouth to the back of his.

"You are what is amazing," he murmured back, his nose nuzzled in my hair and his words slithering across my skin. Slipping in and over and working all the way through.

I rolled over so I could look at his face. Inky eyes stared back at me in the darkness. His hair was a sexy mess and those red lips were swollen.

A shiver rolled through me.

I chewed at my bottom lip.

I'd just had sex with Lyrik West.

Holy shit.

And it'd been exactly that.

Amazing.

Undeniably, extraordinarily amazing.

I hadn't felt lost to fear or panic. I didn't feel a prisoner to the memories.

I felt...liberated.

Beautiful.

Wanted and desired.

He smirked as if he'd just latched onto my thoughts. "You're looking a little...*satisfied.*"

I giggled. Yeah. I giggled.

Then it just got worse and I was giving into this rippling sense of euphoria as I grinned and brushed my fingertips across his chin and thought back to the day when he'd openly challenged me out in the market, provoking me by saying the only thing I needed was to be satisfied.

And God, had this man challenged me. Challenged every belief and fear and hope I'd harbored. Chased me down until I faced them.

"Don't go and get too proud of yourself, rock star." I went for a tease, but there was no keeping the thick emotion from my words.

God. I'd gone and gotten myself in deep.

That smirk. "Oh, I'm feeling pretty proud right about now."

A smile tugged at my mouth. "Oh, you are, huh?"

"Mmm-hmm."

That was the thing. I could see it.

Pride.

But he wasn't proud of himself.

He was proud of me.

"Thank you." My words were hoarse and came from that place within me I'd never thought I'd see again. The place he'd exposed.

He gentled his fingers through my hair, this hard, cryptic man who was so utterly soft. "No…thank you. Thank you for trusting me. For letting me get to see a side of you that nobody else knows. For allowing me to help her shine."

He hooked his finger under my chin and lifted my face to him. "She's incredibly beautiful and I feel honored I was the one who got to meet her."

A million nerves fluttered.

That was the crazy thing. He knew me better than anyone. Maybe it was even crazier I felt as if I knew him best, too. As if only I held the power to understand the veiled truth within him. As if I was so close yet still watching from afar.

My fingertips trailed over his shoulder and ran down to the musical bars winding up his arm. An unsung song crying out to be played.

Feather light, I tapped my fingertips along it. As if playing the chords.

Lyrik winced.

My gaze flitted between the pain written so clearly on his face and the notes engraved on his arm. For a few seconds, I studied his expression, trying to make sense of it. To make sense of him. This menacing, intimidating man who at times seemed shackled and oppressed. I wanted to free him. Maybe return to him a little of what he'd given me.

When I turned to look at my fingers trailing the bars, my voice was quiet and subdued as I spoke my confession. "Sometimes in the middle of the night, when I can't sleep and I'm all alone, I hear you play."

I risked peeking at him.

His eyes were squeezed closed and his body was rigid. Bracing himself.

I turned my attention back to his song. "I'm almost embarrassed to admit this to you…because I would never want you to think I could look at you as anything but the boy next door…the boy who changed me."

I swallowed hard. "It was three years ago when I heard my first *Sunder* song. It was late…I'd come home from work and had been alone in my apartment, lost in the same excruciating loneliness I've lived in for the last four years. This song came on…"

Soft laughter rolled from my tongue. "You'd think it would be forgettable, nothing that would ever be ingrained in my memory, but I remember the tingly feeling I got when the first few chords came through the speakers. I remember sitting propped up in my bed, entranced. I had to find out who it was. I had to know who was singing. To put a face to the voice that was so haunting and comforting at the same time."

Energy rolled across my skin at the memory. "They say music touches us in a way nothing else can, and I swore in that moment it felt as if the person singing it was singing directly to me. That they'd found the words for my loneliness. That they'd tapped into it and for a few minutes I didn't feel so alone."

"Blue," he whispered in effort to shut me down, but I kept speaking. "I found out that song…that song wasn't sung by the lead who normally sings the majority of their songs. It was sung by a gorgeous, black-haired boy. He was singing *Sunday Gone,* a song I learned he wrote. I'd sit for hours in front of my computer and watch him with his black guitar braced on his lap and his mouth pressed to the mic. I'd just hit replay over and over because that was the only time I felt truly understood."

I pulled air into my lungs. "And it turned out it was you, Lyrik."

It was the song I had tortured myself with when I refused to give in to Lyrik's advances. When he'd terrified me simply from the way he'd made me feel. Back when I'd been certain he would use me up and throw me away.

And I knew he would.

Throw me away.

He'd made that much clear. My heart clenched with the promise that this was going to end. That *this* was all he had to give.

But I also knew he wasn't using me up.

He was filling me up.

Would he give me the opportunity to fill him up a little bit, too?

I pressed a hand over his pounding heart. "I hear you, Lyrik."

He trembled.

"I hear your words and I hear your pain. Let me share some of it. The way you're sharing mine. Sing me your song."

In a flash, he had his face buried in my neck. "Goddamn it, Blue. Why do you have to keep doin' this to me? You keep trying and trying to get to the place where I can't let you go."

"What if I'm already there?"

I had to be.

Not all of this could be one-sided and I refused to believe this beautiful boy could be immune.

Not when I'd been touched so wholly.

Not after what we'd just shared.

Not after we'd come so far.

He clutched me tightly. His breaths came harsh and hard and his hands burned into my back as he pulled me tighter.

God, I hurt for him. For me. For us.

"You aren't supposed to make me feel this way," he whispered as if in confession—shamed and ridden with guilt yet still refusing to let go. "This was a terrible idea."

Those five words. If anything, they just reinforced the reasons for my reserve, my need to keep my distance from this devastated man.

He held me, safe and secure, but I could feel part of his spirit detaching and floating away. Just as strongly as he struggled to stay attached.

His voice shook when he finally released it at the sensitive skin of my neck in a torrent of heartbroken passion.

Lyrik sang like he did in the night.

I'd have given it all.
But instead I got lost along the way.

It was only two lines. That was all he gave me of his unsung song.

Two lines from his mystery.

The words coated in uncertainty and obscurity.

Both of us seemed suspended in it, in the echoing silence that followed behind and held fast to the energy clinging to the air.

"I should go," I forced out when I wasn't sure I could remain beneath the crushing weight any longer.

He gathered me closer and tucked my head under his chin, his words just as intense as the song he'd let tumble from his mouth. "No, Blue. No. You definitely should stay."

TAMAR

I gave a quick knock to Lyrik's door. After a couple seconds of no response, I craned my ear toward the wood.

No sound or movement on the other side.

Sucking in a breath, I turned the knob and let myself in. I fought the reckless grin when I thought back to the day when he'd granted me a little more access into the private parts of his life.

"I stopped by this afternoon, but you weren't here."

"Why didn't you just come inside? My place is almost always unlocked." He smirked. *"Hazards of having lazy, nosy, too-comfortable friends like Ash and Zee. Gave up trying to keep them out of my business a long time ago."*

"Feeling awful brave there, aren't you, rock star, giving someone the chance to just waltz into your apartment?"

He shrugged. "Nah, just don't care all that much about stuff. Besides, I kinda like having a reason to kick ass."

Obsidian eyes flashed and he raked just the tip of his fingernail down my cheek. Chills spread like a building avalanche. "But seriously, baby, nothing I'd like better than walking in and finding you lying in my bed. Preferably naked. Next time, don't hesitate."

I mean, giving me free rein in his apartment seemed like a big deal. Right? I couldn't help but hope he was coming around. That maybe he was beginning to want the same things I couldn't help but want, the hopeful ideas that had sprouted and taken residence in my heart and mind.

They rang with words like real and commitment and forever.

So maybe it was stupid and naïve.

A slow, cold shiver rolled through me when I remembered all the promises I'd made myself. That I'd never again find myself in this position. In a place of vulnerability and weakness. It took me all of one second to write the thought off because what Lyrik and I had was entirely different. Not even close to being the same.

Lyrik respected me.

Cared about me.

I knew he did.

When it came to him, there wasn't a whole lot of hesitation on my part. Not anymore. I wanted everything I could get and then I wanted a little more.

Late-afternoon sun blazed through the French doors pouring natural light into his apartment. My arms were weighed down by shopping bags, and I trudged across the space toward the kitchen where I set the bags on the small round table.

Excitement glimmered in a slow dance in my belly as I began to unpack the groceries.

Was it foolish to feel so good that I'd found a little of the old me?

The sound of the shower filtered through the walls from the bathroom tucked within Lyrik's bedroom, and that excitement sharpened. Streaked with desire and lust.

Humming under my breath, I pulled a pot from the bottom cabinet and filled it with water, spun around, my hips striking up their own dance as I swayed across Lyrik's kitchen to the stove on the opposite side.

The gas stove clicked as I turned the knob and a ring of flames came to life. I set the pot over it, and moved back to the other side where I rinsed the red potatoes I'd picked up earlier at the farmers' market. I washed them and dropped them into the water that was beginning to boil.

I moved on to the thick steaks and began to prepare them, figuring we'd toss them on the little grill on Lyrik's balcony.

That excitement flashed when I heard the pipes screech as the water was turned off.

The grin that curled my lips was unstoppable. Was it completely insane that I couldn't wait to see him? Completely insane that I'd slipped so deeply into this non-relationship that my body craved him every second we were apart?

For a while now, it'd seemed all of our time had become the same. But since we'd first had sex two weeks ago? Lyrik and I had become one. Desperate hands. Mind-blowing, incredible sex. Easy conversation.

God, I couldn't get enough of him.

And the man was insatiable, taking me again and again.

So foolishly I didn't want him to stop.

And if what we had was only temporary? We still had two weeks, and I intended to make the most of them.

Footsteps padded on the wooden floor. They creaked beneath his weight.

Barefoot.

I knew he was before he even came into view.

God, was I really that in tune with him?

I felt him stop at the end of the hall. Drawn, I glanced up at him. My breath hitched.

There he was. Rubbing a towel over his damp head. Chest bare. A pair of low-slung jeans hung from his narrow waist.

Barefoot. Just like I thought.

Dark and light. Corrupt and pure.

Energy surged, a cyclone of intensity that spun and twisted and filled up the room.

Goosebumps flashed down my arms.

On all things holy, a man should not be allowed to look that good. My knees rocked and the ground trembled beneath my feet. *The buzz before the strike.*

He smirked and lifted his chin. "Well, well, well, if it isn't *Red* standing in my kitchen, lookin' like my favorite fantasy. Are you trying to wreck me, baby?"

I ripped my gaze from the man standing across the room and let it travel down my attire.

Yeah, I'd dressed for him.

My hair, piled in an intricate twist, was done up in a black bandanna. I wore a tight pair of white jeans that stopped just above my ankles, and a white and black polka-dot blouse tied at the bottom so it exposed a thick strip of skin across my mid-drift, lips painted a vibrant red.

I shrugged like it didn't matter while Lyrik looked at me as if he were two seconds from gobbling me up.

God, I hoped so.

"Not that I'm complaining...finding you standing there." He rounded the countertop and came into the kitchen.

My heart sped, and my breaths became shallow when from behind he wound his arms around my waist. Those big, capable hands went straight to the slip of skin I knew he wouldn't be able to resist, heated palms flat on my flesh.

My stomach dove into a free fall.

He buried his nose in my hair. "You didn't need to do all of this for me, baby. I would have been happy to take you out for dinner."

My shoulders hiked, and I went for blasé. As if it were nothing. But the words slipped free, an uncontrolled statement as I turned my head just enough so we were nose to nose. "Make it if you want it to matter."

For a moment, he stilled, before he wrapped me up tighter. His groan vibrated down my spine. "What am I going to do with you?"

"What aren't you going to do with me?" That time I actually

managed the flirt and tease, because there was nothing feigned about it.

The man gave me multiple personality disorder. Bold and sexy and in control. Soft and kind.

Yet I couldn't help but feel the mix was absolutely me.

I gasped when he pressed his cock to my backside. Big and hard. "You want to find out just what I intend to do to you? What I've been thinking about all week, getting right where I haven't been?"

He rocked against my ass, his tone sharpening in a seductive edge. "All you have to say is no…but I sure as hell hope you don't."

Shivers blazed, a thrill beating a path through my senses and twisting as anticipation swirled in my stomach.

He'd broken down all my barriers. Taken me everywhere and in every way. Except for that. I pressed back. "I'm yours."

He both stilled and managed to hug me a little tighter.

Protective.

I just wasn't sure who he was protecting, anymore.

God, it was getting harder and harder to keep it inside. The way I felt. The way it increased every day and amplified every night.

He dropped a kiss to my temple, stepped back, and ran his fingers through the damp, dark hair on his head. "What can I do to help?"

I twisted the cap to the seasoning and began to sprinkle it over the steaks. "Why don't you go heat up the grill? The potatoes are just starting to boil and I'm getting ready to make a salad."

"Mmm…you spoil me."

"I aim to please," I shot at him, all flirty and filled with innuendo.

He chuckled and touched my nose. "And please you do."

I giggled as he repeated our words, the mood set back to light. Riding with Lyrik required being ready for all the highs and lows.

He pointed at me as he began to walk backward in the direction of the balcony. "Don't move," he said.

"I'm not going anywhere," I promised.

He disappeared into the gleaming light.

I turned to washing the vegetables, patted my hands dry before I opened a drawer to dig around for a utility knife.

Junk drawer.

I started to slam it closed, when a picture shoved in the back caught my attention. So maybe it was buried beneath another stack of papers. The pointy edge was the only thing I saw.

With a brush of my fingers, I nudged the papers covering it aside.

A slick of apprehension beaded as a sheen of sweat across my skin.

Shit. Shit. Shit.

What was I thinking?

Maybe I wasn't at all because I reached inside and pulled it out.

And again I got the sense I was no different than the ditsy girl on a horror flick who was walking right into a trap.

Moments from being gutted.

No, not moments. A flash of a second. Because I didn't even have time for my breath to catch. Instead, the air in my lungs jutted out in some kind of perverted shock. As if I had any right to feel this way. To look on this picture as if it were an insult to me.

As if I'd been betrayed by some kind of illicit affair.

It was a snapshot. Lyrik's face shone. Happy. So goddamned happy and free that it tugged at me from all directions. Ripping me apart. He was without an ounce of the burden and chains that now dragged him down. Without that ever-present ominous and dark aura.

He was wrapped around a girl from behind. Her long brown hair blew in the wind, brushing at his face, her smile just as wide as his.

I attempted to swallow around the lump in my throat.

Impossible.

Because it was too big, too heavy and suffocating and weighted with all the limitations Lyrik continued to hang around our necks.

Because this?

This was limitless.

Forever.

I pressed my hand over my mouth and tried to choke back the

sob. Tried to tamp down the burning behind my eyes as tears rushed to fill them.

God, this girl looked so young. No question, Lyrik looked young in it, too. The image had to be at least five or six years old. But the girl…this gorgeous girl who was beautiful in a seductive way? It was evident in her eyes.

Youth.

"What the fuck do you think you're doing?"

The voice was low and dangerous and dark.

I jerked to look at him. I'd been so wrapped up in the picture I'd not even noticed he'd come back inside.

Anger billowed from him.

"Who's this?"

Stupid, stupid, stupid.

How the hell could I be so insane to ask? Had I really regressed to this point? Needy with zero self-preservation?

The worst part was I wasn't sure I could handle hearing him give the answer.

Because I already knew.

This was love.

His jaw clenched, and I could almost hear the grind of his teeth as he tried to restrain himself. "Asked you what the fuck you think you're doing? Going through my stuff? Told you all along not to go digging where you shouldn't be."

He stalked forward and backed me into the counter.

I held the picture between us. "Who is she?" The question was desperate. Uttered like a fool. A fool who'd run and run and run and then turned right around and let him catch up to me.

"Not. You." His two ugly words pierced me as if he were throwing knives.

At least that's what they felt like when they struck me.

Not. You.

Impaling and cutting.

Excruciating.

I should have been prepared. He told me sex was all he had to give.

Because he belonged to someone else.

217

Slowly, I squeezed my eyes shut, praying I could keep the tears at bay. At least until I made it out his door. That's where I'd crumble and fall. Where I'd lick my wounds and force myself to stand. Where I would refortify the walls I never should have let him knock down.

But first? I gave him one last bit of my honesty. Gently, my gaze traced his face one last time.

"I hear you."

Then I gathered myself and strode out his door.

seventeen

TAMAR

Stealing myself, I walked out my apartment door onto the landing. My head was held high, that old sneer reinstated on my mouth, my lips painted the deepest red. I figured I should always be prepared for what I might stumble upon out here. Because I refused to ever again be caught unaware.

Late afternoon light glinted in my eyes. My body slammed into the hard wall of humidity.

It made it difficult to draw in a full breath.

I shook my head to clear it. Or maybe the motion was done as an admonishment. As a silent command screaming out for me to get my shit together.

I knew I was nothing but a liar if I blamed this feeling on the weather.

As if I didn't know why it felt like there were a thousand bricks piled on my chest. As if they kept raining down from above, pelting and crushing and destroying.

I hated I'd been such a fool to give him the power to make me feel this way.

I knew better.

I knew better.

I knew better.

But it didn't matter how many times I chanted it beneath my breath. Every single one of those feelings remained. The gain and the loss. The renewed confidence he'd given me up against what he'd so easily torn away.

It seemed cruel he was the reason for the first true life I'd felt in years. Glimmers of it were still there, trying to work their way out, the desperate urge to get back some semblance of who I used to be. To go home and be brave. Though all of that was eclipsed by the hurt balled up like a fist at the base of my throat.

It was an old pain whispering its venom.

How could you be so stupid? So careless? How could you have let yourself be used so easily? Taken and tossed out like the morning's trash.

Dirty.

Breaths squeezed in and out of my too-tight lungs as I stood mere feet from his apartment. So close yet there couldn't have been a greater distance between us.

The overabundance of thoughts and worries and hopes swirled around me like a cyclone. I wasn't sure I had the strength left to stand up under the bitter jumble of emotions.

Pulled toward home while this beautiful man pushed me away.

God, this piercing ache never dissipated. Never dimmed or dulled.

No matter how hard I tried, I couldn't escape the unwavering sorrow that chased me through the days and stalked me through the nights.

But standing here ignited a rage of fury and hurt and betrayal so intense my head spun and my heart felt as if it literally might fail. Stutter and bleed out and usher in the end.

My bottom lip trembled as my ear tuned into the heavy metal music blasting from the confines of the old brick walls I knew kept him hidden. The curtains were closed. Exactly the way they'd been for the last two weeks.

I struggled for control, silently screaming the mantra with a hand fisted at my side. *Don't look. Don't look. Don't look.*

But the crazy awareness wouldn't let me go. Dread slid down my spine like the freezing slick of ice. Shaking, my gaze jumped to the stack of moving boxes sitting to the left of his door.

Lyrik West was scratched in Sharpie on the sides.

The sight of them nearly brought everything crashing down. Reality striking home.

Two months.

He couldn't even give me that. And I'd allowed myself to be naïve enough to dream of so much more. That our moments had meant something. Because to me, they'd come to mean everything.

I wobbled on my five-inch heels, and my hand darted out to the wall to keep myself from sinking to the ground. I sucked for nonexistent air. It took everything to keep from falling to my knees.

But I didn't.

Because Tamar King would always stand.

****

Voices shouted in an attempt to be heard over the country band playing onstage. People laughed and shouted. A crush of bodies vied for a spot close to the gleaming wood of the ornate, carved bar, as if touching it gave the promise of a good time.

Typical of a summer Friday night, *Charlie's* was packed.

I couldn't help but be grateful for the distraction. I hustled behind the bar because I was damn good at my job.

So maybe it hadn't been my lifelong dream. Maybe it didn't fill me with hope and awe and the quest for things that could never be.

But it was safe. Void of all the silly, absurd notions Lyrik had incited.

Better to stamp them out now than to have them destroy me in the end.

"How are you holding up, sugar?" Charlie's voice struck me from behind. Softer than normal. As if he needed to approach me with caution and not all the ease he had before Lyrik had messed up the security I'd established in this life.

I really hated that, too.

I glanced at my old friend. At the piece of family I'd found here. The flare of unease trembling my insides warned I was soon to lose *this* false sanctuary, too.

A coy smile spread across my face. Forced. Fake. "Holding up just fine, old man. How about you? Looks like Nathan could use some help rather than you standing looking over my shoulder like you have nothing better to do."

I shot it at him like a teasing taunt, a single eyebrow arching right along with the arch of my upper lip.

A smile flickered beneath his scraggly beard, though his brown eyes remained soft. "Well...I guess since you've got it all under control, I'd better make myself busy."

Under control.

Right.

"You sure you don't need anything?" he added.

I shooed him. "Go on...I've got it handled. The last thing I need is you slowing me down. You know I live for the hustle."

Backing away, he held his hands up in surrender. "All right, all right. Message received. Tamar is just *fine*...all on her own."

I scowled in his direction. I knew what he was doing. What he was implying. The way his tone went fatherly and his words filled with concern.

"Yep. I'm perfectly fine. On my own," I emphasized.

"Whatever you need to tell yourself, sugar. Just know you aren't foolin' anyone but yourself. But I'd bet you aren't even managing that."

Charlie gave me a pointed stare before he turned and headed over to check on Nathan, and I forced my attention back on my job.

And I did just that.

Tried to pretend everything was fine.

To pretend I wasn't falling apart.

Rending.

Splitting.

Crumbling.

Tried to pretend I didn't have the sensation of being fractured in two.

Sophie, one of the weekend waitresses, set her tray down on the bar and leaned over it.

"How's that order coming?" she asked. "Table nineteen is about to lose their shit." She sighed dramatically. "Sometimes I wish the frat boys wouldn't come out to play."

It seemed a miracle, but low laughter rolled from my tongue. I gave her an amused shake of my head. "You and me both. Just give me...two...seconds..." I drew out as I finished pouring tequila across three shot glasses.

I slid the drinks to her. "There you go, gorgeous. Don't let those boys get to you. Not any of them are worth it."

None of them. Not for a second.

"Thank you." She situated them on her tray, shot me a smile, calling over her shoulder as she walked away, "Wish me luck."

"Good lu—" The words locked in my throat when the front doors swung open, which they'd been doing all night. But this time...this time they stopped me in my tracks.

Awareness spread.

Tension wound.

Tighter and harder and faster.

Gaining speed as it barreled forward like a speeding train.

Malicious and dark and foreboding.

My heart stalled before it took off at a sprint. Wild and offbeat.

Ash strode in like he owned the place, his dimpled grin and hungry gaze taking in the churning mayhem dancing within the old walls. It was clear he was all too keen to add to it.

Two steps behind was Zee.

But it was the boy who followed them who might as well have stood out in front.

Eclipsing all.

Like shattering, splintering light.

That sinister man rode in on all his raving intensity. His body was rigid, as if that wild energy was condensed and compounded. Gathering to a pinpoint.

Set to fire.

Cutting down anyone and anything in its path like the devastating shockwave of an atom bomb.

The buzz before the strike.

But this time, the strike just might prove fatal.

How sick was it I still wanted him? That after seeing that photo and hearing his words, I still clung to the moments we'd shared as if they'd somehow counted. When *he'd* laid them all to waste.

Two weeks. Two weeks of *silence.* Silence in the shape of loud, thrashing, violent music through the walls. After all we'd shared physically, emotionally, he'd simply let go. Let *me* go. Not a word. Not an explanation. As if he owed me nothing.

Why did I always want the things that would harm me most?

Furtively, I cut my eyes his way, hoping he wouldn't notice but needing one last image to keep for when he was gone.

Memorizing.

It wasn't so hard. There was no chance I could forget. Tonight he wore a tight white V-neck tee. The tattoos I'd come to know so well vibrated beneath bunched muscle, as if every fiber of him seethed with his own anger.

Emotion burned behind my traitorous eyes, and just as fast as I'd looked, I turned my back before he could catch the anguish I was certain painted every inch of my expression.

For the second time that day, my hands shot forward to keep myself standing, my body jerking as I clutched the edge of the bar and tried to prepare myself to again come face to face with Lyrik West. I tried to find safety behind the walls I had built. To gain solid ground. To fortify and protect.

Never again would I allow him to control me.

With my head dropped, my lips moved soundlessly, as if I were sending up a silent prayer. Reaching for a buoy. A petition to find truth in the words that would allow me to remain afloat.

You are strong. You are nobody's slave. He only has power and effect if you give it to him. And you won't *let him have it.*

Blowing out a breath, I donned that stoic, lofty mask, lifted my chin, and went back to work. The whole time I pretended as if I wasn't painfully aware of him standing there in the haze of light suspended above him. As if I didn't feel the heat of his unfaltering gaze searing into me.

Stark, disbelieving laughter shook my throbbing chest. For a fleeting second, my armor dropped, leaving me vulnerable to his sharp stare.

Why now? Why after two weeks would he show his face when I'd caught nothing more than a glimpse of the back of his head in all that time? It had been as if he'd calculated his every move, ensuring he'd evaded, avoided, and eluded any sight of me.

So easily forgotten.

Dirty.

I could feel the break in the air, the shift, and I knew he'd followed Ash and Zee over to the secluded booth where they liked to hide out. Away from prying eyes and their rock-star fame. Although truthfully, they really didn't seem to have that many issues around here. Most of the locals' tastes slanted country, and they came to the bar in droves on the nights the more popular country bands played.

But that didn't mean the guys didn't garner attention on their appearance alone.

Girls out looking for a good time couldn't resist these boys who looked so bad.

Trouble and disorder and a mind-blowing good time.

Pain stabbed at my stomach as I pictured Lyrik leaving here with one of them. Or more likely, with two. That always seemed to be his style. Images of the side of the boy I really didn't know flashed through my mind, the lusty gleam in his sinful eyes as he was draped in all-too willing women.

I couldn't shake the fear he was out for one last hurrah in the tiny city of Savannah before he left it all behind.

Before he left me behind.

He'd promised he would.

But I'd never imagined it'd be on these terms.

"Hey, Tamar." Sophie broke into my tortured thoughts when she called to me from the other side of the bar. She craned her head back in the direction of the isolated booth. "Your friends are here."

As if I hadn't noticed.

"The cute blond one is insisting you take care of them. He said something about it being an emergency. Of course he did it with a smile on his face, so I'm not so sure what could be so urgent, but I figured you wouldn't mind all that much considering you normally go running that direction the second they step through the door."

Running?

Had it really been that way in those weeks when things were so easy between Lyrik and me? Had I really gone to him so readily?

Just another ignorant lamb willingly led off to the slaughter.

God, I was stupid.

No more.

Strutting across to the boundless array of liquor lined up on the back bar, I grabbed a bottle of vodka. I barely glanced over my shoulder to respond. "Well, I do mind."

She hiked both her shoulders to her ears and began to back away. "Sorry…too late…I told him you'd be happy to."

"Well, then go tell them I'm *not* happy to."

Nervously, she shuffled on her feet and bit at her bottom lip, so transparent and full of guilt. "The blond one kinda sorta invited me back to his place after work tonight if I delivered the message."

Exasperated and fighting the rumbles of fear, I rubbed at my forehead.

She had to be kidding me.

I turned back to her. "Thank you for throwing me under the bus. And in case you wanted to know, the cute blond one is Ash."

There was no missing the bite to my words. But come on. Selling me out for a night with a rock star? Not cool.

She gave me a pleading look. "I'm sorry, Tamar. Really. But he was so insistent."

I guess I had to give her a break. She'd only been working here for a month. And even I knew those dimples were deadly. The guy could probably talk a vegetarian into joining the steak of the month club.

I heaved out a breath. "Fine. I'll take care of them."

An apology crinkled her brow. "Thank you. And for the record, I thought I was doing you a favor."

I scowled. "Please don't do me any more of them."

So maybe I was being a bitch. But I couldn't help it. I couldn't help the way agitation churned in my gut and skimmed across my skin, bristling against the raw, potent energy already saturating the thick air.

Stealing myself, I strode to the end of the bar and slipped out into the main room, strutting across the wooden floorboards on my super-high heels. The vibration sent a rush of shivers up the backs of my legs, like a steady boom, boom, boom pulsing through my body.

The sound only increased the closer I got, that energy going wild as my heart hammered and my stomach both lifted and fell.

Those foolish childhood butterflies decided it was the perfect time to take flight when Lyrik's steely gaze landed on me.

Those sinful eyes seemed to flicker between lust and regret. The spark of need in the flare of his nose and the distress in the pinch of his brow. As if it hurt to look at me.

Shit. Shit. Shit.

This was not okay.

I refused to fall prey to it again.

I knew his games.

Cruel and unjust.

I plastered the old sneer on my face. Tonight, it wasn't so hard to find. Because the truth of it? I was *still* hurt and angered by his callous words. Betrayed in the way he'd cast me aside. In the way he'd let me walk out his door when really he'd been the one pushing me out it.

What I'd done was wrong. I knew that. I knew I shouldn't have snooped. I shouldn't have let the compulsion to know him, to get closer to him—to understand his reservations and sorrow—cloud the respect I had for him. I shouldn't have demanded answers he didn't want to give. Especially when my own jealousy had been the driving force.

But just as strongly, he should have respected me.

Asked me to put it down.

To let it go.

Instead, he'd gone straight for the jugular.

Slicing and cutting me with those deplorable words.

That sneer turned into a perfect, sexy smirk, and I jutted out my hip. "Welcome to *Charlie's*. What brings y'all in tonight?"

I played it off as if I didn't recognize them at all—as if unaffected—while it seemed I was the only thing Lyrik could see.

So maybe a part of me took a little too much pleasure in the way his stare turned greedy.

You threw me away.

Maybe it was wrong I was thanking my stars I'd dressed the way I'd done tonight.

Maybe he'd feel a taste of the hurt he'd left me wallowing in. A taste of that hollow ache amplified by his presence.

But the better part of me—the part he'd resurrected—wanted to touch his cheek, to feel the thready beat of his heart, to tell him I'd take away some of his pain if he promised to take away mine.

If he'd just let me in.

But that was the fool talking.

Ash fumbled out an awkward laugh. "Ahhh…Tam Tam…don't go breaking my heart by pretending you aren't happy to see me. I know you have to have been missing me, because there's no chance these walls are the same without a little Ash. I figured before we packed it up and left for L.A. tomorrow, we'd better get over here and sprinkle a little rock 'n' roll flavor on the place before we have to go."

The look he shot Lyrik belied the statement he made, the way Lyrik grimaced, cringed, and glanced toward the wall.

A new kind of pain cut me open at the realization Lyrik really didn't want to be here. At the realization he'd been dragged through the doors, probably coaxed and prodded and teased by Ash until he gave in, only here to prove he really didn't want me.

God.

Insane. Completely, utterly insane. That was me. Because I

suddenly recognized the niggling hope I'd had that he'd been here for me. That he'd been here to apologize or maybe to tell me goodbye.

At least something.

I'd lost my damned mind.

Right along with my heart.

I forced myself to let my eyes jump around to all three of them, refusing to cower or flinch when it landed on Lyrik.

Red. Red. Red.

I held onto her like a lifeline.

My smirk spread, as forced as it was. "Well, since you're here to spread a little rock 'n' roll cheer, and y'all know exactly how much I like my boys tattooed and screaming…" I glanced down at Lyrik as if it didn't bother me at all. "I'll be happy to help a man out," I continued. "What can I get for you?"

Ash grinned and shot me a wink. "I'll take my regular, darlin'."

My eyes narrowed at him. He was so up to something.

Zee's voice was quiet. "Just a Coke for me. I have to drive these assholes around."

With that sneer firmly set in place, I looked back at Lyrik. "How about you…do you want me to whip you up something extra special?"

The words came out spiteful, though they ached in my throat like some kind of betrayal.

Ash spoke up. "I think our boy here would like a little taste of whatever it is you have to offer. Just as long as you don't make him choke on it. He seems to be a bit out of sorts lately."

God, Ash. As much as I liked the guy, he needed to stop.

"Sure thing," I drawled out, making sure to give Lyrik a good sway of my hips in his face as I turned to leave.

Could anyone blame me?

I was the one pushed up against a wall. Nailed to it, really.

A flash fire of heat jetted up my arm when I felt Lyrik's big hand wrap around my wrist.

Shackling.

Restraining.

An iron fetter I felt around my heart.

Panicked, I jerked to look back at him, my eyes wide and shocked.

I forced myself to narrow them into a glare.

Did he really have the audacity to touch me?

"What?" I spat the word as I yanked my arm free.

Reluctantly, he let me go. His mouth coiled in some sort of misery, and those obsidian eyes flashed. "*Blue.*"

Damn him. Playing games. Winding me up. Watching me spin and spin and spin. I wouldn't let him do this to me again.

Defiance and my last shred of self-preservation squared my jaw. "Sorry, but I have no clue what you're talking about."

Spinning on my heel, I was quick to seek refuge behind the bar. It had to be by some miracle I managed to keep my head held high while I filled their drinks.

I poured Lyrik the same tumbler of Jager as Ash.

He didn't get the best of me. Not anymore. He didn't get what was sacred and special and had only been offered to him. He didn't get my joy or my belief or my hope.

With their drinks arranged on a tray, I headed their way. I stumbled to a stop when I saw Ash walking back to their table.

Three girls in tow.

My stomach plummeted.

No. No. No.

Why would Ash do this to me?

This I could *not* handle. This I could *not* face. A curl of jealousy twisted through me like a nasty viper. Fangs impaling my skin and sinking into my flesh. Pumping me full of poison.

Poison hurt, didn't it?

Burned and stung as it sped through your veins, setting every cell to decay?

Sophie smiled as she passed by. I shoved the tray at her. "Here, take this to my *friends*. Just a warning…it looks like you might have lost your date for the night."

Or maybe Lyrik would take all three of them home.

Shit.

If it wasn't so late, I'd ask Shea if I could come crash at her place.

No way could I stomach stumbling into them at my apartment tonight.

Sophie's attention darted that direction. Her face fell. "What an asshole," she muttered under her breath.

Yeah. What an asshole. I just wasn't entirely sure who I was talking about.

She headed that way carrying about as much spite in her swagger as I'd approached them with ten minutes ago, all the while I struggled not to look that way. Struggled not to care. Struggled to maintain who I'd been before Lyrik had first walked through *Charlie's* door more than a year ago.

But I wasn't sure I knew her anymore.

Wasn't sure which of us was real.

Sophie delivered the drinks, paused as Ash tugged her down so he could whisper something in her ear. She was almost at a sprint when she danced back wearing a smile that couldn't have been pried from her face.

"It's totally still on," she gushed, completely clueless to my torment.

"That's great." I barely managed to voice it without it being loaded down by sarcasm.

"He's really cute," she added.

"Yeah, he is," I agreed, because I totally got Ash's charm, although I seemed to be wholly immune to it considering Lyrik was the only one who held the power to make me *feel*.

"Who's cute?"

I glanced up to find the source of the voice. A man who was nothing more than a boy rested his forearms on the bar top, leaning across it toward me. He couldn't have been a day older than twenty-one, his collar popped, one of those preppy, pretty boys who made their way into the bar from time to time.

I frowned and he just smiled.

Cheeky and bold, he grinned wider as he cocked his head. "I was kinda hoping you were talking about me, since I couldn't help but think the same thing about you while I was sitting *way* over there while you were *way* over here. Seemed a shame, so here I am."

He was cute. I kind of wanted to pat him on the top of the head and send him on his way.

But when I felt Lyrik's fierce, piercing gaze, I was suddenly leaning in the kid's direction.

"You think I'm cute, huh?" So I guessed I was going to play his game.

The guy chuckled, his stare blatant as it dropped to my chest. I tried not to shiver in disgust.

"I could think of a few better ways to describe you," he said. "How about later you let me whisper them in your ear? I've got a room next door."

Wow, was I wrong.

The kid wasn't cute. He was a presumptuous twit.

I leaned in closer and ignored the nausea swirling in my stomach and rising in my throat.

Rise.

I swallowed down that errant thought.

For the last four years, I'd used my body as a weapon. But always as a defense. A tool to keep men just out of reach. Too hot for them to handle. Too dangerous to touch. Giving the impression I'd be all too happy to cut them to pieces if they even tried hurting me in any way, even though in reality I would have been the one shaking in my boots.

But tonight? I hated myself a little more because I used this weapon against Lyrik. Even after he'd destroyed a little of what he'd exposed. I used it against the burning hope that wouldn't stop churning in my spirit.

I reached across the bar and ran the tip of my index finger down the stranger's face. "Sure thing, sweetheart. I get off at three."

As if I was that easy.

I scratched ten digits onto a bar napkin and pressed it into his hand.

Of course they were the wrong ten digits. No chance in hell would I let him touch me.

I hated every second of this.

Back to pretending I was someone I was not.

Messing with this kid, despite how offensively brazen his

advances were.

Vindictive in my actions.

But the only thing that made sense right then was to hurt Lyrik the way he was hurting me.

Slow and agonizing. Sharp and severe.

As if I were slowly bleeding out.

I *had* to build back up the walls. I had to restore the foundation I'd built to survive. I needed to protect and preserve and persevere. And I knew he was watching and I knew he received the message.

You can't hurt me.

In my periphery, I felt more than saw Lyrik stand from the booth. Chest aching, I glanced that way and met with his gaze.

Hard.

Bitter.

Maybe even disappointed.

He stared me down for a few heartbreaking moments. Jaw clenched, the heavy bob of his throat was evident as he swallowed. Then he turned his back on me and walked out the door. He took all that potent energy with him, leaving the cavernous space hollow and vacant.

I slumped forward. The cutting pain was so intense I gasped around it.

You can't hurt me.

But I knew the truth.

Lyrik West was the only one who could.

TAMAR

It was just after three twenty when I finally made it home that night. I plodded up the exterior stairs toward my apartment. Exhaustion and sorrow weighed me down. As if I were bound by chains, my body drained, and my heart sluggish. Darkness clung to the star-studded sky, the trill of bugs a constant hum where they feasted in the trees. The humid air like a mold to my body.

But I felt cold.

Clammy.

As if I might have gone into shock.

Gripping the railing, I forced myself up the stairs. The click of my heels rang out like an exclamation of my loneliness. Like a stark reminder of the solitude.

My hand was shaking as I fumbled to find the right key. I slid it into the lock and let myself into the stark isolation of my apartment.

A dismal sigh worked its way free, and I tossed my keys to the kitchen counter and wandered down the hall into the bathroom so I could wash the mask from my face.

I was getting so goddamned tired of wearing it.

Tired of pretending I was something I was not.

Tired of hiding from the past that rushed to catch up to me, competing to become a part of my future.

I knew the choice was coming.

I'd either have to face it.

Go home and confront my past head on.

Or I'd have to run.

Leave.

I just didn't know if I had the strength to tackle either one and I wasn't quite sure where that left me.

Running a cloth under warm water, I washed my face, erasing the traces of the hard, cold girl.

I dropped it into the sink, and stared at the face devoid of makeup. At the desolation swimming behind the blue eyes that blinked hopelessly back at me.

"You did this," I said aloud. But it wasn't Tamar King who was listening. It was the girl who was screaming, begging me to find her.

Pushing it down, I flicked off the light switch and headed toward my empty bed where I knew I'd toil in the vacancy. Toss with the turmoil. Where I'd be pulled in every direction until I was torn to shreds.

Where I'd wake in the morning and try to pick up the pieces without the first clue of how to put myself back together. Not when I no longer knew the pattern of the puzzle.

A soft knock sounded against my front door. My breath shot from me and I froze in the middle of my room, instinctively knowing it was him.

I swallowed hard, unsure of which direction to follow. My heart begged for one more glimpse before he was gone, while my head said to let him go. It was for the best.

All along, I'd known better.

Known better than to let myself get so deep.

Known better than to let him explore and invade. To get in and under my skin where he'd marked and scarred, like this invisible ink stamped across my heart where he'd left his emblem.

Two more knocks. The second came far behind, the sound trailing off.

As if it were done in resignation.

In defeat.

With a final *please*.

Before I could think better of it, I moved toward the front door, drawn through the darkness.

To the darkness.

To the menacing, malicious man who I knew would be standing on the other side.

Slowly, I turned the lock.

The grinding slide of metal echoed through the quiet.

Even slower, I opened the door.

I guess I liked the pain.

I nearly buckled with the torment just the sight of him summoned, the fiery need and the earth-shattering energy.

That dizzying buzz vibrated in the atmosphere in tiny, explosive shockwaves.

Obsidian eyes stared down at me from where he stood outside my door. Hands shoved in his pockets. Shoulders slack. So different than the bold, untouchable boy. This was someone who'd been *touched*.

I gulped.

God.

He was beautiful.

Gorgeous in a devastating way.

Because that's what I felt, standing there, trembling at his feet.

Devastated.

Stupid girl.

"Hey," he said, his elbows lifting out as he shrugged with his hands still firmly seated in his pockets.

As if maybe this cocky, arrogant boy had no clue what to do with himself.

"Hi." It scraped up my throat.

Moments floated around us, the two of us prisoners to uncertainty and doubt, before he warily peered over my shoulder into the quiet of my apartment. His gaze had gone hard by the time he dragged it back to me. "You alone?"

Shame hit me square in the chest.

I dipped my chin and nodded.

Relief and frustration filled his exhale, and I noticed him look to the ground as he ran a nervous hand through his hair. He looked up, chewing at that bottom lip, that glimpse of vulnerability disappearing with the wind, ushering in his storm. "One thing I never took you for was a tease."

Bastard.

Standing there acting as if this was my fault.

I managed a scoff that I was certain came across broken. "What the hell do you care?"

Humorless laughter vibrated from him. The sound resonated through me as if I was standing too close to a speeding train. "I told you I don't do it often. I don't fucking care because it's not worth the trouble. It's not worth the pain. But I never lied when I said I cared about you. Why, Red? Why should I care about you?"

The last came on a desperate whisper.

The earth shook beneath my feet and I tried to remain on solid ground. But I could feel it cracking. The fissures and fractures. The threat of it breaking away.

He made me so fucking weak.

He leaned in, close enough that his nose brushed mine. His expression verged somewhere between savage and sad as he glared down at me in the shadows. "You gonna hook up with him? Trade me in for a pretty boy before my plane even leaves the ground?"

Guilt simmered because he'd hit it. Spot on. I throttled the feeling. Fought back. "What about the three girls at your table?"

"What about them? Ash goaded me into going to that damned

bar tonight. Asshole thought he had some kind of point to prove, dragging me there, shoving girls in my face who would be all too willing to jump into my bed."

The words constricted into a tight whisper. "Ash thinks it's his God-given right to call me out on my bullshit. Forcing me to look at the truth. And the truth is the only fucking thing I want right now is you. You."

My eyes squeezed closed against his confession. It was so much easier protecting my heart when I hated him.

"You're an asshole." I whimpered it as his hand traced across the distorted heart between my breasts. My body arched, already desperate for more.

"I think we already established that."

"What are you really doing here, Lyrik?" It was difficult to even voice it with him standing there, his boxes packed, at the ready to steal everything away. "What do you want?"

What would it change now?

He huffed a laugh. It was a sound that verged somewhere between hate and disgust. He eyed me. Cautious. Gauging what to say.

"Been lying in bed for the last two hours, staring at the ceiling, tryin' not to listen for your return. For the voices I knew I couldn't stand to hear. Tryin' not to care that little bastard back at the bar might have been in there with you."

I swallowed the pain lodged at the base of my throat and tried to reach for some kind of rational thought when this boy always managed to strip it away.

"You don't really have the right to care about that anymore." It was scarcely a whisper.

He stared across at me. Challenging. "You promised me two months."

"Yeah, you promised them too…and you couldn't even give me that."

"Blue—"

I winced. "Don't call me that."

"Why?" He took a step forward, eclipsing me in his shadow, the man towering over me. "Why, Blue," he demanded. "You think I don't see you? That I don't get what you were trying to pull tonight?"

My hands fisted at my sides. "Tell me what you want...tell me...because I don't think I can take this anymore."

I couldn't stand there and not crumble at his feet.

He hesitated. As if he were trying to hold himself back while everything left unfinished between us built, strengthened, and inflamed. I saw it the second he finally caved.

His hand flew out in frustration, as if he wanted to punch something, and he ducked his head, shocking me by how quickly he got up in my face as the words poured from his mouth like a pissed-off plea.

"I fucking missed you, okay? I fucking missed you and it fucking killed me thinking of you bringing that kid back here. Killed me thinking of you reaching for another man. Killed me to think of that bastard's hands on you, taking what's mine. I was supposed to have two months. *Two months*."

"And now it's too late." The words shook as they slipped from my tongue.

As if he'd been struck, his face jerked to the side. His attention seemed gripped by the night and the unsettled trees and the passing time. Finally he turned back to me, his black hair whipping in the wind, that energy inciting a storm. "We have tonight."

God, I wanted it. To give up and give in.

"What if it hurts when you leave?" I whispered.

Some kind of old sorrow lashed through his expression, and he stepped forward, so gentle as he cradled my face in his hands. The words were so much softer than the first time he'd uttered them to me. "Baby...don't you get it yet? I'm not worth the pain."

I touched his cheek, my fingers fluttering across his lips. They parted with a breath.

I wished he knew how much he was. That I saw so much more.

"Blue," he whispered again.

Soft, gentle seduction.

Cruel.

Manipulation.

"I hate you," I attempted, but tears were already gathering in my eyes.

Exposing. Revealing. Unveiling.

One fell, streaking down my cheek. A single droplet of hazard and hope.

His exhale sounded in relief, and he slowly gathered me in the security of his arms. He pressed my cheek against his heart that ran wild. The man was a bundle of mayhem, pushing and pulling and confounding. Yet in his arms, everything became so clear.

"There she is. *Blue*. My beautiful, brave Blue. I thought I'd lost her." Fingers played through my hair, moving back to my face where he forced me to look at him.

I blinked and more tears fell. The moisture slipped into the webs of his fingers. He squeezed my face, his shoulders bunching and his body swaying in indecision. His gaze flicked between my eyes and my mouth. His tongue swept across that delicious bottom lip, before any timidity vanished.

His mouth came down with the force of a landslide. His tongue drove between my lips, meeting with the resistance in mine. It quickly morphed into surrender.

Because I was already gone.

Lost to this man. To his darkness and his ghosts and his hard, unattainable heart.

I was a fool.

A fool.

A fool.

A fool.

Giving in was only going to hurt me that much more.

But right then, I didn't care.

Because the world was spinning and there was nothing in it that felt better than him. Nothing better than the softness of his lips and the desire on his tongue, his hot hands on my body as his begged against mine.

I clutched his shoulders and pushed up onto my toes.

Dying for more.

That's exactly what it felt like.

As if I would die if I didn't get this one last night.

One last taste.

One last memory.

Because the scars were still there—the old wounds still raw and aching—and confusion still reigned in my heart and mind. My spirit was more unsure of my future now than it'd ever been. But tonight, only this moment mattered.

"I wasn't finished," he growled low. Teeth grazed at my chin, before his kiss took a needy path down my neck. Lyrik sucked at my pulse point. It made me gasp and writhe and moan.

"Two months," he mumbled. "I was supposed to have two months. Two months to erase. Two months to leave my mark. Two months to make you know nothing else but my name."

I shuddered beneath his murmurings. This man had no idea how deeply he had. The eternal impressions he had made and the magnitude of the hole he would leave behind.

"Tell me no, Blue. Tell me no," he begged as he forced me closer, the desperation in his perfect body in direct contrast to his words. His kiss devoured my mouth, just as this man demolished my senses and devastated the last shred of my willpower.

Lyrik West owned me.

But this was my own personal demise.

My choice.

Given on my own accord.

This single night surrendered to him.

Even though I knew the aftermath might destroy me. I had so little left holding me together. But I felt like I needed this to survive.

The overwhelming anger and betrayal, the need and hope, boiled to a tumultuous frenzy. Overflowing. Stripping me bare. "I hate you," I muttered again as delirium hit, my fingers clawing and my mouth demanding, my body pressing and pleading.

I hated him for chasing me.

Hated him for exposing me.

Hated him for making me feel this way.

Hated myself for needing him so much.

And God, how I loved it all.

"You make me forget who I am," he said in return as he hiked me up. Instinctively, I wrapped my legs around his waist.

And Lyrik kissed me like he was never going to kiss me again.

Because we both knew it was the truth.

"Slow." It flowed as a murmur from his soul. A reminder of who we were. Of what he'd given me. Of the security he'd made me feel in these arms that were so strong and comforting when instead I should have perceived their threat.

I wanted to weep—the emotion so dense I choked on it—because tomorrow he'd be gone and he would take it all with him.

My dignity.

My heart.

My soul.

He owned them all.

He carried me into the quiet dimness of my apartment and down the short hall into my bedroom. He set me on the floor and took two steps back. With that potent gaze locked on me, he kicked off his shoes. His heavy pants filled the already thickened air.

"Take off your clothes," he commanded. "I want to see you."

A ragged breath jetted from between my swollen, bruised lips.

There he was. That intimidating man who didn't tiptoe or treat me like glass. The one who didn't treat me like a broken girl. Even when I knew he was getting ready to break me a little more.

He peeled his shirt over his head.

My eyes strayed, dancing across the body I wanted to sink into and disappear forever.

Suppressing a groan, I ate up the magnificent sight in front of me. No doubt, it would be the last one I would get.

"Now," he said.

My attention jerked to those consuming eyes, and I shuddered as I slipped out of my heels, my height dropping by five inches.

The man towered over me.

Impassable.

Impenetrable.

Unattainable.

But for tonight, he was mine.

My fingers trembled and fumbled as I worked free the first button on my blouse, exposing the top portion of the deformed heart tattoo.

Guard your heart.

Too late.

It belonged to him.

Chest heaving, I went for the second. Lyrik's body visibly hardened.

"Do you know how many girls I've been with?" The words were jagged, to the point of anger.

I sucked in a breath and my fingers stalled. "Please, don't," I begged. That was the *last* thing I wanted to know. The countless bodies and faces and girls who'd come before me. The ones who would most definitely come after. Still I managed to free the third button. My lacy white bra came into view.

A strangled sound lodged in his throat. He spoke around it, ignoring my plea. "So many I can't count. So many I didn't even try to keep track. So many I don't *remember.*"

Cruel.

Why did he have to be so cruel?

That same jealousy I'd experienced earlier at the bar ignited a path of fire through me. A spike of the venom that had roiled in me during the last two weeks. The sting coursed through my veins.

I never wanted to be one of those girls.

Forgettable.

Used up and tossed aside.

But not even that could stop me from untying the knot at the bottom of my shirt and letting the fabric fall from my shoulders.

Because I was helpless.

My mind was entranced by his words and the despair coating his expression.

Shivers covered me under his intensity, my spirit wrapped up in the energy, that building storm gaining speed.

"And you…it's you I can't get off my mind. You I can't rid from my thoughts. You I can't wash from my body. It's *you* I can't forget."

With his words, goosebumps sprang to my flesh.

Covering me whole.

Holding me hostage.

"Shut up," I told him weakly. Nothing he said now could possibly matter. This was the end and the seconds were ticking by.

This was our last goodbye.

He flicked the top button of his jeans, and those dark eyes grew darker. The gold and grey flecks dimmed to pitch. Setting like the sun where I was sucked into his endless twilight. Where I floated somewhere between light and his dark. Lost somewhere between the malice, spite, and danger, and this soft, soft boy who'd taken the time to see me.

Taken the time to *care*.

I matched him move for move. We both shrugged out of our pants at the same time.

I went for my bra.

"Don't," he said, stalking forward. He approached, taking up my space and my breath and my reason. My head fell back farther and farther until his too-pretty face hovered an inch above mine. He wrapped one of his arms around my back to keep me from falling.

It was then I knew. I already had.

He'd taken me piece by piece until there was nothing recognizable. Until I didn't know who I was except for his.

Eyes roved, voracious, as if he needed to memorize me the way I'd memorized him.

Inhale.

Exhale.

Those sounds wheezing from his lungs came harder and shorter and faster.

Whatever had been holding him back snapped.

Sheared.

Or maybe Lyrik cracked.

He scooped me up as if I weighed nothing. Arms encircled me. His kiss overpowered. His body prevailed.

"Red," he muttered against my mouth, twisting a hand in my hair and yanking it back to gain him access to my jaw, to my neck, to the disfigured heart that seemed to have come alive. He pushed me back on the bed, and he twisted out of his underwear at the same moment his mouth latched onto my breast.

He sucked hard and I bucked my hips. A pleasured pain shot through my body, pumping fuel to the desire that became a steady beat between my thighs.

"I'd never hurt you, Blue," he murmured softly just before he bit down.

You already have.

"Don't call me that," I implored, low and wispy. One last-ditch effort to cling to *Red*, the girl who couldn't be touched. The one who wasn't vulnerable and trembling in his arms. I cinched my hands in his hair, yanking and tugging and demanding more.

He growled, his dick heavy and hard and more than ready where it pushed at the inside of my thigh. Inches from where I needed him most.

This was the one thing I knew for sure. Of all the things I was certain about.

I'd found freedom in Lyrik's touch.

Gained the belief not all hands were vicious.

The assurance not all touches were vile.

The rest was a mess of confusion and disorder and doubt.

He pushed up onto his hands, his hair as wild as his eyes. My chest rose and fell. As if our hearts had caught time. Both quick and jutted. Intense and free.

He ran his fingers through my hair. A hint of a smile played at the corner of his mouth. "You were sent to torment me, weren't you?" he asked.

The words slid out close to a tease though it rode on the current of the madness he'd provoked within the room. "Always lookin' like my favorite fantasy."

He almost laughed, but the intonation was sad. "Temptation. That's what you are. An angel wrapped up in a demon's body. Heaven and hell. A gift and my greatest demise."

Confusion narrowed my eyes. "I don't understand."

"Not much to get, baby. One look and you win."

Despair clotted, heavy on my chest. "Then why does it feel like I'm going to lose?"

"Fuck…fuck, Blue." His shoulders bunched up as he pushed up onto his hands and dipped down to kiss me, our lips just barely brushing, tongue licking against mine. So, so soft. "If I could, baby, I'd give it all to you."

My spirit ached. It groaned. A muddled turmoil ushered in by the abstract assertion. Questions swirled on the tip of my tongue, silenced by the sudden assault of his.

"Red."

I yelped when he suddenly hauled me up from under my arms. He guided me onto my knees and turned me facing away.

That big body eclipsed mine from behind, and he leaned over and curled my hands close together around the metal frame of my headboard. One hand held me captive by the wrists.

Erratic, my pulse sped, a hammering thunder beating out from every cell.

Oh God.

I whimpered.

His mouth brushed the shell of my ear. "All you have to say is no."

Shivers spread far and free. My body alight. Shuddering, my hands fisted tighter onto the metal. "I can't."

I didn't want to. I wanted him and everything he had to give. For him to mark me and scar me, to leave me with the memories of what he'd taken the time to erase.

My breath hitched when I felt him running the tip of his cock up and down the crease of my ass. The only barrier my black lace underwear.

"Blue," he murmured. He shifted and placed the palm of his free hand flat on my chest. Against the battering roar of my heart, the same as what I felt beating against my back.

Tonight. Tonight. Tonight.

That's all we had, and I leaned back, into the scorching heat of his body. An entreaty for more.

"Please."

My gaze tipped to watch as his tattooed hand explored downward, dragging over my breasts. My stomach quivered as he pressed against my belly, before his fingers dipped into the front of my panties. Gently he brushed between my folds, exhaled against my ear.

"So warm. So soft. So good."

I panted.

On a grunt, he released his hands from my wrists and began to remove my panties. Like I weighed nothing, he lifted me enough to drag them down my legs and free them from my ankles.

"You're mine," rumbled from his mouth.

The sound at my ear sent an electric charge racing down my spine. It gathered low. I could feel it building and building and building. The excitement and the thrill. The flashes of energy in the air. The anticipation thick. A consuming cloud disorienting my senses.

Mine.

I wanted to be.

But that was just a fantasy.

He flicked the clasp at the back of my bra. The straps tickled down my arms that were still pinned to the headboard.

He grunted, his breaths labored, his chest heaving against my back. That motion only served to wind me higher and higher as our skin brushed.

Hot and fevered.

"He tied you up." It was a pained lament at my ear, so low and full of anger I shivered. In anticipation or fear, I wasn't sure which.

I nodded.

Lyrik already knew he did.

"Do you trust me?"

I nodded again.

It should have been in reluctance. But it wasn't. Because I did. I trusted him with my body and *foolishly* trusted him with my heart—my spirit so desperate with longing to feel—to feel close to someone who understood.

Lyrik West was the only one who could.

He wound my bra around my wrists and tied it to the headboard. Loosely. The hold not a restraint but a promise.

He whispered in my ear, "All you have to say is no. All you have to say is no. You are in control. You control me. You own me…" The last trailed off in some kind of misery.

I swayed on my knees, overcome by lust and by this man. He

enclosed me with his body, his darkness a protective shroud.

His hands tightened on the headboard on either side of mine. "What do you want, Red?"

"You. Everything. Everywhere. Take me." It tumbled out like water gushing from a collapsing dam.

Freed.

Sucking in a breath, he positioned himself at my center and thrust into me from behind.

So deep and hard.

I gasped.

Breath gone.

He pulled out and did it again.

"Blue...Blue...Blue." It was a blur of mumbled affection.

I wanted to beg him to call me *Red*. But she was nowhere within the room. Every vulnerability, every fear, and every hope was committed to him.

He drove into me.

Again and Again.

Relentless.

Merciless.

Ruthless.

Hands moved to clutch my hips. Fingers burrowed into my skin.

"Do you trust me?" he demanded again. Desperation had taken over, his movements almost frantic. "Tell me, Blue. Tell me you trust me. Want to take it all the way. Let me."

"I trust you."

He reached over to the nightstand and rummaged in the drawer. The tube he produced made my already erratic pulse take off at breakneck speed. He pulled out of me, and I could feel him shaking. Shaking just as uncontrollably as me. I panted and gripped at the headboard as I waited, my head bowed, the hair falling around my face obscuring my vision.

Yet every move played out in vivid Technicolor that flashed in black and white.

He uncapped the tube and coated himself, before his fingers were on me.

Gentle.

Gentle as he swept them up and down the cleft of my ass.

I stiffened as he slowly pushed one finger inside.

"All you have to say is no." His voice spun around me like a whirlwind. Whipping and whirring.

He knew this was my greatest fear.

A physical barrier.

One I was offering to him.

"It's you, Blue…you." His hand was suddenly back at the front of my neck, under my chin, his mouth next to mine as he forced me to look up at him. His eyes were so dark and hard and tortured. Although when they locked on mine they went soft.

"Do you hear me?" he whispered. "It's you."

"I hear you."

His tongue darted out to wet his lips, and his body shook with restraint as he adjusted and carefully began to press into me.

Darkness flickered at the edges of my eyes.

The spark of a storm.

Streaking light.

"Fuck," Lyrik whispered hoarsely, clutching me tighter. "Tell me you're okay, baby. Tell me, Blue."

"Yes." It barely passed through my trembling lips.

He pushed in deeper, body stretching mine in a searing pleasure, just as my breath stretched thin, the pain scorching and blissful and dangerously dark. I gasped and writhed as he seated himself deeper. Deeper and deeper until I was trembling and shaking.

Forcing himself to keep still, he hugged me closer. There was no space left between us. No room for breaths or thoughts or actions that weren't shared between the two of us.

Dirty.

Memories of the cursed word flitted at the outskirts of my mind.

But, no.

Never before had I felt closer to another soul. Never before had I touched on a beauty quite like this.

The kind found in complete surrender.

In a place where you're defenseless.

Willingly.

Where your preservation comes from the hands that could just as easily crush you.

Emotion gripped every cell of my body, taking up my heart and filling my head. It grew so profound I felt it shatter my spirit. It scattered in a frantic bid to meet with his.

Lyrik had knocked down every wall. Wiped out every physical barrier. Eclipsed every fear.

And he'd replaced them all with himself.

Just like he'd promised from the beginning.

But I knew it was so much greater than that.

This menacing, mysterious boy had completely captured my heart.

"Tell me you're okay." It came through gritted teeth, and I knew he was barely hanging on to a quickly unraveling string. "Tell me you're with me. *Me.*"

"I'm with you."

Because he'd captured all of me.

Taken.

Possessed.

He slowly withdrew before he slid back in. He wrapped an arm just under my breasts, the other winding up at the side of my hair. He tugged me a little to the side, his mouth coming down on my exposed neck, nibbling at the skin, trailing my chin. Oh so soft as he brushed it against my ear.

"Do you have any idea what this feels like? Being in you this way? Fuck…so fucking good, Blue. No girl should feel this good."

He struggled for a breath. "But it's more. You. Trusting me. Letting me take. Fuck…just wish I could give. Do you hear me? What have you done? What have you done?"

I'd fallen.

He began to move in a hypnotizing dance.

Slow and fierce.

Careful and abandoned.

Pained and perfect.

That energy rose up on all sides. Billowing and blistering and building.

The entire world dropped away, and we were in a free fall.

It was the weightlessness that felt so good. No thought given to the ground that would come up so quickly. No consideration for the sharp, jagged rocks waiting to pierce us when we landed.

Lyrik released his hold from under my breasts, his hand so hot against my stomach as he rocked into me, our bodies lost to a heedless, reckless rhythm. Callused fingers played across my lower abdomen, drifting lower until he spread me, stroking my clit.

"Lyrik."

He melted with me until I was lost. Until my head spun with dizziness and my body burned with bliss. Until I was shivering and pushing back against him, wanting more when I wasn't sure how much more I could take.

Until just like he said, the only thing I knew was his name.

Lyrik.

Lyrik.

Lyrik.

I screamed when I came, falling apart in his arms as he clung to me, holding me up as my bound hands went weak in the same moment as my legs.

His hips jerked and his body bowed around mine.

He shuddered and groaned.

"*Blue.*" The whisper caressed like the wisp of a silken sheet.

I sagged against him and he quickly loosed the tie he'd made in my bra and freed my hands.

I crumbled in his hold. Carefully, he shifted to lie us down in the middle of my bed, never letting me go. Up against all his hard and heat and mystery, I curled into a ball. He buried his nose in my hair, exhaled into the night. "My brave, beautiful Blue."

Silence took us over, the only noise the faint whir of a passing car in the distance, the cold air pumping in through the vents, and the erratic beat of our pounding hearts.

God.

I felt it.

Felt it as if it'd become detached.

Physically removed.

That tightly held roughened exterior gone.

Shredded.

That girl I'd run from for so long relieved, as if she'd lain in wait amongst the deepest roots. Dormant for the winter. Blossoming beneath the sun. Sprouting new growth.

Freed.

Lyrik squeezed me closer, and I could feel his hesitation, a suppressed turmoil that pressed against the warmth enveloping us. Like an echo of my own fear and hope. "Come with me to California tomorrow."

Shock froze me, but he continued on, his words pouring out as if maybe he wanted to stop them but couldn't. "We're heading out early and I'm going to visit my family before the show Anthony has organized for tomorrow night. Come with me. Shea's gonna be there one last time before the baby comes. I want you there, too. Stay the weekend. I'm not ready to let this go."

"This?" I hazarded the question, no longer able to camouflage how raw he made me feel. The things he made me want. "Us? Or the sex?"

His swallow was jagged. "I'm not sure anymore."

In confusion, I lifted my head and looked at this volatile man where he lay silhouetted in the glow of moonlight. This boy who I could no longer view as bad.

But I knew.

I knew the words coming from his mouth made him more dangerous than ever. I blinked and tried to orient myself. To find solid ground, even if it was Tamar Gibson who was finding it.

"Who is she?" I whispered as softly as I could to keep him from freaking out. Softer still to hide the jealousy the memory of her wrapped in his arms had flared.

But it was the one thing I needed to know. If I was laying it all on the line. If I was letting this go beyond this night.

I needed to know.

I could feel it trembling. Pulsing in the air. The stir of energy.

Grief struck in his expression, and he cupped the side of my face. "She is the culmination of every mistake I ever made. My every regret. Everything I'll never forget."

Like a fool, I nodded as if I could accept it, as if that alone wouldn't crush me, and let him wrap me in the comfort of his arms, my face pressed into the inked skin of his neck.

Our hearts matched pace, the beating slow as we drifted in the false calm.

He pressed his mouth to the top of my head, the words muted and slurred as he neared sleep. But still, they cut me straight through.

"If my heart was mine to give, I'd give it to you."

TAMAR

"Are you sure you'll be okay?" I clutched the phone to my ear where I sat on the edge of my bed. Just the haze of morning teased at the windows, and Charlie's voice was groggy with the sleep my call had pulled him from.

"Come on, sugar. You really think I'm that helpless?" he teased, and I could almost see him on his back in his bed, tugging at the end of his ratty beard, looking to the ceiling with a smile. Wouldn't be all that surprised if five seconds from now he showed up at my door to help me pack my bags.

"I just don't like the thought of leaving you in the lurch. You know that's not my style."

"Yeah…know exactly what your style is. Holing up behind my bar, pretending like you're happy there. Like you belong there. When you and I both know that's the farthest from the truth."

"Charlie…" I begged. A shiver raced down the skin of my bare back, chasing after Lyrik's callused fingertip that traced my spine.

"Go, Tamar," Charlie urged quietly. "Haven't ever seen you light up the way you do around him. Not ever. Not once. Not gonna act like I know all the details of your story, sugar. Your secrets. But I'm no fool, and I know they're there. Also know when that one's around, suddenly it doesn't seem all that important for you to hide behind them anymore. Go. Find out if he's the one you've been looking for."

Gratitude became one with the lingering fear concealed beneath my ribs. "Thank you."

"Family first, Tamar."

Did Charlie have the first clue what his words did to me? The way they made my insides leap and soar, memories abounding in my mind, spurring me forward.

Toward home.

God, I missed them. Missed their faces and their laughter. The way my mother would look at me as if she already knew what I was thinking before I ever said a word. As if she understood what was happening inside me before I recognized it myself.

The need to be brave had grown so acute, I could feel the faint grasp of the hands of time dragging me back. But once where I'd feared they would hold me down, I now somehow knew they would set me free.

But it was taking the first step that was the hardest.

It was the idea of standing in front of Cameron again that had me drowning in a spiraling wave of panic.

Swiveling, I looked over my shoulder at Lyrik. The gorgeous man was on his back.

In my bed.

That shock of black hair was unruly and wild where he rested on my pillow. My sheets were a jumble of twists and knots where we'd been tangled for the couple hours of sleep we'd managed throughout the night.

Now, in the early morning light, they barely covered his slim waist, revealing his torso and arms and neck where bold ink scripted his fathomless story.

And I wondered…I wondered if there was room for more.

If he had a waiting, unmarked space for me or if all his pages had already been written.

Because I ached to fill him the way he had filled me.

"Is it weird we're doing this?" I asked.

Shifting, Lyrik curled his arms around my waist and brushed a kiss to my hip, before he turned that haunted gaze up at me. "Weird? No. Stupid? Yeah."

I blinked through a new onslaught of confusion. "Stupid?"

He hugged me tighter. "Blue…being with you…it's probably the stupidest thing I've done in a long, long time. Reckless. Just begging for trouble. So fucking selfish. Taking more of you when both of us know I can't keep you. But right now, I don't know how to stop."

I moved to straddle him, my hands on his shoulders, our bodies aligned.

Lyrik grunted and gripped me by the hips as he guided me onto him.

"I don't want you to stop," I whispered down to him.

Never, never stop.

Even if it was stupid.

Because love makes you do stupid things.

An hour and a half later, the car pulled up to the private terminal at Hilton Head Airport. The sun climbed the eastern horizon, rays stretching out to embrace the top of the lush copse of trees outlining the area, the green leaves dusted with dew sparkling like Christmas lights.

Everyone else was already there, gathered around the small chartered jet waiting on us.

I pushed out a nervous breath and glanced at the dark, foreboding man sitting at my side, that delicious mouth quirked up in a knowing smirk, before returning my gaze to the ridiculous show of money flaunted in front of us.

Butterflies assaulted my stomach.

I got the distinct feeling I was about to enter the world of Lyrik I knew nothing about, other than those few glances I'd been granted. The few fans who'd recognized him at the bar. Anthony's beachside mansion. The magazine stories I'd read and the entertainment headlines that had caught my eye.

"Do you guys always go overboard like this?"

Lyrik laughed lightly. "Nah...but it sure is nice when we do."

I looked at him, feigned, wide innocent eyes. "It must be so rough when you subject yourself to commercial first-class instead. The atrocity."

This time it was a thick roll of laughter that left him, before he edged forward and gripped my chin to keep me looking at him. He pressed his nose to mine. "You gonna sit over there and give me a hard time when I was so kind to invite you along? Spoil you with a bit of luxury? Get you backstage to a show?"

Those dark eyes flashed with mischief, a toying threat that sent those butterflies scattering. "I mean, we do know how you like your boys tattooed and screaming, don't we?"

His lips touched mine. Briefly. Wickedly.

I struggled for a breath.

He leaned back, raked his teeth over his bottom lip.

On all things holy. No man should look that good or have the power to effect women that way.

He cocked his head. "Now are you comin' or stayin'?"

Gone were the shadows that'd haunted his eyes last night. In their place was the ruthless man edged with this boyish excitement that skimmed the expression on his face. I couldn't help but feel that way, too.

"Oh, I'm definitely coming."

Chuckling, he shook his head and unlatched his door. "That's what I thought."

Lyrik unloaded our bags from the trunk, grabbing hold of his guitar case and passing me my camera bag. I slung it over my shoulder and followed close behind as he wheeled our suitcases toward our friends.

Shea was grinning when I approached. Her baby belly had grown huge, and she glowed with joy.

I itched to capture the moment, that old need flooding me like a sea cave swilling with the rising tide.

"I can't believe you're coming with us," she squealed as she rushed forward and threw her arms around me. She rocked me in a hug as if she hadn't seen me for ages. She suddenly leaned in close and spoke so no one else could hear. "It's so good to have you back."

Was it possible she read me that easily? That she saw right through the stony façade?

She released me just as quickly. Her words increased in volume as if she were speaking to the entire crowd. "This is going to be the best weekend ever. I always get stuck with all you boys. About time there's another girl there to keep me company."

"Don't get any ideas, Shea." I could feel Lyrik's presence invading me from behind. "Blue here? She's on board for a weekend with me. Not you."

Over my shoulder, I tossed Lyrik a bewildered look. "What are you talking about? You told me Shea was coming. That's the only reason I agreed."

Lyrik wrapped me in his arms, his front to my back. "Is that so?" he questioned, pressing himself a little closer. Teasing me with that body he knew left me defenseless.

"Well…I guess I don't mind spending a little bit of time with you, too."

By the hand, he spun me around. The entirety of that pretty face lifted in a smirk. "Don't mind, huh? You sure didn't seem to *mind* all that much last night." He edged closer, voice dropping. "Or this mornin', for that matter."

I giggled.

Giggled.

Oh. God.

Undone.

That's the way he'd left me.

He swatted my butt. "Now get that sweet ass on the plane."

With a tiny yelp, I jumped right into his arms. A tumble of

excited and joyous nerves skated through my body. Then Lyrik slowed, cupped my cheek as he gazed down at me, then kissed me gently.

Moments like these? They were the ones that left me a mixed-up, muddled mess.

Because they were the times when it felt like *more*.

"Come on," he whispered. Turning, he led me by the hand toward the stairs the rest of the guys and Shea were already climbing.

Well, except for Ash.

He leaned up against the bottom of the railing, arms crossed over his wide chest.

Lyrik passed him, started up the stairs.

Ash gave us a look that was both mocking and sincere.

How the hell did the guy manage that?

"I trust the two of you had a pleasurable evening last night?" he asked. His grin grew in time with the lift of his brow.

Lyrik threw him a look riddled with daggers and knives. "Don't fucking start, man."

Ash smiled, shrugged innocently. "Not starting anything. The two of you just look a little cozier than you did last night, that's all. Can't a guy make an observation?"

"Not that kind, he can't," Lyrik warned, but it was lighter than I expected, his voice carrying as he climbed higher, hauling me up behind him.

Low laughter rolled from Ash as he took to the steps behind us. "I'm just not the type of guy who goes burying his head in the sand. Not fool enough to miss what's right in front of me."

Lyrik didn't look back, just clenched my hand a little tighter in his hold.

Warily, I glanced back at Ash with a scowl. To ask him once to lay off the ribbing.

I was feeling protective of the shaky relationship Lyrik and I had, if you could call it that at all. I sure as hell had no idea what to label *this*.

One minute I'd accepted I would never touch him again and the next I was boarding a plane to spend the weekend in L.A. with him, visiting his family of all things.

But more than that? I was feeling protective of Lyrik.

It was difficult enough for us to maneuver it, wading through uncharted territory. I got the feeling neither of us were sure when one step would be the wrong one. The one that would backfire and incite a chain reaction leading to the end.

Or maybe like that picture, it'd be one disastrous explosion.

But Ash's expression was so much different than I expected. His smile soft. Kind as his attention drifted to the back of Lyrik's head, steady as it latched back on me.

Telling.

He needs you as much as you need him.

Do you see?

Don't give up. Don't let go.

I guess it was the knowledge I wouldn't be the one making that decision that caused the throbbing ache to flare in my gut.

So I was no money-grubbing whore, but I'd be lying if I said flying across country in a private jet wasn't the way to go. The flight was filled with laughter and chatter and unending mimosas, the time so comfortable and natural it was easy to convince myself this was where I belonged.

The guys had jumped into what amounted to an acoustic practice session, running through the set they would play tonight. We stopped for the fastest layover in history to refuel before we were back in the air, then what felt like moments later we were descending yet again.

Los Angeles.

I wrung my hands as I was hit with a rush of jitters.

How crazy, this was supposed to be my home. The place where I'd led everyone to believe I grew up, because it'd been the first city that'd come to mind when Charlie had asked where I was from. It was a familiar place because my family had visited many times for vacations—only an eight-hour drive from the desert city I'd fled four years ago.

I gazed out the small jet window at the jungle of buildings and roads that quickened to meet us from below.

"Are you going to visit any of your family while you're back in town?"

Shea's question pulled me from my trance, and I jerked her direction. Her brown eyes were curious. As if she'd plucked the guilty thoughts right from my head and pointed to my past that got harder and harder to escape the closer I came.

Lyrik looked over at me, too.

Expectantly.

As if maybe since I was going to visit his family, it would only make sense he go to visit mine, too.

Shit. What had I gotten myself into? But I'd known it was coming all along.

The decision.

Run or confront.

But right then I didn't have the strength to step from this limbo, so instead I shook off the haze. Forced a smile and cleared my throat.

"No." I tilted my head at Lyrik. "The trip is short and Lyrik and I are going to visit his family before the show tonight. I doubt there's time."

That in itself should have been enough to make me rethink this whole thing. Label it a really freaking bad idea. The thought of showing up at Lyrik's childhood home without a clue about them or who they were. Being in the dark, not privy or partner to the events that haunted Lyrik, a stranger to what had bred his impervious heart.

A heavy sigh pushed from my lungs. I needed to stop this train of thought before I made more out of this weekend than there actually was.

Lyrik frowned. "We haven't gotten you a ticket to go home yet. We can make time for you to visit your family if you want."

But his words were laden with caution, because only this boy had been allowed to peek over the walls I'd surrounded myself with. Into the place where I harbored my secrets. Now he held the key to completely expose them.

My forced smile trembled, and it was as if he knew. As if he could read me. It simmered around us. The trust that bound us so blatantly clear.

With that deadly smile, he looked at Shea. His words slid out in obvious innuendo. "Pretty sure I'm going to be keeping our girl Tamar here busy all weekend."

But that smile was so utterly soft when he turned it back on me.

Sebastian curled his arms around his wife and whispered something in her ear.

Swiveling into his hold, Shea kissed him.

And that was it, topic diverted.

I was saved.

We landed and debarked. An extra-long, black SUV was waiting to pick us up. Lyrik and I crawled into the very back seat, and he wound me in his arms, our sides pressed together as I rested my head on his shoulder. As if we'd done it a thousand times and I was his and he was mine and this was the way it was always going to be.

Under the blue California sky, grayed at the distant horizon with smog, we headed in the direction of the *Sunder* house.

It was surreal, to say the least.

The number of times I'd listened to their songs, the number of times I'd escaped into the sanctuary of Lyrik's voice as it played from my speakers, while I'd listened and dreamed he were the one person in the world with the ability to understand me.

Crazy how it turned out he was.

Fate.

God.

I was such a fool. A complete, utter fool. Because that's what I wanted it to be.

The city flashed by in a blur of freeways and buildings and stop-and-go traffic, dotted with landmarks that became more and more familiar the closer we came to The Hills. The driver finally exited the freeway and drove us through West Hollywood.

My face was nearly plastered to the side window to take in the scenery.

I cringed. I probably looked like some kind of fangirl, overeager to catch one glimpse of the glitter and limelight that went hand in hand with this city.

But this was me. The old me. The little girl who'd watched the world with wide, innocent eyes. In anticipation and wonder before she found so much of it was actually filled with horror.

I felt his warmth close over me, and from behind, Lyrik slid his arms around my waist and rested his chin on my shoulder. He spoke so low, no one else in the car could hear. "Seems to me, for someone coming home, you're awfully awed by your surroundings."

A soft gasp fell from me, and I turned to look at him, at the intuition glinting in the gold flecks of his eyes.

This boy who knew me like no one else.

Slowly, I shook my head.

No.

I wasn't home.

But I could be.

He exhaled as if releasing some of his reservations, or maybe in acceptance. Then he slung his arm around my shoulder and pulled me against his solid chest and the steady beat of his heart.

Thud.

Thud.

Thud.

I'd once thought it a stampede of destruction.

But no.

It was a chant of safety and security and perfection.

The driver took the winding road leading up into The Hills. It was a place only familiar in movies and in pictures conjured in my mind.

I could only imagine who and what was stowed away behind the rock walls and iron gates, nestled behind the garage faces that seemed so innocuous where they'd been constructed close to the road, camouflaging the homes built on the other side.

The SUV turned left into a driveway tucked away near the top. It led to a massive two-story house sheltered by soaring trees and lush gardens.

We stopped on the cobblestone drive in front of the expansive double doors, the stucco of the exterior walls warm and welcoming. This was where this hard, threatening man sought reprieve from the hustle of his glittering lifestyle within the city below. It was a world apart from the place I expected.

For all of them, really.

I guess the outside could truly be misleading.

Lyrik nudged his nose at my ear. "We're home."

****

"Favorite grade in school?"

"Um..." Memories thumbed through my mind like snapshots in an album. It didn't take me long to land on the correct one. "Sixth."

"Why?" Lyrik asked, stealing a glance at me before he looked back to the road.

Redness swept my cheeks.

Shit.

Now I was blushing? Lyrik really had busted down all the barriers.

"Because that was my first year of middle school. They had a photography club that met twice a week after school. I could barely sit still during class on those days, I was so anxious to get in that darkroom where I could develop the pictures I'd taken that week."

At a red light, he brought his big, rumbling truck to a stop, one he'd left waiting for him in L.A.

Reaching across the middle console, he grabbed my hand and brushed his lips across my knuckles. "It's always been your dream, yeah? Pictures?"

Joy filtered through me like a soft breeze. "Yeah...at least since I understood what dreams were."

I turned the question on him. "What was yours?"

He'd returned to gripping the steering wheel, those tattooed hands wrapped around the leather, the words stamped on his knuckles bold against the other swirling designs.

Sing my soul.

And it was my soul that sang when a lock of that black hair flopped to the side as he gazed across at me, that menacing, beautiful boy looking so powerful behind the wheel of his truck, before he pressed on the gas when the light turned green.

Damn, he was doing crazy things to me.

Crazy, lovely, beautiful things.

By the way he looked at me, there was no question both of us were on uneven ground.

Walking a rope that was tight. High and harrowing.

While our feet felt agile enough to take us at a sprint.

"Ninth grade." He quirked a brow. Those red lips spread like seduction. "Finally got the girl."

A twinge of possessiveness hit me, and his grin only widened as it turned teasing and coy. "Been packing her around with me ever since. My constant companion. She comes with me to every city, is at my side through every show. She's getting a little old and worn, but I love her all the same."

His meaning dawned on me. With playful laughter, I smacked his arm. "Are you trying to make me jealous of your guitar?"

His eyes widened. "Did it work?"

"Maybe…she does seem to be your favorite."

"That she is."

"Who got her for you?" I asked.

His smile softened. "My mom. My fourteenth birthday. I'd worked all summer saving up for it, but I didn't come close to making a dent. Turned out she'd been picking up extra shifts all along so she could give it to me for my birthday."

"She didn't tell you what she was doing?"

He shook his head. "Nah. She wanted to see me work for it. For it to mean something when I finally had it. She always wanted me to understand the best things take effort."

"Did it? Mean something?"

I already knew the answer. But I wanted to hear him say it. For him to let me in a little further.

His spirit dimmed, and he shifted in discomfort. "It meant everything until it cost me everything."

In confusion, my brows drew together. "I don't get it, Lyrik. It's like everything is wrapped up in your band. The guys are your family, and then in the next breath, it seems like you view it as the greatest burden. Does it not make you happy?"

A sigh filtered from his nose. "I don't know, Blue. It does. We all worked so damned hard for it, and being on stage...writing songs and having people sing them back to you like they *get* what you were trying to say? There's something indescribable about that moment, when you catch someone's expression while they're mouthing the words in the crowd. And you think for a fleeting moment they *get* it. That they're feeling the exact same thing you felt when you wrote it. Feeling like it just might make a difference. But everything comes with a cost."

"And you regret paying it?" I hedged, digging in deeper, knowing I was traversing dangerous ground. But God, I wanted to know. I *needed* to understand if I stood any chance of taking some of it away.

He raked an uneasy hand through his hair, the words choked, barely making their way free. "Wasn't really left with much of a choice."

Chaos whipped through me with his admission.

His.

Mine.

Our storms gaining speed. Building and intensifying and baring down. Their paths set on a collision course.

I watched the thick roll of his throat as he swallowed hard, his attention trained on the road. "It was all the choices I made leading up to it that stole it. What *ruined* it. Warned you I did, Blue. I always take the little bits of good I'm given and wreck them. Don't know anything else."

His confession trembled with vehemence. It left me unsure if he'd intended the words for me.

Tentatively, I reached out and touched his arm. "Your songs...they made a difference to me."

You make a difference to me.

I wished I were brave enough to say it.

Brave.

I wanted to be.

He looked at me, that gorgeous face stricken with pain. "Where're you from, Blue?"

My entire being flinched, and slowly I shook my head. "Not here."

"Think I already figured that out."

He was the first person since I'd run who'd sought me out. Searching to find the girl buried beneath the rubble—those tumbled stones covered in brash and hard and bitch.

"Tucson," I finally admitted toward my lap. So low I was sure there was no chance he could hear.

"Arizona," he responded softly. Obviously mostly for confirmation, because he was nodding slowly, as if he were trying to compartmentalize what I was telling him. Committing it to his reality.

He cut those penetrating eyes toward me. "Why hide?"

For a second, I squeezed mine shut, trying to make sense of things. Finally, I looked back at him, at his profile, at the hard, defined curve of his jaw to the soft pout of his mouth. "What are we doing, Lyrik?"

"Talking," he said, but from the way he blanched, he clearly knew I was asking more.

Maybe it was simply because Lyrik was driving us toward his childhood home that reminded him we really didn't know all that much about each other. Both of us were ignorant of the tiny, inconsequential details of the other's lives that added together to become something significant.

The foundations of who we were.

I guessed it was the sum of them, the huge consequence the decisions we had made along the way, that somehow drove the biggest wedge between us. All of it was held back, yet building from below, like magma compressed by a million years of pressure.

Waiting to erupt.

Humorless laughter rolled from him. "You know, sometimes I look at you, and I get this feeling…right here…"

Twice, he knocked the knuckles of his fist at the center of his chest. "Like I know you better than anyone. Like you know *me* better than anyone. And fuck, Blue…I fucking *like* the way that feels."

His voice dropped into a guilty whisper. "And I want more of it. To know you better." Warily, he turned my way. "And that's what scares me most."

At another stoplight, I met the intensity of his gaze. I knew in that moment, this untouchable boy was the most vulnerable he'd ever been. Splayed open wide. For the briefest flash of a second, everything exposed to be seen. As if he were pleading for a reprieve from his demons. For a real chance to be *touched*.

"I hid because when I ran, I ran for my life." My words cracked. "And I never believed in all that time it was safe to turn around."

Faster than I could process, his big hand was on the back of my head, his thumb running along my jaw. "I'll keep you safe, Blue. No one's gonna hurt you. Not ever again."

We stared at each other, both of us prisoners to whatever was happening around us. Binding us. We jumped with the blare of the horn coming from behind.

Lyrik jerked his hand away and accelerated.

Silence filled the cab, restless and agitated.

We both knew he'd crossed an invisible line. *I'll keep you safe, Blue. No one's gonna hurt you. Not ever again.*

I stared out the window at the neighborhoods we passed. The homes had become smaller, interspersed by apartment buildings that appeared a bit rundown as we drew closer to Long Beach.

Lyrik's wistful sigh broke the tension. "Man, do these streets bring back memories. Me and all the guys, nothing more than punks running them, dreaming big. None of us could wait to get out of this place. Thought the world had so much more to offer us. Funny how heading back always feels like coming home."

Looking over at him, I tried to picture him as a boy. "I bet you caused all sorts of trouble."

He laughed. "Always. Wouldn't expect anything less from me, would you?"

"Never." I said it like saying otherwise would be an offense.

He sighed again. This time heavier. "Learned so much on these streets. About life and who I wanted to be. It's where I fucked it all up, too."

He turned the truck down a narrow street lined with tiny houses of every color. Many of them appeared to have been refurbished.

Flipped. Surely stamped with a pretty price tag with the draw of the beaches nearby.

Others were worn and faded, run down with years of neglect.

He pointed to a light blue house. "That was Ash's place before his parents moved back to Ohio. Spent most of our teenage years in his garage. Writing songs. Getting high. Living the life while we dreamed of making ours. Seemed so easy back then."

I wondered when and how it'd gotten out of control.

I didn't pretend not to know the guys were rough.

Sex, drugs, and rock 'n' roll.

That was the one catchphrase synonymous with their name. And it wasn't just rumor. There was no hiding the history of arrests, of overdoses, and the death of their drummer.

But Lyrik kept it all so close to the vest. Isolated and concealed.

About a quarter mile down the road, Lyrik pulled up to the curb in front of a small pink house with white eaves. A tidy lawn stretched between the house and road, and two sprawling trees shaded the front.

A soft smile tugged at my mouth.

This house seemed somewhere between re-fabbed and rundown.

Lived in and loved.

"This is it," Lyrik said as he killed the engine.

Nerves tightened my stomach.

"Are you sure this isn't weird?" I couldn't help but go back to the same question I'd asked early this morning.

Funny, that seemed like an age ago.

"Nah…they're good people. You'll love them."

I nodded and pulled the door handle, just as the front door flew open and a little girl who had to be about Kallie's age came dashing out.

Brown hair in pigtails.

Smile a mile wide.

This time it was my heart's turn to tighten.

Lyrik was already rounding the front of the truck, going straight for her. She bolted toward him. Scooping her up under the arms, he tossed her into the air. She squealed, her sweet voice filling the air. "Uncle 'Lik," she cried as she scrambled to lock her arms around his neck.

"There's my girl," he said, kissing her cheek, nuzzling the side of her face, so at ease with this child it took my breath away. "I've been missing you like crazy, Penny Pie."

"I been missin' you, too."

Feeling out of sorts, I quietly latched my door shut behind me as I stepped onto the sidewalk, trying not to draw any attention to myself.

"Who's dat?" she asked.

Turning my direction, Lyrik hooked the little girl on his hip. "That there is my Blue."

My Blue.

Oh God.

He really was trying to wreck me.

"Bwue? That's a funny name."

"Not as funny as Penny." He tapped her nose.

She howled with laughter, squirming all over the place as he tickled her.

Slowly I approached. I stretched my hand out in front of me as I did.

Right.

Okay.

Was I really going to introduce myself by shaking a little girl's hand? Maybe I really had been hiding out in the bar for too long.

I pulled back my hand and gave her a small wave instead. "Hi there, Penny. It's really nice to meet you."

Shyly, she peered at me from where she had her head buried under Lyrik's chin with eyes that were almost as dark as his.

"Well, well, well, if it isn't my long-lost big brother, coming down from his castle to visit the common folk."

I looked to where the voice hit us from off to the side. Leaning up against the doorjamb with her arms crossed over her chest was a girl who was probably a year or two younger than me. Her mouth stretched into the widest grin when Lyrik turned toward her.

"Ha ha ha, aren't you hysterical?" he answered back, but it was all so clearly done in jest.

The two looked so much alike, I was almost taken aback. Her hair and eyes were just as dark as Lyrik's.

Lyrik wrapped his free hand around my waist and tugged me against him. "Blue...meet my little sister, Mia. She's kind of a pain in the ass, but I like her okay, I guess."

Obviously, the taunt was meant for her.

She was laughing and shaking her head as she walked forward, and I was thanking God for her welcoming smile.

"It's nice to meet you, Mia," I said, unwinding myself from Lyrik's hold. Bits of that old insecurity kept making their play, putting myself on the line this way, wondering just what in the world I was really doing here.

"The pleasure's all mine. It's nice to see someone who can put up with this ass for more than three seconds."

She wrapped both her arms around Lyrik's waist and placed her head on his chest. Everything between them went soft as he drew her into a hug while he still held her daughter in the other arm.

"I missed you so much. Don't stay away so long next time," she said

Um.

Wow.

This I was not expecting.

Unease had me shifting my feet.

He pressed a kiss to the top of her head. "Promise."

She pulled back. "You better get inside. Mom's about to have an aneurysm she's so excited to see you. She's baked the whole damned kitchen and I couldn't say for certain, but I'm pretty sure she knitted you a new pair of underwear or two."

"Underwear?" Penny drew out, like it was the craziest thing she'd ever heard.

Lyrik busted out laughing. "Wouldn't put it past her."

When his sister released him, Lyrik stretched his hand out for me. "Come on, I want you to meet my mom and dad."

I could almost feel the heat of Mia's gaze, the curiosity as her eyes flicked between my face and our entwined hands. Her intensity quite possibly as distinct as her brother's. But different. Warmer and without the old bitterness that seemed to be the fuel to his fire.

Still carrying Penny, Lyrik dragged me the rest of the way up the sidewalk, up the one concrete stair to the door, calling "I'm home" as we stepped through it.

Inside, I froze.

Oh my God.

I felt as if I'd stepped into an alternate universe. Kind of like the day I'd forced my way into Lyrik's apartment uninvited and found him covered in frosting. But this was tenfold.

Hell, probably a hundred.

Memories of my grandmother's house didn't come close to competing with this, and I was sure she'd never gotten rid of one thing she'd collected throughout her entire life.

Sugar and spice hovered in the air—no question the bearing of fresh cinnamon rolls in the oven—the smell so thick I could almost see the scented waves wafting down the hall from the kitchen. Pictures covered every inch of the walls, and every shelf and table was cluttered with knickknacks and artifacts. Crocheted doilies covered the tops of the antique wooden furniture and a colorful afghan was thrown on the back of the couch.

Not one single thing matched.

Make it if you want it to matter.

Adding to the mayhem was the mess of toys strewn across the living room floor, a pop-up princess castle in one corner and a pile of huge pastel blocks in the other.

A man who'd been sitting in an old recliner across from the TV, one who without a doubt was Lyrik's father, climbed to his feet. "Lyrik...there's my boy. Glad to see you're back."

Releasing my hand, Lyrik met him halfway, gave him a shake of the hand and a clap to the back. The man grinned when he pulled away. "Of course, most of it has to do with the fact your mom is about to drive me out of my ever-lovin' mind with her primping and puttering, thinking she has to get things ready for her own son to come home for a visit."

"Not for him, Karl...for his guest," the voice hollered from down the hall.

Redness crawled up my neck and heated my cheeks.

Blushing again.

What had I gotten myself into?

"I'm Tamar," I said, shoving my hand out toward him, praying for even a piece of Tamar King to show.

"Hey…I 'fought your name was Bwue?" Penny demanded.

My attention shot to her. Maybe it was from the tension and strain. Maybe it was from the uncertainty and the questions that had swirled around this whole trip. But I broke out laughing like some kind of crazed lunatic when I saw the confusion on the little girl's too-pretty face.

Too pretty like her uncle's and too pretty like her momma's.

Good God, it wasn't Karl who'd lost his ever-lovin' mind.

If I was worried what they'd think of me before, now they had plenty of arsenal to think I was nuts.

Insane.

But I'd been feeling that way since the moment Lyrik stepped into my life.

Like his weight had caused a shift in my axis.

Ever since, I'd been out of touch with what I'd fought to maintain as my reality.

Lyrik's dad started laughing, too, and instead of returning my handshake, he hugged me. "We're really glad to have you. My name's Karl, in case you didn't hear my woman hollering from the kitchen."

I laughed a little more around the emotion clogged in my chest.

Lyrik was right.

I would love them.

I already knew that from the five seconds I'd spent in their space.

Bustling footsteps echoed down the hall, and Lyrik was already turning around, setting Penny on the floor before he moved forward and lifted his mom in an overbearing hug.

She didn't fight it and let him whip her around like a ragdoll.

Lyrik set her back down and slung his arm around her shoulder. "And this hippie here would be my mom, Katy."

She resembled the rest of them the least, shorter than her daughter by probably five inches, her feet bare, her hair a light brownish blonde, long and flowy, just as flowy as her whimsical skirt and the jewelry she wore.

But her smile.

It was his.

Though it lacked that wickedness.

She smacked his chest and at the same time leaned her head against it. "Oh, hush. You just love giving me a hard time."

"What else are you good for?" With the jibe came pure affection, and he squeezed her a little tighter, as if he wanted to reassure her she was good for so much more.

That she was everything. Because that much was blatantly clear. This was the one place Lyrik was truly free. Unrestrained and without the ghosts that seemed to haunt his every move.

She relaxed into him for a second, before she pushed away with her attention locked on me. Her smile went achingly soft.

"And you must be Tamar." She wrapped my hand in hers, covering them both with the other. "I'm so glad you're here."

"Thank you for having me, especially on such short notice."

She waved me off. "Pssh...I'm always more than ready to have company. Especially if it's someone like you."

A timer buzzed from the kitchen. Her light brown eyes widened. "Lyrik said you two wouldn't be able to stay for dinner because of the show tonight, so I thought I'd whip us up some lunch. I hope you're hungry."

Lyrik rubbed his stomach. "Famished."

"Good then. Come on, let's eat."

When Katy West cooked, Katy West *cooked*.

She'd made ham and potatoes and green beans, a salad, not to mention the cinnamon rolls she served hot out of the oven.

We sat around their small kitchen table, Lyrik at my side. I was pretty sure I wasn't the only one who ate until their stomach was overstuffed, but the laughter was carefree and the conversation light and it felt so good to relax into the atmosphere.

None of them made me feel an outsider. It was only Penny sitting on her knees in her chair who peppered me with questions, which was clearly out of her own need to know every detail of everything, my favorite color and movie and book.

When we finished, I offered to help Katy clear the dishes, but she shooed us out and told me to enjoy my visit. I found myself in the backyard on the thick lawn, Penny screeching as Lyrik pushed her on the swing.

"Higher, Uncle 'Lik!"

I stood aside and watched as they played.

When she'd finally gotten her fill of going down the slide after she'd done it about fifty-two times, she called, "Duck, Duck, Goose time! Momma and Bwue have to play, too, right, Uncle 'Lik?"

She took his hand and looked up at him, that menacing, powerful boy so tall at her side, so striking and bold beneath the California sky, yet so careful with this little girl.

"Right," he answered. He shot a grin our way, looking back after us as he let her haul him over to the grassy spot beneath the leafy ash growing proudly on the right side of the yard.

"You up for this?" Mia asked. "She can be a handful."

"She's wonderful," I said.

Mia's smile was warm, knowing, as if that was a perfectly acceptable answer because she definitely wasn't going to disagree. We headed over to the circle Penny was putting in place.

"You sit right there...and Momma you're right here...and Bwue...you sit there," she said, pointing her tiny finger to the spot beside Lyrik.

"Yeah, you sit right here," Lyrik drawled out just before he yanked my hand.

My feet flew out from under me.

And I was falling.

Right into his arms.

I yelped. "Lyrik...what do you think you're doing? You're so going to pay for that."

But it was the sudden wave of joy rushing me that spun my head and weakened my knees, the ground a rumble, that buzz sizzling in the air. Everything went so rapturously light. This dangerous boy who was so incredibly good.

And I wanted to bask in it, in the excitement and thrill that drew me forward, pushing me into the open space where I had no place to hide.

Did he know?

He held me close, kissed my forehead.

So soft.

So sweet.

So *different.*

I could feel his smile against my skin, and I could feel my own as I clutched my hands in his shirt.

I wanted to hang on to it forever.

"I it!" Penny called, because forever couldn't last, and I forced myself to crawl from Lyrik's lap. I straightened out my shirt and tried to straighten out my emotions that were all tangled and tied.

I turned to catch Mia's knowing smile, the bite of her lip as she looked between us, before she turned back to her daughter. "All ready."

Penny started to skip around the small circle. She touched each of our heads as she passed.

"Duck… Duck… Duck…" She went around three times before she touched my head. "Goose!" she called. She fumbled into a run as I climbed to my feet. Her smile was so carefree as I chased her around the circle.

She jumped into my spot.

"Safe!"

Of course she was.

"Dang it," I drew out, and Lyrik gave me a grin when he gave Penny a high-five. "You're way too fast for our Blue here."

I circled twice before I called "Goose" when I touched Mia's head.

Okay.

So call me a chicken.

But I was taking the safe road.

Because the ones I'd been traveling today had suddenly become perilous. Full of dips and holes and unexpected curves that felt so good. I was sure there had to be an out-of-control truck barreling down on the other side.

I raced around the circle, moving quicker than I anticipated, because damn, Mia was fast. I twisted around, dodging her hand that barely missed my back, before I slid back into her spot.

Penny howled with laughter. "You beat my momma!"

I poked her stomach. "Sure did…you don't have to have those long, gorgeous legs to run fast. Us short girls can do it too."

"Ha," Mia said, starting slow as she began to circle. "I'd give up my height for those curves, any day."

Dark, dark eyes flashed, all mischief and sex as Lyrik glanced my way. "Kinda like those curves myself."

I shot him a warning glare.

Little ears. Little ears.

Mia finally tapped Penny's head and called, "Goose." Penny took off after her, and Mia ran slowly, but never let Penny catch her before she hopped into her spot.

"Made it!"

Penny was all too eager to go again, rounding and rounding and rounding until she touched Lyrik's Head. "Goose!"

Lyrik flew to standing and began to chase after his niece.

Penny squealed and moved her little legs as fast as she could.

"Go, Penny, go! Don't let him get you," I urged as I held out my arms for her to run into to keep her safe.

She flew into them and knocked us back against the grass.

Both of us were laughing, and she was hugging me and I was suddenly hugging her.

It felt so nice.

So natural.

And I missed and I missed and I missed.

A tremble rolled. Working its way from the inside out.

Home.

I wanted to find it.

I wanted to find the pieces I'd lost and shunned and left behind and the ones still waiting to be discovered in the future.

"I *fink* I love you," the tiny voice said as Penny burrowed deeper into my hold.

So innocent and without any doubt. How easily she offered her heart.

I squeezed her tighter, just as tight as I squeezed my eyes shut.

"I think I love you, too," I whispered.

Was that okay? To love freely? Without the fear of it being ripped away?

Intensity blistered the air. A heat so great it was palpable, a tangible weight. My chest squeezed. Shivers covered me whole, magnified by the rays of the sun brushing at my arms and face.

I forced my eyes open and met with the fathomless stare glinting down at me.

The man so gorgeous and hard and terrifying. A storm so wholly beautiful. Dangerous and raw.

More dangerous than he'd ever been.

Because this wasn't the malicious, spiteful man who'd come into my bar a year ago, scarred in bitterness. It wasn't the one I'd run from because he'd reminded me of all the things I should fear.

This was the same boy in the picture I'd found shoved in the back corner of his drawer.

Face shining with pure love and joy and affection.

And he was looking at me.

The last brittle band of my heart broke.

I could feel the snap.

A million pounds gone.

The flood of emotion that swelled in my chest and spun in my spirit.

The shout of my soul.

Love. Love. Love.

Searching for a breath, I peeled Penny from me, gently kissed her on the cheek as I set her aside. "I need to get a glass of water," I said.

Lie.

Lie.

Lie.

I was simply staggered.

Reeling.

I climbed onto shaky feet.

"Are you okay?" Lyrik asked, head cocked in sudden concern.

"I'm fine." I smiled. "Just going to get something to drink. Can I get you anything?"

"Nah…I'm good." He looked to where Penny had climbed onto her mother's lap. "Going to play with my girls for a few more minutes then we'd better get going."

"Okay."

I fumbled my way up the two steps leading to the porch and through the door to the kitchen where it was dim and quiet. Neither of Lyrik's parents were anywhere to be found.

Slowly I made my way over to the kitchen sink and to the window that overlooked the backyard.

Drawn.

Because I couldn't look away.

Lyrik was sitting on the grass, facing across from his sister and niece.

I stared out at everything I wanted. It felt so close. Yet the distance was riddled with obstacles.

"You love him."

A soft gasp left me, and I jerked around to find Lyrik's mother watching me from where she stood at the entrance of the kitchen.

It wasn't a question.

My mouth flapped open and closed, my mind still a buzzing whir of noises and realizations and hope.

"I didn't mean to." It spilled free before I could stop the admission, but as soon as I voiced it, I knew its truth.

I didn't mean to fall in love with Lyrik West.

I'd run from it.

Fought it.

All the while he'd been the one to fight for me.

It was so difficult to reconcile. The boy who I felt as if I could go to for anything, the one who'd protect me with his last dying breath, up against the one who kept himself so shut off. Sheltered and fortified behind his own walls.

Light laughter rippled from her delicate mouth. "We rarely do."

Her brown eyes softened as she tilted her head. "I doubt very much he meant to fall in love with you, either."

Hope whipped into a frenzy.

I shook my head to clear it.

No.

She was wrong.

"I'm pretty sure I'm just along for the ride," I told her, trying to blink away the moisture gathering in my eyes.

Weak.

That's what he made me.

"Are you sure about that? In his entire life, my son has only brought two girls here. And the first one? That boy was head over heels in love with her."

The pain ripping through me was the worst sign. It felt as if my chest was being shorn into a thousand tiny pieces.

I had to be an idiot.

But I knew the risk—coming here—I reminded myself. I learned a long time ago not all skies after a storm are painted in rainbows.

"Has he told you about her?" she asked.

Fiercely, I shook my head.

Her expression lifted in sympathy, but it was clear she wasn't surprised, and she took a tentative step forward. My gaze was drawn back to the window. Outside, I saw Lyrik laugh, the tender way he looked at his sister and niece.

The pain within me only amplified.

"Tamar, I'd never tell you that about her to hurt you or make you feel like you're less, and maybe I shouldn't say anything at all," Katy continued cautiously. She edged in closer behind me.

"I'm telling you because it means something he brought you here. More than something…especially after everything he's been through. And I'm not one to go making excuses for my children. Lyrik made terrible mistakes with her. Mistakes he's been paying for ever since. Mistakes I'm sure he's going to be paying for, for the rest of his life. But he loved her. Loved her like mad. So often, that first love feels like it's the most important thing in the world, when in reality, it's only there to give us a glimpse…to prepare us…for what it's really going to feel like when we meet the one we're supposed to spend our lives with. Because it pales in comparison."

My throat constricted. So tight. I tried to breathe around it.

Katy's tender voice swelled in the room, as if she were lost to the same scene happening in her backyard as I was.

"You know, when Mia got pregnant…she wasn't even eighteen. Lyrik was so protective of her. He'd always been. He would have dropped everything to come take care of his sister when that useless boyfriend of hers dumped her the day she found out about Penny."

Knowingly, she grinned my way. "Little bastard, he was lucky Lyrik didn't skin him alive."

Her voice softened again. "When Penny was born, Baz had just gotten out of jail after all that trouble those boys went and got themselves into."

God, I wanted to ask about that, too.

It was so much more difficult traversing something when you were going in blind.

"Things were just starting to move along for *Sunder*," she mused. "Them gaining national attention and their label picking them up. Lyrik wanted to up and move us into a big house. Take care of us. But this has always been our home. And more important than that, Mia needed to find her own way, even though she's still looking for it."

Everything about her slowed in emphasis as her head inclined toward the window. "Same way as he does. And maybe that way has always been pointing to you."

Stunned by her words, I turned to look at her. She'd only met me today. And I could almost hear *forever* whispering from her tongue.

My gaze trailed out the window. For a moment I stared, before something in my periphery caught my attention.

They were sitting below the window off to the left amid a bunch of other trinkets. There were two of them. The same handmade bears like the one I'd found in Lyrik's apartment. The same kind he'd made for Sebastian and Shea's son. These two were obviously well used, one plainly made for a boy and the other for a girl.

I could almost picture Lyrik as a wild, spirited boy running through the house with a cape on his back, his little sister toddling behind, trying to keep up, as they both dragged the bears along with them.

Make it if you want it to matter.

Overwhelmed by it all, I whipped around to look at her.

"What's the song on his arm? The name?" I demanded it before I could stop myself.

Sadly, she shook her head. "Now that's not my story to tell. But look at you…"

For a second, I recoiled, slammed behind a wall of defensiveness. A flash of *Red*.

But her expression was the furthest from judgmental. "Sweet girl…I see you…trying to cover up the things you wish you could erase."

Could she really tell that just from looking at me?

"And my son? He might not completely understand everything, but that doesn't mean he doesn't *get* it. Just like I know you might not know every single detail of Lyrik's past, but that doesn't mean you don't *get* him. And it's like he's silently begging you to. *See him. Get him.* Even when I know that terrifies him. He doesn't want to forget, Tamar, but it's time he moved beyond it. Maybe you're the one who can help him do that. He deserves to be loved. Every bit as much as you do."

Could she be right? That what Lyrik truly wanted was me?

And she looked at me. Looked at me as if she could see through every day and every moment of the last four years. As if she felt every fear. As if she knew every wound.

"You might have given up on yourselves. Just don't give up on each other."

TAMAR

"*Y*ou sure you're goin' down there?"

Duskiness clung to the enclosed quarters backstage, the hallway narrow and the ceiling low where Lyrik had me pinned against the wall.

People jostled through, moving equipment as the opening band cleared out to make room for *Sunder* to take the stage. Voices yelled demands and directions, and a frenzied excitement bustled through the atmosphere.

"Do I look like I can't take care of myself?" I lifted my chin in defiance and let out a little bit of *Red*. So what if I liked it a little too much that this intimidating boy looked as if he wanted to scoop me up and hide me away.

Protective.

Defensive.

Possessive.

"I just don't get why you'd want to be down there on the floor when you could be back here with Shea, standing at the side of the stage. Best view in the house, baby."

I scoffed. "Watching a video on my computer screen is a pretty good view, too, but you and I both know it's not the same."

"It's a madhouse out there tonight," he warned, as if that bit of information would sway me. "No doubt the pit's gonna be crazy tonight."

"Even better."

He edged in closer. I sucked in a breath, as if I could inhale all the elements of this powerful man. Or maybe as if I could defend myself against them.

Because they were overwhelming.

Consuming.

I pressed back closer to the wall.

His voice was a grumble where he ran his mouth up and down my jaw. "Last thing I need to worry about while I'm on stage is my girl down there, getting trampled underfoot by a bunch of kids who just want to let go."

My girl. My girl. My girl.

Could it be?

It felt so close.

Attainable.

This untouchable boy right within my reach.

My head rocked back against the wall, granting him better access as he started kissing a path up and down the sensitive flesh of my neck. He dug his fingers into my hips and pressed his already straining cock against my belly.

Well then.

"Are you trying to distract me?" I rasped toward the low ceiling, waffling between caving to whatever he asked of me and begging him to take me back to the dressing room.

"Whatever it takes," he muttered against my skin. "Terrible, terrible sacrifice I have to make."

"Right," I drew out. Laughter that hinted at the giddiness his actions stirred within me tumbled up my throat. Finally, I managed to nudge him back, meeting those charcoal eyes. "I'll be careful. I promise. I just…"

I chewed at my lower lip, wondering if he *got* it.

Mouth pressing into a thin line, he seemed to make a decision. With a resigned sigh, he gathered me into a hug. "I hear you, too," he murmured.

Affection wound in my chest, my emotions all over the place as I looked up into the face of this man. This stunning, foreboding man who'd come to mean everything. Staring up at him was the girl who looked at the world with wide eyes and an anticipating, eager spirit.

One who felt as if she was at the verge of experiencing the good things that world had to give.

The thrill and the excitement and the steady hum.

All the while, those hard, hard lessons learned along the way flickered in the distance. In the recesses of my mind that weren't all that rusty. They only fueled the rising flames.

"Lyrik," Ash suddenly called from the end of the hall. "Get your ass over here, man. About time to go on."

Lyrik shot me a menacing grin. "Don't make me have to jump off that stage to kill anyone." He pecked his mouth once against mine. "You know I will."

Butterflies scattered and lifted and flew.

God.

"I'll be sure to stay out of the line of fire." I pushed up onto my toes, kissing him a little longer than he'd kissed me. "I'll see you afterward."

I followed Lyrik down the short hall of the music theater, gave a small wave to Shea who looked at me as if I were crazy as I passed by and headed to the entrance at the side.

So yeah.

Maybe I was a little crazy.

I was totally okay with that.

The bouncer stepped aside to let me through, and I bounded down the five stairs until I became just another indistinguishable face in the unruly crowd.

It was standing room only—everyone crammed together as they vied to get closer to the stage.

Excitement flared. I filled my lungs with it, making myself one with the living, thriving ring of energy spinning through the room.

Bright lights flashed from above the stage.

Anxious, the crowd surged.

Undaunted, I pushed and weaved, making my way through the mass of bodies trying to hold me back until I made it almost all the way to the front.

I took a spot just off to the side where I knew Lyrik would stand. Where his old black, much-loved guitar was propped on a stand in between two others.

Colored lights danced across the faces of the fans. Inciting and stirring.

With a thrust of his drumsticks in the air, Zee burst out onto the stage.

Shouts and yells lifted from the crowd.

Ash appeared next, and that energy sizzled. I felt it build around me, as bright and shimmery as the blue stage lights that twirled and throbbed.

It nearly exploded when Lyrik stepped out from behind the dark maroon curtains.

And that was all it took.

My breath was gone.

Knees weak.

Heart manic.

Pound.

Pound.

Pound.

He was smiling my favorite smile when he strode across the stage. The deadly kind. That arrogant, cocky boy who I'd run from for months was back in full force as he slung the strap of his guitar over his neck.

So powerful and bold.

Stunning.

A beautiful predator who with merely a flick of his finger summoned a flock of willing prey.

God, was I a fool, because I knew right then I adored that part of him, too.

Adored everything about him.

The danger and the dark.

The threat of those big hands.

The soft security of them when he held me in the night.

This convoluted, confusing man who amounted to something brilliant.

The crowd just about lost it when Sebastian stepped out, bringing the whole of *Sunder* standing before them.

No wonder Shea had lost herself to him.

For the briefest flash, the lights completely went dim. The sudden silence only added to the furor.

Energy held fast.

Baited.

Bottled.

Before blinding white spotlights blazed to life.

In that very second, Lyrik slammed into the first erratic chord.

The crowd broke into a riot. As if the ball of energy centered at the foot of the stage burst and rippled out, consuming everything in its path.

Bodies thrashed, bouncing together to the wild, harsh beat and the growling, aggressive lyrics Sebastian screamed into the mic.

I felt a partner to it. Yet elevated above it all as I watched the boy in front of me get lost in the words, in the melody he fed into his own mic, a rugged, razor-sharp edge added to the mayhem.

A dusky haze filtered through the space, and lights strobed as bodies flailed and writhed.

And Lyrik.

Lyrik somehow met my unfaltering gaze.

Dark, piercing eyes.

Penetrating.

Provoking.

As if I were the only thing he could see.

Drawn.

And I wondered if he, too, had felt it all along.

When *Sunder* finally exited the stage, I worked through the maze of bodies to the side entrance leading backstage. Some people stood around chatting as the bouncers tried to herd them toward the front doors. Others lingered, obviously hoping to get that highly coveted invite backstage.

I felt a twig of panic when wondering if the bouncer would recognize me.

That would just be awesome.

Me standing around out back like some kind of wannabe groupie, waiting for Lyrik to realize I wasn't there. My phone was in my purse where I'd left it with his things in the dressing room. I didn't even have a way to call him.

But I should have known better. Lyrik was already there, greedy gaze meeting mine where he waited for me shadowed by the burly bouncer.

With a smile, I offered a couple "excuse me's" as I shouldered through, not caring a bit that I was met with a slew of grumbles and hisses.

All I wanted was to get to my man.

My man.

Could he be? Could he be more than the two months he'd promised? More than this weekend that neither of us could define? Because after the weight of my realization at his parents' earlier today, there was a piece of me that was imploring with myself to pin him down. To make him say the words I could so clearly read in his eyes.

With every step closer to him, emotion pulsed through my veins. But it was a new need unlike anything I'd felt before. As if all the fears and reservations and concerns I'd built up for years had suddenly been loosed and freed. Now they bounded forth like the spill of a waterfall, pouring, meshing, and uniting with the faith he'd created, breeding a flood of devotion that quickly rose to fill every crevice and hole.

Love. Love. Love.

"There you are," he whispered as his big hand came out to grip me from behind my neck, to pull me forward and to kiss me as if he felt the magnitude of what swirled and tumbled through me.

"What'd you think?" he asked when he pulled away.

I clutched his sweaty shirt. "I think you're the most beautiful man I've ever seen."

He laughed a cocky laugh, grin sly as his hand skidded down my arm to my hand where he weaved his tatted fingers through mine, like maybe we were writing our own story. "Know I'm all kinds of irresistible, but I meant about the show."

A playful grin flitted around my mouth. "I do believe you've been hanging out with Ash too much. I think he might be a bad influence."

Lyrik laughed, this deep, melodic sound. He lifted a dark, incredulous brow. "You think it's Ash who's the bad influence?"

His smile softened as my expression drifted into something tender. It was impossible to keep it out.

"You already know what I think about the music," I told him.

"Oh yeah?"

"Yeah…about your voice. About the way you wrap me up when you play. The way I don't feel so alone when I'm surrounded by the words that feel almost like you wrote them just for me."

I lifted a self-deprecating smile, *Red* so far gone I no longer remembered who she was or who I'd been so frantically trying to be.

"Pretty sad, huh, being that girl sitting all alone in her apartment, pressing play again and again to the same song, pretending this untouchable rock star was there and everything didn't seem so bad anymore."

He brushed his fingers through my hair, making my head tilt back as he looked down at me. "Not alone, Blue. Not anymore. You don't have to pretend anymore."

Didn't I? I wanted to beg him as that flood whooshed into a white-capped wave of insecurity.

"Come on," he said. "Four of us have a little tradition after each show. Want you there."

"And what kind of tradition would that be?"

"Shots."

"Surprise, surprise," I mumbled, tone dry.

A smirk played at that delicious mouth, and he turned on his heel and started zigzagging us through the backstage crowd. I clasped my free hand around his wrist, refusing to let him go as I tried to keep up with his long, purposed stride. He gave my hand a squeeze, a silent reassurance that he had me, that he knew where I was.

That maybe he knew who I was.

I hear you.

His voice trembled through my spirit.

People clapped him on the back as we passed, and I took in the whole scene with wide-eyed exuberance.

Balancing on the ledge.

Ready to take that last step over the edge.

To jump.

Straight into a free fall.

Would he be there to catch me at the bottom?

"Great show, man," one of the guys from the opening band said to Lyrik, slowing our progression as he blocked our path in the cramped hallway.

Heat permeated the space, the air dank and dim and thick. In amused appraisal, the guy's brown eyes slithered down to where Lyrik's and my hands were clasped.

"Where's the twin?" he asked with a suggestive twist of his brow.

I cringed.

Wow.

That hurt worse than I thought it would.

But it was no secret or surprise. That was Lyrik's style. In almost every picture I'd seen of Lyrik with a girl, there was never any *girl* about it. It was a pattern in the images captured by the paparazzi, in those snapped by fans.

Lyrik West was always draped in multiple women.

In them, his posture almost suggested he didn't register they were there except for the fact he was getting ready to ravage and annihilate.

Spoil and loot and desolate.

Once he used them up, I was sure there was nothing left behind.

All except for the one I'd found in that picture.

"Fuck off, Brinks." That was Lyrik's only response as he jerked me back into movement. My gaze turned in time to follow the guy's shocked expression staring back at us as Lyrik wound me deeper into the darkened maze.

I guess I was a little shocked too.

And a whole lot relieved.

Lyrik said a few hellos as he walked into one of the reception rooms backstage that had been close to empty when we'd walked through it earlier this afternoon.

Tonight it was packed, overflowing with a crush of people plastered against every wall, some voices loud and raucous, the center of attention, others obviously ill at ease and having no clue what to do with themselves.

Heavy metal blared from the speakers, only adding to the chaotic vibe that vibrated the floors and climbed the walls.

For the most part, Lyrik barely lifted his chin in acknowledgment of someone calling his name, those competing for his attention, this dangerous, volatile man seemingly unaffected and aloof.

He led us to the very back where a bar was set up.

Here, most of the people in the room held back, giving us space.

Anthony appeared off to the side with a grin on his face. He clapped Lyrik on the shoulder. "Lyrik, it's good to see your face. Feel good to be back in town?"

"Sure thing," Lyrik said with a little less enthusiasm than someone might anticipate.

Anthony turned his gaze on me, appraising again, but where the asshole back in the hall had been exactly that...an asshole...Anthony's assessment was soft and without judgment.

Just…curious.

"Nice to see you again, Tamar."

"Nice to see you, too."

Ash squeezed through, bounding onto the scene, always larger than life, cutting off any further conversation. "Anthony, how's it going, man? You outdid yourself this time. Sold out. Guess we can't ask for better than that, now can we?"

"Hell yeah," Sebastian agreed as he sidled up to the bar, his hand wrapped up in Shea's, refusing to let her go.

She eyed me with a knowing smile.

Crazy, huh?

I shook my head with a smile, thinking it truly was crazy, that Lyrik had me wrapped up kind of the way Sebastian had Shea.

Staunch and resolute.

That I was here, and for the moment I was *his*.

That *whole* feeling fluttered through me again. The promise of something good.

Stupid, stupid girl.

Because that thrill trembled with the consequences of leaving myself susceptible and weak.

Right then, I wasn't sure I could much make myself care anymore. Wasn't sure I could conjure the fight.

I squeezed Lyrik's hand, turned my nose to his arm so I could breathe him in.

Maybe it was better to hurt and bleed and cry than to be vacant and alone.

Maybe fear wasn't such a horrible thing, after all.

Ash leaned over the bar and helped himself to a bottle of Jack, lined up a long row of shot glasses, and set to pouring the amber liquid across them.

I felt the curve lifting at the corner of my mouth. "You're making me feel like a slacker, you pouring the drinks while I stand over here pretending like I don't have a thing in the world to do. You sure you don't want a professional to handle that?"

Ash cracked up with a shake of his head, his blue eyes sly as they cut across to me. "Ah now, my Tam Tam…I do appreciate the gesture…"

His attention kept sliding until it landed on the side of Lyrik's profile, Lyrik's head inclined so he could hear whatever Anthony was saying, clearly paying us no mind.

Ash flicked his attention right back to me. "Think you have plenty to keep you busy. My boy there is a handful. Wouldn't want to leave you at a disadvantage."

He said it like a tease, but I didn't miss the undercurrent of warning that made its way into his words.

"I'll keep that in mind," I said, accepting the glass he passed my way.

"I know you will."

Ash nudged Lyrik's arm, and Lyrik turned from his conversation and took the shot glass Ash offered. Everyone seemed to know their routine, each taking a step back or closer, huddling until they'd made a small circle of friends.

These boys who'd always seemed so bad.

The ones who'd shaken my axis the second they'd invaded *Charlie's* bar, because they'd ushered in this black-haired, broken boy who would steal my world.

A beautiful storm.

Still holding my hand, Lyrik slanted me one of this deadly grins and a wink.

My insides went haywire.

A sizzle and a snap.

Ash lifted his glass. "To the future of *Sunder.* May all our roads be paved in gold and may badass songs continue to pour from our souls. Oh yes, and may there always be lots and lots of girls."

He grinned like the Cheshire and tossed back his shot.

Shea smacked him on the chest. "Hey."

He deflected, jumping back and trapping her hand against him. "Don't worry, Beautiful Shea. We know Baz Boy here is locked down tight. No worries. Just leaves more for the rest of us."

Tugging her hand away, she pointed at him. "I still have two hundred bucks saying you're going to be filling up that house with a herd of little Ashes. I've got your card, buddy. This girl needs a new pair of shoes."

Ash gripped his chest like he were in pain.

"Oh…God…you're killing me here, Shea. I'll gladly fill up your whole damned closet with shoes if it'll stop you from this mad delusion."

The entire time, Lyrik was squeezing my hand. Hard. A little hopeless. Like he didn't know where this was going, either, but he couldn't bear the thought of letting me go.

I squeezed back.

Don't let me go. I need you. I want you. I love you.
Do you hear me?

He suddenly looked down at me. "You ready to get out of here?"

"Yeah."

"We're going to call it," Lyrik said offhandedly to the rest of the guys, not waiting around for goodbyes.

He began to lead me back through the crowd. Just before ducking out of the room, Lyrik froze when a middle-aged guy stepped into his path.

He was bald and grinning and so obviously not welcome.

"Eric Banik…" Lyrik seemed to process his presence, before his jaw went rigid. "What the fuck do you think you're doing here? This isn't the time or place for your games."

Eric Banik.

A thread of unease spun through me.

That was the name that had sent Lyrik into a tailspin the night he'd gotten into that fight with Ash. The night Lyrik had lost some of his control. When he'd used me like he'd needed me and not the other way around.

Eric grinned. "Just thought I'd drop by and see if you'd thought any more about my offer."

"Told you a thousand times and not a thing has changed. But if you need a reminder, then fine—" Lyrik edged in closer to him. "Fuck off."

A cold unlike anything I'd ever felt from Lyrik chilled the room. His dark eyes had gone black when he glanced behind him to the guys still talking by the bar.

"Now if I were you, I'd turn around and not ever come back. Pretty sure I gave you a warmer reception than the rest of my crew is going to give."

He laughed as if Lyrik didn't faze him. Not in the least. "Baz's wife sure is pretty, isn't she?"

In a flash, Lyrik had Eric Banik's shirt in his fist, lifting him from the ground. "I'm warning you…turn around and walk out the fucking door. Don't come back. This is me asking *nicely*. And I'm about five seconds from not feeling so friendly. You got me?"

Hands lifted in a placating gesture, Eric backed down. "Fine. Just know the offer's not going to stand forever."

"Real broken up about it," Lyrik mumbled as he pushed around him, and I struggled to keep up as he dragged me out the entry and back down the dingy hall. Anger radiated from him.

And I didn't quite get it. Why an offer would make him so upset. Sure, the guy was obviously a dick. But it wasn't as if he had to accept it.

I was almost surprised Lyrik didn't punch the poor scrawny kid who suddenly stepped out in front of him at the end of the hall. Like a target directly in Lyrik's warpath.

"Lyrik West. Would it be okay if I asked you a couple questions?"

Lyrik just grumbled something about *assholes* beneath his breath, and I gave his hand a small tug. This guy seemed so much better than the paparazzi that had descended on us when we'd stepped from the Escalade when we first pulled up to the theater this afternoon, a swarm of them firing question after question. All of which had been ignored.

"It's fine," I encouraged him, and Lyrik sighed, raked a hand through his unruly hair, agitation still vibrating through his bones. "Make it fast."

The guy gave a timid, but grateful smile as he scrambled to pull out one of those old-fashioned notepads. "Thanks so much for answering my questions. Umm…"

Nervously, he scratched the side of his head. "We know the next *Sunder* album is slated for release this winter. Word is, Sebastian Stone's new wife, Shea Stone, aka Delaney Rhoads, will be a part of that album. Can you confirm or deny?"

"No secret they've written some music together."

"Um…okay…and will she be joining *Sunder* on tour?"

Lyrik huffed. "Doubtful. She's got a family. And the road and family don't exactly mix."

His tone was bitter. I stood at his side, trying to make sense of where all the hostility was coming from, all the while trying to tamp down the frisson of panic that threatened when the reporter's attention kept flicking toward me.

Brows drawn, he inclined his head, assessing. "You look really familiar."

Shit. Shit. Shit.

I'd been too wrapped up in Lyrik's proposal that I'd never even considered someone might recognize me.

Slowly I shook my head and took a step back. That disquiet I'd felt in front of Eric Banik doubled. But I hadn't perfected my mask for nothing. I forced a brilliant smile, all sex and distraction, pushed out an easy laugh. "Nope…I'm nobody. I'm sure you've never seen me before."

He gave a slow nod and turned back to Lyrik. "We've also heard the next album will showcase a few more songs in the style of *Sunday Gone*, your voice as the lead. Is that any indication that Sebastian Stone may be taking a step back from the band?"

Lyrik seemed to itch, antsy on his feet. "Band's in a transition period right now. Don't have all the answers. But I can assure you we'll be making music together. Nothing is gonna change that."

He scribbled something on his notepad, but I could feel the flicker of his eyes as they peeked at me from the side. The curiosity that wouldn't let him go. The awareness.

Almost in frustration, he turned his full attention on me. "Are you sure I don't know you?"

Shaking my head again, I took another step back, slinking behind Lyrik, hating the way I wished his shadows would swallow me up and take me to a place where I could disappear.

Hide.

Hide. Hide. Hide.

I was so damned tired of hiding. Of running from everything that scared me, but I didn't know how to handle this when I'd been running for so long. I didn't know how to bear the brunt of it.

How to stand up under the sudden recognition that lit on his face.

I was peeking out from behind Lyrik when the reporter suddenly shook his index finger my direction, the smile on this guy's face making it clear he had no idea he'd knocked me from the precarious foundation I'd created.

Where I'd balanced on unstable ground.

Knowing one day, one side would eventually give out.

"Yeah…yeah…you're that girl. Tamar Gibson. Madeline Shields…she was from here…L.A. That whole thing is about to go to trial in Arizona, right? Saw something about it come across the feed last week."

He frowned as the full story seemed to dawn, sudden confusion setting in. "Are they still looking for you?"

And that was it.

The bottom finally crumbled out from under me.

Darkness pressed in as a horror of memories came crashing through my mind.

Madeline Shields.

Pain lanced through my being like the cut of a rusted, dulled blade.

Paralyzing.

My legs wobbled as my heart and knees went weak.

All functions gone.

"Blue." Lyrik was suddenly there. Holding me up.

Protectively, he wound his arm around my waist, let me bury my face in his chest. "Think that'll be enough questions for tonight."

He began to guide me through the shadows and voices and bodies. He brought his free hand up to my cheek, pressing me closer, covering the part of my face still exposed.

Blocking.

Shielding and sheltering.

Lyrik squeezed me tighter, his voice an echo on the fringes of the world I'd disappeared to. "It's okay, baby. Ten more feet. Just need to make it out this door. I've got you. Not gonna let you go. I've got you."

My hands curled tighter into his shirt, and I could hear the hushed murmur of his voice mixed with another man's, the scrape of a metal door as it was opened.

Fresh air breezed across my damp, sticky flesh, wiping away the grime of the theater.

But there was no relief.

It was just another layer exposed.

Another sweep across the dirt.

Revealing my forgotten reality.

Madeline.

I hadn't allowed her name to enter my thoughts in years. There was too much guilt. Too much shame.

Now I almost buckled beneath the weight of it.

Lyrik helped me into the backseat of the waiting SUV. The black leather was cold against my already clammy skin. Sliding in, he curled me back in his arms.

"I've got you," he whispered at the top of my head.

"I'm so sorry," I mumbled through the old grief. But I'd kept it in for far too long.

"Shh…don't apologize. You've got nothing to apologize for. Nothing. You're safe. You're safe."

And I remembered that voice and those words.

Lyrik.

The night he'd first found me. When he'd first unearthed everything I'd buried like a cursed relic.

"Lyrik." It was pain. Torment. Regret.

"Shh…baby…I've got you…I'm not gonna let anything happen to you."

"Promise?"

"I promise," he said.

The ride sped by in a blur of memories as I finally fully opened the door.

Opened it for everything to come rushing in.

Every fear.

Every hope.

Every memory.

I opened myself to every wound that had never healed.

I let every single one of them invade.

It was time. It was time. It was time.

I was so tired of being the girl I was not.

And I missed her. Tamar Gibson. The girl Cameron Lucan had tried to destroy.

Just like he'd destroyed Madeline Shields.

It seemed only seconds later when the SUV came to a stop. Lyrik opened the door, quick to slide out, hands careful as he helped me stand.

"Can you walk?"

Through bleary eyes, I nodded, and he wound his arm back around my waist, supported me as we started across the cobblestone drive.

With each step, I somehow felt stronger and stronger.

Braver and braver.

Unchecked, tears streaked down my face.

Once, I'd believed they made me weak.

But now. There was power in their presence.

And I felt a little crazed. Maybe a little insane. To feel so much turmoil and welcome it all the same.

Lyrik fumbled in his pocket and took out his keys. He opened the door to the massive house he called home. The expansive windows on the other side of the huge living area opened up to the pool and the sparkling city below.

He didn't hesitate, just turned me to the right and led me upstairs and down the hall to his room.

I'd only been in it for a few minutes this afternoon before we'd had to leave for his parents'. But it felt so much like him. Dark and filled with mystery, the corners filled with shadows that ached to tell the same story he had written across his skin.

Releasing me, he quietly latched the door shut behind us.

Standing in the middle of his room, I turned to look at him.

For once, I was hiding nothing.

Open and free.

And it hurt and it hurt and it hurt.

And it felt so amazingly right.

He cradled my face.

Softly.

Gently.

"Tell me who you are."

Unable to remain standing, I slowly sank to my knees.

Without releasing my face, Lyrik followed.

Tears clogged my throat. "All I ever wanted to do was forget. But I can't do that anymore, Lyrik. I feel *too* real. Too much like me. Who I used to be."

He nodded like he got it, a prod of encouragement.

I found my voice. "You remember I told you…that I escaped. When I escaped, I escaped from Cameron Lucan."

I hadn't voiced that name in so long.

Lyrik gritted his teeth, the sound an audible grind as he clenched and winced and fought the anger the utterance of it so clearly evoked.

Anger for me.

Was it wrong to love him more for it?

My tongue darted out to wet my lips. "Like I told you, when we first got together, it was good and then it got to where it wasn't so bad. Looking back now, I realize he was acclimating me to his lifestyle. Desensitizing me. Convincing me his twisted desires were my own. Robbing me of all my confidence and self-preservation until I'd completely submitted to his will."

I drew in a breath. "It didn't take him long to persuade me to cut ties with my family. He told me they were only trying to keep us apart. I'd moved in with him before things had gone bad…back when I'd willingly let him use me, even though I knew in my gut something was wrong."

I glanced to the floor, before letting myself look back on the severity of those eyes that had deepened to pitch. "It got so horrible, Lyrik, so bad so fast and I had no idea how to get out. I'd pray for death."

The words had gone raspy. "For it all to end. He'd leave me tied up in this room in the dark where I'd be disoriented for days. Hungry. Not sure when he would return and when he did return if he'd come alone."

Lyrik's muscles twitched. A palpable rage skimmed just below the surface. It lifted and rose and shivered in the air.

Yet there remained a gentle softness to him that had never been there before.

This beautiful boy had always been both cautious and heedless when it came to me. His touch gentle in its aggressive demand.

But I felt the shift as I took him with me to that place where I'd never wanted to return.

Images flashed. I blinked, viewing them like old, faded snapshots I hadn't known were taken yet somehow intimately recognized.

"I lost sense of time, but I would guess it had to have been about six months after he started holding me in that room upstairs when I woke up to him dragging another girl into it."

Old horror circled and circled. I could barely speak. "I guess in the time he'd been isolating me, he'd started the same process with Madeline. Making her fall for him and his lies. Cutting ties with her family. Convincing her she was nothing without him. Making her wholly reliable upon him until he had her where he wanted her. No resources. No fight left to fight."

I squared myself, the words suddenly strong as I looked up at his blistering expression. Anger restrained in agony. As if he both wanted to stand up right then and hunt Cameron down yet refused to leave my side.

I touched his cheek. "But he hadn't broken all my fight, Lyrik. It was still there, buried deep. I watched and waited. Listened. Counted the knots in my ties. Memorized them until I could untie them in my head."

I gulped. "In the corner, he'd…left a video camera on a stand for days. Taunting us."

My skin crawled with the thought of it.

"I waited until I heard his motorcycle start up and drive away. It was so clear in my head. Untying myself. Untying Madeline. Running. Jumping. But she seemed so shocked when I was suddenly out of my bindings, and she screamed when I smashed the window with the camera."

On the waves of the memory, the words broke in my throat and I looked at the bare wall over Lyrik's shoulder as I forced out the confession.

"Madeline…she was too scared, Lyrik. Too scared to jump. Too scared to leave. She begged me to stay. Begged me not to leave her there alone. I'll never forget the defeat in her eyes when I looked at her one last time, giving her one last chance, before I climbed out onto the eaves of the second-story roof."

Everything rushed out. "But I was the coward, Lyrik. I was the coward because I just *left* her. Left her without a word and ran. I never looked back. Madeline had made her choice and I'd made mine. I never picked up the phone because that would mean I'd have to voice what Cameron had done. It was so much easier to pretend it'd never happened. Easier to become someone I wasn't. Someone *no one* could touch."

No one until him.

Lyrik's hold was fierce. Unyielding. Those eyes searched every inch of my face.

Sorrow shook my head. "I didn't know they'd found her body until a year later. I…I was missing my mom so bad. I signed into my old Facebook account…just needing to see her face. There was an article I was tagged in linking all of us…one naming me as a missing person after they'd discovered her. They were looking for Cameron as a person of interest."

Lyrik squeezed me tighter, voice as harsh as broken glass, disbelief and so much hate. "He killed her?"

I shook my head as more tears broke free, begging for him to understand. "No, Lyrik. She killed herself. He dumped her. Just left her like garbage. He was gone when the police showed up at his house. They finally caught up to him and arrested him. He's…he's getting ready to go on trial."

The room swam, the decision dangling over me like a noose. Run.

Or turn around.

"Jesus." Everything about Lyrik softened with a thready caution. He dragged the back of his hand across the tears soaking my cheeks before he knitted his fingers through my hair.

"Blue. I want to destroy him. Never wanted to hurt someone the way I want to hurt him. Can't fucking stand it…thinking about someone hurtin' you. What can I do? Tell me what to do and I'll fucking do it. Say it and it's done."

I gripped him by both wrists and rocked toward him. "Kiss me."

Two months ago, he'd promised to erase Cameron Lucan from my body. To touch me and fill me until I knew nothing but his name.

But it was Lyrik who made me remember mine.

There was zero hesitation. Lyrik hauled me up against the warmth of that strong body. Mouth overwhelming.

But this kiss. This kiss was so excruciatingly slow.

Deliberate.

Measured.

From every wisp and tug of his lips over mine to every flick of his tongue.

An intentional dance.

Unhurried yet brimming with need.

Barely contained.

I felt dizzy on it.

"So brave. So fucking brave."

And we spun and we spun and we spun.

Searching hands. Heedful touches.

Edging back, he dragged my shirt over my head, whispered, "Blue."

A cool rush of air prickled my skin, my flesh covered in chills as he leaned in and kissed across the upper curve of my shoulder.

My head dropped back.

His mouth fell fervid at my neck.

Hot hands at my sides.

I fumbled under his shirt and pulled it free. My hungry gaze roamed, as if I could decipher each bunch of his muscles, the flex and the bow, the smooth skin covered in tantalizing ink.

My eyes wandered, just as greedily as my hands as I touched and explored, drunk on freedom and lust.

My spirit unchained.

Shackles released.

Callused fingertips trailed over the warped heart imprinted on my chest. Translating. Communicating.

Guard your heart.

It was his.

I shivered with his kiss that was just as cautious when he pressed it there.

Oh God. This man.

I arched up on my knees to meet him, my hands fisted in his hair. His mouth moved delicately across the lacy fabric of my bra, his breath like a warm caress across my skin.

A tiny mewl slipped from between my lips and I held him tighter. Closer as he licked then softly sucked.

The need to know him was greater than it'd ever been. His dark, dark spirit taking on shape and form. It snuffed out the air until the only thing I knew was him.

I slid my palms over both his shoulders, slipping down his arms. Across the designs. The pads of my fingers played across the song on his left arm and over the name hidden there.

Tell me who you are.

The question begged at my tongue, but was silenced by his when he suddenly moved to capture my mouth. Hand on the back of my head, he tilted his to the side, kissing me deeper, carrying me away into his twilight.

Tell me who you are.

Lyrik scooped me from the floor and carried me to his bed. He laid me in the middle, never letting me go as he climbed over me.

Enclosing and surrounding and engulfing.

But where Lyrik and I normally lit, we smoldered.

His movements were controlled. Purposed. He edged back, never releasing me from the grip of his gaze as he lifted me by the ankle and unzipped my boot, turned and did the same to the other.

That bold, beautiful body inched forward to flick at the buttons on my jeans, my pulse going wild as I was eclipsed by his shadow.

A sigh puffed from between my lips as I lifted my hips to help him.

He dragged them down, taking my underwear with them.

"Blue," he whispered at my belly, hand palming the apple on my thigh.

"What have you done? What have I done?" It was all a jumbled whir, lost to the energy.

I shuddered, pinned to his bed by the weight of his intensity. His severity so dense and dominant I felt our spirits coalesce.

There was nothing but us.

My head spun, dizzy on this feeling.

Light. Light. Light.

He was suddenly over me, that beautiful body bare, guiding himself into me.

Whole.

Never before had I felt so whole.

He gripped me by the back of the neck, our chests pressed close, the thunder of our hearts the only quickening in the room.

He rocked forward, slow and somehow desperate.

A soft moan fluttered from between my lips.

Those bottomless eyes latched onto mine in the darkness, his mouth a breath from mine.

He pinned my wrists over my head.

His body worked a steady beat, a frenzy barely kept at bay.

A raging storm contained.

Our pants leapt into the air.

"Lyrik," I gasped out.

He swayed and pitched, buried his face in my neck as he released my wrists. My arms were around him, holding him close as he rocked and drove and pled. "Blue...what have you done? What have you done?"

"Lyrik...please..." It was a petition unnecessary, because I was already rising to the top where pleasure gathered fast.

"Blue."

My body stretched tight beneath him as I came undone.

Lost.

Where I floated in the darkest skies. Where I drifted through clouds that rumbled their threat. Where I glided through the danger of this building storm.

The buzz before the strike.

Lyrik jerked and his mouth dropped open, this volatile boy clinging to me. Unhinged. Fingers dug into my skin.

Almost painfully, the words came from his mouth like distress.

"You sing my soul."

So quiet.

Yet deafening.

You sing my soul.

Everything froze. The spin of the room and the hammer of my heart and the panicked boy who lay stock-still on top of me.

It was unmistakable.

The grief that suddenly poured into the room, seeping from his pores and from the shattered breaths from his lungs.

"What did you say?" I didn't mean for it to come out so needy, but I couldn't stop it from fleeing the confines of my mouth.

Because I needed to know.

I tried to edge him back. To see his face.

He jerked his head to the side. Jaw rigid. Throat tight.

Still refusing to look at me, he slowly rolled out of bed.

Nothing was said as he slipped on his underwear and jeans, the silence suffocating as he buttoned them.

He snatched his shirt from the floor and yanked it over his head.

The whole time I lay there with his sheet clutched to my chest. Shocked. Stunned. Both joyed and terrified.

"What did you say?" I begged again.

"Nothin," he mumbled with a rake of his hand through that dark hair.

I clamored off the bed. "Don't tell me it was nothing when we both know it was something."

He looked at me. Hard and furious. "Said it was nothin'. Drop it."

I grabbed his arm. "Lyrik."

He shook me off and headed for the door.

What the hell?

I dressed as fast as I could, on his heels as I chased him down the stairs.

Ash and Zee were just coming through the front door as we hit the landing.

Shit.

But I wasn't letting this go.

I refused to let go of this rigid, impenetrable man who was so obviously broken.

Because God, maybe he needed me just as badly as I needed him.

Maybe he needed a little saving, too.

It didn't matter who was there to witness it.

I didn't care.

Because what I cared about was him.

What I cared about was what he said and what it meant and where it would lead *us*.

"Lyrik, please," I begged as I grasped at the tail of his shirt.

Lyrik spun around. The words he spat from his tongue were low and vicious and vile. "Please, what, *Red?*"

He was looking at me like I was garbage.

Dirty.

"Don't pretend you don't know what this was," he continued. "Two months and you got what you wanted. You fuck like a pro. Congrats."

A strangled gasp wheezed into my lungs and I recoiled. Mortified. Slammed with a misery so great it nearly dropped me to my knees. After everything I'd revealed to him. After what I'd trusted him with. And *this* was his response?

My hand cocked back before I could stop it, and I barely registered the force of it as it flew through the air toward that too-fucking-pretty face.

Guess I was right all along.

Lyrik West was nothing but a bastard.

LYRIK

*T*here are times in your life you know without a doubt you're doing everything wrong.

When you know you're nothing but a liar and a bastard and a cheat.

Hands down, this was one of them.

It was like watching everything go down in slow motion while your mind's still set to real time.

Taking everything in while there's not a fucking thing in the world you can do to stop it.

Especially when you were the piece of shit who'd set it all into motion in the first place.

I could see it coming, and I braced myself for the bitter bite of her hand.

Welcomed it, really.

Hate me, Blue. Hate me.

It was the only option we had left. Not after I'd fucked it all up. The crack echoed off the walls.

Vibrating with the magnitude of the wound I'd just inflicted.

Hate me, Blue. Hate me.

I knew those words would cut her deep. But they were the only ones that could maybe undo the words that had left me without permission upstairs. The only ones that'd maybe keep this gorgeous girl from looking at me as if I were her savior and her light and her life.

Because God knew that's the way I'd come to look at her.

My cheek stung like a bitch when she drew her trembling hand away. Holding her wrist, she cradled her hand against her chest, her expression altogether horrified and hurt and maybe a little bit shocked that she'd actually hit me.

I deserved it.

I fucking deserved every repercussion that would come my way for letting loose *those* words from my mouth.

Both the ones that left me without permission upstairs and the ones spurred by this blinding panic still beating at my heart.

Who didn't deserve it was Blue.

Brave, beautiful Blue.

I wanted to shout a thousand apologies. To drop to my knees like a goddamned beggar and pray for forgiveness. But like she'd told me before, it was a good thing my apologies were rare because they didn't mean all that much anyway. And me opening my mouth now would only hurt her more.

Should have turned around and walked away the first time she made me feel *different*. The first time she filled me with regret and remorse. The first time she made me feel those flickers of joy.

Knew where they would lead.

And like a bastard, I'd chased her all the same. Again and again. Unable to let her go.

Selfish.

That's what I did. I took those bits of good I'd been given and crushed them.

And right now? There was no question that's exactly what I'd done.

Crushed up an innocent girl because I was too fucking weak to stay away.

My red-headed siren who was trying with all her might to stand tall, to pretend I hadn't just slayed her straight.

But it was those warm wells of blue that told no lies.

I felt it in my gut and it trembled around my blackened heart. That feeling I couldn't afford to feel.

You sing my soul.

God, this girl made me want more.

I looked away, to the ground.

Loyalty.

That was the one good thing I had, and it didn't matter how much this was killing me. How badly I was hurting her. This had to end. I had to stop this madness before it was too late. Before I obliterated the lines that I kept pushing and pushing further out. A fool to pretend like I wouldn't eventually cross them.

Slowly, Tamar stepped back, her head shaking as if she were trying to orient herself to the disaster that'd just gone down.

We'd been a bomb waitin' to go off.

That bundle of fireworks just waiting for a match.

And I just loved playing with fire.

"Fuck you," she finally said, her mouth trembling, soaked with the same tears that hadn't stopped falling since that kid had recognized her back at the club.

Yeah.

Fuck me.

Because all I wanted to do was reach out. Hold her. Beg her to stay when without a doubt it was past time for her to go. I'd already let this drag on for far too long.

When I didn't respond, she spun around and ran up the stairs. I could hear her banging around up there, and I was all of a sudden aware of the heat of Ash's glare burning like daggers into my back and the unease radiating off Zee where they stood in the niche of the kitchen entryway.

Just what I needed.

A damned audience while I cut down another life.

She came hurtling back down, suitcase bouncing on each step as she dragged it behind her. She blew by me like a tiny ball of fiery energy, yet so fucking big and profound.

This girl larger than life. All sex and sin. Pure and soft and sweet.

An enigma.

Temptation.

I raked a hand through my hair, feeling like my insides were getting ripped to shreds.

She headed for the door, not even glancing my way.

Panic flapped all around me like frantic wings and before I could stop myself I was calling her name. "Tamar."

She froze.

Shit.

Was that the first time I ever called her that? But I knew anything else would amount to nothin' but a snub. Another insult thrown her way.

Slowly she turned, and my gut clenched, because this girl was so damned beautiful it knocked the breath from my lungs. So damned pretty. And she was looking at me like she was begging me to beg her to stay.

Shit. Shit. Shit.

I dug my wallet from my back pocket and pulled out all the cash I had.

Six neatly pressed hundred dollar bills.

She was just standing there, dazed, lines of confusion darting all over her forehead. I urged them into her hand and closed her fingers around them.

Hopefully that'd be enough to at least get her home. To get her away from this place. Away from me. Where I couldn't hurt her like that bastard Cameron had done.

And I wondered just how different we were, me and him, destroying something so utterly good.

Finally, she looked up at me. Her eyes narrowed. A flash of *Red*. "What the fuck is this?"

I swallowed hard. "Money…to get you home."

Her face twisted. Offended. Words bitter and incredulous. "What? You think I'm your whore now? You think I want your money?" She balled it up, fisted it in front of her, before she threw it in my face. "You can go to hell, Lyrik West."

Not a problem.

I was already there.

She rushed for the double doors, yanked the right side open. It crashed against the interior wall.

She was halfway out it when she flew back around, like she'd changed her mind. "Do you know what?"

As she stared across at me with her chin lifted high, those bits of *Red* that'd tried to make a resurgence were gone.

And it was just my girl.

Blue.

Brave, beautiful Blue.

She pointed at the ground beside her, like she was staking a claim. "No."

No.

My chest tightened.

In all the times I'd begged her to tell me *no*, this was when she was going to use it on me? When I couldn't do anything about it? When I couldn't respect her in the way I knew I should?

Hate me, Blue.

"You don't get to do this," she said, taking a step forward as I took one back. "I've spent years hiding and I know what hiding looks like."

She touched her chest. "And I know you. What you said upstairs…"

I fisted my hands at my sides. Trying not to lose my cool.

"I don't know exactly what it *means* but I *heard* what you meant."

I rubbed my hands down my face, and she just kept on talking, like she didn't get she was completely tearing me apart.

"You asked me for two months. Two months, Lyrik. And in those two months you changed everything. You forced your way into my life, shook up everything I thought was right when the way I'd been living was so very wrong. You breathed the life I didn't know was missing back into me. I thought we had a time stamp. An ending. And it turned out you were just the beginning."

I squeezed my eyes closed, like maybe it could block her words from impaling.

Piercing.

Crucifying.

Except I was no saint.

Hope made its way into the sadness on her face. "I'm going home, Lyrik. Home to Arizona. To the place I've been running from for years. I'm going because you reminded me what it's like to be *brave*. You showed me it's okay to be scared and vulnerable. That sometimes that's the best place to be. And no, I'm not healed. I have a lot of scars to work through…"

She swiped at the tears still streaking like shimmery rivers down her face and sucked in a steeling breath. "And yeah, it's going to fucking *terrify* me to sit on that stand and testify against Cameron. But I'm going to do it because it's the *right* thing to do. Because I can no longer run from who I am. Because you made me stop and look at her."

She took a step back. With a shake of her head, she cast her attention to her feet, her grip firm as she held onto the handle of her suitcase.

Contemplating.

Finally, she looked back up at me.

So brave and bold. Vibrant colors. The darkest dark and the most blinding light.

"I love you, Lyrik West. And when I walk out that door, I promise you, it's going to hurt."

She stared me down. *"But you are worth all the pain."*

Grabbing the door handle, she turned to leave.

I gnashed my teeth so damned hard I was sure they'd be ground to nothing but powder, fucking forcing myself not to respond. Not to give in when that was the only thing in the world I wanted.

Because all I wanted was her.

But I couldn't have her.

Told her before, my heart wasn't mine to give.

But fuck, if it didn't feel like she was taking all of it with her tonight.

Pausing, she slanted one last glance over her shoulder. "And for the record, I think we were the best idea you ever had."

Then she softly clicked the door shut behind her.

And I let her go.

Like Ash said.

Most of us just broke our own damn hearts.

I stood there staring at the blank space where she'd been.

Hating myself.

Hating my choices.

Wishing I could go back and erase it all.

Somehow make it right.

"So that's it…you're really gonna stand there like a straight-up pussy and let her walk out that door?"

My eyes shot to the right where Ash and Zee were standing.

Shit.

I'd all but forgotten they were standing there, bearing witness to the shit-storm that continued to dominate my life.

"Nothing's changed, Ash. Told you that before."

Zee stepped forward, disappointment in the shake of his head. "Fuck you, Lyrik. I'll go make sure your girl is safe at one-fucking-o'clock in the morning."

He stormed out the door, slamming it shut behind him.

I winced with the loud clash of wood. At the truth of his words. At my actions. But I had no fuckin' idea how to make this right.

Ash scoffed low, voice even quieter. "You think everyone around here doesn't know why you always take two, man? Why it's too dangerous for you to have one girl, because you might just get close? Seems to me *something* has changed."

He edged forward. There was something hostile about his approach. A ripple of anger and a rush of disgust.

Or maybe they were just reflections of my own.

Cocking his head to the side, he pinned me with a glare. "You really think Kenzie—"

He might as well have struck me in the face. Kicked me in the gut. My entire body reeled with the impact of her name.

My chest squeezed, heart slamming in its confines.

Ash caught it. His face pinched in slow disbelief, and he huffed out a breath. "You can't even say her fucking name, can you? All this fucking time, and you can't even say her name."

"Stop," I warned. Fighting. Fighting the anger. Just didn't know who I was most angry with.

He kept right on, coming close, digging it in like a razor-sharp prod staked into my spirit. "You really think *Kenzie* is somewhere across town, jabbing needles in a black-haired Voodoo doll? Cursing your name? Hoping you're rotting in hell?"

My laughter was brittle. Breaking like everything else inside me. "After what I did? You really think she's not?"

He scoffed. "The only hell you're in, man? It's the one you created. You sentenced yourself, Lyrik, and that's exactly where you're gonna rot if you don't wake the fuck up and look at what's right in front of you. Look at what you've been given…"

He flung his arm out to the side. "Because you just let the best damned thing that's ever happened to you walk out the front door."

Fucking Ash and the way he saw shit.

I shook my head, voice cold like a slow chill. "You know I can't keep her."

He sobered. "When are you gonna stop blaming yourself?"

I swallowed around the lump sitting like a rock in my throat.

He took another step forward, a move that seemed both pleading and predatory. "What about me, man? You still blamin' me? You think it doesn't kill me to know I had a part in it? Kill me to remember I was the one who'd convinced you to go that night?"

Emphatic and hard, his words were strained where he spat them close to my face. "Kenzie was a nice girl. And yeah, you fucked up. You fucked up bad. We were all so messed up then, doing everything wrong, making mistake after mistake. And I know it cost you the most. But I'm so fucking done with this. So done with you thinking you don't deserve to live. You lost, too, man. She wasn't the only one who got hurt by that whole mess."

I turned my head to the side, tone like grit. "I promised."

315

He took a step back. "Yeah? Tell me what difference that promise has made? Who's it benefited? Not her and sure as hell not you."

"I promised. Not gonna go back on it now."

Not ever.

He laughed, though there was nothing amused about it. "You and your fucked up sense of loyalty. You think I didn't see that bastard Eric at the after show tonight? And you know what, Lyrik. I'm glad you turn your back. That you won't let him fill it with all his bullshit. But you do it for the wrong damned reasons. You do it out of obligation. You might as well sign with them...because we don't need that kind of loyalty. Only thing you're really loyal to is your misery."

I pushed him out of my way, swiping the back of my hand across my mouth like it could wipe away some of the bitterness, forcing down the hatred boiling out. Needing air, I headed for the huge sliding doors that led to the pool.

Yanking the sliding door open wide, I didn't slow, not even when Ash's voice pelted me from behind, "Tell me, Lyrik! What fucking good is that promise? Who's it helping? You here with us because you care about us? About the band? Or are you doin' it because you think you owe us?"

As soon as I was outside, I gripped my head while the sounds of the night shouted around me, the rustle of the cool breeze rolling with the remnants of a party happening below, the dull hum of bugs held fast to the trees. All of it hit me like an echo of the loneliness I felt crawling over me like a disease. That gaping hole just getting larger and larger.

In the distance, thunder rolled.

My chest felt so damned tight. So tight I was sure I couldn't breathe.

I could almost see their faces, flickers of memories sent to test and taunt.

I could almost hear her name on my tongue.

But when I screamed, the name on my tongue was *Blue*.

LYRIK
SIX YEARS EARLIER

It was 11:47 on a Saturday night. Didn't know when life had become one endless party. Maybe it'd been gradual. Maybe overnight. Really, the last year was nothin' but a blur of highs and lows, moving into the small house with the guys, writing music, begging venues to take us, and feeling like we were living the all-American dream at the same damned time.

Music blared from the speakers, and I sat on the dingy, worn-down couch with my baby cradled on my lap, stroking her strings and caressing her body. Feeling that stir inside me, something

A.L. Jackson

powerful, like it was my soul bleeding the song.

Ash was all hyped up, the guy spouting off about how big *Sunder* was going to be as soon as we got our break to a handful of strays who'd made their way in. Kinda the way everyone did. No home. Lost. Feeling abandoned and looking for a purpose to claim.

Apparently, this was the place to find it.

Mark was in the corner, eyes mere slits, getting lost in his own isolated world. In the old recliner inclined to the right of the couch, Sebastian was already nodding out from the poison he'd pumped in his veins, and his kid brother Austin was sitting on the floor, nose pressed to the TV so he could hear above the disorder while he played a video game.

No doubt this wasn't the best atmosphere for him, witnessing shit no thirteen-year-old kid should see. Wasn't the worst, either. Had to be better than him getting knocked around by the asshole who was supposed to be his father, anyway.

Right in front of me was the coffee table. Lined up on top of it in a perfect row were five shots the color of licorice.

Beside them were three fat lines of coke.

I was just getting started.

I barely looked up with the knock at the door and the turn of the knob, the lift of voices as a new group of people piled in. Ash was all welcome and hospitality as he shook a couple hands and patted a few backs.

But it was a tingly awareness that had me lifting my head.

Brown eyes peered back at me.

Wide and curious.

Both shameless and shy.

They wandered my face, over my guitar, down to the shit littered on the coffee table, back up to me.

Whole time, I just stared.

Maybe it was the high getting the best of me.

That rush of adrenaline beating my heart like the roll of a drum, just waiting to propel me on to something great.

But there was no question I had to have this girl.

Her friend touched her arm to get her attention, and reluctantly, she dropped her gaze and followed her into the kitchen. Ash slung his arm around her friend's shoulders, no doubt whispering something saccharine obscene.

Clearly, Ash had done the inviting.

But I was all too happy to participate in the taking.

She accepted a drink Ash poured. They filed back into the living room and grabbed a seat. And I could feel her edging in closer, just like I felt compelled to move her direction.

The night moved on, a blur of shots and lines and shouted voices, the music nonstop.

Still the girl remained my focus. My eyes drawn. Dick hard.

Wanting her more and more with every glimpse of brown eyes below those dark, dark lashes. Her tight little body begging to be devoured, skinny jeans and a ripped-up black T-shirt tied at the back where she constantly teased me with flashes of her milky-white skin.

Ash kept plying her with drinks, and I smiled when she was suddenly sitting next to me, sidling closer with each shot we took. I shared one with her. Wiped the droplet of liquor that clung to the edge of her upper lip. I licked it from my thumb. Then my mouth was on hers, and she was straddling my lap.

Kissing me and kissing me, my hands in her hair, her nails in my skin.

I climbed to my feet, taking her with me, never breaking that kiss.

Swore to God, I'd never tasted anything so sweet.

It was a high unlike anything I'd known.

I carried her to my room, set her on her feet, kicked the door shut behind us. Darkness swam through the room. But this girl was all I could see. A shadowy angel striking like the best kind of sin in the hazy light filtering in from the window.

For a beat, we both just stared, panting, before I edged forward. She gazed up at me with those big brown eyes as she lifted my shirt. Fingers explored across the skin of my stomach, almost cautious, and damn if that wasn't the hottest damn thing I'd ever seen. Then she went to work on the fly of my jeans, and I was kicking off my shoes while ridding her of that top and her plain white bra.

I picked her up and tossed her on my bed.

The remnants of my morning high were sitting on a tray on the nightstand. I swiped my finger through the powder and crawled onto the bed, hovered over her as I licked my lips.

She seemed almost reluctant, those brown eyes wild when I dipped it into her mouth, before she was sucking with a moan and I was kissing her again.

And I felt like a king.

So damned powerful.

Like nothing in this world could touch me.

Nothing but this girl.

Disoriented, I blinked against muted beams of morning light slanting in through the window. A dizzy glaze of glitter tossed what looked like translucent daggers into my room. I blinked, trying to find the source of what'd pulled me from sleep. The sleep I really didn't want to let go of, considering I was pretty sure it couldn't have been more than half an hour since I'd fallen asleep.

Tangled with a girl.

The girl.

That fucking hypnotizing girl from last night.

She was standing at the side of my bed, peering down, looking at me like she was memorizing a secret she was forever gonna keep. Brown eyes intent but confused and a little bit scared.

God.

In the daylight, she was pretty. All lit up in the shimmery haze that danced around her mussed-up hair and cherubic face.

Really fucking pretty.

And really fucking young.

I scrubbed a hand over my face like it might rearrange the picture, then squinted at her. "What are you doing?" I finally managed to ask, my voice like gravel.

Her throat bobbed. Anxiously, her tongue darted out to wet her lips. She started to take a step forward, then seemed to decide against it. "I need to go," she said, so quietly I could barely hear her.

My squinting eyes narrowed. "Why?"

"I have to get home," she whispered, all nervous and agitated. "I'm already late…and if my dad…" She trailed off, leaving me to fill in the rest.

Motherfucker.

I shot all the way up, running both hands over the back of my head with my elbows propped on my knees.

The thin sheet just barely concealed the evidence of my naked body.

I turned my attention her way. "Tell me you're not sayin' what I think you're sayin'."

She winced, swallowed. "Last night…I…I don't do that…I mean…I have before but it was with my ex-boyfriend…but you kept looking at me…"

She waved her hand at me. "*And look at you*…and I was drinking…and…"

Panic started to bubble up in her words, and she shifted on her feet.

Guilt got me in a chokehold.

What the hell did I get myself into?

She was innocent. Yet still a little bit wild. Couldn't quite connect the dots between the two.

"Come here," I finally said.

She hesitated.

"Come here," I insisted again, softer, stretching out my hand, knowing doing so was just asking for all kinds of trouble. But I couldn't stop myself. I wanted to wipe away the shame on her face.

Okay. And I wanted to touch her again.

Yeah.

I really wanted to touch her again.

Finally, she gave. She curled her soft hand in mine and let me pull her back onto the bed. She straddled me, knees supporting her on either side of my waist. She held onto my shoulders and I let my hands go to her hips.

All that long, long hair billowed down around us like a veil.

Hiding away what never should have been.

Us.

Finally got the secret she had planned on stealing away.

My throat felt raw when I finally spoke, not having the first clue how to phrase it. Because damn, this girl had caught me off guard. "Listen…I'm sorry if I took advantage of you in some way last night. I didn't mean to hurt you. Had no clue you were…"

Clueless and a little bit scared of the answer, I looked up at her for help.

"Seventeen," she supplied, biting at her bottom lip.

"Seventeen," I repeated. I let that number roll around in my mind, coming to the conclusion the difference between that and twenty wasn't really all that bad. Right?

I set my palm on the warmth of her neck, feeling the erratic thrum of her pulse, my fingertips gliding into her hair. "I'm sorry if you regret last night."

She chewed at her lip a little more ferociously. "I don't regret it. Not at all. It was—"

"Kinda perfect," I said.

A breathy smile danced all over her mouth. Kind of like relief. Like she'd been wondering if she'd affected me the way I'd affected her.

If she only knew.

"Yeah," she said, eyes downcast and shy and sweet.

She glanced toward the door. "I really should go."

My eyes moved over her face as I made a decision. "What if I said I didn't want you to go?"

Redness splashed her cheeks, and the words rushed from her like a secret. "Then I'd say I really, really want to come back."

With a grin, I brushed the back of my hand down her cheek. "What's your name?" I asked.

She gave me the softest smile. "Kenzie. My name is Kenzie."

Kenzie snuck back into my bed the next night and the night after that, until it became routine. Until it felt strange when she wasn't there. As if I was missing a piece of myself. That piece ached on the nights when she couldn't slip out her window, when she had to hang low because the lies were mounting and her parents were becoming suspicious. The excuses and stories she spouted were beginning to do nothing more than point to our guilt.

She could only say she was staying over at her friend Tricia's house so many times.

She slid right into the scene like she'd belonged there all along. Partying with the best of us. Up all night with me before she'd slink back to her place just before dawn, stealing into her bedroom window she'd broken out of eight hours before.

Most of the time, anyway. This morning I woke with her still wrapped around me. Her head was on my shoulder, all that hair bunched in my face. I pressed my face into it.

"Kenz, baby, what are you still doing here? You have school."

Her head jerked up. Disoriented, she blinked. She looked at the clock on my nightstand. It read *11:48 a.m.* At least we could still call it morning.

"Shit," she muttered. Then she seemed to let the moment of panic go sliding by and she dropped her head back to my shoulder. "I can't do it, Lyrik. It feels like I haven't slept in days. I just want to stay right here…in this bed…all day."

Turning over, I moved to hover over her. "Think I like the sound of that."

She gave me a flirty grin, before we both froze with the sudden pounding at the front door.

"Just ignore it," I said.

But the pounding continued. Her phone lit up on the nightstand. She fumbled for it, then squeezed her eyes shut when she saw the number on the screen. Finally, she opened to me. "It's my dad. And I've missed like…ten calls from him."

She thumbed through her missed texts, shaking her head. "He showed up at school to talk to Tricia. She caved. Told him where I've been going. This is totally my fault," she whispered under her breath. "If I just would have gotten up."

The pounding increased, this incessant, demanding hammer.

I studied her for a beat, before I asked, "How do you want to handle this?"

"I have to go out there. He's just…worried. And I'm sure really, really pissed."

Guilt moved over her face, that innocent girl making a comeback. The one who didn't belong here.

Not at all.

"Coming with you then."

"I don't think that's a good idea."

I touched her face. "We can't hide this forever, Kenz."

"He's going to try to keep you from me."

"I know," I smiled down at her, "but he can't."

Something like affection smoothed her features before dread took her back over, and she gave a tight nod. We quickly dressed. The hammering at the door never ceased. I could almost feel the anxiety and torment that came with it, the desperation fueled by anger and worry and panic.

It only incited my own. My heart rate increased with each thunderous jolt. I was going through a million scenarios in my head, what I would say and what I would do. Because there was no chance I was going to deny Kenzie. Everything about that felt wrong. Not when me and this girl were so fucking right.

That same panic had taken Kenzie whole as she shoved her feet in her shoes and quickly ran her fingers through her hair to straighten it. Desperate to put on a disguise of innocence when it was clear the situation was anything but.

She headed from the bedroom and I followed. In the living room, the curtains were drawn, the place dimmed out but the evidence from the party the night before still strewn all about the room.

For two beats, Kenzie hesitated at the rattling door, sucking in a breath, before she clicked the lock and slowly opened it.

Immediately the knocking ended as a flood of blinding light gushed into the room. A sizzling outline of a single dark figure in the middle of it gave the perception of a man on fire.

No question, that's exactly what he was.

Kenzie just stood there with me five feet behind her, like a monster lurking in the dusky shadows.

For a moment it was utter relief. There was no missing it. Like the only thing in the world her dad wanted was for her to be okay. It took all of a second before the rage came rushing back.

"Get in the car." It was low and full of a threat.

"Daddy." She reached out a hand like she wanted to soothe

him. Ease him and beg him at the same time.

"There's nothing to discuss, Kenzie. Get in the car."

She hesitated and I took a step forward into the light.

Revealing myself.

Brown eyes, the same color as Kenzie's, flew up to clash with mine. But where hers were soft and sweet, his burned with hatred. It was barely contained.

"Get in the car," he gritted again, his attention fully locked on me, that glare holding the strength to cut me in two.

When she didn't move, he grabbed her by the elbow and yanked her out into the day.

She yelped, and I knew he wasn't hurting her, that this guy was only there to protect, but I couldn't stop myself from surging forward. I came to a hard stop when he forced her behind him.

A living wall of aggression.

His eyes wandered, scrutinizing, taking me in, adding me up. I stood there in my super-tight black jeans and ratted-out tee, the new tat I'd just gotten inked on the outside of my upper arm clear and standing out, black hair an unruly disaster.

That hatred deepened.

"You think it's fun to play around with a little girl?" he suddenly spat.

"I'm not a little girl," Kenzie argued quietly.

He threw a warning glance at her, before he was back on me, hostility increasing with every second that passed.

He pointed at me. "Stay away from my daughter."

I rubbed my fingers across my mouth, dropped my focus to my feet like they held an answer. Slowly I looked back at him, trying to keep any animosity from my tone. "That's gonna be a problem."

"A problem?" he seethed, stepping forward and jutting out his chest. "You are the problem, and I promise you, the next time you even look at my daughter, the police are getting involved."

Didn't mean to scoff, but it was there. "You and I both know nothing will come of that. You really think they care about a girl who's gonna turn eighteen in a few months and a guy who's twenty? No disrespect, but your daughter isn't a little girl anymore."

"Yeah? Well, she's *my* little girl. A girl who used to be a straight-A student. One I could trust not to tell me lies. And since she's been hanging out with the likes of you, that's all I get. A bunch of lies. Calls about her skipping school. Grades falling through the floor."

Like he'd just been struck with the thought to do it, his attention drifted into the living room. It left me wishing I'd done a quick sweep. So no, there was nothing concrete laying out, but the remnants were damned near incriminating enough.

It was blatant.

The intense pain that slammed him, gripping him whole like he'd had the sudden onslaught of a heart attack.

He seemed to have trouble standing. "You really want to drag *her* into your mess? Ruin her life? Look at you," he wheezed. It was something between an insult and him pleading with me to see reason.

Guilt spun through me again.

Winding me tight.

She *was* too good for this life.

"If you care about her at all, stay away from my daughter." The command was hard, lined with steel, sustained by his love for her.

And it fucking hurt. Standing there like a punk.

Knowing he was right.

Wanting to fight back, all the same.

Guess we both heard her crying softly at the same time, because the two of us cringed in response, before we tightened again.

The words were spoken barely above a breath. "Daddy…I love him."

I love him.

She'd never said those words before. And they terrified me, filled me up and left me flat.

What had I done?

He didn't respond to her, resentment still aimed at me. "Stay away from her."

He took her by the arm and dragged her out to the car waiting at the curb.

Kenzie pleaded with me from over her shoulder.

Do something.

And I wanted to. To change something. Just had no idea what that was.

Three weeks passed in a desolate confusion, me missing her like mad and filling my veins full of anything that might soothe it. So fucking high. So fucking low. Needing more and more and more. Of course, no one in the house noticed because they were all just as fucked up.

Sex, drugs, and rock 'n' roll, baby.

Never really knew what that meant until then. It was an endless cycle that gobbled you up before you even knew what was happening.

Just a bunch of heedless rats jumping on the rodent wheel.

Spin.

Spin.

Spin.

Of course, I was missing out on the *sex* part because no matter how many girls walked through the door, I was only waiting for her.

I texted her too many times and kept calling the same number that had been disconnected. Over and over again, like a fool expecting a different result.

They say that's the definition of insanity.

Wasn't going to argue the logic of that. I felt it. My brain slowly coming unhinged as my body gave.

In the bathroom, I regarded the red-eyed reflection staring back at me, splashed some cold water on my face as if it might clear the daze. Knocking my forehead into the bathroom mirror, I groaned.

God, I had to get myself together.

Scratching my head, I shuffled out, crossed the hall, and opened my bedroom door. I faltered to a stop and the breath punched from my lungs.

Sitting on the floor, leaning up against the far wall under the window, was Kenzie. She was a mess, cheeks stained with tears, hair matted in chunks where it clung to her soaked skin.

I shot across the room and dropped to my knees. Praying she

wasn't some sort of hallucination. I took her by the face. "Kenz...baby...you're here."

I was wiping away her tears with my thumbs, knowing it was stupid I was simultaneously smiling like a fool when she looked this way, but I couldn't help it.

She was here.

She sniffled and shuddered, breaking my hold as she brought her arm up to wipe away the tears with the sleeve of her shirt.

I ran my fingers through her hair. "What's wrong, baby, you don't look happy to see me." I tried to tease, hating the way she flinched when I said it. A slow dread laced with the relief I'd felt at finding her there.

She looked down, and I hooked my finger under her chin, forcing her to look at me. "Tell me what's wrong."

Her face pinched. "I'm pregnant."

I stumbled back. Knocked on my ass. "What? How?"

Incredulous, she laughed like I might be a little dense, the words oozing out like an accusation. "In the four months we've been sleeping together, did you ever use a condom? Did you ever take me to get pills?"

She pressed her fingertips into both eyes. "God. We're so stupid," she whispered. "So reckless and irresponsible. Just like my dad told me. He was right, Lyrik. He was totally right. I got so caught up in being with you, I never even thought about the consequences."

I'd backed into the bed, propped up on it as I looked at her. Helpless.

Tears kept streaming down her face, and I wanted to ask her what she wanted to do—what I could do—but all of a sudden she thrashed, like she were in physical pain. She wrapped her arms around her stomach, voice a flood of torment. "What if I hurt him?"

Jesus.

I guessed that was my answer, because Kenzie was holding herself like she was *holding* it.

And I was kind of in shock. Had no clue what I'd gotten myself into. How to manage the shift from five minutes ago to now.

But there was one thing I knew.

I moved to her, climbed to my feet while picking her up at the same time, one arm under her back and the other under her knees. I carried her to my bed and lay down with her curled up against me, whispered at her head. "I'm in this with you, Kenz. We can do this."

Gaze intense, she inched back so she could see my face. "I know we can, Lyrik. But I need to know if you *want* to."

A soft smile pulled all around my mouth. Maybe there should have been hesitation. There wasn't. "Yeah, I do."

She chewed at her bottom lip, hard…hard like it was difficult for her to say. "We have to stop."

I knew exactly what she was saying. What she was implying. Leaving the mess behind that was close to consuming me, the constant parties and drugs and endless nights.

"I know. I will." I kissed across her knuckles. "I promise."

A fresh round of tears slipped from her eyes, but these weren't so sad. "Tell me you love me."

I brushed the hair back from her face so I could see those brown eyes. Big and wide and full of trust. I gave her the complete and utter truth.

"You sing my soul."

I lay curled on the cold linoleum floor. Naked. Shaking. Freezing cold and sweating all the same.

I lurched, just making it back onto my knees to puke some more.

Everything hurt.

But they were worth it.

"What the fuck, man, you can't just leave."

Ash was on my heels, chasing me from room to room while I packed my things, like it was going to alter my decision.

I hoisted my guitar case to the table and lay my baby in the velvet. I snapped it closed. "Yes, I can."

"What about the band?"

A nagging ache tugged somewhere deep in my chest. It was

from that place where I'd grown up dreaming about me and the rest of the guys making it big. Dreams of playing the music I loved widespread enough that someone else might love it, too. It was all mixed up with my loyalty to the guys, my friends that had always been more like family than anything else.

But none of that mattered now. I glanced at Ash who was fisting his hair like it might wake him up from a nightmare.

I gave him a shrug that was somehow loaded with guilt. "You know I can't go on livin' this life and have a family. Two just don't mix."

"Why not? I mean, come on. You're just going to up and leave us hanging…after everything? We're so close, man. So fucking close I can taste it, and we can't do it without you."

I hefted the case from the table. "I'm sorry, but you're going to have to."

It was always a little bit awkward pulling up in front of the house of a guy you knew hated your guts.

For the last two months, I'd chilled at my parents' place, working my ass off at the shop where I'd gotten a job. I loved cars and bikes about as much as I loved my guitar, so it really wasn't all that bad of a gig. I'd saved every damn penny I'd earned except for the bit I gave my mom to cover my stay, scrimping enough together for the deposit and the first and last month's rent on a tiny one-bedroom apartment.

Maybe I shouldn't have been all that surprised when we found out Kenzie had pretty much gotten pregnant straight off. Could I really have expected anything else? But I guess when you're living in a haze day after day, you remain out of touch of reality, little thought given to repercussions and results.

But honestly, I couldn't say I regretted it or wished I could change it, even if ours wasn't the most ideal situation in the world. She made me fucking happy and I knew I made her that way, too.

I clicked open my door and she came running out. She was just now showing, her tiny frame giving way to her five-month bump.

After tonight she'd be going home with me. She was eighteen and finally mine.

Not that her parents hadn't thrown up all kinds of roadblocks, trying to keep us apart.

Maybe they wanted to see if I'd stick around.

Maybe they wanted to see if she'd change her mind.

But my dedication had never wavered or faltered in that time, even when I'd been threatened with arrest and a record tied to my name. Of course, that's all any of it had turned out to be.

Threats.

She threw herself in my arms, and I lifted her, swinging her around. "Happy Birthday, Kenz."

"Best birthday ever," she squealed through her excitement.

Yeah. She most definitely had not changed her mind.

Laughing, I set her down, wrapped my hand up in hers. "You're really gonna put me through this, huh?"

She stepped out in front of me, still holding my hand, grinning as she walked backward and led me up the walk. "How are they supposed to fall in love with you if they don't know you?"

"I can think of quite a few things I'm sure your dad would rather do to me than *fall in love*," I said, letting the sarcasm drip free.

She giggled. "Oh, come on, don't be a wuss. There's a whole lot to love. On both sides. They're not all that bad. You'll see. My dad wants the best for me. He just doesn't always know what that is."

I gave her a wry grin. "And you think that's me?"

"I know that's you."

That was the thing about Kenz. She loved her family, and she'd been their sweet, innocent girl, destined for great things, until she'd run too fast into the speed bump that was me.

I shoved off the niggle of guilt.

The fact I'd derailed the direction of her life.

But I guess she'd done a little derailing herself.

"Don't be nervous," she mouthed as she opened the door.

She wanted all of us close, and I was willing to suffer through a night with her parents if it made her happy.

It was her birthday, after all, and after this evening, I was stealing her away. I knew that fact couldn't come easy for either of them.

I adjusted the collar on my button-up shirt, shifted in the dress slacks I'd worn to put my best foot forward.

"He's here," she called as she led me through the living room toward the kitchen. Their place was nice, everything in order and tidy and clean, so much different than the chaos that reigned at my parents' place. Her dad was a public defender, so he wasn't close to raking in the bucks, but I knew it kept them comfortable.

What wasn't comfortable was the silence that solidified the air in the kitchen when we walked in.

Her mom was at the stove, frozen mid-turn, her father with one hip leaned up against the counter and his arms crossed over his chest.

Going rigid and hard the second his sight caught on me.

Sure.

I'd spoken to them both before.

Multiple times.

But it'd never exactly been on friendly terms.

It was her mother, Deborah, who finally broke. A stiff smile cracked her face. "Lyrik…welcome to our home."

Kenzie gave me an encouraging glance.

See.

"Thank you for having me," I returned, gaze sliding to her father then back to her.

In what seemed like disgust, he shook his head, before he seemed to come to a decision. He breathed out heavily as he extended his hand. "It's nice to see you again, Lyrik."

I was hoping someday that might actually be true. That he'd really think it nice to see me. I mean, I'd dropped the band. The lifestyle. Got clean. All for them. Was hoping eventually he'd see that when it came to his daughter, all my intentions were good.

I shook his hand. "Thank you, sir."

He eyed me warily, before he shook his head again, this time with a resigned laugh. "Come on, let's eat."

It really wasn't as bad as I thought it would be, making conversation with Kenzie's parents, seeing how much they cared, so much like mine. All any of them wanted was for our lives to be good. Of course, there would be some differences on what that looked like, but I was going to do my all to make sure Kenzie's life was good. To make sure *his* life was good.

Yeah. *His.* We'd seen him on an ultrasound two weeks ago. It was kind of mind-blowing, seeing just what was happening inside her, that he was real and whole. Heart beating. They said everything looked good. He was strong and growing fine. Since then, the shrouded fear and guilt Kenzie had seemed to wear the whole time had vanished.

After we ate dinner, Deborah brought out a round cake and set it in the middle of the table. A ring of eighteen candles burned around it. Kenzie glanced at me before she closed her eyes for a beat, making her wish, then blew them out.

Deborah's cake was all kinds of delicious. I told her so and she grinned a genuine smile. Kenzie moved to her father sitting in his chair, wrapped her arms around his neck, and kissed his cheek. "Thank you, Daddy."

He sighed, then smiled. "Anything for my girl."

"I love it," she said as she spun in the living room furnished with the shabby couch my parents had given me, a scratched-up coffee table I'd picked up at a used store, and the TV from my bedroom back at the house I'd shared with the guys.

"It's small." It almost came out a pout as I felt a sudden rush of self-consciousness.

She smiled. "It's ours."

She turned fully toward me. Sobering. Voice soft.

"Tell me you love me."

I took a single step forward. Touched her face. "You sing my soul."

"I'm so grateful for everything we got today, but I have to admit, this is my favorite," Kenzie whispered into the calm, clutching the mismatched patchwork teddy bear.

A smile fluttered around her mouth, eyes flicking down to meet mine. "I can't believe you made this."

It was a murmur. Deep and reverent.

That's what tonight felt like, as we lay curled up in the quiet darkness on our bed.

Knew the day had been both exciting and exhausting for Kenz. We'd had the baby shower my mom, sister, and Kenzie's mom had thrown together. Kind of liked it that the guys had been included, because I didn't want to miss out on watching her open her gifts.

Especially the one I'd made for our son.

She clutched the lanky bear, holding it close to her huge belly where Brendon grew. Her tank top was pushed up so that big bump was bare, her skin pulled taut, rivers of stretch marks forever signed on her skin. I was lying just a little lower than her, arms wrapped around both of them.

"Make it if you want it to matter." I chuckled softly as I repeated my mom's mantra. Kenzie did the same, those brown eyes warm and contented.

I ran my fingertips over the bear. It was an inconsistent pattern of blues, deep navy all the way down to ghost white. It was sewn with sapphire yarn, the pattern a little off because my hands could never quite get it right. Not the way my mother had mastered.

"It's not very pretty, but they're supposed to represent a family being stitched together by a new birth. Each piece of fabric represents the people who make up that family, the yarn the love that binds it all together. Mom says they're good luck."

Mom had always been a little out there. Subscribing to a kind of faith I wasn't sure I could ever have. But I sure couldn't disagree with her on this.

Kenzie whispered, "Your mom's amazing."

"She loves you," I told her.

Fingertips brushed down my face. "Because I love you."

Brendon kicked against my hand, and I couldn't contain the force of my smile as I pressed my mouth to her belly, the crazy amount of love palpitating within my heart. Shaking me all the way through. Seemed impossible to love someone I hadn't even met. Not the way I loved him.

Less than two months and he'd be here.

God, I couldn't wait.

"Come on, man, it's a one-time thing. Once. It's not gonna hurt anything."

I slid out from under the car I was working on. Ash sat above me on a stool, grinning with those dimples like I was some chick who couldn't resist his charm.

Idiot.

Still, I smiled, shaking my head. Because hell, I'd missed him. Had missed them all, that piece of my family that no longer quite fit.

"No can do, my friend. I've got a shit-ton to do and…well…"

Didn't finish up the rest.

Didn't need to.

All of them knew why I had to keep my distance.

Ash rubbed his hand over his face. "Listen, man, I totally get your reservations, but Justin totally bailed. We've gone through like five guitarists since you. And this show is big. Word is, house is gonna be crawling with labels and agents. We need you."

I wiped my hands with a greasy rag, feeling bad, knowing I'd left them in a jam.

"Five hundred bucks, Lyrik. Five hundred bucks for one night and you can walk. You know there's not a soul who's ever gonna fill your shoes. But I promise, we'll figure our shit out from there. We just can't miss out on this chance."

Five hundred dollars.

I could get that crib for Kenz, the one she'd been eyeing, the one we sure as shit couldn't afford. She'd settled on the bassinet my mom had given us. It'd work fine. For now.

Ash could sense my interest, my slow surrender, and he jumped on it. "One night," he promised.

I pinned him with a glare. "One night."

Sebastian clapped me on the back before he pulled me into a hug. "Lyrik…holy shit, man, I've missed the hell outta you."

"Shit, I've missed you, too," I said, grinning wide as I stepped back to take in the venue. It was bigger than anything we'd ever played, backstage set up like we were royalty, dressing rooms, bottled water, and a bar full of booze.

Okay, so maybe not royalty.

But sure as shit better than the holes we'd been playing the last three years.

The vibe was intense. I watched a little wide-eyed as roadies ran around to get things set up for the headlining band. A band I'd actually learned to play my guitar to when I was thirteen, sitting in my room and picking out the chords to some of their songs.

Never in a million years would I have imagined one day we'd be opening for them.

Loud music pumped from the speakers, people rushing this way and that.

Muted light seem to thrum with the beat.

My heart latched on to it, this awesome feeling spreading fast.

This had to be one of the coolest things to ever happen in my life.

Totally fucking surreal.

Ash was right.

This was an opportunity that couldn't be missed.

I shucked off the guilt trying to gain its voice, that little white lie sitting like a rock in the pit of my stomach. One I'd told Kenzie so I could get out of the apartment tonight, not to mention the fact I'd had to sneak my guitar into the trunk of my car while she'd been taking a nap.

My little sister needs me, baby. She's been having a rough time at school. Gonna hang with her a bit. One on one.

I just didn't want her to worry, and if she knew where I really was, she would.

Ash was jumping around, completely stoked. "Everyone ready to go on?"

"Hell yeah," Baz replied, slanting me a glance. "Feels like a reunion...way it's supposed to be...with Lyrik here."

And it did.

It felt fucking right, and when I stepped on that stage, I was feeling so damned high. Floating on those old dreams that I'd had to let go. But for one night, I was going to cling to them. *Live them.* I could only hope this would give something good back to the guys when I was the one who'd bailed.

The crowd was absolutely wild. Eating us up. Their bodies a living, breathing pulse where they thrashed on the floor in front of us.

It felt so good.

So right.

I played so hard it felt like my fingers would bleed—so out of practice—sang until my throat was raw and my spirit was soaring. The place was completely lit by the time we wrapped the last song on our set.

We all fumbled off the stage, high fives going up, everyone backstage telling us the show was as kickass as it felt.

Shots were passed around.

I hesitated with the tiny glass clasped in my hand.

"To the future," Ash said as he lifted his, and Sebastian and Mark repeated the same. I lifted mine. All four of us clinked them in the middle.

What the hell? It was tradition.

I tossed it back.

It burned sliding down my throat, pooled like fire in the welcoming well of my stomach.

I heaved a harsh breath through my nose.

Damn.

That tasted good.

And I didn't have a fucking clue why, but I was throwing back another. Then another. I found myself in a room backstage. The headlining band had just gone on, but the after-party was already in full swing.

I fucking twitched at the sight of the pile of coke Adrian was cutting on the table. Had known him for years, and the kid was nothing but a straight punk, following the hardcore scene, party to party, club to club, always at the ready with a supply.

He'd even been back at the house I'd shared with the guys a few times, more there for a delivery, though he played it off like it was his job to have a good time.

Didn't trust him.

Not at all.

But that didn't mean my mouth wasn't watering. That I didn't itch.

I forced my attention away, back to Sebastian who was talking to some agent. He'd introduced him as Anthony, and I struggled to engage in their small talk, doing my best to focus on anything but Adrian.

But there was no stopping it, the way my gaze kept getting drawn, my mind already there, kneeling at the table.

What could one little hit hurt?

I crossed the space, fisting my hands as I stared down at Adrian where he sat on the sofa.

Looking up, he grinned. "Well, well, well, if it isn't the infamous Lyrik West. Thought you'd gone and decided you were too good for us."

I wanted to tell him to fuck off.

Instead, I dropped to my knees. No different than a cheap whore, taking the rolled up bill and the proffered line.

But that was all it took for everything in my world to come into sharp focus. Tonight had to be right. My conscious sprinted ahead of the nagging wrong. The show. That fucking amazing show. Right here was where I belonged.

The rest of my crew joined in, the party raging on, growing by the minute. Between the four of us, we spent everything laid out on the table.

"What do you got?" Sebastian asked, swiping under his nose as he lifted his chin at Adrian, asking for more.

Adrian clucked. "You're at five hundred bucks, bro. Gotta see some cash."

Sebastian's eyes flashed. "What the fuck, man? You trying to rip us off now?" He flung his hand at the table. "That was like…two hundred…max."

"You still owe me from back at *Benny's* a couple of weeks ago."

"Paid you for that."

Adrian sneered. "What? You're calling me a liar now?"

Faster than anyone could make sense of it, Sebastian shoved the table forward. Adrian howled like a bitch when it rammed his shins. "Fuck yeah, I am."

Weren't usually a whole lot of people dumb enough to go up

against us, but this asshole climbed to his feet, glaring down like he was all too happy to take us on. He spat in Baz's direction. "Promise you, you don't want to start thinking you're gonna cut me short. That's a story that's not gonna end well."

Anger radiated from Sebastian. Seeping out. This diseased venom he'd caught the day one of his brother's had died.

Contagious.

Because I could feel those fangs sinking into me. It'd always been like that between us. Me and Sebastian feeding off the other, taking it out on whatever asshole got in our way.

Tonight it was Adrian.

Sebastian slowly stood, rising to the full height of his hulking mass.

"And just what exactly do you think you're going to do about it?"

I pushed to my feet beside him.

Aggression curled through my muscles, twisting and twisting until I was wound tight. That old feeling I hadn't felt in so damned long took me over. Something powerful and big. Bigger than life. Heart pounding wild, heavy in my hands and heavy in my fists.

Ash was suddenly a sensation in my periphery, everything else zeroed in on Adrian. His words just barely cut through the violence skimming beneath my skin. "Go home, Lyrik. You've got a baby coming. This night wasn't supposed to go down this way. You know you don't want this."

Kenzie.

Brendon.

Thoughts of them tried to break through to my rationale. Screaming at me to step back. But Adrian smirked, a looked so self-satisfied, nausea curled in my stomach. "Heard you knocked up that *Sunder* slut."

The scowl screwing up my face was almost painful, and I edged forward, pushing off Ash who tried to get in my way. "What did you say?"

Adrian laughed. "What…tell me you all didn't pass her around first. Bet you all still are. We all know how things roll with girls like that."

He smirked a little wider. "Know what…forget what you owe me…I'll head over to your place and collect from her."

It was like getting struck by an inciting fire, a bolt of energy that snapped you in half.

Because that's exactly what I did.

I snapped.

I had the bastard by the throat, pinned against the wall, squeezing like I didn't give two shits about his no-good life.

Deadbeat.

Sounded about right to me.

He was gasping, writhing at the wall, tips of his toes barely brushing the floor.

Sebastian landed three quick punches to his side.

I could feel the muscles in his neck rippling as he tried to catch a breath through the pain.

Ash got between us and pushed me back.

Scumbag slid to the floor, and Sebastian was on him, patting him down, pulling the bags filled with powder from his jacket pockets.

Figured it wouldn't hurt to grab a couple myself. I shoved three in my front pocket, shot the bastard my own smug grin. "You can count that as my payment. Think you're gonna say something about my girl? Think again."

I slanted one last kick to his stomach. A gurgled moan wept from his mouth, dude a balled-up sack on the grimy floor.

"Goddamn it." Ash dragged both his hands through his hair, eyes completely wild, rolling with fear as he looked at the crowd who'd gathered.

It was just then I noticed the entire room was watching us in horror. Like they'd just gotten a front-row seat to the freak show.

What have you done?

A voice pushed into my racing mind as my high started to ebb. I took a single step back with the shot of anxiety that hit me. Sebastian squeezed my shoulder. "Let's get out of here."

We started for the side door. Something like remorse and regret tickled through my senses, the bags in my pocket burning like guilt. The mistakes I'd been making all night long started to run through my mind as if on a reel. Mistakes I'd been making since the second I'd agreed to coming tonight.

What have you done?

A voice shouted out behind us, and I froze at the words, choppy as he coughed, but clear as day. "You better run, assholes, because you aren't getting away with this. You fucked with the wrong guy."

For a beat, I mashed my eyes closed, before Ash grabbed me by the arm and dragged me out, swearing under his breath. We stumbled into the late, late night. Cool air flashed against my sweat-slicked skin.

Jarring.

A waking slap to the face.

"What the fuck do you think you're doing?" Ash demanded as he shoved me away from him. He paced, huffed, brow curled up when he looked between me and Baz. "Taking his shit? You got some kind of death wish? Because I sure as hell don't."

Sebastian threw out a sound of scorn. "Guy's nothin' but a pussy. He's not going to do anything."

"Yeah," Ash shot back, "what about Benny? You really think he's just gonna sit tight after you ripped him off? This is stupid, man. Don't act like it wasn't. And in front of all those agents. I'm done with this bullshit."

Ash was done?

Agitation was setting in, and I dragged my hands over my head. "Gonna go get Kenz. Take her to her parents' for the night."

Shit. Shit. Shit.

I walked a couple circles as reality came sinking in. Was that what I was really going to do? Drag my pregnant girl out in the middle of the night?

"Said he's just a pussy, man," Sebastian tossed out, all nonchalant, leaning back on my car and shoving his hands in his pockets like he didn't have a damned care in the world.

"Not taking that chance with her."

"Go with him, Baz." Ash gestured to my car. "I'm gonna take Mark home. Dude can barely stand."

Sebastian shrugged. "All right then."

He climbed into my car and I sped the short distance back to my apartment building. Dread sloshed through me, sure and thick.

Fuck.

What have you done?

I hopped out and bounded upstairs, let myself into the quiet darkness of the apartment. This tiny home we had made that was supposed to be protected. Safe.

I slipped into our room and stuffed a couple things into a bag. Kenzie was asleep on her side, and I nudged her hip. "Kenz, baby, wake up."

She stirred just a little, squinting, before she smiled that soft smile. "Hey, you're home."

Guilt. Guilt. Guilt.

I swallowed around it. "Come on, baby, need to get you out of here."

Confused, she shook her head. "What are you talking about?"

"Come on. Please...just...trust me."

Trust me.

I bit back the cynical laughter, and instead focused on helping her out of bed, her belly so swollen it was amazing she could stand. She only had four weeks left and I wasn't sure how her tiny body could get any bigger. She wobbled, and I steadied her, trying to keep my cool, that frantic edge that nipped at my nerves as I helped her slip on a shoe.

"Tell me what's happening." She whispered her growing fear into the darkness. I could feel it. The tremble that rolled through her as she clung to my shoulders while I slipped on the second shoe.

I didn't respond, just grabbed her hand and started to haul her out of the house.

"Is Mia hurt?" She asked it as if the thought drew torment, this girl always thinking of someone else.

I wanted to say something. To come up with an excuse or another lie that would make this okay, but I was pulling her out into the deepest night, that quiet hour when the air held still in anticipation of the breaking day.

We started down the concrete exterior steps.

"Lyrik, please," she begged, but stumbled a step when she saw Baz climbing out the front passenger and moving into the back seat.

A surprised breath left her, and she was shaking her head and tugging against me as I towed her toward the car.

"Why's Sebastian here?" Her voice was quiet but tinged with accusation.

Didn't answer. Just jerked open the front passenger door and got her in, buckled her as fast as I could, tossed her bag on the floorboards at her feet.

I rounded the front of the car and climbed into the driver's seat. Engine still idling, I threw it in reverse. I was just short of peeling out of the parking lot as we flew out onto the road.

A bottled silence suffocated the air, like a carbonated toxin, shaken and shaken and shaken. Ready to explode.

Kenzie stared at me from the side, twisted with her back pressed to the door as if she could read me, her breaths sharp and barely controlled. "Lyrik, look at me."

Knuckles white, I gripped the steering wheel tighter, keeping my attention trained ahead.

"I said look at me," she demanded harder.

For a second, I resisted, head shaking several times, before I cut my gaze over to her.

Teeth clenched.

Jaw rigid.

Pain rushed up her throat. Strangled and hurt. "You're high?" She wheezed it as tears filled her eyes. "Oh my God. You're high. You promised…you promised."

She started struggling in her seat, fighting to get to the seatbelt latch. "Stop the car, let me out."

"No. Taking you to your parents'."

"I said stop the car and let me out," she wailed.

"Kenzie, cool it," I yelled. Didn't mean for it to come out the way it did, like I was lashing out, but she was freaking the fuck out, yanking at the door handle like she was going to bolt.

"Let me out!" she screamed.

Maybe it was the screech of her voice that let me know I'd

shattered our thinly set mold. Broken this good thing we could have had.

Crack.

Crack.

Crack.

At least my fucked-up mind thought it was her, physically rending our bond, my stupid mistakes cutting us in two. Until the blacked-out car sped around us on the left, Adrian leaning out and firing from the passenger-side window.

The windshield shattered.

I sucked in a shocked breath, yanking the wheel all the way to the right as I slammed on the brakes.

Sebastian was totally wrong.

Adrian wasn't a pussy.

He was crazy.

Out for revenge.

Because of pride and money.

Money.

That's what'd gotten me here in the first place.

Or maybe it was just my pride.

Base and vile.

Needing one more taste of everything I shouldn't have.

The car skidded and careened, the wheel jerking as I fought and pulled against it.

A street lamp pole came up fast. Streaks of light glinted in the splintered windshield. Head on, we slammed into it. The car came to a grinding halt.

Only sound was the ringing in my ears.

Stunned, I sat there still gripping the wheel as my mind raced to catch up with what'd just gone down.

Slow realization filtered in. We hadn't hit all that hard. The airbags hadn't even deployed.

I breathed out relief, shaking my head to orient myself, to clear the muddled hum deafening my left ear.

I blinked through that high-pitched trill, tried to focus on Kenzie who stared back at me with those wide brown eyes.

Wild and frozen.

Shocked.

Completely shocked.

"Kenz, baby, are you okay?" I finally whispered through the clogging fear. I was fumbling for my seatbelt when everything went completely numb.

Kenzie lifted her hand that been pressed to her side.

She was shaking so badly as she held it up in front of her. Confused. The color was so bright, almost shimmery as it glistened in the street lamp glaring from above.

Her fingers were dripping with blood.

"Kenzie! Baby! Kenz…where are you hurt?"

Frantic, I searched her.

High on her side, a red stain climbed fast across her shirt.

"Oh my God, Kenzie."

Hands shaking so damned bad, I fumbled with my phone and dialed 911.

What do I do?

What do I do?

"Please, hurry," I begged when the dispatcher answered.

What do I do?

Silence.

The ticking of the engine as it cooled. The hiss of the radiator.

Silence.

I wrenched open my door and stumbled out. Paced. Gripping my hair. I finally made it around the car.

Sirens blared in the distance.

I pulled open her door.

"Kenzie." It was a plea.

Lights blinded me from behind and paramedics came stampeding forward. Pushing me out of the way.

Suddenly, a flashlight was glaring against my eyes. It twisted me in knots, the look in the cop's eyes as he took me in.

Suspecting.

Adding.

Kenzie.

Her name was the only thing I could think.

I batted the flashlight out of my face.

345

Another officer was ordering Baz to get out of the car. Sebastian resisted, a snide "Fuck off" sliding from his mouth.

Next thing I knew, I was being shoved to the ground. Face down on the pavement.

"Stay down," a hard voice shouted as he stepped on the back of my neck when I fought to get to my feet, boot cutting into the skin, arms being wrenched behind my back.

My eyes were locked open wide in horror. Lights flashed and flashed and flashed, a dizzying whorl of colors and blips of sirens and pounding feet.

"Kenzie," I kept screaming as paramedics moved by, voices obscured and lifted and drowned out by the panic still ringing in my ears.

"Kenzie!"

Next to me, Sebastian was face down on the pavement, too. Wrists cuffed behind his back. The cop standing over him pulled the bags out of his pockets, one by one, at the same time another was patting me down.

Discovering my guilt.

Someone was reading me my rights, but the words were garbled together like I was hearing them underwater. Didn't care if they locked me up forever. Didn't fucking care. Just needed to know she was okay. That *he* was okay.

The officer dragged me to my feet.

"Kenzie...please...Kenzie. Please...just tell me she's okay. Please."

Please.

Hours passed. Each minute excruciating. Every second complete torture. In a holding cell, I sat on a bench with my back propped against the block wall, knees pulled to my chest, eyes closed in a silent prayer I didn't have any right to pray.

In it, I bartered my life.

As if it was worth anything at all.

The hands on the round clock sitting high on the far wall told me more than twelve hours had gone by since they'd left me in here without a word. Without any idea of what'd happened to either of them. Left me to my thoughts and self-hatred and fear.

Agony.

Hadn't slept in close to two days, and that low after my high was begging me to find sleep. To curl up so maybe I could just die.

Fighting the fatigue, I banged my head against the wall and shouted out another unheard plea.

"Kenzie."

Startled, I jumped when the lock buzzed and the heavy door gave.

I scrambled to my feet.

"Got a visitor, West. Let's go."

They shackled my wrists in the front, leading me down one long hall then another, before they ducked me into a small room, the walls the same dingy white like the cell.

But this one had a table in the middle, a single chair on the side closest to me and two on the other.

Doug Cartwright sat in one of the far two chairs, brown hair sticking up all over the place like he'd run his hands through it a million times, cheap suit wrinkled, tie loose, eyes red.

Dread shook me to the core, and my knees went weak. I stumbled. The guard huffed and grabbed me by an elbow, forcing me up and shoving me forward where I slumped into the chair facing Doug. I closed my eyes, throat so fucking thick and dry I was pretty sure it was going to strangle me.

"Tell me they're okay."

I begged it against the blackness of my lids, unable to look at Kenzie's father if he told me anything different.

There was a charged silence before he finally spoke, his voice rough, reticent. "They both made it."

There was nothing I could do. My entire body collapsed forward, bones dislodged in relief. A sob erupted from a place so deep, so intense, I felt it ripping from me, fracturing as I expelled the pent-up, festered agony. It echoed off the walls, torment and relief as my forehead rocked against the cold table.

Didn't care I probably sounded like a sniveling bitch.

That I knew Doug was watching me crumble into a million

splintered pieces.

Disintegrating.

Viewing it with disgust.

I forced myself to find a breath, to sit up, to look at this man who'd done everything in his power to keep me away from his daughter.

How could I have ever blamed him?

He cleared his throat, though everything coming from him was still craggy and pitted with grief. "They took Brendon by C-section. He was born at 6:12 this morning. He had no issues other than mild fetal distress, probably brought on by Kenzie's trauma. They delivered him and transitioned her straight into surgery to repair her abdominal wall."

His bottom lip trembled. "Inch lower, and they'd both be dead."

My eyes dropped closed again. Thinking if I closed them long enough, it might set time in rewind. Take me back to where it all started. To that one decision I'd made.

One mistake.

All it took was one mistake for the world to fall down around you.

One mistake to set you on a collision course with yourself.

Knew it all along.

Kenz didn't belong in my world, hard as I'd tried to keep her there.

Doug leaned forward. Anger eclipsed the sorrow and exhaustion that'd sagged his shoulders just a minute before. He rammed his index finger into the table. "One inch, Lyrik...one inch and you would've killed my baby and yours."

I couldn't even respond, because what was I going to say?

Knew I was to blame.

Guilt swallowed me like a ship going down in the middle of an icy ocean.

A shiver slicked down my spine.

He flipped open the folder sitting on the table.

I tried to breathe.

To sit still and accept my punishment when I somehow realized the executioner had come to collect.

I blinked long, focus blurry yet somehow excruciatingly clear.

On the top was a sheet where my charges were listed, and he pushed it across the table toward me.

Possession of cocaine and heroin with intent to distribute. Two counts of reckless endangerment.

I gave him a slight nod of understanding.

He pulled out a short stack of papers clipped together at the top, hand shaking when he slid it my way.

It was a plea bargain.

What the fuck?

My attention jerked up to meet the weariness lining his face.

"What, you're my attorney now?" Didn't mean it to sound so bitter.

"Just want the best for all parties involved."

"What's that supposed to mean?"

He hefted a shoulder. "Read it."

I lifted my shackled wrists to the table, metal clanging as I pulled the papers closer so I could see the details.

The bitter fucking details.

I got a free pass.

No doubt, there were all kinds of strings being pulled, and it was Doug who held them like a puppeteer.

I could walk as long as I signed away my parental rights.

As long as I agreed to never see Kenzie again.

Didn't even know if this shit was legal.

I shook my head. Blinking. Unseeing.

"You want me to walk away from them." It wasn't a question.

He kept his voice even. "I just want the best for them."

On a heavy exhale, he shifted, dug into the inside pocket of his jacket, and pulled out an envelope. "Can't have this on record, but sign and it's yours. It's all the money I have to give. You walk away and I promise I'll take care of them. I'll make sure they have the kind of life you could never give them. Or you can sit and rot in jail for the next five to ten years and you won't have her anyway. Your choice."

Your choice? There was no fucking choice. Either way, I'd lost my family.

Ruined it all.

He set the thin envelope next to the agreement.

Overwhelming grief formed in every cell of my being. But I pushed it down, and instead let each inch of me harden to the point of pain. Brittle and broken and harsh. I welcomed it. Could feel the grit of my teeth. "And Baz?"

"Your friend's going to jail one way or the other. Got him down to a couple of years, and he'll probably be out in less than a year if he keeps his nose clean on the inside."

I ran my finger under the open edge of the envelope, lifting it enough so I could peek inside. Not that I gave a shit what the number read.

One hundred thousand dollars.

No doubt, this was their entire life savings.

"Need to talk to Baz…" I swallowed over the razors in my throat. "And I want to tell Kenzie myself."

He hesitated, and I shook my head. "Won't do it any other way."

It seemed in reluctance, but finally he nodded. Quickly, I scanned through the agreement then scribbled my name on the line, not giving two fucks if I was unknowingly signing away my life. I'd just paid for the one thing I wanted.

One minute with Kenzie.

One minute with my son.

I picked up the envelope and shot Doug a grin.

He dropped his gaze.

Like he couldn't stand to look at me.

Seemed about right, because I couldn't stand myself.

"You expect somethin' different?" I asked, that bitterness baring its teeth.

He looked up and met my stare straight on. "Yeah…guess maybe I did."

"Last thing I meant was to sell you out, leave you in this hole by yourself when I belong here, too, but this is the one thing I need."

My voice was desperate, my demeanor the same. "The one thing I'm asking of you. I need to see them once. I'll spend the rest of my life making it up to you."

I just needed to see them once.

Baz gripped me, his hug a stranglehold, his voice a harsh whisper in my ear. "Don't, man. This is my fault. Everything. Dragging my whole crew down and into this bullshit lifestyle. You know it's on me." Pulling back, he studied my face. "Are you sure this is what you want?"

Of course it wasn't.

I'd taken the good I was given. Trampled it like it was nothing. Thrown it away in one reckless night.

But I was going to do one thing good.

I was going to let the good go.

"Yeah."

Baz stepped back and gripped me by both shoulders. "Take whatever time they'll give you. Then go...step up and take my place while I'm in here. Keep the band together. Make sure all this nonstop partying bullshit ends. Take care of the guys. Watch over my baby brother. Need you, man."

I jerked through a nod. "Anything. It's done."

The door buzzed and I shuffled out into the emerging night.

Freedom.

But I'd never felt more chained.

I'd gone back to our tiny apartment, showered and changed, fighting the loneliness that moaned from within the walls, tentacles burrowing into my skin and hunting for a way to become one with me.

It would.

I knew it.

But I had one task left before I could let it.

I took a cab to the hospital and stepped onto the sidewalk. Night in full bloom, the sky seemed a tired, drooping canvas, grayed with the reflection of city lights. A thick fog stretched across the space and meshed with the clouds encroaching in the distance.

Tumultuous.

Fierce.

Energy held fast, something ominous and dense.

A dark warning I was getting ready to sell my soul.

Welcome to hell.

Sucking in a breath, I found my way inside, anxious as I jabbed at the elevator button. It lifted me to the seventh floor, and I ducked by the nurses, headed down the hall to the room number Doug had supplied.

Outside her room, I had to take a minute to convince myself what I was doing was right. When that didn't work, I just fed myself a few lies, drew in a breath, and cracked open the door.

Kenzie was propped up in the hospital bed, gown slung down over one shoulder with our son flailing a bit where he was pressed to her breast.

Grief slammed me. Another stake to my blackened soul.

Forcing myself to step forward, I let the door click shut behind me.

Startled, Kenzie's attention flew my way. Her face transformed into an expression of sheer relief. Her mouth parted, smile tilting at the corner. She heaved out a breath, wiped at her face, and I was just seeing then the tears that had been making a slow path down her face.

I wanted to drink her in. Memorize her sweet, soft face. Because I wouldn't ever get to see her again.

"You're here."

"Yeah."

I stood over them, and she looked down, away from me, tender as she touched his face. This tiny thing with swollen eyes and pouty lips, this little boy that tore everything I had left inside apart.

Shredded.

Soggy laughter tumbled from her, and she grinned between us, vacillating somewhere between awe and sorrow. "This is so much harder than they make it out to be...the breastfeeding thing..." She started to ramble. "I've been trying all afternoon, and he just keeps falling asleep...and I keep trying...and..."

Her voice broke on the last, and she heaved a sob.

Overridden by shame, I moved across the room and sat down on a chair, stared over at her.

"I'm so mad at you," she finally whispered through her tears.

"I know."

"Lyrik...you can't—"

I cut her off by quickly standing again, because I couldn't take it. Couldn't take her pleading with me to be someone I obviously couldn't be.

I inched back over to them, the back of my finger caressing Brendon's cheek. "Can I?"

She frowned. "Of course you can...he's your son."

Only he wasn't really. Not anymore.

Carefully, I lifted his tiny body that was wrapped in a blanket, a blue and pink cap on his head. The weight of him was next to nothing yet wholly profound.

I rested him on my shoulder, inhaling as deeply as I could when I breathed him in.

Memorizing everything I'd lost. Pouring anything I had left back into him.

Loved him with everything I had.

Silent promises began to rush out.

My heart. It belongs to you. Won't ever give it to anyone again. You're the last. I won't ever fall in love again. Not after you.

My son.

He made this gurgling, sweet sound. With my hand, I guarded his head when I pulled him away so my eyes could trace his face. So I could commit it to memory.

His tiny mouth opened in an exaggerated yawn as he leaned back into my hold, tongue poking out, then he was trying to shove his fist in his mouth.

Warm laughter spilled from my chest.

"He's perfect, Kenz."

"Yeah." A soft smile pulled at her tired face.

"You're gonna be okay," I told her, hugging Brendon a little closer.

"I know," she said like she didn't get what I was trying to say. And I knew she didn't. This innocent, sweet girl had no clue she was getting ready to be crushed.

Fuck, I'd do anything to go back. Erase it. Change everything I'd done.

But Doug was right.

I wasn't ever gonna be good enough.

I held my son as close as I could.

Rocking him slowly, because God, I didn't want to let him go.

The back of my throat burned like a bitch, and I fought the moisture welling behind my eyes. Quickly, before I lost my nerve, I moved back to that hypnotizing girl, settled our son back across her chest, and kissed through the hair matted to her forehead. I didn't move away, just let my words penetrate there.

"I'm leaving, Kenz. Leaving you and Brendon because you both deserve so much better than anything I could ever give."

She jerked. "No."

"Yes."

I could feel the rush of panic swell around her. "No...Lyrik...no don't. We can—"

"No, we can't. Your dad got me off, Kenz. Paid me off too, and I'm taking that money. Band and the boys need it. You'll be just fine without me."

Trembles of revulsion and denial rolled through her body. "No. You're lying. You're lying."

Yeah. I was. But she wasn't ever going to know.

It was better this way.

Hate me, Kenz. Hate me.

And as fucking hard as I tried to keep it in, to hold it back, to just *leave* because I knew it'd be easier on her that way, I got selfish and pressed one last kiss to her wet lips. I closed my eyes as I gave her the complete and utter truth. "You sing my soul."

Took everything I had to rip myself away.

She was screaming my name when I tore open the door and flew out.

"Lyrik!"

A shrill, startled cry from that tiny, innocent boy vibrated the walls, like he was a partner to his mom's torment—to mine—like something vital had been cut away from his soul.

"Lyrik…please…no…don't leave me."

I didn't slow down or acknowledge her father where he sat like a broken guardian outside her door, head bowed between his shoulders and elbows on his knees.

I just fled.

Bright lights blinded from above and gleamed against the stark white floor. I hurtled down the narrow hall, desperate for escape.

With every pounding step, I felt the separation grow. A chasm rending and ripping until I felt myself splitting in two.

Don't leave us.

Impossible, but I could still hear her even when it wasn't real. When she was too far and I couldn't touch.

Lyrik…please.

Knew my battered, blackened soul would always *hear* her.

Gasping for breath, I stumbled out of the building and into the vacancy of the deep, deep night. Wind gusted, tumbling along the surface of the ground, a stir of agitation at my feet.

Above, the storm raged. Clouds dark and heavy and ominous.

Beside me, lightning struck. A crackle of energy shocked through the air. Wrapping me in coils of white-hot agony.

For a moment, I gave into it and let myself feel. I lifted my face to the tormented sky, hands gripping my hair as I screamed.

Screamed in anguish.

Screamed in regret.

Screamed loud enough I would never forget.

A crack of thunder opened the sky.

Rain poured.

I took the check from my pocket, heart heaving as I tore it to shreds, flying pieces impaled by fat drops of rain as I chucked them into the disordered air.

Hands fisted at my sides, I buried the memory of the way he'd felt in my arms, the memory of his face, in the deepest part of me, sealed it off and cemented my heart.

My spirit grasped and wove with the promise I had made him.

I will never fall in love again.

Not ever again.

Not after tonight.

TAMAR

Dawn touched the sky, just a whisper of pink lifting at the horizon and kissing the earth. The house sat silent like a prisoner of the night. Quiet and still.

The mountains I loved so much were framed behind it. As if they stood guard over those taking refuge within.

Eyes bleary, I swiped at them, my heart rising to my throat and sinking in my stomach, pulse throbbing everywhere.

Home.

It'd felt so far away.

Like a fairytale, and when I'd awoken as Tamar King, it'd only been a dream.

It appeared that way now. So warm and quaint and welcoming, it could only be a fantasy.

But Lyrik reminded me this could be my reality.

I killed the engine of the rental car and slowly opened the door, my knees feeling weak when I stepped out onto the desert floor and quietly latched it shut behind me.

Bugs trilled in the emerging day and the warmth of the rising sun wrapped me in its arms.

Home.

I edged toward my childhood house, boots quieted as I climbed the two wooden steps onto the front porch, hand gripping the railing for support.

Home.

Everything locked inside me when I lifted my fist and rapped it against the door.

Subdued yet strong.

It felt like an eternity passed before there was rustling on the other side. The turn of the lock. The creak of the door.

My mother, frozen at the threshold.

Hands at her mouth.

Moisture gathering fast in her eyes.

She dropped to her knees.

I followed suit.

I guessed all the tears I'd bottled for years had been unleashed. Because it felt as if I hadn't stopped crying for days. Because my heart was broken yet somehow in this moment made whole.

Love filled me everywhere while the hollow space Lyrik left ached.

She grabbed me by the face, her touch gentle and encouraging. Firm and unyielding.

"Tamar. My baby girl. You came home to me. You're here."

My father rushed out from the end of the hall, fumbling to a stop when he found my mother and me kneeling on the floor, the breath visibly knocked from his lungs.

I felt like the prodigal child, on my knees and begging

forgiveness for what I'd wasted.

Their love and belief and undying support. I should have always known it would be great enough to hold me strong. To see me through. But I was coming to accept not every bad choice was the wrong one. That maybe I'd needed that time to grow before I'd ever be strong enough to stand.

"You're here," she said again.

Yeah.

I was there.

Because of a boy.

A boy who reminded me I was brave.

LYRIK

What does it take to define a person?

How many moments?

How many choices?

How many mistakes?

Maybe it's the first time you step out on your own when you realize you're getting there. No longer in need of that comforting guidance of your parents.

Maybe it's the day you're struck with what you want to be. When that spec of ambition blossoms within you and you know you'll do whatever it takes to achieve what you want most.

Maybe it's the first time you fall in love.

Maybe it's the last.

Maybe it's the sum of them.

What I did know was walking out on Kenzie and Brendon had become my definition.

Didn't know if my doing so was the result of years of bad choices or one fatal mistake.

Because losing them? It'd felt like a death penalty.

My soul cursed to a living hell.

I'd left that hospital bitter and hard. Sentenced to a life of regret and self-hatred. It didn't take all that long for it to shape me. *Reshape me.* Shallow and selfish and lashing out. Only good things I had were my family, the guys, and my loyalty to the band.

My songs my single true joy.

Along the way, I'd allowed myself two vices. An endless string of women and bottomless bottles of booze. Of course, both those things only served to leave me a little more hollowed out than before.

That hollow space? That's where I shored up all that hate and hostility. Where I festered with memories of what I had done.

Figured that definition would be forever unchanged.

That was until Tamar had come on like a hurricane. A rising storm gathering in the distance. Stronger than anticipated. Fierce and savage in the most beautiful way.

Blowing over me with the force of a gale wind.

Reshaping and rewriting and redefining.

Eclipsing all that dark with so many hues—reds and blues—and that brilliant, blinding white.

Until I no longer recognized who I was. Because somewhere along the way, without my permission, I had become hers.

A gentle breeze rustled through the trees, just shy of being cool. Brimming with an innuendo of the approaching winter and dimming the heat of the warm California sky.

I'd lost them then.

Just at the cusp of winter.

That's when all things had gone cold.

Five years later, it was when I lost Blue, too.

I scrubbed a weary hand down my face.

Fuck.

I no longer knew how to live through the loss.

So here I waited like some kind of twisted stalker.

Waiting.

Watching.

Wondering if this was the right or wrong thing to do.

But I'd done so many damned wrongs in my life, I needed to make something right.

And I'd be willing to lay down bets this moment would be defining, too.

Chills spread like a crippling freeze when I saw the silver Toyota Highlander approaching then slow.

Innocuous.

Yet something about it felt absolute.

It pulled into the drive directly across from where I sat in the small neighborhood park. Red brake lights flashed as the SUV eased into the garage before the engine shut off.

My pulse spiked and sped.

God. What was I doing? But I couldn't stop what I'd already set into motion. What my heart had already proclaimed. So I stood, drawn across the road when the driver's side door opened and Kenzie climbed out.

Knew it'd only be her.

Just like it'd been the last three days when I'd sat in this same spot studying her routine. Because as damned much as I needed to see my son, knew I had to get her approval first. Knew I couldn't come forcing my way back into his life if there was no chance I fit in it. And sure as hell not if it hurt Kenzie any more than I already had.

Completely unaware, she leaned back in through the car door and gathered her things, slung a laptop case over her shoulder, did the same with her purse, the girl all dressed up in work clothes and heels.

A lump knotted at the base of my throat. Heavy. Just as heavy as the boulder that sat in my stomach.

She stepped back and slammed the door. Took a single step

toward the interior garage door leading into the house.

"Kenzie." It was ragged.

Broken.

Bristling with blame.

With her back to me, she froze, her shoulders stuttering up and down. Like she was trying to find the breath I'd knocked from her. Trying to find the ground I'd yanked from beneath her feet.

Kinda sucked when just your presence held the power to cause that effect.

Slowly she turned, the straps of her bags sliding down her arm. They dropped with a thud to the floor.

Face ashen.

Eyes wide.

Soul shocked.

"Kenzie," I chanced again, taking a step forward, hoping it was soft enough she'd get I wasn't there to cause her more pain.

Even though I wasn't fool enough to think this encounter wasn't going to hurt.

She took one step back, blinked like she were trying to focus, before she started shaking her head. "No."

"Kenzie...please...not here to cause you trouble."

A sob tore from her and she fisted her hand at her mouth. Like she was trying to hold it in. Her eyes pinched so deeply at the corners I got the feeling she was doing her best to shut me out but didn't trust me enough to look away.

Couldn't blame her.

That was all on me.

"Then what are you doing here?" she finally demanded, voice a rasp of accusation and tears.

I cleared my throat. "I'm here because five years ago I made the biggest mistake of my life. Five years ago I signed away my son."

Desperation had me taking another step forward. "And I know I don't have the right to be here, Kenzie. That all those mistakes I made cost me that right. But I need to know he's okay. Need to know that you're both okay."

Nerves pricked my flesh. I raked a hand through my hair,

doing my best to contain it. To, for once, stand up and really be a man. I met the fear in her gaze. "I need to see him, Kenz. If you'll let me, I *need* to see my son."

The last was a breath, and with the claim she flinched like I'd struck her.

"Why now?" she asked, mouth trembling. "Why now, after all this time?"

Glancing to the ground off to the side, I rubbed a hand over my face to clear the tension that stretched taut between us.

Anger.

Hostility.

And old, old pain I wasn't sure would ever go away.

"Because someone showed me recently what it's like to be brave."

Brave.

Brown eyes moved over me. Like maybe she was just then realizing how different I looked since the last time she saw me, the ink now covering almost every exposed inch of skin.

The torment I'd written there.

Hers.

Mine.

She winced when she locked on Brendon's name that was woven through his song.

She finally tore her attention up to my eyes that probably told more than the ink ever could.

Because I was sorry.

So fucking sorry.

But I didn't know if that made a damned difference in the grand scheme of things.

If it was worth the upheaval of their lives. Because no question, the house behind her was a home. A place she lived with our son and the guy she'd married two years ago, something I'd discovered when I got on-line to track her down.

They were a family and I wasn't sure how I was ever gonna fit because I sure as hell wasn't there to break it up.

Wasn't lying when I told her I didn't come to bring her trouble. But that rarely mattered much since trouble seemed to be tacked to my name.

She chewed at her bottom lip, the way she always used to do when she didn't know what to do with herself. "I always knew you would come."

Uneasily, I shifted on my feet and shoved my hands a little deeper in my pockets. "Yeah? Because I never thought I would."

I watched the heavy bob of her throat. "Because you didn't want to?"

I gave her a jerk of my head. "No, Kenzie. Because it was the only thing in the world I wanted to do."

She nodded like she got it, looked me square. "Okay."

Okay.

I puffed out the breath I didn't know I'd been holding.

Okay.

She lifted her chin toward the neighborhood park where I'd been waiting. "I'll bring him out...wait for us at the park."

She turned around, then paused. Wavered. Warily, she looked at me from over her shoulder. "Lyrik...he doesn't..."

She trailed off like she couldn't bring herself to say it aloud.

Not needing clarification, my head rocked with acceptance.

Of course he didn't.

Didn't expect him to know who I was.

I lifted my shoulders in a hapless shrug. "Introduce me however you need to, Kenz. Whatever makes sense. I don't care. I just want to see him."

A mournful smile lifted just the corner of her mouth, and she swiped at the moisture clouding her eyes. "I'll be out in a minute. Brad needs to know."

Something like jealousy grabbed me.

Yeah.

I'd seen Brad returning with Brendon every day, too, even though I'd never gotten a real look at my son. Just the vague awareness he was in the backseat of the truck that pulled into the garage an hour earlier than Kenzie got home.

I wandered back to the park, took a seat on the bench with my elbows propped on my knees. Same way as I'd done the last three days. Though this time...this time my insides shook and my heart thundered. Throbbed with regret same as it raced with hope.

With the hope of something different.

The hope of something good.

That something good came when the door opened about ten minutes later. Over the cars in the garage, I could only see the top of Kenzie's head and the guy emerging behind her. They edged down the space between the car and the garage wall before they stepped into the waning light as the day got sucked away.

Same as the air in my lungs.

My breath and my heart and my spirit caught.

Everything timeless yet speeding ahead.

A small hand was clutched tight in Kenzie's.

Brendon.

My entire being pulsed.

Emotion after emotion.

Pain.

Loss.

Regret.

Love. Love. Love.

They stood frozen across the space, because maybe time needed to catch up to them too. His free arm was tucked full of toys, the kid wearing a button-up collared shirt and jeans cuffed at the ankles, looking like a little badass with the checkered Vans on his feet.

I felt the grin pulling all over my face while my spirit flailed in every direction.

The breeze whipped through his hair.

Black.

Just like mine.

I stood.

Drawn.

Emotion gathered thick as Kenzie began to lead him across the street. Her husband hung back with his arms crossed over his chest. Stare wary and hard and full of warning.

Didn't blame him a bit.

If I were him, I'd want to kick my ass too.

Didn't matter anyway. Because this kid…this kid was all I

could see. The way his mouth twisted up in welcome, eyes so dark they were almost black, sparking with mischief I knew all too well. It was like looking at all those pictures my mom kept plastered on her walls.

This boy was mine.

They stopped just a couple feet away from where I stood under a shade tree near the bench. He kept peering up at me with this unending smile that twisted through me like chains and ropes and indestructible ties.

An unbreakable bond.

Curiosity played in his dark, dark eyes, and his mom dropped to her knees in front of him, something shaky and frantic about her as she brushed the too-long bangs from his forehead. "Baby, I want you to meet someone really important, okay?"

"Okay," he agreed, grinning toward me.

"This is Lyric." She said it like a secret, and I was dropping to my knees, too, completely laid bare when he turned the full force of his attention on me.

His grin showcased a straight row of baby teeth. One missing on the bottom.

And I wanted to weep when I looked at him.

When I looked at all the years gone, and the wonder in his gaze and at what came spilling out of his arms when he suddenly dumped his stash of toys to the ground. He rummaged through his pile, snatching it upside down by a leg.

That fucking bear that was supposed to be good luck.

Binding a family together.

The thing was a complete disaster and probably should have been tossed years ago, tattered and torn and frayed.

He held it up like a prize. "You made this!"

For a second, every part of me seized.

My eyes pinched at the sides, dents cutting into my forehead as I fought against the unbearable pain. I shifted my gaze to Kenzie for help because I didn't quite know how to make sense of this.

Tears just kept sliding down her face. She remained silent. Like she *trusted* me to handle this right. For me to get the situation was fragile and I could either foster it or shatter it into a million unrecognizable pieces.

"Yeah, buddy, I did."

He turned back to his pile and dug out a blue car. "Hey, do you like cars? This one's my favorite."

A low chuckle rumbled in my chest. "I like them a lot."

His grin grew. "Me, too. My dad says this kind goes so fast."

Did my damned best not to flinch, but I couldn't help it, that slam of jealousy I knew I'd feel. But I'd accepted that was probably something I was gonna feel when I'd made another *choice*. When I'd switched paths and headed a different direction.

When I came here.

I forced some lightness into the gravel grinding up the words. "Your dad's totally right. It is super-fast. Any faster and it'd be a race car."

His eyes went wide. "Whoa, that's way fast. Do you know what green means?"

A little bewildered, I lifted my shoulders. "Go?"

"Yep!"

He made a revving noise and pushed the car along the ground, totally unaware he was completely crumbling my world.

"Go!" he shouted, then asked, "How about yellow?"

"Um…slow down?"

He glanced at me with a smile. "Right again, 'cuz that's what my teacher tells me when I have to flip my card from green to yellow. *Slow down*," he acted out with a grin, those eyes glinting with mischief again. "Because when you get on red? That means stop and you don't get to play at recess. No way is that gonna happen!"

Kenzie choked out a laugh below her breath.

Yeah.

I was right.

He was a total badass.

So fucking cute.

I was betting he was a little handful and unruly and a whole lot perfect.

He started driving that car up my arm and over his song. A song I'd never sang for anyone. It was one reserved for the loneliest hours of the night. One I'd played what felt like a thousand times. One I played like some kind of fucked-up tribute. When I'd pray more of those prayers I didn't have the right to pray.

Begging for his joy.

"Hey, that's my name," he suddenly said, running the wheels back and forth over his name forever etched on my arm.

Affection gripped my throat.

"Yeah, it is, little man, it is."

He grinned again, and it took about all I had not to scoop him up and steal him away.

Instead I sat there while he talked, showing me all his favorite toys that he obviously took with him everywhere, his chatter nonstop, animated, and unbridled. He talked to me like he'd known me forever.

Like I was his best friend.

My gaze drifted to Kenzie who had taken a seat on the small bench, elbows on her knees as she watched us. Her expression was soft and sad and knowing.

Silently I told her what an amazing job she'd done with this kid. Just like I'd known she would.

And I couldn't stop myself from wondering what it would have been like if I'd been there, if I'd gotten to witness it all, if I'd somehow been a partner to it.

The hardships and joys and accomplishments.

The little things.

Everything I'd given away for one night of revelry.

I watched as Brendon got lost in his own play, pushing his car through the blades of grass, then plopped it in his pocket as he stood and raced for the slide.

Silence swirled around me and Kenzie as she gave me time. But honestly, no amount of time was ever gonna be enough.

"Thank you," I finally said. Because I'd had no clue how her reception was going to be. Not when she didn't owe me anything at all. Especially when I'd given her no warning at all of my intrusion into her life. Wrapping my arms around my knees, I rocked, working my way through the discomfort, gauging what to say.

"So…he does know…about me?"

A slow breath leaked from between her pursed lips. "I was being honest when I said I knew one day you'd come. And yes, it was definitely a shock turning around and finding you there, but once the shock wore off, I can't say I was really surprised."

She tipped her head toward her husband who still stood guard across the street. I wondered just how damned difficult this had to be for him, because it sure as shit was hell for me.

"We've been preparing him for this day, Lyrik. For the day when you'd come back into our lives. And even if you never did, we still knew one day he'd figure out Brad isn't his biological father. We weren't going to lie to him about that."

I rubbed the tension from the back of my neck, trying to brace myself for the impression Brendon might have already made about me. "What does he know, Kenz?"

She looked down at me through bleary eyes. "Lyrik...he knows that he has your eyes and your hair and that you made him that bear." She choked over the admission. "He knows you put him in my tummy. He just hasn't figured out what that means yet."

Everything throbbed and ached.

And I wasn't sure I could breathe.

Not through the remorse and sorrow and gratitude.

A wistful smile tugged at her mouth as she looked at Brendon. "Even after I fell out of love with you, that didn't mean I didn't still love you, Lyrik. That I didn't have faith in you. That after all the horrible mistakes you made, that one day you wouldn't make the right one. So I told him stories about you...the good ones...about the guy I knew before I didn't know you at all."

That smile tipped down, and more tears fell down her face. "But I guess I did know you, after all, didn't I?"

Unsure, I turned my full attention on her.

"I know you didn't cash that check. My dad finally admitted it to me...the night before I married Brad. He wanted to be sure I was sure. That I was marrying for my heart rather than marrying because I thought some guy would be good for me and my son."

Her voice lowered to a whisper. "He wanted to give me the chance to go back to you."

"And you chose him," I supplied through a nod with a subtle

gesture in Brad's direction.

For two weeks I'd wondered how I'd feel when I got here. About Kenzie. About this girl I'd thought would forever hold my heart.

Guess that was my answer.

The fact her choosing the other guy when she knew I'd been lying when I left her and Brendon didn't hurt. Instead it filled me with this strange sense of comfort.

A simple joy found in the fact she was happy.

That's all I wanted for her.

I guess just like her, even though there would always be a part of me that loved her…cared for her…I wasn't *in love* with her anymore.

Guess that's what my stupid heart had been telling me for the last two months. Why those words had come spilling free.

Blue.

You sing my soul.

A warm ache filled my chest.

No longer was there a question of who owned me anymore.

That girl.

My brave, beautiful Blue.

Self-conscious laughter trickled from her, and she blushed. "I think what we had was real, Lyrik. But I think it was just preparing me for what I was going to feel when I met the man I was supposed to live my life with."

Tenderly, she looked at the man across the street.

I chuckled. "Why does that sound like something my mother would say?"

She laughed. "Because your mom is amazing."

And God, it was weird. Sitting comfortably with Kenzie this way.

She sobered, eyes roaming my face. "Are you happy, Lyrik?"

Exhaling, I pushed back the hair blowing in my face. "No, Kenz. I'm not happy. I haven't let myself be since the night I walked out on you and Brendon."

The words locked somewhere deep, before they came rushing out in a quiet confession. "But I'm…almost there."

Yeah.

That was weird, too.

Realizing that.

"I watched you," she admitted, "watched you as *Sunder* made it. I saw the tabloids…the success and the parties and the women. You should have been happier than anyone. But I knew, Lyrik. I knew. I saw it on your face."

She met her husband's gaze. "I want you to know it's okay. It's okay to let it go. The guilt I saw in every picture." She looked at me. Expression wistful. "I let you go a long time ago."

My world spun on fast forward. In slow motion. Everything becoming clear.

So fucking clear.

You sing my soul.

"You'd better go," she finally said with a tender smile. "Brad's the best guy you'll ever meet, but even he has his limits."

Nodding through the daze, I stood and brushed off the grass and leaves from my pants.

Brendon came hurtling back over. His arms were lifted over his head and there was nothing I could do but swoop him up.

I squeezed him and breathed him in like I'd done that night, and he giggled as he edged back and pulled at a strand of my hair, like he was remembering what his mom had told him, this strange connection filling up our air.

Energy and light and life.

This tugging pull. Tying me to him. Leading me to *her*.

"I'll miss you, little man," I murmured in his ear.

"I'll see you soon," he said as if he held a clue. As if he were telling me not to worry. That maybe that gaping distance between us had just become narrow.

Close enough to cross.

"Yeah…I sure hope so."

Carefully, I set him down, shoved my hands in my pockets. Brendon went running to his dad who was already crossing the street, going straight for Brendon with love and protection in his eyes.

Whole and absolute.

Slowly, I began to back away, taking in the last couple seconds of my son I could get.

Kenzie's and my eyes met. "He's going to ask questions after you're gone. And I'm going to tell him, Lyrik. I really hope you do the right thing with it."

The words were subdued and filled with the promise as I continued to walk backward. "Whenever he's ready to find me, whenever he knows what all that means, please don't stop him. I'll be waiting."

She nodded, and I gave her the gentlest of smiles. I spun around and started climbing the small hill.

"Hey, Lyrik," Kenzie called. She was grinning wide when I slanted my attention to her over my shoulder. "Whoever she is…she's a lucky girl."

I returned her grin, shaking my head.

I increased my pace, breaking out in a sprint as I ran for my truck.

Because Blue wasn't the lucky one.

But if I managed to win her back? I'd be one lucky guy.

TAMAR

My mother squeezed my hand. It was a silent show of encouragement as she stood at my side. The world rushed around us, people traversing the busy downtown streets, while I stood stock still right in the middle of the sidewalk in front of the short stack of steps leading to the court building.

Sweat slicked my hands and beaded at the back of my neck.

Run. Run. Run.

It was that small, terrified voice that whispered the tortured plea within the confines of my muddled head.

Begging me to go.

To spare myself the torture waiting behind those doors.

Brave.

But it was the memory of that deep, haunting voice that convinced me to stay. The lingering warmth of his presence.

Funny how Lyrik had been the one to reveal my inner courage, to embrace it, to show me I no longer had to live behind walls when he'd just kept building his own.

Brick after brutal brick.

Deflecting and avoiding and protecting a mashed-up heart I'd learned kept so much hidden good. I knew it was there. Lurking in his ominous shadows.

That didn't mean his savage heart didn't hold the power to decimate.

I was still reeling from the fact he'd chosen to decimate *me.*

I'd thought we'd been so close…so close to finding who we were supposed to be. Together. But I guessed that was the problem.

Lyrik had gotten too close and it was too much.

This boy who didn't have his heart to give.

But he held mine, anyway.

My mother squeezed my hand again. "We need to go inside."

"I know," I whispered, still unmoving.

She turned to me, her expression pure and understanding as she tenderly brushed back the long locks of my hair that whipped around my head, stirred by the wind.

Hair now so dark brown it was nearly black.

Red gone.

I should have known when Lyrik forced his way into my life *she* could never stay.

I'd dyed it back to my natural color. The color it'd been before I'd run. Before I'd masked and cloaked and camouflaged.

The same way it'd be when I climbed the stand and stood against Cameron Lucan.

No.

I'd realized since I'd come home I wasn't ashamed of the tattoos that covered my scars or the way I'd dyed my hair.

But when he saw me sitting there, it wouldn't be under veil

or disguise.

It would be me.

Tamar Gibson.

The girl he'd so nearly destroyed.

In all those years of running, I'd never realized by hiding, I was allowing him to keep her that way.

Broken.

Hidden.

Submissive.

And as scared as I was to face him, he would no longer hold me down or hold me back.

"You can do this, Tamar," my mother said. Emphatic. "I know you can, and I know it has to be one of the most terrifying feelings you've ever had to contend with. But you're already more than halfway there. You're *here*. You *came*."

Tears welled, and I trembled a smile. In the two weeks since I'd knocked on their door at dawn, my mother had been my constant support. There for me when I'd needed someone to talk to and there for me in the silence when she'd known I'd needed to be left alone.

She pulled her bottom lip between her teeth and wiped away the single tear that slid down my cheek. "I'm so proud of you. Have I told you that?"

I laughed a soggy laugh. "Only about a thousand times."

She smiled. "Then I'll gladly tell you a thousand more."

"Thank you," I whispered, more grateful to her than she could ever know.

"Oh, sweet girl. I'm your mother. No matter how far you go, I will always be right here. Waiting for you. You are a gift, not a burden. Don't ever think otherwise."

Her saying that just made me want to grab onto her, hug her and thank her again and again. Instead, I nodded. "Okay. Let's do this."

We headed into the building and through security. I'd declined sitting through other testimonies and questioning. Declined putting myself through the presentation of evidence. I was here to tell my story. And I was here to stand in the place of

Madeline since Cameron had robbed her of telling her own.

That didn't mean my stride didn't slow as we approached the courtroom. That I couldn't feel my heart pounding in my chest, so hard I was sure it was visible beneath my white blouse, each step inciting a panic that quickened through my veins.

It only amplified when I was led through the double wooden doors.

Tingles flashed across my skin.

Evil and vile.

Oh God.

I gulped down the bile that threatened to rise in my throat, the fear that threatened to bring me to my knees.

Run.

But I'd done it for so long and I was so tired of hiding. So tired of pretending.

Just like I'd known I would, I'd reached a crossroads.

Decision made.

I'd turned in the direction of my past.

An anxious energy trembled in the room, voices muted and subdued as they awaited my arrival. Paneled wood lined the walls, even darker where it gleamed from the judge's and jurors' boxes, the same wood making up the benches where people were squeezed shoulder to shoulder.

It made everything appear dark.

Sinister.

Cold.

A shiver skidded down my spine, and I forced up my chin, searched for the strength and courage that had set me on this path in the first place.

Brave, beautiful Blue.

I clung to her, that girl Lyrik had exposed, even though I felt so weak, so scared as I tentatively made my way down the narrow aisle. Heads swiveled and eyes gawked as this restless energy crawled across the floor and clawed at the walls. It pressed at the domed ceiling that only seemed to echo it back.

Amplified.

It was suffocating.

But it was nothing compared to the moment when *he* turned to look at me.

I felt as if I literally might die as I got trapped in the vile glare of Cameron Lucan.

Those dark eyes held no warmth and that heart held no capacity to care.

Reeling back, I ran into my father who was following close behind. He held me up while I wanted to crumble to the floor, his support always staunch and stoic.

How had I ever compared the two?

Lyrik and Cameron.

Because I recognized the difference. The difference between broken and depraved.

I was sworn in and took the stand. I could feel the weight of those terrorizing eyes locked on me. As if with just a look, he could back me into another corner. Hold me hostage in that dirty, disgusting room.

Memories spun.

Pain.

I couldn't look up. Couldn't bring myself to meet his eye.

Trembling, I gripped the edge of the chair to keep myself from fleeing. Feet aching to move.

I couldn't do this.

I couldn't do this.

Sickness clawed at my spirit, breath locked in my throat.

Panic welled.

But I had to stay.

For me.

For Madeline.

For the shame. For the guilt I had born. To put away this man who had belittled and oppressed and abused. To ensure he could never do it again.

I just didn't know how to lift my head.

"Ms. Gibson, can you tell us when you first met Cameron Lucan?" The female prosecutor stood a couple feet away from me, prodding me with sympathy woven through her voice.

"Ms. Gibson?"

Run.

I squeezed my eyes shut. Tighter than before.

Trembles rolled as awareness spread, my heart rate kicking up a notch, this disoriented comfort soothing across my skin.

I puffed out a breath and slowly lifted my head.

Drawn.

That magnet that wouldn't let me go.

Inky eyes stared back at me, that intimidating, confusing boy like a vision where he stood just inside the courtroom door. My pulse hammered and sped, my mind and heart at war, fighting the stark relief in his presence and the echo of his cutting words.

Silently, he took two steps forward, his gaze unwavering as he slid into the very back bench. Still, he may as well have been under a spotlight, all that wicked beauty a lure, tattoos standing out against his crisp, dark gray suit.

Gritty and straight-laced.

Hard and so unbearably soft.

Edged in hostility and bleeding calm.

A blatant, bold contradiction.

So destructive and compelling it was impossible to look away, the man poised to strike and set you aflame.

But I was already on fire.

Burned by this man.

And I ached beneath his stare that filled with sorrow, that pouty mouth tipped down at the corners.

Why?

I blinked, and tears streaked down my face.

Why?

Why are you here?

Why do you keep doing this to me?

My tongue darted out to wet my bottom lip as I tried to get myself together. To focus on the reason I was here.

"Ms. Gibson," the prosecutor said again, this time a prod.

Lyrik tipped his head. Gently.

Brave, beautiful Blue.

Promising me I had the strength.

Reminding me I'd had it all along.

I blinked myself away from that comforting face and turned my attention back to the prosecutor. "I'm sorry," I whispered.

She shook her head. "It's okay. I understand this is difficult for you. Let's start again. Can you tell us when you first met Cameron Lucan?"

I cleared the lump from my throat, though the words trembled. "I was nineteen. It was summer and I was working at a diner when he first came in…"

Throat raw. Mouth dry. Fingers twisted in knots. That's how I delivered my testimony, the memories brought to life with the power of a projection on a 3-D movie screen. Bile churned in my stomach as I relived every moment, the way he'd twisted and manipulated until my will was no longer my own. How the physical scars ran almost as deep as the emotional. The confession slid like venom from my tongue. Sharp as a dagger and heavy as a stone.

Horror and hate.

"Thank you, Ms. Gibson," she said quietly. As quiet as the rest of the room that seemed to hold a collective breath, for a moment also prisoners to the atrocities meted at Cameron's hand.

Caution laced her tone. "Ms. Gibson, do you recognize the person you just described in your testimony to be seated in this courtroom?"

"Yes," I whispered, even though up to that point, I'd still refused to look that way.

"Can you please point to where that person is seated?"

My eyes dropped closed and the pressure built. So strong and intense. Because even after all the words that had flowed from my mouth, this felt like the culmination of it all.

The moment I finally took a stand.

The moment I stood against Cameron Lucan.

My eyes fluttered open, landing on the boy. My boy. Even if he would never truly belong to me. His jaw was rigid, anger rippling from him in waves that touched like soft encouragement.

And I didn't give myself time to question the reason Lyrik West was here. To question his motives or desires or needs.

Because right then, I knew he was there for me.

I lifted my chin, my gaze, and my hand.

Cameron sat across the room unmoving in his chair. As if he sensed the end and willed me to be the one to end it. With so much evidence stacked against him, there was virtually no chance of acquittal. I doubted aiming my attention at him would make a difference either way.

But it didn't matter.

Because I would no longer remain silent.

I would no longer hide or mask or run.

I pointed a finger at Cameron Lucan.

The rest of her questions were a blur. "Can you please describe what that person is wearing for the court?"

I mumbled the answer and slumped forward when I did.

Gasping.

Reeling.

Free.

"Let the court record reflect that the witness has just identified the defendant, Cameron Lucan."

I was completely shaking when I was excused from the stand, the cross-examination nothing but a muted whir at the fringes of my mind.

From the back of the room, Lyrik West smiled at me.

So damned soft and filled with understanding.

And I saw it there.

Written all over the edges of that convoluted man.

Pride.

I stumbled into my seat where my mother pulled me into her embrace, pressing wet kisses into my hair, her face soaked in tears. "I'm so proud of you. I'm so proud of you."

And when I looked back over my shoulder, Lyrik was gone.

Mom edged out onto the back porch and handed me a hot cup of tea.

"Thank you." I blew at the cup as I sat on a wooden rocking chair watching the sun melt against the mountains, a reflection of its passing as it dropped down the horizon at the opposite end of the sky.

These mountains had always been one of my favorite parts of home. Watching the storms build above them, witnessing a beauty unlike anything I'd ever seen. So strong and powerful and dangerous.

Mom settled in the seat next to me and propped up her feet on the railing. "How are you holding up?"

Two days had passed since my testimony. One day since Cameron Lucan's conviction.

I took a sip and let it soothe my aching throat. "It feels…good."

I eyed her with a half-smile. "Weird. The day I escaped, I'd accepted the fact it would be something that chased me forever. That I'd have to look behind at every turn. Always be ready to run again. It feels so odd to put it to rest."

"Yet you're not settled." When it came to me, she'd always been this way. Intuitive.

I shook my head. "No."

"Where do you go from here?"

I hefted a single shoulder. "I don't know, Mom. I just feel so…lost. I'm not sure where I belong anymore."

"I'd keep you here forever if you'd let me." It came out almost a tease, although I recognized the honesty behind it.

"I know you would. And you know I love it here, but—"

"I know, Tamar. I know. You'll find your place."

Her smile was knowing. "Are you about ready to tell me about this boy who broke my baby's heart?" She lifted a brow. "I want to know whose ass I have to kick."

Wistful laughter fumbled from me and my smile trembled. "Maybe that's the hardest part of it all. He broke it in the best way. He found me when I didn't know I was lost. Turned me in the right direction. It was him who pointed me home."

"You're here because of him?"

I gave a small shrug. "No…but in some ways, yes. He forced me to see myself. To *hear* where I was being called."

"It takes someone brave to listen."

I choked over the swell of emotion. "He used to call me that… Brave."

Sympathy clouded her blue eyes that were the same color as mine, her voice soft as she reached out to play with a few stray strands of my hair. "You love him?"

My insides shuddered and screamed and flailed.

Searching for a way to fill up the hole he'd left behind. Carved out and bleeding.

Hollow.

Every time he barged into my life, he took a little more when he left me behind.

"So much," I whispered as I released the tears Lyrik had taken the time to show me weren't a weakness.

They were ones I deserved to shed.

And God. I missed him so much it reminded me of death. His name equating to loss and grief and sorrow. And still, his touch had been my resurrection.

This beautiful, tormented boy.

He'd both wrecked me and breathed the life back into me.

The conflicting emotions got locked up in my chest. Because the deepest part of me knew where I belonged was with him.

And I remembered.

I remembered.

Even after he was gone.

He was worth every second of the pain.

Light tapping at my door roused me from sleep. It was the drifting kind, where I hovered just above full coherency, as if watching my life suspended above it all.

It felt so strange, this broken heart up against the overwhelming feeling of being free. Missing him and being so thankful to be home.

The door creaked open. "Hey," my mother said as she slipped into my room. Late afternoon light bled in through the parted drapes, shadows playing on the vista, dancing up and down the peaks and ridges of the mountains.

"Hi," I said as I tried to establish my bearings. I blinked through the daze as I sat up.

She sank down on the bed next to me, ran her fingers through my hair. "I'm sorry to wake you."

"No…it's fine."

She hesitated. "I thought you might want this."

My attention traveled to the small yellow mailer she held in her hands.

Dread and hope.

They slammed me.

God, what was wrong with me?

She glanced at me from the side. "It's for you…I think."

Unease rustled through my dim room, and I pulled in a deep breath as I gathered the courage to peek at what was written across the front. Somehow already knowing what would be there.

There was no address.

No first or last name.

It simply said *Blue.*

That statement was written in his bold script. As if he were reaching out. Touching me. This boy who chased me in my dreams and haunted my nights.

"Where did you find this?" I managed.

Her lips thinned. "It was sitting at the front door. I'm guessing it's from him?"

I nodded. "Yeah."

She touched my chin. "Okay…I'll give you some time."

"Thank you," I whispered as I accepted the padded envelope. I held it against my chest until she snapped the door closed behind her. Silence stole over the room, my breaths increasing to a pant.

Anxiety. Emotions running wild.

Was I really going to allow him to do this to me again? Pull and pull and pull until he pushed me away?

Swallowing, I ripped open the seal. A disk fell out. *Blue* was again scripted across it.

Warily, I stood, paced, wondered. Before I gave and sat down at the small desk and lifted my laptop lid, shaking as I slid the disk inside.

There was one file on it.

A video.

Fumbling, I pressed my headphones into my ears, my pulse

at a sprint and my spirit in a frenzy, while the rational, logical side screamed at me to toss the disk in the trash. To protect. To find some semblance of those walls.

But I couldn't stop myself from pressing play.

The screen filled with Lyrik.

So big and bold and beautiful.

My breath caught and my heart skipped.

He was sitting on a hotel bed with an acoustic guitar balanced on his lap. Those eyes were sad and brimming with remorse, his mouth vacant of that smirk. He scratched at his temple, as if this menacing, malicious man didn't know what to do with himself.

"Blue."

My insides quaked with it falling like a plea from his tongue.

Eyes dropping closed, he looked away, before he turned his attention to the camera. "I've written a lot of songs in my life. For a long damn time, they were the only real joy I had. And this one...it's the most important one I've ever written, even though I could never bring myself to get to the end."

He strummed a single chord and cleared his throat. "You know a song says more than any words I could ever speak. Listen, Blue. Fuck..." He raked a hand through his hair. "Please...just...listen."

Quietly, he plucked through another chord, and when he opened that pretty mouth, the words were raw. Rough. Coarse and bleeding emotion.

Trembles rolled when I recognized the haunting cadence of the music.

He was playing the unsung song. The song coiling his arm, wrapping him in mystery and unseen misery.

Tears blurred my eyes.

Will you ever know
Just what it meant
Holding you high
Now I'm down on my knees
Begging for the pieces
That no longer belong to me

I'd have given it all
But instead I got lost along the way

The intensity of the song increased as he drove into the chorus.

But I'm coming…
I'm coming home to you
Finally found forever
It's been waiting all around
I'm coming…
I'm coming home to you
Tell me what I have to do
To get the chance
Say you'll let me spend it with you

Tears poured free, and my chest ached and throbbed while my shaky world spun.

I'd once thought he'd laugh when he watched me fall.

But I knew now. There was a huge part of Lyrik that wanted to hold me up.

I just wasn't sure he knew how.

His fingers stumbled across the frets, and a pained breath left him. "Blue." He leaned forward, as if he could get to me from across the space. "Blue…I wrote the beginning of that song a long damn time ago. But it's not finished. I know it now. Let me end it with you."

The screen went blank.

A sob shot from my mouth.

Let me end it with you.

I climbed from the chair and paced the quiet of my room. I gripped my hair, feeling like I had to be insane. Completely, entirely insane.

Because that's the way this boy made me.

Weak.

But I refused to be a fool.

Not because I was rigid and forging walls.

No.

Because I wanted to be loved. Loved the way I deserved to be.

So confused, I fumbled from my room and down the hall, hand darting out to the wall to keep myself from falling.

That intensity swelled. I nearly choked over it.

Thick.

Heavy.

Dense.

Needing a breath, clarity, I flew out the front door and down the steps to the thatch of grass lining the front.

I faltered to a staggered stop.

That dark, foreboding boy stood at the edge of the graveled drive. Tattooed hands stuffed in his pockets. Hair wild as it whipped around his head.

My mouth went dry and I took a single step back.

He took a pleading one forward. "Blue."

My head shook as another gust of wind blasted through.

Those dark eyes swallowed me whole, his voice hard. "Been sittin' in that hotel room for the last three days, since the moment I saw you on the stand. Being brave."

My face pinched. As if it could protect me from his words. From this boy who held the power to desolate and destroy.

To build me up or break me.

"All these months…" His head shook, as if he were trying to make sense of it. "The way I felt? Feeling like I wanted to wrap you up and protect you? Hunt down that bastard and make him pay for what he did to you? Didn't get it, Blue. Didn't get what it meant. Not until that night back at my place in L.A."

I took another step back. Wanting to run. To him. Or away. I didn't know.

"I can't let you do this to me, Lyrik. Not again." I fisted my hand at my chest. "I can't take it…you drawing me closer before you push me away. I don't know what you want from me."

He laughed this bemused sound, mouth pulling up at the side. "You know…when I first met you…thought that was what I liked about you most. The push and the pull. All that attracting and repelling. That crazy contradiction I felt around you. Was something I just couldn't resist."

His expression turned somber. "But it was so much more than that. And as much as I wanted to launch myself across that courtroom and tear that piece of shit to shreds, I knew you sitting up there on that stand, doing it yourself? It's what *you* needed. Even when I knew I wanted to be the one there if you needed me. To catch you if you fell, even when I knew my girl was gonna stand."

My girl.

The air whipped into a frenzy.

And that feeling blazed.

The thrill.

I shivered as it rolled over me.

Wave after wave.

"I need to tell you something, Blue."

"You can't—" I attempted.

He edged forward, so damned tall and strong and so ridiculously soft. Those dark eyes were tormented as he reached out and grabbed both my wrists, hauling me forward.

And I felt so small and vulnerable.

Caged.

"Please…listen to me."

I struggled and he held tighter though his tone softened. "Listen to me, Blue…I need you to *hear* this."

I gave. So fucking weak. Because that's the way this boy made me.

He gathered me closer and his voice dropped to a whisper as he uttered the confession at my ear. "I have a son."

His words slammed into me like a freight train that had no time to slow.

They just blew straight through me.

Impacting everything.

"Brendon." It scraped from my throat as that awareness took hold. The name woven through his song. The heart of his story.

The word was reverent when he murmured it back. "Brendon."

He shifted, still holding me tight as he stared down at me.

"Told you I fuck everything up, Blue. I take the good things I'm given then crush them. First day I met him? That was the day I had to tell him goodbye."

Pain radiated from him. A crestless wave. Endless. "I got to hold him once. Once, Blue. I didn't get to keep him. Fuck, I wanted to so bad…but I had to give him up because it was the only thing I could do. The best thing I could do for him."

Tears soaked my face as he kept talking, "I made him a promise…I promised him he'd be the last person I ever fell in love with. In some twisted way, I thought it'd make up for something, condemning myself to my own personal hell."

I was shaking. Shaking all over.

My heart breaking.

For him.

For the child.

For the girl in the photo.

Just the same as it swelled with jealousy.

"You have a son," I whimpered.

He tried to draw me closer, as if that might be the only way he could get me to understand. "How could I go and find happiness after I'd left him? How could I, Blue?"

Edging back, his brow twisted and pinched, gaze relentless. "But then there was you. This beautiful, bold, brave girl. Think I knew from the get go you were off limits. That I shouldn't touch you. That I should stay away. Because I knew if I did, I wasn't ever gonna be the same. And I'm not, Blue. I'm not. Because you *changed* everything."

My spirit thrashed, stirred by a sudden gust of wind. Tension winding fast.

His expression locked in sorrow. "Look at you…"

He brushed his knuckles across my cheeks, sending a rush of chills spiraling through my senses.

Body and soul.

"All I fuckin' do is make you cry. Hurt you more. But I'm done, Blue. So fucking done with that. I know you think my apologies don't count for anything, but this one…this one is all I have to give. I'm so fucking sorry for the things I said. For the things I did. I won't try to make excuses or pretend the way I treated you was right...but I need you to know I was trying to protect my heart because I thought it could only belong to my son."

My chest heaved and he drew in a ragged breath. "And there you were, breaking up all the broken, brittle parts and making room for something different. For something better. Waking me up from the dead. Making me realize what it's like to feel again. Making me feel things I've *never* felt before. You were making room for *you*."

"Lyrik." It was so soft. Broken like this boy.

Energy swelled. The storm gained speed.

The buzz before the strike.

My entire body shook, all my hopes floating to the surface, clashing with my fears. With that image branded in my memory, the picture of him and the girl, the words he'd said when I found it.

Not you.

"If you still love her—"

He gripped my jaw, forcing me to stop talking and to look up at him. "No, Blue. I don't. It's you. It's you."

Lyrik suddenly dropped to his knees on the grass.

An offering.

"Do you hear me?"

And for the first time, I was the one towering above this intimidating man.

Wind whipped through. Gathering strength.

It was as if nitrogen and oxygen had come alive.

Every element in the dense air combustible.

Explosive.

Chills raced up my spine.

"I don't know how to trust you."

But God, I wanted to.

I wanted this boy as much as I wanted breath.

But more than that, I wanted love. The real kind. I wouldn't settle for anything less.

His words were hoarse. "Let me prove it, Blue. Let me show

you that every night, I want to be the one making love to you, and when you wake up in the morning, I want it to be me who has their arms wrapped around you."

His tongue darted out. Nervous but sure. "And when you wear a ring on your finger, I want to be the one who put it there."

Emotion swam in those eyes the color of pitch. Twilight and the sunrise. "And when you become a mother, I want you to be holding my child."

I panted.

Overwhelmed by this man.

This time it was my turn to drop to my knees.

Floored.

Gone.

His.

He gathered my face in his hands. Thumbs brushed the tears from my cheeks. "I'm in love with you, Tamar Gibson. Do you hear me?"

I hear you.

I hear you.

"Be with me, Blue. Tell me you're mine. Because I don't think I can let you go. And there's a good chance my son's gonna be a part of my life. Because it was *you* who taught me what it's like to be brave. That if I was gonna move on, I had to face my past. Share it with me, Blue. My past and my future."

He buried his face in my hair, mouth at my ear. "Please...don't tell me no."

My voice was a rasp. "I couldn't."

With Lyrik, I never could.

He gasped out in relief, and he pressed a thick lock of my dark hair against his nose and laughed out this disbelieving sound. Breathed me in. Then he inched back so those unyielding eyes could take me in. The softest smirk lifted at one side of his mouth. But it lacked the threat. Warmed me through.

This intimidating, malicious man who was so utterly soft.

His words twisted with awe. "You're so damned pretty."

Then that mouth was on mine.

Kissing me in a way that was wholly profound.

Soft and deep.

Slow and hard.

With a promise he would never let me go.

The air crackled with energy.

Light lit up at the edges of my eyes.

Intense and alive.

With the force of a thunderbolt.

Where lightning strikes.

And I felt so small. Scared. Yet strong at the same time. Witnessing this beauty unseen. Touching on an experience I only thought I'd observe from afar.

Love.

It was blinding.

Powerful.

It turned out this boy was the perfect storm.

"Say it again," I whispered at his mouth.

Lyrik pulled back. I watched the heavy bob of his throat. The heave of his chest. The severity in those pitch-black eyes.

"Blue, you sing my soul."

.

epilogue

LYRIK

*Y*ou'd think with the guitar playing and all, I'd be good at this.

Nimble fingers.

Quick hands.

Not so much.

A chuckle left me just under my breath, and I bit my bottom lip in concentration as I weaved the fat needle through the fabric. Creating a patchwork design. Every shade of pink. Ginghams and calicoes and solids.

So, yeah. Guys might call me a pussy considering I know the names of all those prints. But you know. My mom.

I gripped the needle between clumsy fingers, trying to keep it straight.

Brendon laughed like it was the funniest thing he'd ever seen. "Dad…you're doin' it all wrong."

"What do you mean, I'm doing it wrong?"

Against the table in the kitchen nook where we were working, he leaned in closer. Place looked like an entire craft fair had exploded in here. So maybe the kid and I had gotten a little carried away at the store.

Sue me.

"You're putting the ear on backwards."

"Crap," I muttered under my breath, and he cracked up. I rustled a hand through his hair. "Where's your grandma when we need her?"

Dark, dark eyes widened in my direction. Full of mischief. "Good thing not here, because she'd be rollin' her eyes."

My jaw dropped in feigned offense.

The kid was a little whip. Testing just how far he could take that sarcasm at every turn. Couldn't help it. I thought it was the cutest damned thing in the world.

"I'll have you know, I made that bear…all by myself." I pointed at the ratty, mangled thing he still refused to give up. "It's been lastin' for years. How's that for someone who has no clue what they're doing?"

"You got lucky?" he shot back with a lift of his brow.

"Oh, dude…you're so going down for that."

He was grinning, getting ready to run, when my girl's voice came floating through the heavy wooden door separating the kitchen from the rest of the house. "Knock, knock."

Guess most wouldn't describe it as sweet, considering it was throaty and sexy as all fuck, just the sound of it raising chills. But that didn't mean it didn't land on me like honey.

"Don't come in," Brendon yelled, slanting me a wry grin.

"Are you still not finished?" she called back.

"Nope," he shouted.

I could hear her exaggerated sigh, almost see her smile. "All right then. I'll just be out here…lonely…waiting…by myself…all alone."

"Someone's feeling a little overdramatic," I playfully said with a wink at my son, and Brendon snickered quietly.

"Think she just likes us," he said a little innocently.

But fuck.

Yeah.

Guess I got lucky enough, that after everything I'd done, that gorgeous girl did.

"Here, buddy, why don't you weave this one through?" I suggested as I fed a piece of pink ribbon through the eye of the needle.

Tongue darted out to the side, Brendon finished weaving the last bit through the bear, then helped me sew in the eyes and mouth with black thread.

"You think she'll like it?" he whispered.

"Think she'll love it."

Both of them.

"You ready to give it to her?"

He scrambled down. "Yep."

He hid it behind his back as we made our way across the huge kitchen. It was a little country, done as a throwback to Savannah where we'd met, the cabinets white and the island sage, countertops gray. Felt homey. Lived in.

Really, the entire expansive place felt that way.

Warm.

Home.

Never really thought I'd get one.

Never thought I'd deserve one.

Thought I'd messed up too many times. Ruined too much good.

And somehow…somehow I'd gotten it all.

I followed Brendon through the sweeping foyer. Night pressed in over the windows—the city resting below—twinkling through the bank of floor-to-ceiling windows in the living and formal dining rooms.

We passed by and ducked into the den that seemed to be Tamar's favorite spot in the house. Cozy with a fireplace and plush carpet. Walls covered in big blown-ups of some of her favorite shots she'd taken over the years. Some of lightning. Others of us and the rest of our families and friends.

A ton of Brendon.

As I rounded the corner, my damned breath caught in my throat.

Didn't matter how many times I saw her. It was always a violent jar to my senses. She was bold and brash, a flash of a million brilliant colors shimmering in the night.

Erotic and seductive.

Pure and sweet.

Angel with a little demon woven in between.

So maybe I didn't mind it all that much when *Red* came out to play.

Tamar West was all those things.

This perfect contradiction who would always hold me in the palm of her hand.

She was sitting crisscrossed on the floor, her huge belly resting in the well of her legs, wearing a black tank top that hugged all her curves, mouth curving up as she saw us walk in.

Well, I was walking in. Brendon was running. He slid onto his knees on the floor beside her. "We finished your surprise!"

She pushed her fingers through his locks of dark hair. "You did, huh?"

She slanted me a glance that sent a ripple of affection through me.

Gripping my heart.

Filling me with joy.

Couldn't quite explain what it did to me to see her with my kid. Seeing the way she loved him wholly, took him on as a part of her because he was a part of me, as shocking and sudden as his emergence into our lives had been.

A week after I went to Arizona to get Tamar back, I'd gotten a call from Kenzie that Brendon wanted to see me. That she and Brad had explained to him who I was, as well as someone his age could understand.

We'd taken things slow so Brendon could get used to me

being a part of his life. All of their lives, really. I didn't want to go barging in like some kind of selfish bastard, demanding time I didn't deserve.

Honestly, I had been surprised Kenzie and Brad were willing to give any at all. But Kenzie had always been that way, kind and wanting the best for everyone, and she thought the best for Brendon would be me being a part of his life.

During that first handful of months, we'd established a routine. I'd go over to take him someplace cool a couple times a week when I was in town and have him spend the night at our place at least once on the weekend.

Even after two years, we still didn't have some court-appointed visitation. I just respected Kenzie and she respected me, and we let things take their course.

No.

Didn't get to see him nearly as much as I wanted. But I cherished every single second I got.

Blue tickled his sides. "Let me see," she playfully demanded. She was doing her best not to laugh.

Brendon messed with her for a few seconds, keeping it hidden behind his back, before that same tender expression climbed across his face. Same look he got when you knew he was feeling something deep. He stilled before he pulled the bear out.

A little gasp shot from her. Even though she knew what we were making, considering she'd seen the two my mom still kept in her kitchen a thousand times, and Brendon's, which he never let out of his sight.

Still, moisture gathered in her eyes, and she accepted it from Brendon's cupped hands, moving to gently cradle it on her lap.

"I love it," she whispered.

"Really?" he asked.

"Really."

Not able to stay away, I climbed down beside them. Brendon sat on his knees where he hovered over Blue, and I lay low on the other. Just taking in the moment.

"Do you know what it means?" he asked, like he was getting ready to tell her the greatest secret.

"Tell me," she murmured back.

"Grandma says it represents a family being stitched together by a new birth." He traced his finger over the blocks of pink. "Each piece of fabric represents the people who make up that family, and the ribbon is the love that binds it all together. She says they're really good luck."

A wistful smile pulled along her mouth. "It's beautiful. I bet this is going to be your sister's favorite bear."

He touched a bright pink patch. "This is you," he whispered, and moved onto another. "And this is Dad."

His grin was wide and excited. "And this is my baby sister."

She smiled at him. "And where are you?"

"Right here," he said, touching the small block of fabric.

Making this family whole.

Seemed crazy after how many years I'd lived alone, committing myself to suffering day after day in debt for what I'd done, that all those hollow places would be filled. So full I could scarcely remember what they felt like.

There was a piece of me that hung onto them, though. No. Not because I remained in that tortured hell.

These two?

They'd resurrected me from it.

But I did keep them as daily reminders to be thankful. To never forget family was a blessing. Never to be neglected or disregarded or treated as anything less than the most important thing in life.

Because that's what they were.

Life.

We all just hung out on the floor for a bit, chatting, the hour growing late. "All right, buddy, it's time for bed," I finally said.

"Ah man," he exaggerated. "Are you sure you're a rock star? Because you're not any fun at all."

Like I said.

A little whip.

Girls were going to be putty in this boy's hands. Of course, Sebastian didn't appreciate it all that much when I suggested Brendon and Kallie were the perfect match, the two thick as thieves and kinda perfect every time they were together.

Chuckling, I hopped up onto my feet. "Oh, dude, you're really gonna pay for that."

He was on his feet and racing from the room, flying up the curved stairs leading to the second floor. I chased him, reaching out and just *missing* him every time.

Some games I was just always gonna let the kid win.

Flying into his room, he hopped onto his bed. I wandered in, pulled his covers up to his chest, and brushed a kiss to his forehead.

Clutching the top of his blankets, he lifted his chin and leaned into it, grinning so fucking wide I felt it right in the center of my chest.

Peace.

Happiness.

Calm.

Tamar was leaning against the doorjamb, arms crossed over her chest, watching us with that small, tender smile. She finally fumbled forward, that belly that drove me a little wild setting her a bit off balance. She leaned in and ran her fingers through Brendon's hair.

This kid who'd become our son.

Affection thick.

Real.

Intense.

"Night, Momma Blue," he said.

"G'night, sweetheart." She pressed her lips to his cheek, brushing her hand across my chest as she left the room.

I smiled at my son. "Love you, buddy."

"Love you the most," he said through that giddy grin.

I let my smile bleed free. Nah. Not even close. But I'd give him that. I kissed his forehead again. "Sleep tight. See you in the morning."

I crossed his room, flipping the light switch, leaving his door open a crack.

Drawn, I headed toward our room. Knowing she was there. She stood just outside the balcony doors, looking out over the city

398

blinking up at us from below. Black hair blowing in the breeze.

This girl so fucking gorgeous, she turned my heart and ripped my gut, brought me to my knees.

Owned.

Should have known it the first time I saw her.

But sometimes those leading lessons are needed.

Required so we get just how important one person can be.

So we understand they were *meant* to be.

Just thanked my lucky damned stars she'd agreed.

Things with *Sunder* had gotten…crazy. The band had gotten bigger than we ever could have dreamed. Had known it'd been coming for a long damned time, but Sebastian finally stepped down a little more than a year ago.

Couldn't hardly blame the guy. The time he wanted with his family was not time he wanted to spend on the road. But he hadn't left us entirely. He'd purchased Anthony's place out on Tybee Island, recording studio already intact, and had turned his talent to producing. Mostly he worked with us, but he had a few other bands that wanted to record away from the fast pace of the city.

Nah.

I didn't step up and take his place. Truth was, I didn't want to lead. That role? It belonged to someone else. Someone I'd put down bets had belonged there all along.

Blue and I kept a house in Savannah, too.

But we mostly hung in L.A., being closer to her family, closer to mine, and what mattered more than anything was this was Brendon's home. Of course, Tamar had never minded jumping on a plane and traveling with me, the girl all too eager to get out on the floor and get lost in the music.

Guess this girl was my biggest fan.

She never went anywhere without that camera. Her inspiration found every day. Everywhere. In the way she looked at the world.

With the baby coming in just a few weeks, things had to change. Knew she couldn't simply up and leave whenever she wanted.

But I'd been wrong.

Faulty in thinking I couldn't have a family and *Sunder*, too.

Because this girl had given me it all. My dreams. Playing. Making music. Loving her.

I got them both.

I got it all.

I edged up behind her and gathered her up, her back pressing to my chest, her belly in my hands.

I held them.

Protective.

Possessive.

That baby girl jumped and kicked.

Fuck.

I was so in love. Couldn't wait to hold her in my arms. To do it *right*.

I nuzzled my nose into Blue's hair. "Hey, baby."

She sighed, a sound so content it wrung me through.

"You know what it does to me? Finding you standing out here like this? Lookin' like my favorite fantasy?"

She giggled. "Hardly."

But that's where this girl was wrong.

She was everything I liked.

Everything I wanted.

Just touching her, my dick was already hard. Needing to touch. Explore. Feel. Take this girl because she was *mine*.

So damned deliciously hot.

Lust-inducing and heart-inspiring.

She was every single thing I'd had no clue I was going to need.

My lips caressed her temple. "You're so damned beautiful. So sexy. Wanna spend my life buried in you."

She giggled again, but this time it was a seductive sound. "What do you mean, want? Pretty sure you're giving that a good go."

A soft chuckle rumbled from my chest. "Can you blame me?"

She snuggled deeper into my hold. "How'd we get this life?"

I held her a little closer. God, she smelled so good, all cinnamon and spice with a dash of sweet.

"Think we were just meant to be. From the second I saw you,

there was something pulling at me. Everywhere. Not sure I could have ever stayed away. Feel like one way or another, I would have found you."

Her voice was wistful. "Or I would have found you."

My lips caressed along the delicate slope of her neck. "Because you would have heard me calling…didn't even know you, and already you were written in my songs."

She threaded her fingers through mine, the words stamped across my knuckles on display where our clamped hands were pressed against her chest.

Sing my soul.

I'd thought it a curse.

Loving someone. Just making yourself susceptible to heartache and sorrow and pain.

All the burdened bullshit I could no longer bear.

"And I always would have *heard* you," she murmured into the night.

But loving her?

This girl?

She eased all the pain.

Erased that overwhelming sorrow.

Filled up the hollow void.

Showed me how to live.

Once I'd thought her the worst kind of temptation. Destruction and blinding light. The kind of girl who could wreck every last thing I believed.

Blue…

Guess she was.

Temptation.

She'd tempted me to live.

Now, I was gonna spend this life living it for her.

With her.

She swiveled in my arms and hiked up on her toes, the girl so short she struggled to get to me. I could feel my smile where it was pressed to her mouth. So damned sweet.

Could feel her racing through my veins.

Fire.

This girl was a bundle of fireworks.

Waiting for a match.

I swooped her into my arms and carried her to our bed, set her in the middle of it.

Gazed down on this girl staring up at me.

Hard and soft.

Tainted and pure.

Vixen and angel.

She touched my face just as sure as she touched my heart.

She was every hue of color, reds and blues, the darkest black and blinding white.

Energy and life.

Boom.

the end

Did you love Lyrik & Tamar's story? Help spread the word by leaving a short review - I would appreciate it so much! I knew Lyrik & Tamar's story will leave a lasting impression on my heart. I hope it touched you, too.

Xoxo ~ Amy

MORE FROM A.L. JACKSON

ABOUT THE AUTHOR

A.L. Jackson is the New York Times & USA Today Bestselling author of contemporary romance. She writes emotional, sexy, heart-filled stories about boys who usually like to be a little bit bad.

Her bestselling series include THE REGRET SERIES, CLOSER TO YOU, BLEEDING STARS, FIGHT FOR ME, CONFESSIONS OF THE HEART, FALLING STARS, and REDEMPTION HILLS.

If she's not writing, you can find her hanging out by the pool with her family, sipping cocktails with her friends, or of course with her nose buried in a book.

Be sure not to miss new releases and sales from A.L. Jackson - Sign up to receive her newsletter http://smarturl.it/NewsFromALJackson or text "aljackson" to 33222 to receive short but sweet updates on all the important news.

Connect with A.L. Jackson online:

FB Page **https://geni.us/ALJacksonFB**
Newsletter **https://geni.us/NewsFromALJackson**
Angels **https://geni.us/AmysAngels**
Amazon **https://geni.us/ALJacksonAmzn**
Book Bub **https://geni.us/ALJacksonBookbub**
Text "aljackson" to 33222 to receive short but sweet updates on all the important news.

Printed in Great Britain
by Amazon

23248988R00229